VICTOR HUGO
Ninety-Three

Translated by Frank Lee Benedict

Carroll & Graf Publishers, Inc.
New York

First Carroll & Graf edition 1988
Second printing 1989

Carroll & Graf Publishers, Inc.
260 Fifth Avenue
New York, NY 10001

ISBN: 0-88184-405-5

Manufactured in the United States of America

CONTENTS

CONTENTS

PART II.— IN PARIS.

BOOK I.— Cimourdain.

BOOK II.— The Public House of the Rue du Paon.

BOOK III.— The Convention.

CONTENTS

PART III.—LA VENDEE.

BOOK I.—La Vendée.

BOOK II.—The Three Children.

BOOK III.—The Massacre of Saint Bartholomew.

CONTENTS

NINETY-THREE

PART I

AT SEA

BOOK I

THE WOOD OF LA SAUDRAIE

IN the latter part of May, 1793, one of the Paris battalions
sent into Brittany by Santerre, searched the much dreaded
forest of La Saudraie, in Astillé. There were only about
three hundred men in the reconnoitring party, for the battalion had been well-nigh annihilated in the fierce conflicts in
which it had engaged.

It was after the battles of Argonne, Jemmapes, and Valmy,
and of the First Paris Regiment, which consisted originally of
six hundred volunteers, only twenty-seven men remained, of
the Second Regiment only thirty-three, of the Third only
fifty-seven. It was unquestionably a time of epic strife.

Each of the battalions sent from Paris to the Vendée numbered nine hundred and twelve men, and was provided with
three field-pieces. The force had been very hastily organized.
On the 25th of April,— Gohier being minister of Justice, and
Bouchotte minister of war,— the Committee of Public Welfare
urged the necessity of immediately dispatching a large body

1

of troops to Vendée. Lubin, a member of the Commune, reported the bill favourably; and on the 1st of May, Santerre had twelve thousand men, thirty cannon, and a corps of gunners ready for the field.

These battalions, though organized so hurriedly, were organized so well that they serve as models even at the present day. Regiments of the Line are yet organized in the same manner; the relative proportion between the number of soldiers and non-commissioned officers has been changed,— that is all.

On the 28th of April, the Commune of Paris gave Santerre's volunteers this order: "No mercy; no quarter." By the end of May, of the twelve thousand men that left Paris, eight thousand were dead.

The troops who were exploring the forest of La Saudraie held themselves on the alert. They advanced slowly and cautiously. Each man cast furtive glances to the right and to the left of him, in front of him and behind him. It was Kléber who said: "A soldier has one eye in his back." They had been marching a long while. What time of day could it be? It was difficult to say, for a dim twilight always pervades these dense forests. It is never really light there.

The forest of La Saudraie was tragic. It was in its copses that, from the month of November, 1792, civil war commenced its crimes. Mousqueton, the ferocious cripple, came out of its fatal shades. The list of the murders that had been committed there was enough to make one's hair stand on end. There was no place more to be dreaded. The soldiers moved cautiously forward. The depths were full of flowers; on each side was a trembling wall of branches and dew-wet leaves. Here and there rays of sunlight pierced the green shadows. The gladiola, that flame of the marshes, the meadow narcissus, the little wood daisy, harbinger of spring, and the vernal crocus, embroidered the thick carpet of vegetation, crowded with every form of moss, from that resembling velvet (*chenille*) to that which looks like a star. The soldiers advanced in silence, step by step, pushing the brushwood softly aside. The birds twittered above the bayonets.

In former peaceable times La Saudraie was a favourite place for the *Houiche-ba*, the hunting of birds by night; now they hunted men there.

The thicket was one of birch-trees, beeches, and oaks; the ground flat; the thick moss and grass deadened the sound of the men's steps; there were no paths, or only blind ones, which quickly disappeared among the holly, wild sloes, ferns, hedges of rest-harrow, and high brambles. It would have been impossible to distinguish a man ten steps off.

Now and then a heron or a moor-hen flew through the branches, indicating the neighbourhood of marshes.

They pushed forward. They went at random, with uneasiness, fearing to find that which they sought.

From time to time they came upon traces of encampments, — burned spots, trampled grass, sticks arranged crosswise, branches stained with blood. Here soup had been made; there, Mass had been said; yonder, they had dressed wounds. But all human beings had disappeared. Where were they. Very far off, perhaps; perhaps quite near, hidden, blunderbuss in hand. The wood seemed deserted. The regiment redoubled its prudence. Solitude — hence distrust. They saw no one; so much more reason for fearing some one. They had to do with a forest with a bad name. An ambush was probable.

Thirty grenadiers, detached as scouts, and commanded by a sergeant, marched at a considerable distance in front of the main body. The vivandière of the battalion accompanied them. The vivandières willingly join the vanguard; they run risks, but they have the chance of seeing whatever happens. Curiosity is one of the forms of feminine bravery.

Suddenly the soldiers of this little advance party started like hunters who have neared the hiding-place of their prey. They had heard something like a breathing from the centre of a thicket, and seemed to perceive a movement among the branches. The soldiers made signals.

In the species of watch and search confided to scouts, the officers have small need to interfere; the right thing seems done by instinct.

In less than a minute the spot where the movement had been noticed was surrounded; a line of pointed muskets encircled it; the obscure centre of the thicket was covered on all sides at the same instant; the soldiers, finger on trigger, eye on the suspected spot, only waited for the sergeant's order. Notwithstanding this, the vivandière ventured to peer through the underbrush, and at the moment when the sergeant was about to cry, " Fire! " this woman cried, " Halt! "

Turning toward the soldiers, she added, " Do not fire, comrades! "

She plunged into the thicket; the men followed.

There was, in truth, some one there.

In the thickest of the brake, on the edge of one of those little round clearings left by the fires of the charcoal-burners, in a sort of recess among the branches, a kind of chamber of foliage, half open like an alcove, a woman was seated on the moss, holding to her breast a nursing babe, while the fair heads of two sleeping children rested on her knees.

This was the ambush.

" What are you doing here, you? " cried the vivandière.

The woman lifted her head.

The vivandière added furiously:—

" Are you mad, that you are there?   A little more and you would have been blown to pieces! "

Then she addressed herself to the soldiers,—

" It is a woman."

" Well, that is plain to be seen," said a grenadier.

The vivandière continued,—

" To come into the wood to get yourself massacred!   The idea of such stupidity! "

The woman, stunned, petrified with fear, looked about like one in a dream at these guns, these sabres, these bayonets, these savage faces.

The two children awoke, and cried.

" I am hungry," said the first.

" I am afraid," said the other.

The baby was still suckling; the vivandière addressed it.

" You are in the right of it," said she.

The mother was dumb with terror. The sergeant cried out to her:—

" Do not be afraid; we are the battalion of the Bonnet Rouge."

The woman trembled from head to foot. She stared at the sergeant, of whose rough visage there was nothing visible but the moustaches, the brows, and two burning coals for eyes.

" Formerly the battalion of the Red Cross," added the vivandière.

The sergeant continued: " Who are you, madame?"

The woman scanned him, terrified. She was slender, young, pale, and in rags; she wore the large hood and woollen cloak of the Breton peasant, fastened about her neck by a string. She left her bosom exposed with the indifference of an animal. Her feet, shoeless and stockingless, were bleeding.

" It is a beggar," said the sergeant.

The vivandière began anew, in a voice at once soldierly and feminine, but sweet,—

" What is your name?"

The woman stammered so that she was scarcely intelligible.

" Michelle Fléchard."

The vivandière stroked the little head of the sleeping babe with her large hand.

" What is the age of this mite?" demanded she.

The mother did not understand. The vivandière persisted.

" I ask you, how old is it?"

" Ah!" said the mother; " eighteen months."

" It is old," said the vivandière; " it ought not to suckle any longer. You must wean it; we will give it soup."

The mother began to feel a certain confidence. The two children, who had awakened, were rather curious than scared. They admired the plumes of the soldiers.

" Ah," said the mother, " they are very hungry."

Then she added, " I have no more milk."

" We will give them something to eat," cried the sergeant; " and you too. But that's not all. What are your political opinions? "

The woman looked at him, but did not reply.

" Did you hear my question? "

She stammered,—

" I was put into a convent very young — but I am married — I am not a nun. The sisters taught me to speak French. The village was set on fire. We ran away so quickly that I had not time to put on my shoes."

" I ask you, what are your political opinions? "

" I don't know what that means."

The sergeant continued,—

" There are such things as female spies. We shoot spies. Come, speak! You are not a gipsy? Which is your side? "

She still looked at him as if she did not understand.

The sergeant repeated,—

" Which is your side? "

" I do not know," she said.

" How? You do not know your own country."

" Ah, my country! Oh, yes, I know that."

" Well, where is it? "

The woman replied,—

" The farm of Siscoignard, in the parish of Azé."

It was the sergeant's turn to be stupefied. He remained thoughtful for a moment, then resumed: " You say —"

" Siscoignard."

" That is not a country."

" It is my country," said the woman; and added, after an instant's reflection, " I understand, sir. You are from France; I belong to Brittany."

" Well? "

" It is not the same neighbourhood."

" But it is the same country," cried the sergeant.

The woman only repeated,—

" I am from Siscoignard."

" Siscoignard be it," returned the sergeant. " Your family belong there? "

" Yes."

" What is their occupation? "

" They are all dead; I have nobody left."

The sergeant, who thought himself a fine talker, continued his interrogatories:—

" What? the devil! One has relations, or one has had. Who are you? Speak!"

The woman listened, astounded by this: " *Or one has had!* " which was more like the growl of an animal than any human sound.

The vivandière felt the necessity of interfering. She began again to caress the babe, and to pat the cheeks of the two other children.

" How do you call the baby? " she asked. " It is a little girl — this one? "

The mother replied, " Georgette."

" And the eldest fellow? For he is a man, the small rascal! "

" René-Jean."

" And the younger? He is a man, too, and chubby-faced into the bargain."

" Gros-Alain," said the mother.

" They are pretty little fellows," said the vivandière; " they already look as if they were somebody."

Still the sergeant persisted. " Now, speak, madame! Have you a house? "

" I had one."

" Where was it? "

" At Azé."

" Why are you not in your house? "

" Because they burned it."

" Who? "

" I do not know — a battle."

" Where did you come from? "

" From there."

" Where are you going? "

" I don't know."

" Get to the facts!   Who are you? "

" I don't know."

" You don't know who you are? "

" We are people who are running away."

" What party do you belong to? "

" I don't know."

" Are you Blues? Are you Whites? Who are you with? "

" I am with my children."

There was a pause.   The vivandière said,—

" As for me, I have no children; I have not had time."

The sergeant began again: —

" But your parents?   See here, madame! give us the facts about your parents.   My name is Radoub; I am a sergeant, from the street of Cherche Midi; my father and mother belonged there.   I can talk about my parents; tell us about yours.   Who were they? "

" Their name was Fléchard,— that is all."

" Yes; the Fléchards are the Fléchards, just as the Radoubs are the Radoubs.   But people have a calling.   What was your parents' calling?   What was their business, these Fléchards of yours? "

" They were labourers.   My father was sickly, and could not work on account of a beating that the lord — his lord — our lord — had given to him.   It was a kindness, for my father had poached a rabbit,— a thing for which one was condemned to death; but the lord showed him mercy, and said, ' You need only give him a hundred blows with a stick; ' and my father was left crippled."

" And then? "

" My grandfather was a Huguenot.   The curé had him sent to the galleys.   I was very little at the time."

" And then? "

" My husband's father smuggled salt.   The king had him hung."

" And your husband,— what did he do? "

" Lately, he fought."

" For whom? "

" For the king."

" And afterward? "

" Well, for his lordship."

" And next? "

" Well, then for the curé."

" A thousand names of brutes! " cried a grenadier.

The woman gave a start of terror.

" You see, madame, we are Parisians," said the vivandière, graciously.

The woman clasped her hands, and exclaimed,—

" O my God and blessed Lord! "

" No superstitious ejaculations! " growled the sergeant.

The vivandière seated herself by the woman, and drew the eldest child between her knees. He submitted quietly. Children show confidence as they do distrust, without any apparent reason; some internal monitor warns them.

" My poor, good woman of this neighbourhood," said the vivandière, " you brats are very pretty,— babies are always that. I can guess their ages. The big one is four years old; his brother is three. Upon my word! the little suckling poppet is a greedy one. Oh, the monster! Will you stop eating up your mother? See here, madame, do not be afraid. You ought to join the battalion. Do like me. I call myself Houzarde. It is a nickname; but I like Houzarde better than being called Mamzelle Bicorneau, like my mother. I am the canteen woman; that is the same as saying, ' she who offers drink when they are firing and stabbing.' Our feet are about the same size. I will give you a pair of my shoes. I was in Paris the 10th of August. I gave Westermann drink too. How things went! I saw Louis XVI. guillotined,— Louis Capet, as they call him. It was against his will. Only just listen, now! To think that the 13th of January he roasted chestnuts and laughed with his family. When they forced him down on the see-saw, as they say, he had neither coat nor shoes, nothing but his shirt, a quilted waistcoat, grey cloth breeches, and grey silk stockings. I saw that, I did! The hackney-coach they brought him in was painted green. See here! come with us; the battalion are good fellows. You shall be canteen number two; I will teach you the business. Oh, it is very simple! You have your can and your hand-bell; away you go into the hubbub, with the platoons firing, the cannon thundering,— into the thickest of the row; and you cry, 'Who'll have a drop to drink, my children?' It 's no more trouble than that. I give everybody and anybody a sup, yes, indeed,— Whites the same as Blues, though I am a Blue myself, and a good Blue, too; but I serve them all alike. Wounded men are all thirsty. They die without any difference of opinions. Dying fellows ought to shake hands. How silly it is to go fighting! Do you come with us. If I am killed, you will step into my place. You see I am only so-so to look at; but I am a good woman, and a brave chap. Don't you be afraid."

When the vivandière ceased speaking, the woman murmured,—

"Our neighbour was called Marie Jeanne, and our servant was named Marie Claude."

In the mean time the sergeant reprimanded the grenadier:—

"Hold your tongue! You frighten madame. One does not swear before ladies."

"All the same; it is a downright butchery for an honest man to hear about," replied the grenadier; "and to see Chinese Iroquois, that have had their fathers-in-law crippled by a lord, their grandfathers sent to the galleys by the priest, and their fathers hung by the king, and who fight — name of the little Black Man!— and mix themselves up with revolts, and get smashed for his lordship, the priest, and the king!"

"Silence in the ranks!" cried the sergeant.

"A man may hold his tongue, Sergeant," returned the grenadier; "but that doesn't hinder the fact that it's a pity to see a pretty woman like this running the risk of getting her neck broken for the sake of a dirty robber."

"Grenadier," said the sergeant, "we are not in the Pike-club of Paris; no eloquence!"

He turned toward the woman.

"And your husband, madame? What is he at? What has become of him?"

"There hasn't anything become of him, because they killed him."

"Where did that happen?"

"In the hedge."

"When?"

"Three days ago."

"Who did it?"

"I don't know."

"How? You do not know who killed your husband?"

"No."

"Was it a Blue? Was it a White?"

"It was a bullet."

"Three days ago?"

"Yes."

"In what direction?"

"Toward Ernée. My husband fell,— that is all."

"And what have you been doing since your husband was killed?"

"I bear away my children."

"Where are you taking them?"

"Straight ahead."

"Where do you sleep?"

"On the ground."

"What do you eat?"

"Nothing."

The sergeant made that military grimace which makes the moustache touch the nose.

"Nothing?"

"That is to say, sloes and dried berries left from last year, myrtle seeds, and fern shoots."

"Faith! you might as well say ' nothing.' "

The eldest of the children, who seemed to understand, said, "I am hungry."

The sergeant took a bit of regulation bread from his pocket, and handed it to the mother. She broke the bread into two fragments, and gave them to the children, who ate with avidity.

"She has kept none for herself," grumbled the sergeant.

"Because she is not hungry," said a soldier.

"Because she is a mother," said the sergeant.

The children interrupted the dialogue.

"I want to drink," cried one.

"I want to drink," repeated the other.

"Is there no brook in this devil's wood?" asked the sergeant.

The vivandière took the brass cup which hung at her belt beside her hand-bell, turned the cock of the can she carried slung over her shoulder, poured a few drops into the cup, and held it to the children's lips in turn.

The first drank and made a grimace. The second drank and spat it out.

"Nevertheless, it is good," said the vivandière.

"Is it some of the old cut-throat?" asked the sergeant.

"Yes, and the best; but these are peasants." And she wiped her cup.

The sergeant resumed: —

"And so, madame, you are trying to escape?"

"There is nothing else left for me to do."

"Across fields — going whichever way chance directs?"

"I run with all my might, then I walk, then I fall."

"Poor villager!" said the vivandière.

"The people fight," stammered the woman. "They are shooting all around me. I do not know what it is they wish. They killed my husband; that is all I understood."

The sergeant grounded the butt of his musket till the earth rang, and cried,—

"What a beast of a war — in the hangman's name!"

The woman continued,—

" Last night we slept in an *émousse*."

" All four? "

" All four."

" Slept? "

" Slept."

" Then," said the sergeant, " you slept standing."

He turned toward the soldiers: " Comrades, what these savages call an *émousse* is an old hollow tree-trunk that a man may fit himself into as if it were a sheath. But what would you? We cannot all be Parisians."

" Slept in a hollow tree? " exclaimed the vivandière. " And with three children! "

" And," added the sergeant, " when the little ones howled, it must have been odd to anybody passing by and seeing nothing whatever, to hear a tree cry, ' Papa! mamma!' "

" Luckily it is summer," sighed the woman.

She looked down upon the ground in silent resignation, her eyes filled with the bewilderment of wretchedness.

The soldiers made a silent circle round this group of misery. A widow, three orphans; flight, abandonment, solitude, war muttering around the horizon; hunger, thirst; no other nourishment than the herbs of the field, no other roof than that of heaven.

The sergeant approached the woman, and fixed his eye on the sucking baby. The little one left the breast, turned its head gently, gazing with its beautiful blue orbs into the formidable hairy face, bristling and wild, which bent toward it, and began to smile.

The sergeant raised himself, and they saw a great tear roll down his cheek and cling like a pearl to the end of his moustache.

He lifted his voice: —

" Comrades, from all this I conclude that the regiment is going to become a father. Is it agreed? We adopt these three children? "

" Hurrah for the Republic! " chorused the grenadiers.

"It is decided!" said the sergeant.

He stretched his two hands above the mother and her babes.

"Behold the children of the battalion of the Bonnet Rouge!"

The vivandière leaped for joy.

"Three heads under one bonnet!" cried she.

Then she burst into sobs, embraced the poor widow wildly, and said to her, "What a rogue the little girl looks already!"

"Vive la République!" repeated the soldiers.

And the sergeant said to the mother: —

"Come, citizeness!"

BOOK II

THE CORVETTE "CLAYMORE."

CHAPTER I

ENGLAND AND FRANCE IN CONCERT

IN the spring of 1793, at the moment when France, simultaneously attacked on all its frontiers, suffered the pathetic distraction of the downfall of the Girondists, this was what happened in the Channel Islands.

At Jersey, on the evening of the 1st of June, about an hour before sunset, a corvette set sail from the solitary little Bay of Bonnenuit, in that kind of foggy weather which is favourable to flight because pursuit is rendered dangerous. The vessel was manned by a French crew, though it made part of the English fleet stationed on the look-out at the eastern point of the island. The Prince de la Tour d'Auvergne, who was of the house of Bouillon, commanded the English flotilla; and it was by his orders, and for an urgent and special service, that the corvett had been detached.

This vessel, entered at Trinity House under the name of the " Claymore," had the appearance of a transport or trader, but was in reality a war corvette. She had the heavy, pacific look of a merchantman; but it would not have been safe to trust to that. She had been built for a double purpose,—cunning and strength: to deceive if possible, to fight if necessary. For the service before her this night, the lading of the lower deck had been replaced by thirty carronades of

15

heavy calibre. Either because a storm was feared, or because it was desirable to prevent the vessel having a suspicious appearance, these carronades were housed,— that is to say, securely fastened within by triple chains, and the hatches above shut close. Nothing was to be seen from without. The ports were blinded; the slides closed; it was as if the corvette had put on a mask. Armed corvettes only carry guns on the upper deck; but this one, built for surprise and cunning, had the deck free, and was able, as we have just seen, to carry a battery below. The "Claymore" was after a heavy, squat model, but a good sailer nevertheless,— the hull of the most solid sort used in the English navy,— and in battle was almost as valuable as a frigate, though for mizzen she had only a small mast of brigantine rig. Her rudder, of a peculiar and scientific form, had a curved frame, of unique shape, which cost fifty pounds sterling in the dockyards of Southampton.

The crew, all French, was composed of refugee officers and deserter sailors. They were tried men; not one but was a good sailor, good soldier, and good royalist. They had a threefold fanaticism,— for ship, sword and king.

A half-regiment of marines, that could be disembarked in case of need, was added to the crew.

The corvette "Claymore" had as a captain chevalier of Saint Louis, Count du Boisberthelot, one of the best officers of the old Royal Navy; for second, the Chevalier La Vieuville, who had commanded a company of French guards in which Hoche was sergeant; and for pilot, Philip Gacquoil, the most skilful mariner in Jersey.

It was evident that the vessel had unusual business on hand. Indeed, a man who had just come on board had the air of one entering upon an adventure. He was a tall old man, upright and robust, with a severe countenance, whose age it would have been difficult to guess accurately, for he seemed at once old and young,— one of those men who are full of years and of vigour; who have white hair on their heads and lightning in their glance; forty in point of energy and eighty in power and authority. As he came on deck his sea-cloak blew open, exposing his large loose breeches and top-boots, and a goat-skin vest which had one side tanned and embroidered with silk, while on the other the hair was left rough and bristling,— a complete costume of the Breton peasant. These old-fashioned jackets answered alike for working and holidays: they could be turned to show the hairy or embroidered side, as one pleased,— goat-skin all the week, gala accoutrements on Sunday. As if to increase a resemblance which had been carefully studied, the peasant dress worn by the old man was threadbare at the knees and elbows, and seemed to have been long in use, while his coarse cloak might have belonged to a fisherman. He had on his head the round hat of the period,— high, with a broad rim, which, when turned down, gave the wearer a rustic look, but took a military air when fastened up at the side with a loop and a cockade. The old man wore his hat with the brim flattened forward, peasant fashion, without either tassels or cockade.

Lord Balcarras, the governor of the island, and the Prince de la Tour d'Auvergne, had in person conducted and installed him on board. The secret agent of the princes, Gélambre, formerly one of the Count d'Artois's body-guard, had superintended the arrangement of the cabin; and, although himself a nobleman, pushed courtesy and respect so far as to walk behind the old man, carrying his portmanteau. When they left him to go ashore again, Monsieur de Gélanbre saluted the peasant profoundly; Lord Balcarras said to him, " Good luck, General! " and the Prince de la Tour d'Auvergne added, " *Au revoir*, my cousin! "

" The peasant " was the name by which the crew immediately designated their passenger during the short dialogues which seamen hold; but without understanding further about the matter, they comprehended that he was no more a peasant than the corvette was a common sloop.

There was little wind. The " Claymore " left Bonnenuit, and passed in front of Boulay Bay, and was for some time

2

in sight, tacking to windward; then she lessened in the gathering night, and finally disappeared.

An hour after, Gélambre, having returned to his house at Saint Helier, sent by the Southampton express the following lines to the Count d'Artois, at the Duke of York's headquarters, —

MONSEIGNEUR, — The departure has just taken place. Success certain. In eight days the whole coast will be on fire from Granville to Saint Malo.

Four days previous, Prieur, the representative of Marne, on a mission to the army along the coast of Cherbourg, and momentarily residing at Granville, had received by a secret emissary this message, written in the same hand as the dispatch above: —

CITIZEN REPRESENTATIVE, — On the 1st of June, at the hour when the tide serves, the war corvette "Claymore," with a masked battery, will set sail for the purpose of landing upon the shore of France a man of whom this is a description: tall, old, white hair, peasant's dress, hands of an aristocrat. I will send you more details to-morrow. He will land on the morning of the 2d. Warn the cruisers; capture the corvette; guillotine the man.

CHAPTER II

NIGHT ON THE VESSEL AND WITH THE PASSENGER

THE corvette, instead of going south and making for Saint Catherine's, headed north, then veered to the west, and resolutely entered the arm of the sea between Sark and Jersey, called the Passage de la Deronte. At that time there was no lighthouse upon any point along either coast. The sun had set clear; the night was dark, — darker than summer nights ordinarily are; there was a moon, but vast clouds, rather of the equinox than the solstice, veiled the sky, and according to all appearance the moon would not be visible

till she touched the horizon at the moment of setting. A few
clouds hung low upon the water and covered it with mist.

All this obscurity was favourable.

The intention of Pilot Gacquoil was to leave Jersey on the
left and Guernsey on the right, and to gain, by bold sailing
between the Hanois and the Douvree, some bay of the Saint
Malo shore,— a route less short than that by the Minquiers,
but safer, as the French cruisers had standing orders to keep
an especially keen watch between Saint Helier and Granville.
If the wind were favourable, and nothing occurred, Gacquoil
hoped by setting all sail to touch the French coast at day-
break.

All went well. The corvette had passed Gros-Nez. Toward nine o'clock the weather looked sulky, as sailors say,
and there were wind and sea; but the wind was good and the
sea strong without being violent. Still, now and then the
waves swept the vessel's bows.

The " peasant," whom Lord Balcarras had called " General," and whom the Prince de la Tour d'Auvergne addressed
as " My cousin," had a sailor's footing, and paced the deck
with tranquil gravity. He did not even seem to notice that
the corvette rocked considerably. From time to time he took
a cake of chocolate out of his pocket and munched a morsel:
his white hair did not prevent his having all his teeth.

He spoke to no one, except now and then a few low quick
words to the captain, who listened with deference, and seemed
to consider his passenger, rather than himself, the commander.

The " Claymore," ably piloted, skirted unperceived in the
fog the long escarpment north of Jersey, hugging the shore
on account of the formidable reef Pierres de Leeq, which is in
the middle of the channel between Jersey and Sark. Gacquoil,
standing at the helm, signalled in turn the Grève de Leeq,
Gros-Nez, and Plémont, and slipped the corvette along among
this chain of reefs, feeling his way to a certain extent, but
with certitude, like a man familiar with the course and acquainted with the disposition of the sea. The corvette had no
light forward, from a fear of betraying its passage through

these guarded waters. The fog was a cause for rejoicing. They reached the Grande Etaque. The mist was so thick that the outlines of the lofty pinnacle could scarcely be made out. Ten o'clock was heard to sound from the belfry of Saint Ouen, a proof that the wind was still abaft. All was yet going well. The sea grew rougher on account of the neighbourhood of La Corbière.

A little after ten. Count de Boisberthelot and the Chevalier La Vieuville reconducted the man in the peasant's garb to his cabin, which was in reality the captain's stateroom. As he went in, he said to them in a low voice: —

" Gentlemen, you understand the importance of secrecy. Silence up to the moment of explosion. You two are the only ones here who know my name."

" We will carry it with us to the tomb," replied Boisberthelot.

" As for me," added the old man, " were I in face of death, I would not tell it."

He entered his cabin.

CHAPTER III

NOBLE AND PLEBEIAN IN CONCERT

THE commander and the second officer returned on deck and walked up and down, side by side, in conversation. They were evidently talking of their passenger, and this was the dialogue which the wind dispersed among the shadows.

Boisberthelot grumbled in a half-voice in the ear of La Vieuville: —

" We shall see if he is really a leader."

La Vieuville replied, " In the mean time he is a prince."

" Almost."

" Nobleman in France, but prince in Brittany."

" Like the La Trémoilles; like the Rohans."

" With whom he is connected."

Boisberthelot resumed : —

" In France, and in the king's carriages, he is marquis, as I am count, and you are chevalier."

" The carriages are far off ! " cried La Vieuville. " We have got to the tumbrel."

There was a silence.

Boisberthelot began again : —

" For lack of a French prince, a Breton one is taken."

" For lack of thrushes,— no, for want of an eagle,— a crow is chosen."

" I should prefer a vulture," said Boisberthelot.

And La Vieuville retorted,—

" Yes, indeed ! a beak and talons."

" We shall see."

" Yes," resumed La Vieuville, " it is time there was a head. I am of Tinteniac's opinion : *'A true chief, and — gunpowder!'* ' See, Commander ; I know nearly all the leaders, possible and impossible,— those of yesterday, those of to-day, and those of to-morrow ; there is not one with the sort of headpiece we need. In that accursed Vendée it wants a general who is a lawyer at the same time. He must worry the enemy, dispute every mill, thicket, ditch, pebble ; quarrel with him ; take advantage of everything ; see to everything ; slaughter plentifully ; make examples ; be sleepless, pitiless. At this hour there are heroes among that army of peasants, but there are no captains. D'Elbée is *nil;* Lescure is ailing ; Bonchampe shows mercy,— he is kind, that means stupid ; La Rochejacquelein is a magnificent sub-lieutenant ; Silz an officer for open country, unfit for a war of expedients ; Cathelineau is a simple carter ; Stofflet is a cunning gamekeeper ; Bérard is inept ; Boulainvilliers is ridiculous ; Charette is shocking. And I do not speak of the barber Gaston. For, in the name of Mars ! what is the good of opposing the Revolution, and what is the difference between the republicans and ourselves, if we set hairdressers to command noblemen ? "

" You see that beast of a Revolution has infected us also."

" An itch that France has caught."

" An itch of the Third Estate," replied Boisberthelot.

" It is only England that can cure us of it."

" And she will cure us, do not doubt it, Captain."

" In the meanwhile it is ugly."

" Indeed, yes.   Clowns everywhere!   The monarchy which has for commander-in-chief Stofflet, the game-keeper of M. de Maulevrier, has nothing to envy in the republic that has for minister, Pache, son of the Duke de Castrie's porter. What men this Vendean war brings out against each other! On one side Santerre the brewer, on the other Gaston the wig-maker! "

" My dear Vieuville, I have a certain respect for Gaston. He did not conduct himself ill in his command of Gueménée. He very neatly shot three hundred Blues, after making them dig their own graves."

" Well and good; but I could have done that as well as he."

" Zounds! no doubt; and I also."

" The great acts of war," resumed La Vieuville, " require to be undertaken by noblemen.   They are matters for knights and not hairdressers."

" Still, there are some estimable men among this ' Third Estate,' " returned Boisberthelot.   " Take, for example, Joby the clockmaker.   He had been a sergeant in a Flanders regi-ment; he gets himself made a Vendean chief; he commands a coast band; he has a son who is a Republican, and while the father serves among the Whites, the son serves among the Blues.   Encounter.   Battle.   The father takes the son pris-oner, and blows out his brains."

" He's a good one," said La Vieuville.

" A royalist Brutus," replied Boisberthelot.

" All that does not hinder the fact that it is insupportable to be commanded by a Coquereau, a Jean-Jean, a Mouline, a Focart, a Bouju, a Chouppes! "

" My dear chevalier, the other side is equally disgusted. We are full of plebeians; they are full of nobles.   Do you suppose the *san-sculottes* are content to be commanded by the

Count de Canclaux, the Viscount de Miranda, the Viscount de Beauharnais, the Count de Valence, the Marquis de Custine, and the Duke de Biron."

" What a hash! "

" And the Duke de Chartres! "

" Son of Egalité. Ah, then, when will he ever be king? "

" Never."

" He mounts toward the throne. He is aided by his crimes."

" And held back by his vices," said Boisberthelot.

There was silence again; then Boisberthelot continued:

" Still, he tried to bring about a reconciliation. He went to see the king. I was at Versailles when somebody spat on his back."

" From the top of the grand staircase? "

" Yes."

" It was well done."

" We call him Bourbon the Bourbeux."

" He is bald; he has pimples; he is a regicide — poh! "

Then La Vieuville added,—

" I was at Ouessant with him."

" On the ' Saint Esprit ' ? "

" Yes."

" If he had obeyed the signal that the Admiral d'Orvilliers made him, to keep to the windward, he would have kept the English from passing."

" Certainly."

" Is it true that he was hidden at the bottom of the hold? "

" No; but it must be said all the same."

And La Vieuville burst out laughing.

Boisberthelot observed,—

" There are idiots enough. Hold! That Boulainvilliers you were speaking of, La Vieuville,— I knew him. I had a chance of studying him. In the beginning, the peasants were armed with pikes: if he did not get it into his head to make pikemen of them! He wanted to teach them the manual of exercise, *de la pique-en biais et de la pique-trainante-le-fer*

dévant. He dreamed of transforming those savages into soldiers of the Line. He proposed to show them how to mass
battalions and form hollow squares. He jabbered the old-
fashioned military dialect at them; for ' chief of a squad,' he
said *un cap d'escade,* which was the appellation of corporals
under Louis XIV. He persisted in forming a regiment of
those poachers: he had regular companies. The sergeants
ranged themselves in a circle every evening to take the countersign from the colonel's sergeant, who whispered it to the sergeant of the lieutenants; he repeated it to his neighbour, and
he to the man nearest; and so on, from ear to ear, down to the
last. He cashiered an officer because he did not stand bare-
headed to receive the watchword from the sergeant's mouth.
You can fancy how all succeeded. The booby could not understand that peasants must be led peasant fashion, and that
one cannot make drilled soldiers out of woodchoppers. Yes,
I knew that Boulainvilliers."

They moved on a few steps, each pursuing his own thoughts.
Then the conversation was renewed.

" By the way, is it true that Dampierre is killed? "

" Yes, Commander."

" Before Condé? "

" At the camp of Pamars, by a gunshot."

Boisberthelot sighed.

" The Count de Dampierre. Yet another of ours who went
over to them! "

" A good journey to him," said La Vieuville.

" And the princesses — where are they? "

" At Trieste."

" Still? "

" Still. Ah, this republic! " cried Vieuville. " What havoc
from such slight consequences! When one thinks that this
revolution was caused by the deficit of a few millions."

" Distrust small outbreaks," said Boisberthelot.

" Everything is going badly," resumed La Vieuville.

" Yes; La Rouarie is dead; Du Dresnay is an idiot. What
pitiful leaders all those bishops are,— that Concy, Bishop of

Rochelle; that Beaupoil Saint-Aulaire, Bishop of Poitiers; that Mercy, Bishop of Luçon and lover of Madame de l'Eschasserie —"

"Whose name is Servanteau, you know, Commander; L'Eschasserie is the name of an estate."

"And that false Bishop of Agra, who is curé of I know not what."

"Of Dol. He is called Guillot de Folleville. At least he is brave, and he fights."

"Priests when soldiers are needed! Bishops who are not bishops! Generals who are no generals!"

La Vieuville interrupted Boisberthelot.

"Commander, have you the 'Moniteur' in your cabin?"

"Yes."

"What are they playing in Paris just now?"

"'Adèle and Poulin,' and 'The Cavern.'"

"I should like to see that."

"You will be able to. We shall be at Paris in a month." Boisberthelot reflected a moment, and added,—

"At the latest. Mr. Windham said so to Lord Hood."

"But then, Captain, everything is not going so ill."

"Zounds! everything would go well, on condition that the war in Brittany could be properly conducted."

La Vieuville shook his head.

"Commander," he asked, "do we land the marines?"

"Yes, if the coast is for us, not if it is hostile. Sometimes war must break down doors, sometimes slip in quietly. Civil war ought always to have a false key in its pocket. We shall do all in our power. The most important is the chief."

Then Boisberthelot added thoughtfully:—

"La Vieuville, what do you think of the Chevalier de Dieugie?"

"The younger?"

"Yes."

"For a leader?"

"Yes."

"That he is another officer for open country and pitched battles. Only the peasant understands the thickets."

"Then resign yourself to General Stofflet and to General Cathelineau."

La Vieuville mused a while, and then said, "It needs a prince,— a prince of France, a prince of the blood, a true prince."

"Why? Whoever says prince —"

"Says poltroon. I know it, Captain. But one is needed for the effect on the big stupid eyes of the country lads."

"My dear chevalier, the princes will not come."

"We will get on without them."

Boisberthelot pressed his hand upon his forehead with the mechanical movement of a man endeavouring to bring out some idea. He exclaimed,—

"Well, let us try the general we have here."

"He is a great nobleman."

"Do you believe he will answer?"

"Provided he is strong."

"That is to say, ferocious," said Boisberthelot.

The count and the chevalier looked fixedly at each other.

"Monsieur du Boisberthelot, you have said the word,— ferocious. Yes; that is what we need. This is a war without pity. The hour is to the bloodthirsty. The regicides have cut off Louis XVI.'s head; we will tear off the four limbs of the regicides. Yes, the general necessary is General Inexorable. In Anjou and Upper Poitou the chiefs do the magnanimous; they dabble in generosity: nothing moves on. In the Marais and the country of Retz, the chiefs are ferocious: everything goes forward. It is because Charette is savage that he holds his own against Parrein: it is hyæna against hyæna."

Boisberthelot had no time to reply; La Vieuville's words were suddenly cut short by a desperate cry, and at the same instant they heard a noise as unaccountable as it was awful. The cry and this noise came from the interior of the vessel.

The captain and lieutenant made a rush for the gun-deck,

but could not get down.   All the gunners were hurrying frantically up.

A frightful thing had just happened.

CHAPTER IV

TORMENTUM BELLI

ONE of the carronades of the battery, a twenty-four pounder, had got loose.

This is perhaps the most formidable of ocean accidents. Nothing more terrible can happen to a vessel in open sea and under full sail.

A gun that breaks its moorings becomes suddenly some indescribable supernatural beast.   It is a machine which transforms itself into a monster.   This mass turns upon its wheels, has the rapid movements of a billiard-ball; rolls with the rolling, pitches with the pitching; goes, comes, pauses, seems to meditate; resumes its course, rushes along the ship from end to end like an arrow, circles about, springs aside, evades, rears, breaks, kills, exterminates.   It is a battering-ram which assaults a wall at its own caprice.   Moreover, the battering-ram is metal, the wall wood.   It is the entrance of matter into liberty.   One might say that this eternal slave avenges itself. It seems as if the power of evil hidden in what we call inanimate objects finds a vent and bursts suddenly out.   It has an air of having lost patience, of seeking some fierce, obscure retribution; nothing more inexorable than this rage of the inanimate.   The mad mass has the bounds of a panther, the weight of the elephant, the agility of the mouse, the obstinacy of the axe, the unexpectedness of the surge, the rapidity of lightning, the deafness of the tomb.   It weighs ten thousand pounds, and it rebounds like a child's ball.   Its flight is a wild whirl abruptly cut at right angles.   What is to be done?

How to end this? A tempest ceases, a cyclone passes, a wind falls, a broken mast is replaced, a leak is stopped, a fire dies out; but how to control this enormous brute of bronze? In what way can one attack it?

You can make a mastiff hear reason, astound a bull, fascinate a boa, frighten a tiger, soften a lion; but there is no resource with that monster,— a cannon let loose. You cannot kill it,— it is dead; at the same time it lives. It lives with a sinister life bestowed on it by Infinity.

The planks beneath it give it play. It is moved by the ship. which is moved by the sea, which is moved by the wind. This destroyer is a plaything. The ship, the waves, the blasts, all aid it; hence its frightful vitality. How to assail this fury of complication? How to fetter this monstrous mechanism for wrecking a ship? How foresee its comings and goings, its returns, its stops, its shocks? Any one of these blows upon the sides may stave out the vessel. How divine its awful gyrations! One has to deal with a projectile which thinks, seems to possess ideas, and which changes its direction at each instant. How stop the course of something which must be avoided? The horrible cannon flings itself about, advances, recoils, strikes to the right, strikes to the left, flees, passes, disconcerts ambushes, breaks down obstacles, crushes men like flies. The great danger of the situation is in the mobility of its base. How combat an inclined plane which has caprices? The ship, so to speak, has lightning imprisoned in its womb which seeks to escape; it is like thunder rolling above an earthquake.

In an instant the whole crew were on foot. The fault was the chief gunner's; he had neglected to fix home the screw-nut of the mooring-chain, and had so badly shackled the four wheels of the carronade that the play given to the sole and frame had separated the platform, and ended by breaking the breeching. The cordage had broken, so that the gun was no longer secure on the carriage. The stationary breeching which prevents recoil was not in use at that period. As a heavy wave struck the port, the carronade, weakly attached, recoiled, burst its chain, and began to rush wildly about. Conceive, in order to have an idea of this strange sliding, a drop of water running down a pane of glass.

At the moment when the lashings gave way the gunners were in the battery, some in groups, others standing alone, occupied with such duties as sailors perform in expectation of the command to clear for action. The carronade, hurled forward by the pitching, dashed into this knot of men, and crushed four at the first blow; then, flung back and shot out anew by the rolling, it cut in two a fifth poor fellow, glanced off to the larboard side, and struck a piece of the battery with such force as to unship it. Then rose the cry of distress which had been heard. The men rushed toward the ladder; the gundeck emptied in the twinkling of an eye. The enormous cannon was left alone. She was given up to herself. She was her own mistress, and mistress of the vessel. She could do what she willed with both. This whole crew, accustomed to laugh in battle, trembled now. To describe the universal terror would be impossible.

Captain Boisberthelot and Lieutenant Vieuville, although both intrepid men, stopped at the head of the stairs, and remained mute, pale, hesitating, looking down on the deck. Some one pushed them aside with his elbow and descended.

It was their passenger, the peasant,— the man of whom they had been speaking a moment before.

When he reached the foot of the ladder, he stood still.

CHAPTER V

VIS ET VIR

THE cannon came and went along the deck. One might have fancied it the living chariot of the Apocalypse. The marine-lantern, oscillating from the ceiling, added a dizzying whirl of lights and shadows to this vision. The shape

of the cannon was undistinguishable from the rapidity of its
course; now it looked black in the light, now it cast weird
reflections through the gloom.

It kept on its work of destruction. It had already shattered
four other pieces, and dug two crevices in the side, fortunately
above the water-line, though they would leak in case a squall
should come on. It dashed itself frantically against the
frame-work; the solid tie-beams resisted, their curved form
giving them great strength, but they creaked ominously under
the assaults of this terrible club, which seemed endowed with a
sort of appalling ubiquity, striking on every side at once.
The strokes of a bullet shaken in a bottle would not be madder
or more rapid. The four wheels passed and repassed above
the dead men, cut, carved, slashed them, till the five corpses
were a score of stumps rolling about the deck; the heads
seem to cry out; streams of blood twisted in and out of the
planks with every pitch of the vessel.. The ceiling, damaged
in several places, began to gape. The whole ship was filled
with the awful tumult.

The captain promptly recovered his composure, and at his
order the sailors threw down into the deck everything which
could deaden and check the mad rush of the gun,— mattresses,
hammocks, spare sails, coils of rope, extra equipments, and
the bales of false assignats of which the corvette carried a
whole cargo; an infamous deception which the English considered a fair trick in war.

But what could these rags avail? No one dared descend to
arrange them in any useful fashion, and in a few instants they
were mere heaps of lint.

There was just sea enough to render an accident as complete as possible. A tempest would have been desirable,—
it might have thrown the gun upside down; and the four
wheels once in the air, the monster could have been mastered.
But the devastation increased. There were gashes and even
fractures in the masts, which, imbedded in the woodwork of
the keel, pierce the decks of ships like great round pillars.
The mizzen-mast was cracked, and the main-mast itself was

injured under the convulsive blows of the gun. The battery
was being destroyed. Ten pieces out of the thirty were disabled; the breaches multiplied in the side, and the corvette
began to take in water.

The old passenger, who had descended to the gun-deck,
looked like a form of stone stationed at the foot of the stairs.
He stood motionless, gazing sternly about upon the devastation. Indeed, it seemed impossible to take a single step forward.

Each bound of the liberated carronade menaced the destruction of the vessel. A few minutes more and shipwreck
would be inevitable.

They must perish or put a summary end to the disaster.
A decision must be made — but how?

What a combatant — this cannon!

They must check this mad monster. They must seize this
flash of lightning. They must overthrow this thunderbolt.

Boisberthelot said to La Vieuville: —

" Do you believe in God, Chevalier? "

La Vieuville replied,—

" Yes. No. Sometimes."

" In a tempest? "

" Yes; and in moments like this."

" Only God can aid us here," said Boisberthelot.

All were silent: the cannon kept up its horrible fracas.

The waves beat against the ship; their blows from without
responded to the strokes of the cannon.

It was like two hammers alternating.

Suddenly, into the midst of this sort of inaccessible circus,
where the escaped cannon leaped and bounded, there sprang
a man with an iron bar in his hand. It was the author of
this catastrophe,— the gunner whose culpable negligence had
caused the accident; the captain of the gun. Having been the
means of bringing about the misfortune, he desired to repair
it. He had caught up a handspike in one fist, a tiller-rope
with a slipping-noose in the other, and jumped down into
the gun-deck.

Then a strange combat began, a titanic strife,— the struggle of the gun against the gunner; a battle between matter and intelligence; a duel between the inanimate and the human.

The man was posted in an angle, the bar and rope in his two fists; backed against one of the riders, settled firmly on his legs as on two pillars of steel, livid, calm, tragic, rooted as it were in the planks, he waited.

He waited for the cannon to pass near him.

The gunner knew his piece, and it seemed to him that she must recognize her master. He had lived a long while with her. How many times he had thrust his hand between her jaws! It was his tame monster. He began to address it as he might have done his dog.

"Come!" said he. Perhaps he loved it.

He seemed to wish that it would turn toward him.

But to come toward him would be to spring upon him. Then he would be lost. How to avoid its crush? There was the question. All stared in terrified silence.

Not a breast respired freely, except perchance that of the old man who alone stood in the deck with the two combatants, a stern second.

He might himself be crushed by the piece. He did not stir.

Beneath them, the blind sea directed the battle.

At the instant when, accepting this awful hand-to-hand contest, the gunner approached to challenge the cannon, some chance fluctuation of the waves kept it for a moment immovable, as if suddenly stupefied.

"Come on!" the man said to it. It seemed to listen.

Suddenly it darted upon him. The gunner avoided the shock.

The struggle began,— struggle unheard of. The fragile matching itself against the invulnerable. The thing of flesh attacking the brazen brute. On the one side blind force, on the other a soul.

The whole passed in a half-light. It was like the indistinct vision of a miracle.

A soul,— strange thing; but you would have said that the
cannon had one also,— a soul filled with rage and hatred.
This blindness appeared to have eyes. The monster had the
air of watching the man. There was — one might have fancied so at least — cunning in this mass. It also chose its moment. It became some gigantic insect of metal, having, or
seeming to have, the will of a demon. Sometimes this colossal
grasshopper would strike the low ceiling of the gun-deck,
then fall back on its four wheels like a tiger upon its four
claws, and dart anew on the man. He, supple, agile, adroit,
would glide away like a snake from the reach of these lightning-like movements. He avoided the encounters; but the
blows which he escaped fell upon the vessel and continued the
havoc.

An end of broken chain remained attached to the carronade. This chain had twisted itself, one could not tell how;
about the screw of the breech-button. One extremity of the
chain was fastened to the carriage. The other, hanging loose,
whirled wildly about the gun and added to the danger of its
blows.

The screw held it like a clinched hand, and the chain mul-
tiplying the strokes of the battering-ram by its strokes of a
thong, made a fearful whirlwind about the cannon,— a whip
of iron in a fist of brass. This chain complicated the battle.

Nevertheless, the man fought. Sometimes, even, it was the
man who attacked the cannon. He crept along the side, bar
and rope in hand, and the cannon had the air of understanding, and fled as if it perceived a snare. The man pursued it,
formidable, fearless.

Such a duel could not last long. The gun seemed suddenly
to say to itself, " Come, we must make an end! " and it paused.
One felt the approach of the crisis. The cannon, as if in suspense, appeared to have, or had,— because it seemed to all a
sentient being,— a furious premeditation. It sprang unexpectedly upon the gunner. He jumped aside, let it pass, and
cried out with a laugh, " Try again! " The gun, as if in a
fury, broke a carronade to larboard; then, seized anew by the

3

invisible sling which held it, was flung to starboard toward the man, who escaped.

Three carronades gave way under the blows of the gun; then, as if blind and no longer conscious of what it was doing, it turned its back on the man, rolled from the stern to the bow, bruising the stem and making a breach in the plankings of the prow. The gunner had taken refuge at the foot of the stairs, a few steps from the old man, who was watching.

The gunner held his handspike in rest. The cannon seemed to perceive him, and, without taking the trouble to turn itself, backed upon him with the quickness of an axe-stroke. The gunner, if driven back against the side was lost. The crew uttered a simultaneous cry.

But the old passenger, until now immovable, made a spring more rapid than all those wild whirls. He seized a bale of the false assignats, and at the risk of being crushed, succeeded in flinging it between the wheels of the carronade. This manœuvre, decisive and dangerous, could not have been executed with more adroitness and precision by a man trained to all the exercises set down in Durosel's "Manual of Sea Gunnery."

The bale had the effect of a plug. A pebble may stop a log, a tree-branch turn an avalanche. The carronade stumbled. The gunner, in his turn, seizing this terrible chance, plunged his iron bar between the spokes of one of the hind wheels. The cannon was stopped.

It staggered. The man, using the bar as a lever, rocked it to and fro. The heavy mass turned over with a clang like a falling bell, and the gunner, dripping with sweat, rushed forward headlong and passed the slipping-noose of the tiller-rope about the bronze neck of the overthrown monster.

It was ended. The man had conquered. The ant had subdued the mastodon; the pigmy had taken the thunderbolt prisoner.

The marines and the sailors clapped their hands.

The whole crew hurried down with cables and chains, and in an instant the cannon was securely lashed.

The gunner saluted the passenger.

" Sir," he said to him, " you have saved my life."

The old man had resumed his impassible attitude, and did not reply.

CHAPTER VI

THE TWO SCALES OF THE BALANCE

THE man had conquered, but one might say that the cannon had conquered also. Immediate ship-wreck had been avoided, but the corvette was by no means saved. The dilapidation of the vessel seemed irremediable. The sides had five breaches, one of which, very large, was in the bow. Out of the thirty carronades, twenty lay useless in their frames. The carronade, which had been captured and rechained, was itself disabled; the screw of the breech-button was forced, and the levelling of the piece impossible in consequence. The battery was reduced to nine pieces. The hold had sprung a leak. It was necessary at once to repair the damages and set the pumps to work.

The gun-deck, now that one had time to look about it, offered a terrible spectacle. The interior of a mad elephant's cage could not have been more completely dismantled.

However great the necessity that the corvette should escape observation, a still more imperious necessity presented itself, — immediate safety. It had been necessary to light up the deck by lanterns placed here and there along the sides.

But during the whole time this tragic diversion had lasted, the crew were so absorbed by the one question of life or death that they noticed little what was passing outside the scene of the duel. The fog had thickened; the weather had changed; the wind had driven the vessel at will; it had got out of its route, in plain sight of Jersey and Guernsey, farther to the south than it ought to have gone, and was surrounded by a troubled sea. The great waves kissed the gaping wounds of

the corvette,— kisses full of peril. The sea rocked her men-
acingly. The breeze became a gale. A squall, a tempest
perhaps, threatened. It was impossible to see before one four
oars' length.

While the crew were repairing summarily and in haste the
ravages of the gun-deck, stopping the leaks and putting back
into position the guns which had escaped the disaster, the
old passenger had gone on deck.

He stood with his back against the main-mast.

He had paid no attention to a proceeding which had taken
place on the vessel. The Chevalier La Vieuville had drawn
up the marines in line on either side of the main-mast, and at
the whistle of the boatswain the sailors busy in the rigging
stood upright on the yards.

Count du Boisberthelot advanced toward the passenger.

Behind the captain marched a man, haggard, breathless,
his dress in disorder, yet wearing a satisfied look under it all.
It was the gunner who had just now so opportunely shown
himself a tamer of monsters, and who had got the better of
the cannon.

The count made a military salute to the unknown in peasant
garb, and said to him: —

" General, here is the man."

The gunner held himself erect, his eyes downcast, standing in a soldierly attitude.

Count du Boisberthelot continued,—

" General, taking into consideration what this man has
done, do you not think there is something for his commanders
to do? "

" I think there is," said the old man.

" Be good enough to give the orders," returned Boisberthelot.

" It is for you to give them. You are the captain."

" But you are the general," answered Boisberthelot.

The old man looked at the gunner.

" Approach," said he.

The gunner moved forward a step. The old man turned

toward Count du Boisberthelot, detached the cross of Saint Louis from the captain's uniform and fastened it on the jacket of the gunner.

"Hurrah!" cried the sailors.

The marines presented arms. The old passenger, pointing with his finger toward the bewildered gunner, added,—

"Now let that man be shot."

Stupor succeeded the applause.

Then, in the midst of a silence like that of the tomb, the old man raised his voice. He said,—

"A negligence has endangered this ship. At this moment she is perhaps lost. To be at sea is to face the enemy. A vessel at open sea is an army which gives battle. The tempest conceals, but does not absent itself. The whole sea is an ambuscade.

"Death is the penalty of any fault committed in the face of the enemy. No fault is reparable. Courage ought to be rewarded and negligence punished."

These words fell one after the other, slowly, solemnly, with a sort of inexorable measure, like the blows of an axe upon an oak.

And the old man, turning to the soldiers, added,—

"Do your duty."

The man upon whose breast shone the cross of Saint Louis bowed his head.

At a sign from Count du Boisberthelot, two sailors descended between decks, then returned, bringing the hammock winding-sheet. The ship's chaplain, who since the time of sailing had been at prayer in the officers' quarters, accompanied the two sailors; a sergeant detached from the line twelve marines, whom he arranged in two ranks, six by six; the gunner, without uttering a word, placed himself between the two files. The chaplain, crucifix in hand, advanced and stood near him.

"March!" said the sergeant.

The platoon moved with slow steps toward the bow. The two sailors who carried the shroud followed.

A gloomy silence fell upon the corvette. A hurricane moaned in the distance.

A few instants later there was a flash; a report followed, echoing among the shadows; then all was silent; then came the thud of a body falling into the sea.

The old passenger still leaned back against the mainmast with folded arms, thinking silently.

Boisberthelot pointed toward him with the forefinger of his left hand, and said in a low voice to La Vieuville:

" The Vendée has found a head! "

CHAPTER VII

HE WHO SETS SAIL PUTS INTO A LOTTERY

BUT what was to become of the corvette?

The clouds, which the whole night through had touched the waves, now lowered so thickly that the horizon was no longer visible; the sea seemed to be covered with a pall. Nothing to be seen but fog,— a situation always perilous, even for a vessel in good condition.

Added to the mist came the surging swell.

The time had been used to good purpose: the corvette had been lightened by throwing overboard everything which could be cleared from the havoc made by the carronade,— the dismantled guns, the broken carriages, frames twisted or unnailed, the fragments of splintered wood and iron; the portholes had been opened, and the corpses and parts of bodies, enveloped in tarpaulin, were slid down planks into the waves.

The sea was no longer manageable. Not that the tempest was imminent; it seemed, on the contrary, that the hurricane rustling behind the horizon decreased, and the squall was moving northward; but the waves were very high still, which indicated disturbance in the depths. The corvette could offer slight resistance to shocks in her crippled condition, so that the great waves might prove fatal to her.

Gacquoil stood thoughtfully at the helm.

To face ill-fortune with a bold front is the habit of those accustomed to rule at sea.

La Vieuville, who was the sort of man that becomes gay in the midst of disaster, accosted Gacquoil.

"Well, pilot," said he, "the squall has missed fire. Its attempt at sneezing comes to nothing. We shall get out of it. We shall have wind, and that is all."

Gacquoil replied, seriously, "Where there is wind there are waves."

Neither laughing nor sad, such is the sailor. The response had a disquieting significance. For a leaky ship to encounter a high sea is to fill rapidly. Gacquoil emphasized his prognostic by a frown. Perhaps La Vieuville had spoken almost jovial and gay words a little too soon after the catastrophe of the gun and its gunner. There are things which bring bad luck at sea. The ocean is secretive; one never knows what it means to do; it is necessary to be always on guard against it.

La Vieuville felt the necessity of getting back to gravity.

"Where are we, pilot?" he asked.

The pilot replied,—

"We are in the hands of God."

A pilot is a master; he must always be allowed to do what he will, and often he must be allowed to say what he pleases. Generally this species of man speaks little.

La Vieuville moved away. He had asked a question of the pilot; it was the horizon which replied. The sea suddenly cleared.

The fogs which trailed across the waves were quickly rent; the dark confusion of the billows spread out to the horizon's verge in a shadowy half-light, and this was what became visible:—

The sky seemed covered with a lid of clouds, but they no longer touched the water; in the east appeared a white-

ness, which was the dawn; in the west trembled a corresponding pallor, which was the setting moon.   These two ghostly
presences drew opposite each other narrow bands of pale lights
along the horizon, between the sombre sea and the gloomy
sky.

Across each of these lines of light were sketched black
profiles, upright and immovable.

To the west, against the moonlight sky, stood out sharply
three lofty rocks, erect as Celtic cromlechs.

To the east, against the pale horizon of morning, rose
eight sail, ranged in order at regular intervals in a formidable array.

The three rocks were a reef; the eight ships, a squadron.

Behind the vessel was the Minquiers,— a rock of an evil
renown; before her, the French cruisers.   To the west, the
abyss; to the east, carnage: she was between a shipwreck and
a combat.

For meeting the reef, the corvette had a broken hull, rigging disjointed, masts tottering in their foundations; for
facing battle, she had a battery where one-and-twenty cannon
out of thirty were dismounted, and whose best gunners were
dead.

The dawn was yet faint; there still remained a little night
to them.   This might even last for some time, since it was
principally made by thick, high clouds presenting the solid
appearance of a vault.

The wind, which had succeeded in dispersing the lower
mists, was forcing the corvette toward the Minquiers.

In her excessive feebleness and dilapidation, she scarcely
obeyed the helm; she rolled rather than sailed, and, smitten
by the waves, she yielded passively to their impulse.

The Minquiers, a dangerous reef, was still more rugged
at that time than it is now.   Several towers of this citadel
of the abyss have been razed by the incessant chopping of the
sea.

The configuration of reefs changes.   It is not idly that
waves are called the swords of the ocean; each tide is the

stroke of a saw. At that period, to strike on the Minquiers was to perish.

As for the cruisers, they were the squadron of Cancale, afterward so celebrated under the command of that Captain Duchesne whom Léquinio called Father Duchesne.

The situation was critical. During the struggle of the unchained carronade, the corvette had, unobserved, got out of her course, and sailed rather toward Granville than Saint Malo. Even if she had been in a condition to have been handled and to carry sail, the Minquiers would have barred her return toward Jersey, and the cruisers would have prevented her reaching France.

For the rest, tempest there was none. But, as the pilot had said, there was a swell. The sea, rolling under a rough wind and above a rocky bottom, was savage.

The sea never says at once what it wishes. The gulf hides everything, even trickery. One might almost say that the sea has a plan. It advances and recoils; it proposes and contradicts itself; it sketches a storm and renounces its design; it promises the abyss, and does not hold to it; it threatens the north, and strikes the south.

All night the corvette " Claymore " had had the fog and the fear of the storm. The sea had belied itself, but in a savage fashion; it had sketched in the tempest, but developed the reef. It was shipwreck just the same, under another form.

So that to destruction upon the rocks was added extermination by combat,— one enemy complementing the other.

La Vieuville cried amid his brave merriment:—

" Shipwreck here — battle there! We have thrown the double fives! "

CHAPTER VIII

9 = 380

THE corvette was little more than a wreck.

In the wan, dim light, midst the blackness of the clouds, in the confused, changing line of the horizon, in the mysterious sullenness of the waves, there was a sepulchral solemnity. Except for the hissing breath of the hostile wind, all was silent. The catastrophe rose with majesty from the gulf. It resembled rather an apparition than an attack. Nothing stirred among the rocks; nothing moved on the vessels. It was an indescribable, colossal silence. Had they to deal with something real? One might have believed it a dream sweeping across the sea; there are legends of such visions. The corvette was in a manner between the demon reef and the phantom fleet.

Count du Boisberthelot gave orders in a half-voice to La Vieuville, who descended to the gun-deck; then the captain seized his telescope and stationed himself at the stern by the side of the pilot.

Gacquoil's whole effort was to keep the corvette to the wind; for if struck on the side by the wind and the sea, she would inevitably capsize.

" Pilot," said the captain, " where are we? "

" Off the Minquiers."

" On which side? "

" The bad one."

" What bottom? "

" Small rocks."

" Can we turn broadside on? "

" We can always die," said the pilot.

The captain levelled his glass toward the west and examined the Minquiers; then he turned to the east and studied the sail in sight.

The pilot continued, as if talking to himself:—

" It is the Minquiers. It is where the laughing sea-mew and the great black-hooded gull rest, when they make for Holland."

In the mean time the captain counted the sail.

There were, indeed, eight vessels, drawn up in line, and lifting their warlike profiles above the water. In the centre was seen the lofty sweep of a three-decker.

The captain questioned the pilot.

" Do you know those ships? "

" Indeed, yes! " replied Gacquoil.

" What are they? "

" It is the squadron."

" Of France? "

" Of the devil."

There was a silence. The captain resumed:—

" The whole body of cruisers are there."

" Not all."

In fact, on the 2d of April, Valazé had announced to the Convention that ten frigates and six ships-of-the-line were cruising in the Channel. The recollection of this came into the captain's mind.

" Right," said he; " the squadron consists of sixteen vessels. There are only eight here."

" The rest," said Gacquoil, " are lagging below, the whole length of the coast, and on the look-out."

The captain, still with his glass to his eye, murmured:

" A three-decker, two first-class frigates, and five second-class."

" But I, too," growled Gacquoil, " have marked them out."

" Good vessels," said the captain. " I have done something myself toward commanding them."

" As for me," said Gacquoil, " I have seen them close by. I do not mistake one for the other. I have their description in my head."

The captain handed his telescope to the pilot.

" Pilot, can you make out the three-decker clearly? "

" Yes, Captain; it is the ' Côte d'Or.' "

" Which they have rebaptized," said the captain. " She was formerly the ' Etats de Bourgogne.' A new vessel; a hundred and twenty-eight guns."

He took a pencil and note-book from his pocket, and made the figure 128 on one of the leaves.

He continued,—

" Pilot, what is the first sail to larboard? "

" It is the ' Expérimentée.' The —"

" First-class frigate. Fifty-two guns. She was fitted out at Brest two months since."

The captain marked the figure 52 on his note-book.

" Pilot," he asked, " what is the second sail to larboard? "

" The ' Dryade.' "

" First-class frigate. Forty eighteen-pounders. She has been in India. She has a good naval reputation."

And beneath the 52 he put the figure 40; then lifting his head:—

" Now, to starboard."

" Commander, those are all second-class frigates. There are five of them."

" Which is the first, starting from the three-decker? "

" The ' Résolute.' "

" Thirty-two pieces of eighteen. And the second? "

" The ' Richemont.' "

" Same. The next? "

" The ' Athéiste.' " [1]

" Odd name to take to sea. What next? "

" The ' Calypso.' "

" And then? "

" ' La Preneuse.' "

" Five frigates, each of thirty-two guns."

The captain wrote 160 below the first figures.

" Pilot," said he, " you recognize them perfectly."

[1] Marine Archives: State of the Fleet in 1793.

" And you," replied Gacquoil —" you know them well,
Captain. To recognize is something; to know is better."

The captain had his eyes fixed on his note-book, and added
between his teeth:—

" One hundred and twenty-eight, fifty-two, forty, a hundred and sixty."

At this moment La Vieuville came on deck again.

" Chevalier," the captain cried out to him, " we are in sight
of three hundred and eighty cannon."

" So be it," said La Vieuville.

" You come from the inspection, La Vieuville: how many
guns, exactly, have we fit for firing? "

" Nine."

" So be it," said Boisberthelot, in his turn.

He took the telescope from the pilot's hands and studied
the horizon.

The eight vessels, silent and black, seemed motionless, but
they grew larger.

They were approaching imperceptibly.

La Vieuville made a military salute.

" Commander," said he, " this is my report. I distrusted
this corvette ' Claymore.' It is always annoying to embark
suddenly on a vessel that does not know you or that does not
love you. English ship — traitor to Frenchman. That slut
of a carronade proved it. I have made the round. Anchors
good. They are not made of half-finished iron, but forged
bars soldered under the tilt-hammer. The flukes are solid.
Cables excellent, easy to pay out; regulation length, a hundred and twenty fathoms. Munitions in plenty. Six gunners dead. A hundred and seventy-one rounds apiece."

" Because there are but nine pieces left," murmured the
captain.

Boisberthelot levelled his telescope with the horizon. The
squadron was still slowly approaching.

The carronades possess one advantage,— three men are
enough to work them; but they have one inconvenience,—
they do not carry so far nor aim so true as guns. It would

be necessary to let the squadron get within range of the carronades.

The captain gave his orders in a low voice. There was silence throughout the vessel. No signal to clear for battle had been given, but it was done. The corvette was as much disabled for combat with men as against the waves. Everything that was possible was done with this ruin of a war-vessel. By the gangway near the tiller-ropes were heaped all the hawsers and spare cables for strengthening the masts in case of need. The cockpit was put in order for the wounded. According to the naval use of that time, the deck was barricaded, which is a guaranty against balls but not against bullets. The ball-gauges were brought, although it was a little late, to verify the calibres; but so many incidents had not been foreseen. Each sailor received a cartridge-box, and stuck into his belt a pair of pistols and a dirk. The hammocks were stowed away, the artillery pointed, the musketry prepared, the axes and grapplings laid out, the cartridge and bullet stores made ready, and the powder-room opened. Every man was at his post. All was done without a word being spoken, like arrangements carried on in the chamber of a dying person. All was haste and gloom.

Then the corvette showed her broadside. She had six anchors, like a frigate. The whole six were cast,— the cockbill anchor forward, the kedger aft, the flood-anchor toward the open, the ebb-anchor on the side to the rocks, the bower-anchor to starboard, and the sheet-anchor to larboard.

The nine carronades still in condition were put into form; the whole nine on one side,— that toward the enemy.

The squadron had on its part not less silently completed its manœuvres. The eight vessels now formed a semicircle, of which the Minquiers made the chord. The " Claymore," enclosed in this semicircle, and into the bargain tied down by her anchors, was backed by the reef,— that is to say, by shipwreck.

It was like a pack of hounds about a wild boar, not yet giving tongue, but showing their teeth.

It seemed as if on the one side and the other they awaited some signal.

The gunners of the " Claymore " stood to their pieces.

Boisberthelot said to La Vieuville:—

" I should like to open fire."

" A coquette's whim," replied La Vieuville.

CHAPTER IX

SOME ONE ESCAPES

THE passenger had not quitted the deck; he watched all the proceedings with the same impassible mien.

Boisberthelot approached.

" Sir," he said to him, " the preparations are complete. We are now lashed fast to our tomb; we shall not let go our hold. We are the prisoners of either the squadron or the reef. To yield to the enemy, or founder among the rocks: we have no other choice. One resource remains to us,— to die. It is better to fight than be wrecked. I would rather be shot than drowned; in the matter of death, I prefer fire to water. But dying is the business of the rest of us; it is not yours. You are the man chosen by the princes; you are appointed to a great mission,— the direction of the war in Vendée. Your loss is perhaps the monarchy lost; therefore you must live. Our honour bids us remain here; yours bids you go. General, you must quit the ship. I am going to give you a man and a boat. To reach the coast by a detour is not impossible. It is not yet day; the waves are high, the sea is dark; you will escape. There are cases when to fly is to conquer."

The old man bowed his stately head in sign of acquiescence.

Count du Boisberthelot raised his voice:—

" Soldiers and sailors ! " he cried.

Every movement ceased; from each point of the vessel all faces turned toward the captain.

He continued:—

"This man who is among us represents the king. He has been confided to us; we must save him. He is necessary to the throne of France; in default of a prince he will be — at least this is what we try for — the leader in the Vendée. He is a great general. He was to have landed in France with us; he must land without us. To save the head is to save all."

"Yes! yes! yes!" cried the voices of the whole crew.

The captain continued:—

"He is about to risk, he also, serious danger. It will not be easy to reach the coast. In order to face the angry sea the boat should be large, and should be small in order to escape the cruisers. What must be done is to make land at some safe point, and better toward Fougères than in the direction of Coutances. It needs an athletic sailor, a good oarsman and swimmer, who belongs to this coast, and knows the Channel. There is night enough, so that the boat can leave the corvette without being perceived. And besides, we are going to have smoke, which will serve to hide her. The boat's size will help her through the shallows. Where the panther is snared, the weasel escapes. There is no outlet for us; there is for her. The boat will row rapidly off; the enemy's ships will not see her: and moreover, during that time we are going to amuse them ourselves. Is it decided?"

"Yes! yes! yes!" cried the crew.

"There is not an instant to lose," pursued the captain. "Is there any man willing?"

A sailor stepped out of the ranks in the darkness, and said, "I."

CHAPTER X

DOES HE ESCAPE?

A FEW minutes later, one of those little boats called a "gig," which are especially appropriate to the captain's service, pushed off from the vessel. There were two men in this boat,— the old man in the stern, and the sailor who had volunteered in the bow. The night still lingered. The sailor, in obedience to the captain's orders, rowed vigorously in the direction of the Minquiers. For that matter, no other issue was possible. Some provisions had been put into the boat,— a bag of biscuit, a smoked ox-tongue, and a cask of water.

At the instant the gig was let down, La Vieuville, a scoffer even in the presence of destruction, leaned over the corvette's stern-post, and sneered this farewell to the boat:—

" She is a good one if one want to escape, and excellent if one wish to drown."

" Sir," said the pilot, " let us laugh no longer."

The start was quickly made, and there was soon a considerable distance between the boat and the corvette. The wind and waves were in the oarsman's favour; the little bark fled swiftly, undulating through the twilight, and hidden by the height of the waves.

The sea seemed to wear a look of sombre, indescribable expectation.

Suddenly, amid the vast and tumultuous silence of the ocean, rose a voice, which, increased by the speaking-trumpet as if by the brazen mask of antique tragedy, sounded almost superhuman.

It was the voice of Captain Boisberthelot giving his commands: " Royal marines," cried he, " nail the white flag to the main-mast. We are about to see our last sunrise."

And the corvette fired its first shot.

4

"Long live the king!" shouted the crew.

Then from the horizon's verge echoed an answering shout, immense, distant, confused, yet distinct nevertheless:—

"Long live the Republic!"

And a din like the peal of three hundred thunderbolts burst over the depths of the sea.

The battle began.

The sea was covered with smoke and fire. Streams of foam, made by the falling bullets, whitened the waves on every side.

The "Claymore" began to spit flame on the eight vessels. At the same time the whole squadron, ranged in a half-moon about the corvette, opened fire from all its batteries. The horizon was in a blaze. A volcano seemed to have burst suddenly out of the sea. The wind twisted to and fro the vast crimson banner of battle, amid which the ships appeared and disappeared like phantoms.

In front the black skeleton of the corvette showed against the red background.

The white banner, with its *fleur-de-lis*, could be seen floating from the main.

The two men seated in the little boat kept silence. The triangular shallows of the Minquiers, a sort of submarine Trinacrium, is larger than the entire island of Jersey. The sea covers it. It has for culminating point a platform which even the highest tides do not reach, from whence six mighty rocks detach themselves toward the northeast, ranged in a straight line, and producing the effect of a great wall, which has crumbled here and there. The strait between the plateau and the six reefs is only practicable to boats drawing very little water. Beyond this strait is the open sea.

The sailor who had undertaken the command of the boat made for this strait. By that means he put the Minquiers between the battle and the little bark. He manoeuvred the narrow channel skilfully, avoiding the reefs to larboard and starboard. The rocks now masked the conflict. The lurid light of the horizon, and the awful uproar of the cannonading, began to lessen as the distance increased; but the continuance of the reports proved that the corvette held firm, and meant to exhaust to the very last her one hundred and seventy-one broadsides. Presently the boat reached safe water, beyond the reef, beyond the battle, out of reach of the bullets.

Little by little the face of the sea became less dark; the rays, against which the darkness struggled, widened; the foam burst into jets of light, and the tops of the waves gave back white reflections.

Day appeared.

The boat was out of danger so far as the enemy was concerned, but the most difficult part of the task remained. She was saved from grape-shot, but not from shipwreck. She was a mere egg-shell, in a high sea, without deck, without sail, without mast, without compass, having no resource but her oars, in the presence of the ocean and the hurricane,— an atom at the mercy of giants.

Then, amid this immensity, this solitude, lifting his face, whitened by the morning, the man in the bow of the boat looked fixedly at the one in the stern, and said:

" I am the brother of him you ordered to be shot."

BOOK III

HALMALO

———

CHAPTER I

SPEECH IS THE "WORD"

THE old man slowly raised his head. He who had spoken was a man of about thirty. His forehead was brown with sea-tan; his eyes were peculiar: they had the keen glance of a sailor in the open pupils of a peasant. He held the oars vigorously in his two hands. His air was mild.

In his belt were a dirk, two pistols, and a rosary.

" Who are you? " asked the old man.

" I have just told you."

" What do you want with me? "

The sailor shipped the oars, folded his arms, and replied,—

" To kill you."

" As you please," said the old man.

The other raised his voice:—

" Get ready! "

" For what? "

" To die."

" Why? " asked the old man.

There was a silence. The sailor seemed for an instant confused by the question. He repeated:—

" I say that I mean to kill you."

" And I ask you, what for? "

The sailor's eyes flashed lightning:—

" Because you killed my brother."

The old man replied with perfect calmness:—

" I began by saving his life."

" That is true. You saved him first, then you killed him."

" It was not I who killed him."

" Who, then? "

" His own fault."

The sailor stared open-mouthed at the old man; then his eyebrows met again in their murderous frown.

" What is your name? " asked the old man.

" Halmalo; but you do not need to know my name in order to be killed by me."

At this moment the sun rose. A ray struck full upon the sailor's face, and vividly lighted up that savage countenance. The old man studied it attentively.

The cannonading, though it still continued, was broken and irregular. A vast cloud of smoke weighed down the horizon. The boat, no longer directed by the oarsman, drifted to leeward.

The sailor seized in his right hand one of the pistols at his belt, and the rosary in his left.

The old man raised himself to his full height.

" You believe in God? " said he.

" Our Father which art in heaven," replied the sailor; and he made the sign of the cross.

" Have you a mother? "

" Yes."

He made a second sign of the cross. Then he resumed:

" It is all said. I give you a minute, my lord." And he cocked the pistol.

" Why do you call me ' my lord ' ? "

" Because you are a lord. That is plain enough to be seen."

" Have you a lord — you? "

" Yes, and a grand one. Does one live without a lord? "

" Where is he? "

" I don't know.   He has left this country.   He is called
the Marquis de Lantenac, Viscount de Fontenay, Prince in
Brittany; he is the lord of the Seven Forests.   I never saw
him, but that does not prevent his being my master."

" And if you were to see him, would you obey him? "

" Indeed, yes.   Why, I should be a heathen if I did not
obey him.   I owe obedience to God; then to the king, who is
like God; and then to the lord, who is like the king.   But we
have nothing to do with all that.   You killed my brother; I
must kill you."

The old man replied,—

" Agreed; I killed your brother.   I did well."

The sailor clinched the pistol more tightly.

" Come," said he.

" So be it," said the old man.   Still perfectly composed, he
added, " Where is the priest? "

The sailor stared at him.

" The priest? "

" Yes; the priest.   I gave your brother a priest; you owe
me one."

"I have none," said the sailor.   And he continued, " Are
priests to be found out at sea? "

The convulsive thunderings of battle sounded more and
more distant.

" Those who are dying yonder have theirs," said the old
man.

" That is true," murmured the sailor; " they have the
chaplain."

The old man continued: " You will lose me my soul; that
is a serious matter."

The sailor bent his head in thought.

" And in losing me my soul," pursued the old man, " you
lose your own.   Listen.   I have pity on you.   Do what you
choose.   As for me, I did my duty a little while ago,— first,
in saving your brother's life, and afterward in taking it from
him; and I am doing my duty now in trying to save your soul.

Reflect. It is your affair. Do you hear the cannon-shots at this instant? There are men perishing yonder, there are desperate creatures dying, there are husbands who will never again see their wives, fathers who will never again see their children, brothers who, like you, will never again see their brothers. And by whose fault? Your brother's — yours! You believe in God, do you not? Well, you know that God suffers in this moment; he suffers in the person of his Most Christian Son the King of France, who is a child as Jesus was, and who is a prisoner in the fortress of the Temple. God suffers in his Church of Brittany; he suffers in his insulted cathedrals, his desecrated Gospels, in his violated houses of prayer, in his murdered priests. What did we intend to do, we, with that vessel which is perishing at this instant? We were going to succour God's children. If your brother had been a good servant, if he had faithfully done his duty like a wise and prudent man, the accident of the carronade would not have occurred, the corvette would not have been disabled, she would not have got out of her course, she would not have fallen in with this fleet of perdition, and at this hour we should be landing in France,— all, like valiant soldiers and seamen as we were, sabre in hand, the white flag unfurled, numerous, glad, joyful; and we should have gone to help the brave Vendean peasants to save France, to save the king; we should have been doing God's work. This was what we meant to do; this was what we should have done. It is what I — the only one who remains — set out to do. But you oppose yourself thereto. In this contest of the impious against the priests, in this strife of the regicides against the king, in this struggle of Satan against God, you are on the devil's side. Your brother was the demon's first auxiliary; you are the second. He commenced; you finish. You are with the regicides against the throne; you are with the impious against the Church. You take away from God his last resource. Because I shall not be there,— I, who represent the king,— the hamlets will continue to burn, families to weep, priests to bleed, Brittany to suffer, the king to remain in prison, and Jesus

Christ to be in distress. And who will have caused this? You! Go on; it is your affair. I depended on you to help bring about just the contrary of all this. I deceived myself. Ah, yes! it is true,— you are right: I killed your brother. Your brother was courageous; I recompensed that. He was culpable; I punished that. He had failed in his duty; I did not fail in mine. What I did, I would do again. And I swear by the great Saint Anne of Auray, who sees us, that in a similar case I would shoot my son just as I shot your brother. Now you are master. Yes, I pity you. You have lied to your captain. You, Christian, are without faith; you, Breton, are without honour. I was confided to your loyalty and accepted by your treason; you offer my death to those to whom you had promised my life. Do you know who it is you are destroying here? It is yourself. You take my life from the king, and you give your eternity to the devil. Go on; commit your crime,— it is well. You sell cheaply your share in Paradise. Thanks to you, the devil will conquer; thanks to you, the churches will fall; thanks to you, the heathen will continue to melt the bells and make cannon of them. They will shoot men with that which used to warn souls! At this moment in which I speak to you, perhaps the bell that rang for your baptism is killing your mother. Go on; aid the devil,— do not hesitate. Yes, I condemned your brother; but know this: I am an instrument of God. Ah, you pretend to judge the means God uses! Will you take it on yourself to judge Heaven's thunderbolt? Wretched man, you will be judged by it! Take care what you do. Do you even know whether I am in a state of grace? No. Go on, all the same. Do what you like. You are free to cast me into hell, and to cast yourself there with me. Our two damnations are in your hand. It is you who will be responsible before God. We are alone; face to face in the abyss. Go on — finish — make an end. I am old and you are young; I am without arms and you are armed; kill me!"

While the old man stood erect, uttering these words in a voice louder than the noise of the sea, the undulations of the

waves showed him now in the shadow, now in the light.   The
sailor had grown lividly white; great drops of sweat fell from
his forehead; he trembled like a leaf; he kissed his rosary
again and again.   When the old man finished speaking, he
threw down his pistol and fell on his knees.

"Mercy, my lord!   Pardon me!" he cried; "you speak
like God.   I have done wrong.   My brother did wrong.   I
will try to repair his crime.   Dispose of me.   Command; I
will obey."

"I give you pardon," said the old man.

CHAPTER II

THE PEASANT'S MEMORY IS AS GOOD AS THE CAPTAIN'S SCIENCE

THE provisions which had been put into the boat proved
most acceptable.   The two fugitives, obliged to make
long detours, took thirty-six hours to reach the coast.   They
passed a night at sea; but the night was fine, though there
was too much moon to be favourable to those seeking concealment.

They were obliged first to row away from France, and gain
the open sea toward Jersey.

They heard the last broadside of the sinking corvette as
one hears the final roar of the lion whom the hunters are killing in the wood.   Then a silence fell upon the sea.

The "Claymore" died like the "Avenger," but glory has
ignored her.   The man who fights against his own country
is never a hero.

Halmalo was a marvellous seaman.   He performed miracles
of dexterity and intelligence; his improvisation of a route amid
the reefs, the waves, and the enemy's watch was a masterpiece.   The wind had slackened and the sea grown calmer.
Halmalo avoided the Caux des Minquiers, coasted the Chaus-

sée-aux-Bœufs, and in order that they might have a few hours'
rest, took shelter in the little creek on the north side, practicable at low water; then, rowing southward again, found
means to pass between Granville and the Chausey Islands without being discovered by the look-out either of Granville or
Chausey.

He entered the bay of Saint-Michael,— a bold undertaking,
on account of the neighbourhood of Cancale, an anchorage for
the cruising squadron.

About an hour before sunset on the evening of the second
day, he left Saint Michael's Mount behind him, and proceeded
to land on a beach deserted because the shifting sands made
it dangerous.

Fortunately the tide was high.

Halmalo drove the boat as far up as he could, tried the
sand, found it firm, ran the bark aground, and sprang
on shore. The old man strode over the side after him and
examined the horizon.

" Monseigneur," said Halmalo, " we are here at the mouth
of the Couesnon. There is Beauvoir to starboard, and Huisnes to larboard. The belfry in front of us is Ardevon."

The old man bent down to the boat and took a biscuit,
which he put in his pocket, and said to Halmalo:

" Take the rest."

Halmalo put the remains of the meat and biscuit into the
bag and slung it over his shoulder. This done, he said:—

" Monseigneur, must I conduct or follow you? "

" Neither the one nor the other."

Halmalo regarded the speaker in stupefied wonder.

The old man continued:—

" Halmalo, we must separate. It will not answer to be
two. There must be a thousand or one alone."

He paused, and drew from one of his pockets a green silk
bow, rather like a cockade, with a gold *fleur-de-lis* embroidered
in the centre. He resumed:—

" Do you know how to read? "

" No."

"That is fortunate. A man who can read is troublesome. Have you a good memory?"

"Yes."

"That will do. Listen, Halmalo. You must take to the right and I to the left. I shall go in the direction of Fougères, you toward Bazouges. Keep your bag; it gives you the look of a peasant. Conceal your weapons. Cut yourself a stick in the thickets. Creep among the fields of rye, which are high. Slide behind the hedges. Climb the fences in order to go across the meadows. Leave passers-by at a distance. Avoid the roads and the bridges. Do not enter Pontorson. Ah! you will have to cross the Couesnon. How will you manage?"

"I shall swim."

"That's right. And there is a ford — do you know where it is?"

"Between Ancey and Vieux-Viel."

"That is right. You do really belong to the country."

"But night is coming on. Where will Monseigneur sleep?"

"I can take care of myself. And you — where will you sleep?"

"There are hollow trees. I was a peasant before I was a sailor."

"Throw away your sailor's hat; it will betray you. You will easily find a woollen cap."

"Oh, a peasant's thatch is to be found anywhere. The first fisherman will sell me his."

"Very good. Now listen. You know the woods?"

"All of them."

"Of the whole district?"

"From Noirmoutier to Laval."

"Do you know their names too?"

"I know the woods; I know their names; I know about everything."

"You will forget nothing?"

"Nothing."

" Good! At present, attention. How many leagues can you make in a day? "

" Ten, fifteen — twenty, if necessary."

" It will be. Do not lose a word of what I am about to say. You will go to the wood of Saint-Aubin."

" Near Lamballe? "

" Yes. On the edge of the ravine between Saint-Reuil and Plédiac there is a large chestnut-tree. You will stop there. You will see no one."

" Which will not hinder somebody's being there. I know."

" You will give the call. Do you know how to give the call? "

Halmalo puffed out his cheeks, turned toward the sea, and there sounded the " to-whit, to-hoo " of an owl.

One would have said it came from the night-locked recesses of a forest. It was sinister and owl-like.

" Good! " said the old man. " You have it."

He held out the bow of green silk to Halmalo.

" This is my badge of command. Take it. It is important that no one should as yet know my name; but this knot will be sufficient. The *fleur-de-lis* was embroidered by Madame Royale in the Temple prison."

Halmalo bent one knee to the ground. He trembled as he took the flower-embroidered knot, and brought it near to his lips, then paused, as if frightened at this kiss.

" Can I? " he demanded.

" Yes, since you kiss the crucifix."

Halmalo kissed the *fleur-de-lis*.

" Rise," said the old man.

Halmalo rose and hid the knot in his breast.

The old man continued:—

" Listen well to this. This is the order: Up! Revolt! No quarter! On the edge of this wood of Saint-Aubin you will give the call. You will repeat it thrice. The third time you will see a man spring out of the ground."

" Out of a hole under the trees. I know."

" This man will be Planchenault, who is also called the

King's Heart. You will show him this knot. He will understand. Then, by routes you must find out, you will go to
the wood of Astillé; there you will find a cripple, who is surnamed Mousqueton, and who shows pity to none. You will
tell him that I love him, and that he is to set the parishes in
motion. From there you will go to the wood of Couesbon,
which is a league from Ploërmel. You will give the owl-cry;
a man will come out of a hole. It will be Thuault, seneschal
of Ploërmel, who has belonged to what is called the Constituent
Assembly, but on the good side. You will tell him to arm the
castle of Couesbon, which belongs to the Marquis de Guer, a
refugee. Ravines, little woods, ground uneven,— a good
place. Thuault is a clever, straightforward man. Thence you
will go to Saint-Guen-les-Toits, and you will talk with Jean
Chouan, who is, in my mind, the real chief. From thence
you will go to the wood of Ville-Anglose, where you will see
Guitter, whom they call Saint Martin; you will bid him have
his eye on a certain Courmesnil, who is the son-in-law of old
Goupil de Préfeln, and who leads the Jacobinery of Argentan.
Recollect all this. I write nothing, because nothing should
be written. La Rouarie made out a list; it ruined all. Then
you will go to the wood of Rougefeu, where is Miélette, who
leaps the ravine on a long pole."

" It is called a leaping-pole."

" Do you know how to use it?"

" Am I not a Breton and a peasant? The *ferte* is our
friend. She widens our arms and lengthens our legs."

" That is to say, she makes the enemy smaller and shortens
the route. A good machine."

" Once on a time, with my *ferte*, I held my own against
three salt-tax men who had sabres."

" When was that?"

" Ten years ago."

" Under the king?"

" Yes, of course."

" Then you fought in the time of the king?"

" Yes, to be sure."

" Against whom? "

" My faith, I do not know!   I was a salt-smuggler."

" Very good."

" They called that fighting against the excise officers. Were they the same thing as the king? "

" Yes.   No.   But it is not necessary that you should understand."

" I beg Monseigneur's pardon for having asked a question of Monseigneur."

" Let us continue.   Do you know La Tourgue? "

" Do I know La Tourgue?   Why, I belong there."

" How? "

" Certainly, since I come from Parigné."

" In fact, La Tourgue is near Parigné."

" Know La Tourgue!   The big round castle that belongs to my lord's family?   There is a great iron door which separates the new part from the old that a cannon could not blow open.   The famous book about Saint Bartholomew, which people go to look at from curiosity, is in the new building. There are frogs in the grass.   When I was little, I used to go and tease them.   And the underground passage, I know that; perhaps there is nobody else left who does."

" What underground passage?   I do not know what you mean."

" It was made for old times, in the days when La Tourgue was besieged.   The people inside could escape by going through the underground passage which leads into the wood."

" There is a subterranean passage of that description in the castle of Jupellière, and the castle of Hunaudaye, and the tower of Champéon; but there is nothing of the sort at La Tourgue."

" Oh, yes, indeed, Monseigneur!   I do not know the passages that Monseigneur spoke of; I only know that of La Tourgue, because I belong to the neighbourhood.   Into the bargain, there is nobody but myself who does know it.   It was not talked about.   It was forbidden, because it had been

used in the time of Monsieur de Rohan's wars. My father
knew the secret, and showed it to me. I know how to get in
and out. If I am in the forest, I can go into the tower, and
if I am in the tower, I can go into the forest, without anybody's seeing me. When the enemy enters, there is no longer
any one there. That is what the passage of La Tourgue is.
Oh, I know it!"

The old man remained silent for a moment.

" It is evident that you deceive yourself. If there were
such a secret, I should know it."

" Monseigneur, I am certain. There is a stone that turns."

" Ah, good! You peasants believe in stones that turn and
stones that sing, and stones that go at night to drink from
the neighbouring brook. A pack of nonsense!"

" But since I have made the stone turn —"

" Just as others have heard it sing. Comrade, La Tourgue
is a fortress, sure and strong, easy to defend; but anybody
who counted on a subterranean passage for getting out of it
would be silly indeed."

" But, monseigneur —"

The old man shrugged his shoulders.

" We are losing time; let us talk of what concerns us."

The peremptory tone cut short Halmalo's persistence.

The unknown resumed:—

" To continue. Listen. From Rougefeu you will go to
the wood of Montchevrier; Benedicité is there, the chief of
the Twelve. There is another good fellow. He says his
Bénédicité while he has people shot. War and sensibility do
not go together. From Montchevrier, you will go —"

He broke off.

" I forgot the money."

He took from his pocket a purse and a pocket-book, and
put them in Halmalo's hand.

" There are thirty thousand livres in assignats in the
pocket-book (something like three pounds); it is true the
assignats are false, but the real ones are just as worthless.
In the purse — attention — there are a hundred gold louis.

I give you all I have.   I have no need of anything here.
Besides, it is better that no money should be found on me.
I resume.   From Montchevrier you will go to Antrain, where
you will see Monsieur de Frotté; from Antrain to La Jupellière, where you will see De Rochecotte; from La Jupellière to
Noirieux, where you will find the Abbé Baudoin.   Can you
recollect all this? "

" Like my paternoster."

" You will see Monsieur Dubois-Guy at Saint-Bricen-en-
Cogles, Monsieur de Turpin at Morannes, which is a fortified
town, and the Prince de Talmont at Château-Gonthier."

" Shall I be spoken to by a prince? "

" Since I speak to you."

Halmalo took off his hat.

" Madame's *fleur-de-lis* will ensure you a good reception
everywhere.   Do not forget that you are going into the country of mountaineers and rustics.   Disguise yourself.   It will
be easy to do.   These republicans are so stupid that you may
pass anywhere with a blue coat, a three-cornered hat, and a
tricoloured cockade.   There are no longer regiments, there
are no longer uniforms; the companies are not numbered;
each man puts on any rag he pleases.   You will go to Saint-
Mhervé; there you will see Gaulier, called Great Peter.   You
will go to the cantonment of Parné, where the men blacken
their faces.   They put gravel into their guns, and a double
charge of powder, in order to make more noise.   It is well
done; but tell them, above all, to kill — kill — kill!   You
will go to the camp of the Vache Noire, which is on a height;
to the middle of the wood of La Charnie, then to the camp
Avoine, then to the camp Vert, then to the camp of the
Fourmis.   You will go to the Grand Bordage, which is also
called the Haut de Pré, and is inhabited by a widow whose
daughter married Treton, nicknamed the Englishman.   Grand
Bordage is in the parish of Quelaines.   You will visit
Epineux-le-Chevreuil, Sillé-le-Guillaume, Parannes, and all
the men in all of the woods.   You will make friends, and you
will send them to the borders of the high and the low Maine;

you will see Jean Treton in the parish of Vaisges, Sans Regret at Bignon, Chambord at Bonchamps, the brothers Corbin at Maisoncelles, and the Petit-sans-Peur at Saint-John-on-Erve. He is the one who is called Bourdoiseau. All that done, and the watch-word — Revolt! No quarter! — given everywhere, you will join the grand army, the Catholic and royal army, wherever it may be. You will see D'Elbée, De Lescure, De la Rochejacquelein, all the chiefs who may chance to be still living. You will show them my token of command. They all know what it means. You are only a sailor, but Cathelineau is only a carter. This is what you must say to them from me: 'It is time to join the two wars, the great and the little. The great makes the most noise; the little does the most execution. The Vendée is good; *Chouannerie* is worse; and in civil war the worst is the best. The goodness of a war is judged by the amount of bad it does.'"

He paused.

"Halmalo, I say all this to you. You do not understand the words, but you comprehend the things themselves. I gained confidence in you from seeing you manage the boat. You do not understand geometry, yet you perform sea-manœuvres that are marvellous. He who can manage a boat can pilot an insurrection. From the way in which you have conducted this sea intrigue, I am certain you will fulfil all my commands well. I resume. You will tell the whole to the chiefs, in your own way, of course; but it will be well told. I prefer the war of the forest to the war of the plain; I have no wish to set a hundred thousand peasants in line, and expose them to Carnot's artillery and the grape-shot of the Blues. In less than a month I mean to have five hundred thousand sharpshooters ambushed in the woods. The Republican army is my game. Poaching is our way of waging war. Mine is the strategy of the thickets. Good; there is still another expression you will not catch; no matter, you will seize this: *No quarter, and ambushes everywhere.* I depend more on bush fighting than on regular battles. You will add that the English are with us. We catch the Republic between two

5

fires. Europe assists us. Let us make an end of the Revolution. Kings will wage a war of kingdoms against it; let us wage a war of parishes. You will say this. Have you understood?"

"Yes. Put all to fire and sword."

"That is it."

"No quarter."

"Not to a soul. That is it."

"I will go everywhere."

"And be careful, for in this country it is easy to become a dead man."

"Death does not concern me. He who takes his first step uses perhaps his last shoes."

"You are a brave fellow."

"And if I am asked Monseigneur's name?"

"It must not be known yet. You will say you do not know it, and that will be the truth."

"Where shall I see Monseigneur again?"

"Where I shall be."

"How shall I know?"

"Because all the world will know. I shall be talked of before eight days go by. I shall make examples; I shall avenge religion and the king, and you will know well that it is I of whom they speak."

"I understand."

"Forget nothing."

"Be tranquil."

"Now go. May God guide you! Go."

"I will do all that you have bidden me. I will go. I will speak. I will obey. I will command."

"Good!"

"And if I succeed?"

"I will make you a knight of Saint Louis."

"Like my brother. And if I fail, you will have me shot?"

"Like your brother."

"Done, monseigneur."

The old man bent his head and seemed to fall into a sombre

reverie. When he raised his eyes he was alone. Halmalo was only a black spot disappearing on the horizon.

The sun had just set.

The sea-mews and the hooded gulls flew homeward from the darkening ocean.

That sort of inquietude which precedes the night made itself felt in space. The green frogs croaked; the kingfishers flew whistling out of the pools; the gulls and the rooks kept up their evening tumult; the cry of the shore birds could be heard, but not a human sound. The solitude was complete. Not a sail in the bay, not a peasant in the fields. As far as the eye could reach stretched a deserted plain. The great sand-thistles shivered. The white sky of twilight cast a vast livid pallor over the shore. In the distance, the pools scattered over the plain looked like great sheets of pewter spread flat upon the ground. The wind hurried in from the sea with a moan.

BOOK IV

TELLMARCH

CHAPTER I

THE TOP OF THE DUNE

THE old man waited till Halmalo disappeared, then he drew his fisherman's cloak closely about him and set out on his course. He walked with slow steps, thinking deeply. He took the direction of Huisnes, while Halmalo went toward Beauvoir.

Behind him, an enormous black triangle, with a cathedral for tiara and a fortress for breastplate, with its two great towers to the east, one round, the other square, helping to support the weight of the church and village, rose Mount Saint Michael, which is to the ocean what the Pyramid of Cheops is to the desert.

The quicksands of Mount Saint Michael's Bay insensibly displace their dunes. Between Huisnes and Ardevon there was at that time a very high one, which is now completely effaced. This dune, levelled by an equinoctial storm, had the peculiarity of being very ancient; on its summit stood a commemorative column, erected in the twelfth century, in memory of the council held at Avranches against the assassins of Saint Thomas of Canterbury. From the top of this dune the whole district could be seen, and one could fix the points of the compass.

The old man ascended it.

When he reached the top, he sat down on one of the projections of the stones, with his back against the pillar, and began to study the kind of geographical chart spread beneath his feet. He seemed to be seeking a route in a district which had once been familiar. In the whole of this vast landscape, made indistinct by the twilight, there was nothing clearly defined but the horizon stretching black against the sky.

He could perceive the roofs of eleven towns and villages; could distinguish for several leagues' distance all the bell-towers of the coast, which were built very high, to serve in case of need as landmarks to boats at sea.

At the end of a few minutes the old man appeared to have found what he sought in this dim clearness. His eyes rested on an enclosure of trees, walls, and roofs, partially visible midway between the plain and the wood; it was a farm. He nodded his head in the satisfied way a man does who says to himself, " There it is," and began to trace with his finger a route across the fields and hedges. From time to time he examined a shapeless, indistinct object stirring on the principal roof of the farm, and seemed to ask himself, " What can it be?" It was colourless and confused, owing to the gloom; it floated — therefore it was not a weather-cock; and there was no reason why it should be a flag.

He was weary; he remained in his resting-place, and yielded passively to the vague forgetfulness which the first moments of repose bring over a tired man.

There is an hour of the day which may be called noiseless: it is the serene hour of early evening. It was about him now. He enjoyed it; he looked, he listened — to what? The tranquillity. Even savage natures have their moments of melancholy.

Suddenly this tranquillity was not troubled, but accentuated by the voices of persons passing below,— the voices of women and children. It was like a chime of joy-bells unexpectedly ringing amid the shadows. The underbrush hid the group from whence the voices came, but it was moving slowly along the foot of the dune toward the plain and the forest. The clear, fresh tones reached distinctly the pensive old man; they were so near that he could catch every word.

A woman's voice said,—

" We must hurry ourselves, Flécharde. Is this the way? "

" No, yonder."

The dialogue went on between the two voices,— one high-pitched, the other low and timid.

" What is the name of the farm we are stopping at? "

" L'Herbe-en-Pail."

" Will it take us much longer to get there? "

" A good quarter of an hour."

" We must hurry on to get our soup."

" Yes; we are late."

" We shall have to run. But those brats of yours are tired. We are only two women; we can't carry three brats. And you — you are already carrying one, my Flécharde; a regular lump of lead. You have weaned the little gormandizer, but you carry her all the same. A bad habit. Do me the favour to make her walk. Oh, very well — so much the worse! The soup will be cold."

" Oh, what good shoes these are that you gave me! I should think they had been made for me."

" It is better than going barefooted, eh? "

" Hurry up, René-Jean! "

" He is the very one that hindered us. He must needs chatter with all the little peasant girls he met. Oh, he shows the man already! "

" Yes, indeed; why, he is going on five years old."

" I say, René-Jean, what made you talk to that little girl in the village? "

A child's voice, that of a boy, replied,—

" Because she was an acquaintance of mine."

" What, you know her? " asked the woman.

" Yes, ever since this morning; she played some games with me."

" Oh, what a man you are! " cried the woman. " We have only been three days in the neighbourhood; that creature there is no bigger than your fist, and he has found a sweetheart already!"

The voices grew fainter and fainter; then every sound died away.

CHAPTER II

AURES HABET, ET NON AUDIET

THE old man sat motionless. He was not thinking, scarcely dreaming. About him was serenity, rest, safety, solitude. It was still broad daylight on the dune, but almost dark in the plain, and quite night in the forest. The moon was floating up the east; a few stars dotted the pale blue of the zenith. This man, though full of preoccupation and stern cares, lost himself in the ineffable sweetness of the infinite. He felt within him the obscure dawn of hope, if the word hope may be applied to the workings of civil warfare. For the instant it seemed to him that in escaping from that inexorable sea and touching land once more, all danger had vanished. No one knew his name; he was alone, escaped from the enemy, having left no trace behind him, for the sea leaves no track; hidden, ignored; not even suspected. He felt an indescribable calm; a little more and he would have fallen asleep.

What made the strange charm of this tranquil home to that man, a prey within and without to such tumults, was the profound silence alike in earth and sky.

He heard nothing but the wind from the sea; but the wind is a continual bass, which almost ceases to be a noise, so accustomed does the ear become to its tone.

Suddenly he started to his feet.

His attention had been quickly awakened; he looked about the horizon. Then his glance fixed eagerly upon a particular point. What he looked at was the belfry of Cormeray, which rose before him at the extremity of the plain. Something very extraordinary was indeed going on within it.

The belfry was clearly defined against the sky; he could see the tower surmounted by the spire, and between the two the cage for the bell, square, without pent-house, open at the four sides after the fashion of Breton belfries.

Now this cage appeared alternately to open and shut at regular intervals; its lofty opening showed entirely white, then black; the sky could be seen for an instant through it, then it disappeared; a gleam of light would come, then an eclipse, and the opening and shutting succeeded each other from moment to moment with the regularity of a hammer striking its anvil.

This belfry of Cormeray was in front of the old man, about two leagues from the place where he stood. He looked to his right at the belfry of Baguer-Pican, which rose equally straight and distinct against the horizon; its cage was opening and shutting, like that of Cormeray.

He looked to his left, at the belfry of Tanis: the cage of the belfry of Tanis opened and shut, like that of Baguer-Pican.

He examined all the belfries upon the horizon, one after another; to his left those of Courtils, of Précey, of Crollon, and the Croix-Avranchin; to his right the belfries of Raz-sur-Couesnon, of Mordrey, and of the Pas; in front of him, the belfry of Pontorson. The cages of all these belfries were alternately white and black.

What did this mean?

It meant that all the bells were swinging. In order to appear and disappear in this way they must be violently rung.

What was it for? The tocsin, without doubt.

The tocsin was sounding, sounding madly, on every side, from all the belfries, in all the parishes, in all the villages; and yet he could hear nothing.

This was owing to the distance and the wind from the sea, which, sweeping in the opposite direction, carried every sound of the shore out beyond the horizon.

All these mad bells calling on every side, and at the same time this silence; nothing could be more sinister.

The old man looked and listened. He did not hear the tocsin; he saw it. It was a strange sensation, that of seeing the tocsin.

Against whom was this rage of the bells directed?

Against whom did this tocsin sound?

CHAPTER III

USEFULNESS OF BIG LETTERS

ASSUREDLY some one was snared.

Who?

A shiver ran through this man of steel.

It could not be he? His arrival could not have been discovered. It was impossible that the acting representative should have received information; he had scarcely landed. The corvette had evidently foundered, and not a man had escaped. And even on the corvette, Boisberthelot and La Vieuville alone knew his name.

The belfries kept up their savage sport. He mechanically watched and counted them; and his meditations, pushed from one conjecture to another, had those fluctuations caused by a sudden change from complete security to a terrible consciousness of peril. Still, after all, this tocsin might be accounted for in many ways; and he ended by reassuring himself with the repetition of, " In short, no one knows of my arrival, and no one knows my name."

During the last few seconds there had been a slight noise above and behind him. This noise was like the fluttering of leaves. He paid no attention to it at first, but as the sound continued — one might have said insisted on making itself heard — he turned round at length. It was in fact a leaf, but a leaf of paper. The wind was trying to tear off a large placard pasted on the stone above his head. This placard had been very lately fastened there, for it was still moist, and offered a hold to the wind, which had begun to play with and was detaching it.

The old man had ascended the dune on the opposite side, and had not seen this placard as he came up.

He mounted the coping where he had been seated, and laid his hand on the corner of the paper which the wind moved. The sky was clear, for the June twilights are long; the bottom of the dune was shadowy, but the top in light. A portion of the placard was printed in large letters, and there was still light enough for him to make it out. He read this:—

THE FRENCH REPUBLIC, ONE AND INDIVISIBLE.

We, Prieur, of the Marne, acting representative of the people with the army of the coast of Cherbourg, give notice: The *ci-devant* Marquis de Lantenac, Viscount de Fontenay, so-called Breton prince, secretly landed on the coast of Granville, is declared an outlaw. — A price is set on his head. — Any person bringing him, alive or dead, will receive the sum of sixty thousand livres. — This amount will not be paid in assignats, but in gold. — A battalion of the Cherbourg coast-guards will be immediately dispatched for the apprehension of the so-called Marquis de Lantenac.

The parishes are ordered to lend every assistance.

Given at the Town-Hall of Granville, this 2d of June, 1793.

(Signed) PRIEUR, DE LA MARNE.

Under this name was another signature, in much smaller characters, and which the failing light prevented the old man's deciphering.

The old man pulled his hat over his eyes, closed his sea-jacket up to his chin and rapidly descended the dune.

It was unsafe to remain longer on this summit.

He had perhaps already stayed too long; the top of the dune was the only point in the landscape which still remained visible.

When he reached the obscurity of the bottom, he slackened his pace.

He took the route which he had traced for himself toward

the farm, evidently having reason to believe that he should be safe in that direction.

The plain was deserted. There were no passers-by at that hour.

He stopped behind a thicket of underbrush, undid his cloak, turned his vest the hairy side out, refastened his rag of a mantle about his neck by its cord, and resumed his way.

The moon was shining.

He reached a point where two roads branched off; an old stone cross stood there. Upon the pedestal of the cross he could distinguish a white square, which was most probably a notice like that he had just read. He went toward it.

" Where are you going? " said a voice.

He turned round.

A man was standing in the hedge-row, tall like himself, old like himself, with white hair like his own, and garments even more dilapidated,— almost his double. This man leaned on a long stick.

He repeated,—

" I ask you where you are going."

" In the first place, where am I? " returned he, with an almost haughty composure.

The man replied,—

" You are in the seigneury of Tanis. I am its beggar; you are its lord."

" I? "

" Yes, you, my lord Marquis de Lantenac."

CHAPTER IV

THE CAIMAND

THE Marquis de Lantenac — we shall henceforth call him by his name — answered quietly:—

" So be it. Give me up."

The man continued:—

" We are both at home here: you in the castle, I in the bushes."

" Let us finish. Do your work. Betray me," said the marquis.

The man went on:—

" You were going to the farm of Herbe-en-Pail, were you not? "

" Yes."

" Do not go."

" Why? "

" Because the Blues are there."

" Since how long? "

" These three days."

" Did the people of the farm and the hamlet resist? "

" No; they opened all the doors."

" Ah! " said the marquis.

The man pointed with his finger toward the roof of the farm-house, which could be perceived above the trees at a short distance.

" You can see the roof, Marquis? "

" Yes."

" Do you see what there is above it? "

" Something floating? "

" Yes."

" It is a flag."

" The tricolour," said the man.

This was the object which had attracted the marquis's attention as he stood on the top of the dune.

" Is not the tocsin sounding? " asked the marquis.

" Yes."

" On what account? "

" Evidently on yours."

" But I cannot hear it."

" The wind carries the sound the other way."

The man added,—

" Did you see your placard? "

" Yes."

" They are hunting you; " and casting a glance toward the farm, he added, " There is a demi-battalion there."

" Of republicans? "

" Parisians."

" Very well," said the marquis; " march on."

And he took a step in the direction of the farm.

The man seized his arm.

" Do not go there."

" Where do you wish me to go? "

" Home with me."

The marquis looked steadily at the mendicant.

" Listen, my lord marquis. My house is not fine, but it is safe. A cabin lower than a cave. For flooring a bed of sea-weed, for ceiling a roof of branches and grass. Come. At the farm you will be shot; in my house you may go to sleep. You must be tired; and to-morrow morning the Blues will march on, and you can go where you please."

The marquis studied this man.

" Which side are you on? " he asked. " Are you republican? Are you royalist? "

" I am a beggar."

" Neither royalist nor republican? "

" I believe not."

" Are you for or against the king? "

" I have no time for that sort of thing."

" What do you think of what is passing? "

" I have nothing to live on."

" Still you come to my assistance."

" Because I saw you were outlawed. What is the law? So one can be beyond its pale. I do not comprehend. Am I inside the law? Am I outside the law? I don't in the least know. To die of hunger, is that being within the law? "

" How long have you been dying of hunger? "

" All my life."

" And you save me? "

" Yes."

" Why? "

" Because I said to myself, ' There is one poorer than I. I have the right to breathe; he has not.' "

" That is true. And you save me? "

" Of course; we are brothers, monseigneur. I ask for bread: you ask for life. We are a pair of beggars."

" But do you know there is a price set on my head? "

" Yes."

" How did you know? "

" I read the placard."

" You know how to read? "

" Yes; and to write, too. Why should I be a brute? "

" Then, since you can read, and since you have seen the notice, you know that a man would earn sixty thousand livres by giving me up? "

" I know it."

" Not in assignats."

" Yes, I know; in gold."

" Sixty thousand livres! Do you know it is a fortune? "

" Yes."

" And that anybody apprehending me would make his fortune? "

" Very well; what next? "

" His fortune! "

" That is exactly what I thought. When I saw you, I said, ' Just to think that anybody by giving up that man yonder would gain sixty thousand livres, and make his fortune!' Let us hasten to hide him."

The marquis followed the beggar.

They entered a thicket; the mendicant's den was there. It was a sort of chamber which a great old oak had allowed the man to take possession of within its heart; it was dug down among its roots, and covered by its branches. It was dark, low, hidden, invisible. There was room for two persons.

" I foresaw that I might have a guest," said the mendicant.

This species of underground lodging, less rare in Brittany than people fancy, is called in the peasant dialect a *carnichot.*

The name is also applied to hiding-places contrived in thick walls.

It was furnished with a few jugs, a pallet of straw or dried wrack, with a thick covering of kersey; some tallow-dips, a flint and steel, and a bundle of furze twigs for tinder.

They stooped low,— crept rather,— penetrated into the chamber, which the great roots of the tree divided into fantastic compartments, and seated themselves on the heap of dry sea-weed which served as a bed. The space between two of the roots, which made the doorway allowed a little light to enter. Night had come on; but the eye adapts itself to the darkness, and one always finds at last a little day among the shadows. A reflection from the moon's rays dimly silvered the entrance. In a corner was a jug of water, a loaf of buckwheat bread, and some chestnuts.

" Let us sup," said the beggar.

They divided the chestnuts; the marquis contributed his morsel of biscuit. They bit into the same black loaf, and drank out of the jug, one after the other.

They conversed.

The marquis began to question this man.

" So, no matter whether anything or nothing happens, it is all the same to you? "

" Pretty much. You are the lords, you others. Those are your affairs."

" But after all, present events —"

" Pass away up out of my reach."

The beggar added presently:—

" Then there are things that go on still higher up; the sun that rises, the moon that increases or diminishes; those are the matters I occupy myself about."

He took a sip from the jug, and said,—

" The good fresh water! "

Then he asked,—

" How do you find the water, monseigneur? "

" What is your name? " inquired the marquis.

" My name is Tellmarch, but I am called the Caimand."

" I understand. *Caimand* is a word of the district."

" Which means beggar. I am also nicknamed Le Vieux. I have been called ' the old man ' these forty years."

" Forty years! But you were a young man then."

" I never was young. You remain so always, on the contrary, my lord marquis. You have the legs of a boy of twenty; you can climb the great dune. As for me, I begin to find it difficult to walk; at the end of a quarter of a league I am tired. Nevertheless, our age is the same. But the rich, they have an advantage over us,— they eat every day. Eating is a preservative."

After a silence the mendicant resumed:—

" Poverty, riches — that makes a terrible business. That is what brings on the catastrophes,— at least, I have that idea. The poor want to be rich; the rich are not willing to be poor. I think that is about what it is at the bottom. I do not mix myself up with matters. The events are the events. I am neither for the creditor nor for the debtor. I know there is a debt, and that it is being paid. That is all. I would rather they had not killed the king; but it would be difficult for me to say why. After that, somebody will answer, ' But remember how they used to hang poor fellows on trees for nothing at all.' See; just for a miserable gunshot fired at one of the king's roebucks, I myself saw a man hung who had a wife and seven children. There is much to say on both sides."

Again he was silent for a while. Then:—

" I am a little of a bone-setter, a little of a doctor, I know the herbs, I study plants. The peasants see me absent, preoccupied, and that makes me pass for a sorcerer. Because I dream, they think I must be wise."

" You belong to the neighbourhood? " asked the marquis.

" I never was out of it."

" You know me? "

" Of course. The last time I saw you was when you passed through here two years ago. You went from here to England. A little while since I saw a man on the top of the dune, — a very tall man. Tall men are rare; Brittany is a country

of small men. I looked close; I had read the notice; I said
to myself, 'Ah ha!' And when you came down there was
moonlight, and I recognized you."

" And yet I do not know you."

" You have seen me, but you never looked at me."

And Tellmarch the Caimand added,—

" I looked at you, though. The giver and the beggar do
not look with the same eyes."

" Had I encountered you formerly? "

" Often; I am your beggar. I was the mendicant at the
foot of the road from your castle. You have given me alms.
But he who gives does not notice; he who receives examines
and observes. When you say mendicant, you say spy. But
as for me, though I am often sad, I try not to be a malicious
spy. I used to hold out my hand; you only saw the hand, and
you threw into it the charity I needed in the morning in order
that I might not die in the evening. I have often been twenty-
four hours without eating. Sometimes a penny is life. I
owe you my life; I pay the debt."

" That is true; you save me."

" Yes, I save you, monseigneur."

And Tellmarch's voice grew solemn as he added,—

" On one condition."

" And that? "

" That you are not come here to do harm."

" I come here to do good," said the marquis.

" Let us sleep," said the beggar.

They lay down side by side on the sea-weed bed. The
mendicant fell asleep immediately. The marquis, although
very tired, remained thinking deeply for a few moments; he
gazed fixedly at the beggar in the shadow, and then lay back.
To lie on that bed was to lie on the ground,— which sug-
gested to him to put his ear to the earth and listen. He could
hear a strange buzzing underground. We know that sound
stretches down into the depths: he could hear the noise of
the bells.

The tocsin was still sounding.

The marquis fell asleep.

6

CHAPTER V

SIGNED GAUVAIN

IT was daylight when he awoke. The mendicant was standing up,— not in the den, for he could not hold himself erect there, but without, on the sill. He was leaning on his stick. The sun shone upon his face.

" Monseigneur," said Tellmarch, " four o'clock has just sounded from the belfry of Tanis. I could count the strokes, therefore the wind has changed: it is the land breeze. I can hear no other sound, so the tocsin has ceased. Everything is tranquil about the farm and hamlet of Herbe-en-Pail. The Blues are asleep or gone. The worst of the danger is over; it will be wise for us to separate. It is my hour for setting out."

He indicated a point in the horizon.

" I am going that way."

He pointed in the opposite direction.

" Go you this way."

The beggar made the marquis a gesture of salute. He pointed to the remains of the supper.

" Take the chestnuts with you, if you are hungry."

A moment after, he disappeared among the trees.

The marquis rose and departed in the direction which Tellmarch had indicated.

It was that charming hour called in the old Norman peasant dialect " the song-sparrow of the day." The finches and the hedge-sparrows flew chirping about. The marquis followed the path by which they had come on the previous night. He passed out of the thicket and found himself at the fork of the road, marked by the stone cross. The placard was still there, looking white, fairly gay, in the rising sun. He remembered that there was something at the bottom of the placard which he had not been able to read the evening before, on account of the twilight and the size of the letters. He went up to the pedestal of the cross. Under the signature " PRIEUR, DE LA MARNE," there were yet two other lines in small characters:—

The identity of the *ci-devant* Marquis de Lantenac established, he will be immediately shot.

(Signed)
GAUVAIN,
*Chief of battalion commanding
the exploring column.*

" Gauvain ! " said the marquis. He stood still, thinking deeply, his eyes fixed on the notice.

" Gauvain ! " he repeated.

He resumed his march, turned about, looked again at the cross, walked back, and once more read the placard.

Then he went slowly away. Had any person been near, he might have been heard to murmur, in a half-voice, " Gauvain ! "

From the sunken paths into which he retreated he could only see the roofs of the farm, which lay to the left. He passed along the side of a steep eminence covered with furze, of the species called long-thorn, in blossom. The summit of this height was one of those points of land named in Brittany a *hure.*

At the foot of the eminence the gaze lost itself among the trees. The foliage seemed bathed in light. All Nature was filled with the deep joy of the morning.

Suddenly this landscape became terrible. It was like the bursting forth of an ambuscade. An appalling, indescribable trumpeting, made by savage cries and gunshots, struck upon these fields and these woods filled with sunlight, and there could be seen rising from the side toward the farm a great smoke, cut by clear flames, as if the hamlet and the farm buildings were consuming like a truss of burning straw. It was sudden and fearful,— the abrupt change from tranquillity to fury; an explosion of hell in the midst of dawn; a horror without transition. There was fighting in the direction of Herbe-en-Pail. The marquis stood still.

There is no man in a similar case who would not feel curiosity stronger than a sense of the peril. One must know what is happening, if one perish in the attempt. He mounted the eminence along the bottom of which passed the sunken path by which he had come. From there he could see, but he could also be seen. He remained on the top for some instants. He looked about.

There was, in truth, a fusilade and a conflagration. He could hear the cries, he could see the flames. The farm appeared the centre of some terrible catastrophe. What could it be? Was the farm of Herbe-en-Pail attacked? But by whom? Was it a battle? Was it not rather a military execution? Very often the Blues punished refractory farms and villages by setting them on fire. They were ordered to do so by a revolutionary decree; they burned, for example, every farm-house and hamlet where the tree-cutting prescribed by law had been neglected, or no roads opened among the thickets for the passage of the republican cavalry. Only very lately, the parish of Bourgon, near Ernée, had been thus destroyed. Was Herbe-en-Pail receiving similar treatment? It was evident that none of the strategic routes called for by the decree had been made among the copses and enclosures. Was this the punishment for such neglect? Had an order been received by the advance-guard occupying the farm? Did not this troop make part of one of those exploring divisions called the " infernal columns "?

A bristling and savage thicket surrounded on all sides the eminence upon which the marquis had posted himself for an outlook. This thicket, which was called the grove of Herbe-en-Pail, but which had the proportions of a wood, stretched to the farm, and concealed, like all Breton copses, a network of ravines, by-paths, and deep cuttings, labyrinths where the republican armies lost themselves.

The execution, if it were an execution, must have been a ferocious one, for it was short. It had been, like all brutal deeds, quickly accomplished. The atrocity of civil wars admits of these savage vagaries. While the marquis, multiply-

ing conjectures, hesitating to descend, hesitating to remain,
listened and watched, this crash of extermination ceased, or,
more correctly speaking, vanished. The marquis took note of
something in the thicket that was like the scattering of a wild
and joyous troop. A frightful rushing about made itself
heard beneath the trees. From the farm the band had thrown
themselves into the wood. Drums beat. No more gunshots
were fired. Now it resembled a battue; they seemed to search,
follow, track. They were evidently hunting some person.
The noise was scattered and deep; it was a confusion of words
of wrath and triumph; of indistinct cries and clamour. Suddenly, as an outline becomes visible in a cloud of smoke, something is articulated clearly and distinctly amid this tumult: it
was a name,— a name repeated by a thousand voices,— and
the marquis plainly heard this cry:—

" Lantenac! Lantenac! The Marquis de Lantenac!"
It was he whom they were looking for.

CHAPTER VI

THE WHIRLIGIGS OF CIVIL WAR

SUDDENLY all about him, from all sides at the same
time, the copse filled with muskets, bayonets, and
sabres, a tricoloured flag rose in the half-light, the cry of
" Lantenac!" burst forth in his very ear, and at his feet, behind the brambles and branches, savage faces appeared.

The marquis was alone, standing on a height, visible from
every part of the wood. He could scarcely see those who
shrieked his name; but he was seen by all. If a thousand
muskets were in the wood, there was he like a target. He
could distinguish nothing among the brush-wood but burning
eyeballs fastened upon him.

He took off his hat, turned back the brim, tore a long, dry

thorn from a furze-bush, drew from his pocket a white cockade, fastened the upturned brim and the cockade to the hat with the thorn, and putting back on his head the hat, whose lifted edge showed the white cockade, and left his face in full view, he cried in a loud voice that rang like a trumpet through the forest:—

"I am the man you seek. I am the Marquis de Lantenac, Viscount de Fontenay, Breton prince, lieutenant-general of the armies of the king. Now make an end! Aim! Fire!"

And tearing open with both hands his goat-skin vest, he bared his naked breast.

He looked down, expecting to meet levelled guns, and saw himself surrounded by kneeling men.

Then a great shout arose:—

"Long live Lantenac! Long live Monseigneur! Long live the general!"

At the same time hats were flung into the air, sabres whirled joyously, and through all the thicket could be seen rising sticks on whose points waved caps of brown woollen. He was surrounded by a Vendean band.

This troop had knelt at sight of him.

Old legends tell of strange beings that were found in the ancient Thuringian forests,— a race of giants, more and less than men, who were regarded by the Romans as horrible monsters, by the Germans as divine incarnations, and who, according to the encounter, ran the risk of being exterminated or adored.

The marquis felt something of the sentiment which must have shaken one of those creatures when, expecting to be treated like a monster, he suddenly found himself worshipped as a god.

All those eyes, full of terrible lightnings, were fastened on him with a sort of savage love.

This crowd was armed with muskets, sabres, scythes, poles, sticks; they wore great beavers or brown caps, with white cockades, a profusion of rosaries and amulets, wide breeches open at the knee, jackets of skins, leather gaiters, the calves

of their legs bare, their hair long: some with a ferocious look,
all with an open one.

A man, young and of noble mien, passed through the kneeling throng, and hurried toward the marquis. Like the peasants, he wore a turned-up beaver and a white cockade, and
was wrapped in a fur jacket; but his hands were white and
his linen fine, and he wore over his vest a white silk scarf, from
which hung a gold-hilted sword.

When he reached the *hure* he threw aside his hat, untied
his scarf, bent one knee to the ground, and presented the
sword and scarf to the marquis, saying:

"We were indeed seeking you, and we have found you.
Accept the sword of command. These men are yours now.
I was their leader; I mount in grade, for I become your
soldier. Accept our homage, my lord. General, give me
your orders."

Then he made a sign, and some men who carried a tricoloured flag moved out of the wood. They marched up to
where the marquis stood, and laid the banner at his feet. It
was the flag which he had just caught sight of through the
trees.

"General," said the young man who had presented to him
the sword and scarf, "this is the flag we just took from the
Blues, who held the farm of Herbe-en-Pail. Monseigneur, I
am named Gavard. I belong to the Marquis de la Rouarie."

"It is well," said the marquis. And, calm and grave, he
put on the scarf.

Then he drew his sword, and waving it above his head, he
cried,—

"Up! Long live the king!"

All rose. Through the depths of the wood swelled a wild
triumphant clamour: "Long live the king! Long live our
marquis! Long live Lantenac!"

The marquis turned toward Gavard:—

"How many are you?"

"Seven thousand."

And as they descended the eminence, while the peasants

cleared away the furze-bushes to make a path for the Marquis de Lantenac, Gavard continued:—

" Monseigneur, nothing more simple.   All can be explained in a word.   It only needed a spark.   The reward offered by the Republic, in revealing your presence, roused the whole district for the king.   Besides that, we had been secretly warned by the mayor of Granville, who is one of our men, the same who saved the Abbé Ollivier.   Last night they sounded the tocsin."

" For whom? "

" For you."

" Ah! " said the marquis.

" And here we are," pursued Gavard.

" And you are seven thousand? "

" To-day.   We shall be fifteen thousand to-morrow.   It is the Breton contingent.   When Monsieur Henri de la Roche-jacquelein set out to join the Catholic army, the tocsin was sounded, and in one night six parishes — Isernay, Corqueux, the Echaubroignes, the Aubiers, Saint-Aubin, and Nueil — brought him ten thousand men.   They had no munitions; they found in the house of a quarry-master sixty pounds of blast-ing-powder, and M. de la Rochejacquelein set off with that.

" We were certain you must be in some part of this forest, and we were seeking you."

" And you attacked the Blues at the farm of Herbe-en-Pail? "

" The wind prevented their hearing the tocsin.   They sus-pected nothing; the people of the hamlet, who are a set of clowns, received them well.   This morning we surrounded the farm; the Blues were asleep, and we did the thing out of hand.   I have a horse.   Will you deign to accept it, Gen-eral? "

" Yes."

A peasant led up a white horse with military caparisons. The marquis mounted without the assistance Gavard offered him.

" Hurrah!" cried the peasants.   The cries of the English were greatly in use along the Breton coast, in constant communication as it was with the Channel Islands.

Gavard made a military salute, and asked,—

" Where will you make your headquarters, monseigneur? "

" At first in the Forest of Fougères."

" It is one of your seven forests, my lord marquis."

" We must have a priest."

" We have one."

" Who? "

" The curate of the Chapelle-Erbrée."

" I know him.   He has made the voyage to Jersey."

A priest stepped out of the ranks, and said,—

" Three times."

The marquis turned his head.

" Good-morning, Monsieur le Curé.   You have work before you."

" So much the better, my lord marquis."

" You will have to hear confessions,— those who wish; nobody will be forced."

" My lord marquis," said the priest, " at Guéménée, Gaston forces the republicans to confess."

" He is a hairdresser," said the marquis; " death ought to be free."

Gavard, who had gone to give some orders, returned.

" General, I wait your commands."

" First, the rendezvous in the Forest of Fougères.   Let the men disperse, and make their way there."

" The order is given."

" Did you not tell me that the people of Herbe-en-Pail had received the Blues well? "

" Yes, General."

" You have burned the house? "

" Yes."

" Have you burned the hamlet? "

" No."

" Burn it."

" The Blues tried to defend themselves, but they were a hundred and fifty, and we were seven thousand."

" Who were they? "

" Sañterre's men."

" The one who ordered the drums to beat while the king's head was being cut off?   Then it is a regiment of Paris? "

" A half-regiment."

" Its name? "

" General, it had on its flag, ' Battalion of the Bonnet Rouge.' "

" Wild beasts."

" What is to be done with the wounded? "

" Put an end to them."

" What shall we do with the prisoners? "

" Shoot them."

" There are about eighty."

" Shoot the whole."

" There are two women."

" Them also."

" There are three children."

" Carry them off.   We will see what shall be done with them."

And the marquis rode on.

CHAPTER VII

" NO MERCY! " (WATCHWORD OF THE COMMUNE).   " NO QUARTER! " (WATCHWORD OF THE PRINCES).

WHILE all this was passing near Tanis, the mendicant had gone toward Crollon. He plunged into the ravines, among the vast silent bowers of shade, inattentive to everything and attentive to nothing, as he had himself said; dreamer rather than thinker, for the thoughtful man has an

aim, and the dreamer has none; wandering, rambling, paus-
ing, munching here and there a bunch of wild sorrel; drinking
at the springs, occasionally raising his head to listen to the
distant tumult, again falling back into the bewildering fasci-
nation of Nature; warming his rags in the sun; hearing sometimes the noise of men, but listening to the song of the birds.

He was old, and moved slowly. He could not walk far; as
he had said to the Marquis de Lantenac, a quarter of a league
fatigued him. He made a short circuit to the Croix-Avranchin, and evening had come before he returned.

A little beyond Macey, the path he was following led to a
sort of culminating point, bare of trees, from whence one could
see very far, taking in the whole stretch of the western horizon
to the sea.

A column of smoke attracted his attention.

Nothing calmer than smoke, but nothing more startling.
There are peaceful smokes, and there are evil ones. The
thickness and colour of a line of smoke marks the whole difference between war and peace, between fraternity and hatred,
between hospitality and the tomb, between life and death. A
smoke mounting among the trees may be a symbol of all that
is most charming in the world,— a heart at home; or a sign of
that which is most awful,— a conflagration. The whole
happiness of man, or his most complete misery, is sometimes
expressed in this thin vapour, which the wind scatters at will.

The smoke which Tellmarch saw was disquieting.

It was black, dashed now and then with sudden gleams of
red, as if the brasier from which it flowed burned irregularly,
and had begun to die out; and it rose above Herbe-en-Pail.

Tellmarch quickened his steps, and walked toward this
smoke.

He was very tired, but he must know what this signified.

He reached the summit of a hill, against whose side the
hamlet and the farm were nestled.

There was no longer either farm or hamlet.

A heap of ruins was burning still; it was Herbe-en-Pail.

There is something which it is more painful to see burn

than a palace,— it is a cottage. A cottage on fire is a lamentable sight. It is a devastation swooping down on poverty, the vulture pouncing upon the worms of the ground; there is in it a contradiction which chills the heart.

If we believe the Biblical legend, the sight of a conflagration changed a human being into a statue. For a moment Tellmarch seemed thus transformed. The spectacle before his eyes held him motionless. Destruction was completing its work amid unbroken silence. Not a cry arose; not a human sigh mingled with this smoke. This furnace laboured, and finished devouring the village, without any noise being heard save the creaking of the timbers and the crackling of the thatch. At moments the smoke parted, the fallen roofs revealed the gaping chambers, the brasier showed all its rubies; rags turned to scarlet, and miserable bits of furniture, tinted with purple, gleamed amid these vermilion interiors, and Tellmarch was dizzied by the sinister bedazzlement of disaster.

Some trees of a chestnut grove near the house had taken fire, and were blazing.

He listened, trying to catch a sound of a voice, an appeal, a cry. Nothing stirred except the flames; everything was silent, save the conflagration. Was it that all had fled?

Where was the knot of people who had lived and toiled at Herbe-en-Pail? What had become of this little band? Tellmarch descended the hill.

A funereal enigma rose before him. He approached without haste, with fixed eyes. He advanced toward this ruin with the slowness of a shadow; he felt like a ghost in this tomb.

He reached what had been the door of the farm-house, and looked into the court, which had no longer any walls, and was confounded with the hamlet grouped about it.

What he had before seen was nothing. He had hitherto only caught sight of the terrible; the horrible appeared to him now.

In the middle of the court was a black heap, vaguely outlined on one side by the flames, on the other by the moonlight. This heap was a mass of men; these men were dead.

All about this human mound spread a great pool which smoked a little; the flames were reflected in this pool, but it had no need of fire to redden it,— it was blood.

Tellmarch went closer. He began to examine these prostrate bodies one after another: they were all dead men.

The moon shone; the conflagration also.

These corpses were the bodies of soldiers. All had their feet bare; their shoes had been taken. Their weapons were gone also; they still wore their uniforms, which were blue. Here and there he could distinguish among these heaped-up limbs and heads shot-riddled hats with tricoloured cockades. They were republicans. They were those Parisians who on the previous evening had been there, all living, keeping garrison at the farm of Herbe-en-Pail. These men had been executed: this was shown by the symmetrical position of the bodies; they had been struck down in order, and with care. They were all quite dead. Not a single death-gasp sounded from the mass.

Tellmarch passed the corpses in review without omitting one; they were all riddled with balls.

Those who had shot them, in haste probably to get elsewhere, had not taken the time to bury them.

As he was preparing to move away, his eyes fell on a low wall in the court, and he saw four feet protruding from one of its angles.

They had shoes on them; they were smaller than the others. Tellmarch went up to this spot. They were women's feet. Two women were lying side by side behind the wall; they also had been shot.

Tellmarch stooped over them. One of the women wore a sort of uniform; by her side was a canteen, bruised and empty: she had been vivandière. She had four balls in her head. She was dead.

Tellmarch examined the other. This was a peasant. She was livid: her mouth open. Her eyes were closed. There was no wound in her head. Her garments, which long marches, no doubt, had worn to rags, were disarranged by her fall, leaving her bosom half naked. Tellmarch pushed her dress aside, and saw on one shoulder the round wound which a ball makes; the shoulder-blade was broken. He looked at her livid breast.

"Nursing mother," he murmured.

He touched her. She was not cold.

She had no hurts besides the broken shoulder-blade and the wound in the shoulder.

He put his hand on her heart, and felt a faint throb. She was not dead.

Tellmarch raised himself, and cried out in a terrible voice,—

"Is there no one here?"

"Is it you, Caimand?" a voice replied, so low that it could scarcely be heard.

At the same time a head was thrust out of a hole in the ruin. Then another face appeared at another aperture. They were two peasants, who had hidden themselves,— the only ones who survived.

The well-known voice of the Caimand had reassured them, and brought them out of the holes in which they had taken refuge.

They advanced toward the old man, both still trembling violently.

Tellmarch had been able to cry out, but he could not talk; strong emotions produce such effects.

He pointed out to them with his finger the woman stretched at his feet.

"Is there still life in her?" asked one of the peasants.

Tellmarch gave an affirmative nod of the head.

"Is the other woman living?" demanded the second man.

Tellmarch shook his head.

The peasant who had first shown himself continued:

"All the others are dead, are they not? I saw the whole. I was in my cellar. How one thanks God at such a moment for not having a family! My house burned. Blessed

Saviour! They killed everybody. This woman here had three children — all little. The children cried, ' Mother! ' The mother cried, ' My children! ' Those who massacred everybody are gone. They were satisfied. They carried off the little ones, and shot the mother. I saw it all. But she is not dead,— didn't you say so? She is not dead? Tell us, Caimand, do you think you could save her? Do you want us to help carry her to your *carnichot?* "

Tellmarch made a sign, which signified " Yes."

The wood was close to the farm. They quickly made a litter with branches and ferns. They laid the woman, still motionless, upon it, and set out toward the copse, the two peasants carrying the litter, one at the head, the other at the feet, Tellmarch holding the woman's arm, and feeling her pulse.

As they walked, the two peasants talked; and over the body of the bleeding woman, whose white face was lighted up by the moon, they exchanged frightened ejaculations.

" To kill all! "

" To burn everything! "

" Ah, my God! Is that the way things will go now? "

" It was that tall old man who ordered it to be done."

" Yes; it was he who commanded."

" I did not see while the shooting went on. Was he there? "

" No. He had gone. But no matter; it was all done by his orders."

" Then it was he who did the whole."

" He said, ' Kill! burn! no quarter! ' "

" He is a marquis."

" Of course, since he is our marquis."

" What do they call him now? "

" He is M. de Lantenac."

Tellmarch raised his eyes to heaven, and murmured:

" If I had known! "

PART II

IN PARIS

BOOK I

CIMOURDAIN

CHAPTER I

THE STREETS OF PARIS AT THAT TIME

PEOPLE lived in public: they ate at tables spread outside the doors; women seated on the steps of the
churches made lint as they sang the " Marseillaise." Park
Monceaux and the Luxembourg Gardens were parade-grounds.
There were gunsmiths' shops in full work; they manufactured
muskets before the eyes of the passers-by, who clapped their
hands in applause. The watchword on every lip was, " Patience; we are in revolution." The people smiled heroically.
They went to the theatre as they did at Athens during the
Peloponnesian war. One saw play-bills such as these pasted
at the street corners: " The Siege of Thionville; " " A
Mother saved from the Flames; " " The Club of the Care-
less; " " The Eldest of the Popes Joan; " " The Philosopher-
Soldiers; " " The Art of Village Love-Making."

The Germans were at the gates; a report was current that

the King of Prussia had secured boxes at the Opera. Everything was terrible, and no one was frightened. The mysterious law against the suspected, which was the crime of
Merlin of Douai, held a vision of the guillotine above every
head. A solicitor named Séran, who had been denounced,
awaited his arrest in dressing-gown and slippers, playing his
flute at his window. Nobody seemed to have leisure: all the
world was in a hurry. Every hat bore a cockade. The
women said, " We are pretty in red caps." All Paris seemed
to be removing. The curiosity-shops were crowded with
crowns, mitres, sceptres of gilded wood, and *fleur-de-lis* torn
down from royal dwellings: it was the demolition of monarchy
that went on. Copes were to be seen for sale at the old-
clothesmen's, and rochets hung on hooks at their doors. At
Ramponneau's and the Porcherons, men dressed out in sur-
plices and stoles, and mounted on donkeys caparisoned with
chasubles, drank wine at the doors from cathedral ciboria.
In the Rue Saint Jacques, barefooted street-pavers stopped the
wheelbarrow of a peddler who had boots for sale, and clubbed
together to buy fifteen pairs of shoes, which they sent to the
Convention " for our soldiers."

Busts of Franklin, Rousseau, Brutus, and, we must add, of
Marat, abounded. Under a bust of Marat in the Rue Cloche-
Perce was hung in a black wooden frame, and under glass,
an address against Malouet, with testimony in support of the
charges, and these marginal lines:

These details were furnished me by the mistress of Silvain Bailly, a
good patriotess, who has a liking for me.
(Signed) MARAT.

The inscription on the Palais Royal fountain —" Quantos
effundit in usus ! "— was hidden under two great canvases
painted in distemper, the one representing Cahier de Gerville
denouncing to the National Assembly the rallying cry of the
" Chiffonistes " of Arles; the other, Louis XVI. brought back
from Varennes in his royal carriage, and under the carriage
a plank fastened by cords, on each end of which was seated
a grenadier with fixed bayonet.

7.

Very few of the larger shops were open; peripatetic haberdashery and toy shops were dragged about by women, lighted by candles, which dropped their tallow on the merchandise. Open-air shops were kept by ex-nuns, in blond wigs. This mender, darning stockings in a stall, was a countess; that dressmaker, a marchioness. Madame de Boufflers inhabited a garret, from whence she could look out at her own hotel. Hawkers ran about offering the " papers of news." Persons who wore cravats that hid their chins were called " the scrofulous." Street-singers swarmed. The crowd hooted Pitou, the royalist song-writer, and a valiant man into the bargain; he was twenty-two times imprisoned and taken before the revolutionary tribunal for slapping his coat-tails as he pronounced the word *civism*. Seeing that his head was in danger, he exclaimed: " But it is just the opposite of my head that is in fault; "— a witticism which made the judges laugh, and saved his life. This Pitou ridiculed the rage for Greek and Latin names; his favourite song was about a cobbler, whom he called *Cujus*, and to whom he gave a wife named *Cujusdam*. They danced the Carmagnole in great circles. They no longer said " gentleman and lady," but " citizen and citizeness." They danced in the ruined cloisters with the church-lamps lighted on the altars, with cross-shaped chandeliers hanging from the vaulted roofs, and tombs beneath their feet. Waistcoats of " tyrant's blue " were worn. There were " liberty-cap " shirt-pins made of white, blue, and red stones. The Rue de Richelieu was called the Street of Law; the Faubourg Saint Antoine was named the Faubourg of Glory; a statue of Nature stood in the Place de la Bastille. People pointed out to one another certain well-known personages,— Chatelet, Didier, Nicholas and Garnier-Delaunay, who stood guard at the door of Duplay the joiner; Voullant, who never missed a guillotine-day, and followed the carts of the condemned,— he called it going to " the red mass; " Montflabert, revolutionary juryman, and a marquis, who took the name of " Dix Août [Tenth of August]. People watched the pupils of the Ecole Militaire file past, de-

scribed by the decrees of the Convention as " aspirants in the
school of Mars," and by the crowd as " the pages of Robespierre." They read the proclamations of Fréron denouncing
those suspected of the crime of " negotiantism." The dandies
collected at the doors of the mayoralties to mock at the civil
marriages, thronging about the brides and grooms as they
passed, and shouting " Married *municipaliter!* " At the Invalides the statues of the saints and kings were crowned with
Phrygian caps. They played cards on the curb-stones at the
crossings. The packs of cards were also in the full tide of
revolution: the kings were replaced by genii, the queens by the
Goddess of Liberty, the knaves by figures representing Equality, and the aces by impersonations of Law. They tilled the
public gardens; the plough worked at the Tuileries. With
all these excesses was mingled, especially among the conquered
parties, an indescribable haughty weariness of life. A man
wrote to Fouquier-Tinville, " Have the goodness to free me
from existence. This is my address." Champcenetz was arrested for having cried in the midst of the Palais Royal garden: " When are we to have the revolution of Turkey? I
want to see the republic *à la Porte.*" Newspapers appeared
in legions. The hairdressers' men curled the wigs of women
in public, while the master read the " Moniteur " aloud.
Others, surrounded by eager groups, commented with violent
gestures upon the journal " Listen to Us," of Dubois Crancé,
or the " Trumpet " of Father Bellerose. Sometimes the bar-
bers were pork-sellers as well, and hams and chitterlings might
be seen hanging side by side with a golden-haired doll. Deal-
ers sold in the open street " wines of the refugees; " one merchant advertised wines of fifty-two sorts. Others displayed
harp-shaped clocks and sofas *à la duchesse.* One hairdresser
had for sign: " I shave the clergy; I comb the nobility; I
arrange the Third Estate."

People went to have their fortunes told by Martin, at No.
173, in the Rue d'Anjou, formerly Rue Dauphine. There
was a lack of bread, of coals, of soap. Herds of milch-cows
might be seen coming in from the country. At the Vallée,

lamb sold for fifteen francs the pound. An order of the
Commune assigned a pound of meat per head every ten days.
People stood in rank at the doors of the butchers' shops.
One of these files has remained famous: it reached from a
grocer's shop in the Rue du Petit Carreau to the middle of
the Rue Montorgueil. To form a line was called " holding
the cord," from a long rope which was held in the hands of
those standing in the row. Amid this wretchedness, the
women were brave and mild; they passed entire nights awaiting their turn to get into the bakers' shops. The Revolution
resorted to expedients which were successful; she alleviated
this widespread distress by two perilous means,— the assignat
and the maximum. The assignat was the lever, the maximum
was the fulcrum. This empiricism saved France. The
enemy, whether of Coblentz or London, gambled in assignats.
Girls came and went, offering lavender water, garters, false
hair, and selling stocks. There were jobbers on the Perron of
the Rue Vivienne, with muddy shoes, greasy hair, and fur
caps decorated with fox-tails; and there were swells from the
Rue Valois, with varnished boots, toothpicks in their mouths,
and long-napped hats on their heads, to whom the girls said
" thee " and " thou." Later, the people gave chase to them
as they did to the thieves, whom the royalists styled " active
citizens." For the time, theft was rare. There reigned a
terrible destitution and a stoical probity. The barefooted and
the starving passed with lowered eyelids before the jewellers'
shops of the Palais Egalité. During a domiciliary visit that
the Section Antoine made to the house of Beaumarchais, a
woman picked a flower in the garden; the crowd boxed her
ears. Wood cost four hundred francs in coin per cord; people could be seen in the streets sawing up their bedsteads.
In the winter the fountains were frozen; two pails of water
cost twenty sous: every man made himself a water-carrier. A
gold louis was worth three thousand nine hundred and fifty
francs. A course in a hackney-coach cost six hundred francs.
After a day's use of a carriage, this sort of dialogue might be
heard: " Coachman, how much do I owe you? " " Six thou-

sand francs." A green-grocer woman sold twenty thousand francs' worth of vegetables a day. A beggar said, " Help me, in the name of charity! I lack two hundred and thirty francs to finish paying for my shoes." At the ends of the bridges might be seen colossal figures sculptured and painted by David, which Mercier insulted. " Enormous wooden Punches!" said he. The gigantic shapes symbolized Federalism and Coalition overturned.

There was no faltering among this people. There was the sombre joy of having made an end of thrones. Volunteers abounded; each street furnished a battalion. The flags of the districts came and went, every one with its device. On the banner of the Capuchin district could be read, " Nobody can cut our beards." On another, " No other nobility than that of the heart." On all the walls were placards, large and small, white, yellow, green, red, printed and written, on which might be read this motto: " Long live the Republic!" The little children lisped " Ca ira."

These children were in themselves the great future.

Later, to the tragical city succeeded the cynical city. The streets of Paris have offered two revolutionary aspects entirely distinct,— that before and that after the 9th Thermidor. The Paris of Saint-Just gave place to the Paris of Tallien. Such antitheses are perpetual; after Sinai the Courtille appeared.

An attack of public madness made its appearance. It had already been seen eighty years before. The people came out from under Louis XIV. as they did from under Robespierre, with a great need to breathe; hence the regency which opened that century and the directory which closed it,— two saturnalia after two terrorisms. France snatched the wicket-key and got beyond the Puritan cloister just as it did beyond that of monarchy, with the joy of a nation that escapes.

After the 9th Thermidor Paris was gay, but with an insane gaiety. An unhealthy joy overflowed all bounds. To the frenzy for dying succeeded the frenzy for living, and grandeur eclipsed itself. They had a Trimalcion, calling himself

Grimod de la Reynière: there was the " Almanac of the Gour-
mands." People dined in the entresols of the Palais Royal
to the din of orchestras of women beating drums and blowing trumpets; the " rigadooner " reigned, bow in hand. People supped Oriental fashion at Méot's surrounded by perfumes. The artist Boze painted his daughters, innocent and
charming heads of sixteen, *en guillotinées;* that is to say, with
bare necks and red shifts. To the wild dances in the ruined
churches succeeded the balls of Ruggieri, of Luquet-Wenzel,
Mauduit, and the Montansier; to grave citizenesses making
lint succeeded sultanas, savages, nymphs; to the naked feet
of the soldiers covered with blood, dust, and mud, succeeded
the naked feet of women decorated with diamonds. At the
same time, with shamelessness, improbity reappeared; and it
had its purveyors in high ranks, and their imitators among the
class below. A swarm of sharpers filled Paris, and every
man was forced to guard well his *luc,*— that is, his pocket-
book. One of the amusements of the day was to go to the
Palace of Justice to see the female thieves; it was necessary
to tie fast their petticoats. At the doors of the theatres the
street boys opened cab doors, saying, " Citizen and citizeness, there is room for two." The " Old Cordelier " and the
" Friend of the People " were no longer sold. In their places
were cried " Punch's Letter " and the " Rogues' Petition."
The Marquis de Sade presided at the Section of the Pikes,
Place Vendôme. The reaction was jovial and ferocious. The
Dragons of Liberty of '92 were reborn under the name of
the Chevaliers of the Dagger. At the same time there appeared in the booths that type, Jocrisse. There were " the
Merveilleuses," and in advance of these feminine marvels
came " the Incroyables." People swore by strange and affected oaths; they jumped back from Mirabeau to Bobêche.
Thus it is that Paris sways back and forth; it is the enormous
pendulum of civilization; it touches either pole in turn,—
Thermopylæ and Gomorrah. After '93 the Revolution traversed a singular occultation; the century seemed to forget to
finish that which it had commenced. A strange orgy inter-

posed itself, took the foreground, swept back to the second
place the awful Apocalypse, veiled the immeasurable vision;
and laughed aloud after its fright. Tragedy disappeared
in parody, and, rising darkly from the bottom of the horizon,
a smoke of carnival effaced Medusa.

But in '93, where we are, the streets of Paris still wore the
grandiose and savage aspect of the beginning. They had
their orators, such as Varlet, who promenaded in a booth on
wheels, from the top of which he harangued the passers-by;
they had their heroes, of whom one was called the " Captain
of the iron-pointed sticks; " their favourites, among whom
ranked Guffroy, the author of the pamphlet " Rougiff."
Certain of these popularities were mischievous, others had a
healthy tone; one among them all was honest and fatal,— it
was that of Cimourdain.

CHAPTER II

CIMOURDAIN

CIMOURDAIN had a conscience pure but sombre.
There was something of the absolute within him. He
had been a priest, which is a grave matter. A man may, like
the sky, possess a serenity which is dark and unfathomable; it
only needs that something should have made night within
his soul. The priesthood had made night in that of Cimourdain. He who has been a priest remains one.

What makes night within us may leave stars. Cimourdain
was full of virtues and verities, but they shone among shadows.

His history is easily written. He had been a village curate,
and tutor in a great family; then he inherited a small legacy,
and gained his freedom.

He was above all an obstinate man. He made use of
meditation as one does of pincers; he did not think it right

to quit an idea until he had followed it to the end; he thought stubbornly. He understood all the European languages, and something of others besides. This man studied incessantly, which aided him to bear the burden of celibacy; but nothing can be more dangerous than such a life of repression.

He had from pride, chance, or loftiness of soul been true to his vows, but he had not been able to guard his belief. Science had demolished faith; dogma had fainted within him. Then, as he examined himself, he felt that his soul was mutilated; he could not nullify his priestly oath, but tried to remake himself man, though in an austere fashion. His family had been taken from him; he adopted his country. A wife had been refused him; he espoused humanity. Such vast plenitude has a void at bottom.

His peasant parents, in devoting him to the priesthood, had desired to elevate him above the common people; he voluntarily returned among them.

He went back with a passionate energy. He regarded the suffering with a terrible tenderness. From priest he had become philosopher; and from philosopher, athlete. While Louis XV. still lived, Cimourdain felt himself vaguely republican. But belonging to what republic? To that of Plato perhaps, and perhaps also to the republic of Draco.

Forbidden to love, he set himself to hate. He hated lies, monarchy, theocracy, his garb of priest; he hated the present, and he called aloud to the future; he had a presentiment of it, he caught glimpses of it in advance; he pictured it awful and magnificent. In his view, to end the lamentable wretchedness of humanity required at once an avenger and a liberator. He worshipped the catastrophe afar off.

In 1789 this catastrophe arrived, and found him ready. Cimourdain flung himself into this vast plan of human regeneration on logical grounds,— that is to say, for a mind of his mould, inexorably; logic knows no softening. He lived among the great revolutionary years, and felt the shock of their mighty breaths,—'89, the fall of the Bastille, the end of the torture of the people; on the 4th of August, '90, the end of feudalism; '91, Varennes, the end of royalty; '92, the birth of the Republic. He saw the Revolution loom into life; he was not a man to be afraid of that giant,— far from it. This sudden growth in everything had revivified him; and though already nearly old,— he was fifty, and a priest ages faster than another man,— he began himself to grow also. From year to year he saw events gain in grandeur, and he increased with them. He had at first feared that the Revolution would prove abortive; he watched it. It had reason and right on its side; he demanded success for it likewise. In proportion to the fear it caused the timid, his confidence strengthened. He desired that this Minerva, crowned with the stars of the future, should be Pallas also, with the Gorgon's head for buckler. He demanded that her divine glance should be able at need to fling back to the demons their infernal glare, and give them terror for terror.

Thus he reached '93.

'93 was the war of Europe against France, and of France against Paris. And what was the Revolution? It was the victory of France over Europe, and of Paris over France. Hence the immensity of that terrible moment, '93,— grander than all the rest of the century. Nothing could be more tragic: Europe attacking France, and France attacking Paris! A drama which reaches the stature of an epic. '93 is a year of intensity. The tempest is there in all its wrath and all its grandeur. Cimourdain felt himself at home. This distracted centre, terrible and splendid, suited the span of his wings. Like the sea-eagle amid the tempest, this man preserved his internal composure and enjoyed the danger. Certain winged natures, savage yet calm, are made to battle the winds,— souls of the tempest: such exist.

He had put pity aside, reserving it only for the wretched. He devoted himself to those sorts of suffering which cause horror. Nothing was repugnant to him. That was his kind of goodness. He was divine in his readiness to succour what was loathsome. He searched for ulcers in order that he might kiss them. Noble actions with a revolting exterior are the

most difficult to undertake; he preferred such.   One day at the
Hôtel Dieu a man was dying, suffocated by a tumour in the
throat,— a fetid, frightful abscess,— contagious perhaps,—
which must be at once opened.   Cimourdain was there; he put
his lips to the tumour, sucked it, spitting it out as his mouth
filled, and so emptied the abscess and saved the man.   As he
still wore his priest's dress at the time, some one said to him,
" If you were to do that for the king, you would be made a
bishop."   " I would not do it for the king," Cimourdain
replied.   The act and the response rendered him popular in
the sombre quarters of Paris.

They gave him so great a popularity that he could do
what he liked with those who suffered, wept, and threatened.
At the period of the public wrath against monopolists,— a
wrath which was prolific in mistakes,— Cimourdain by a word
prevented the pillage of a boat loaded with soap at the quay
Saint Nicholas, and dispersed the furious bands who were
stopping the carriages at the barrier of Saint Lazare.

It was he who, two days after the 10th of August, headed
the people to overthrow the statues of the kings.   They
slaughtered as they fell: in the Place Vendôme, a woman called
Reine Violet was crushed by the statue of Louis XIV., about
whose neck she had put a cord, which she was pulling.   This
statue of Louis XIV. had been standing a hundred years.
It was erected the 12th of August, 1692; it was overthrown
the 12th of August, 1792.   In the Place de la Concorde, a
certain Guinguerlot was butchered on the pedestal of Louis
XV.'s statue for having called the demolishers scoundrels.
The statue was broken in pieces.   Later, it was melted to coin,
— into sous.   The arm alone escaped,— it was the right arm,
which was extended with the gesture of a Roman emperor.
At Cimourdain's request the people sent a deputation with
this arm to Latude, the man who had been thirty-seven years
buried in the Bastille.   When Latude was rotting alive, the
collar on his neck, the chain about his loins, in the bottom
of that prison where he had been cast by the order of that
king whose statue overlooked Paris, who could have prophesied

to him that this prison would fall, this statue would be destroyed; that he would emerge from the sepulchre and monarchy enter it; that he, the prisoner, would be the master of this hand of bronze which had signed his warrant; and that of this king of Mud there would remain only his brazen arm?

Cimourdain was one of those men who have an interior voice to which they listen. Such men seem absent-minded; no, they are attentive.

Cimourdain was at once learned and ignorant. He understood all science, and was ignorant of everything in regard to life. Hence his severity. He had his eyes bandaged, like the Themis of Homer. He had the blind certainty of the arrow, which, seeing not the goal, yet goes straight to it. In a revolution there is nothing so formidable as a straight line. Cimourdain went straight before him, fatal, unwavering.

He believed that in a social Genesis the farthest point is the solid ground,— an error peculiar to minds which replace reason by logic. He went beyond the Convention; he went beyond the Commune; he belonged to the Evêché.

The society called the Evêché, because its meetings were held in a hall of the former episcopal palace, was rather a complication of men than a union. There, as at the Commune, those silent but significant spectators were present who, as Garat said, " had as many pistols as pockets."

The Evêché was a strange mixture,— a crowd at once cosmopolitan and Parisian. This is no contradiction, for Paris is the spot where beats the heart of the peoples. The great plebeian incandescence was at the Evêché. In comparison to it, the Convention was cold and the Commune lukewarm. The Evêché was one of those revolutionary formations similar to volcanic ones; it contained everything,— ignorance, stupidity, probity, heroism, choler, spies. Brunswick had agents there. It numbered men worthy of Sparta, and men who deserved the galleys. The greater part were mad and honest. The Gironde had pronounced by the mouth of Isnard, temporary president of the Convention, this monstrous warning: —

"Take care, Parisians! There will not remain one stone upon another of your city, and the day will come when the place where Paris stood shall be searched for."

This speech created the Evêché. Certain men — and as we have just said, they were men of all nations — felt the need of gathering themselves close about Paris. Cimourdain joined this club.

The society reacted on the reactionists. It was born out of that public necessity for violence which is the formidable and mysterious side of revolutions. Strong with this strength, the Evêché at once began its work. In the commotions of Paris it was the Commune that fired the cannon; it was the Evêché that sounded the tocsin.

In his implacable ingenuousness, Cimourdain believed that everything in the service of truth is justice, which rendered him fit to dominate the extremists on either side. Scoundrels felt that he was honest, and were satisfied. Crime is flattered by having virtue to preside over it; it is at once troublesome and pleasant. Palloy, the architect who had turned to account the demolition of the Bastille, selling its stones to his own profit, and who, appointed to whitewash the cell of Louis XVI., in his zeal covered the wall with bars, chains, and iron rings: Gonchon, the suspected orator of the Faubourg Saint Antoine, whose quittances were afterward found; Fournier, the American, who on the 17th of July fired at Lafayette a pistol-shot, paid for, it is said, by Lafayette himself; Henriot, who had come out of Bicêtre, and who had been valet, mountebank, robber, and spy before being a general and turning the guns on the Convention; La Reynie, formerly grand-vicar of Chartres, who had replaced his breviary by "The Père Duchesne,"— all these men were held in respect by Cimourdain; and at certain moments, to keep the worst of them from stumbling, it was sufficient to feel his redoubtable and believing candour as a judgment before them. It was thus that Saint-Just terrified Schneider. At the same time the majority of the Evêché, composed principally as it was of poor and violent men who were honest,

believed in Cimourdain and followed him. He had for curate or *aide-de-camp*, as you please, that other republican priest,
Danjou, whom the people loved on account of his height, and
had christened Abbé Six-Foot. Cimourdain could have led
where he would that intrepid chief called General La Pique,
and that bold Truchon named the Great Nicholas, who had
tried to save Madame de Lamballe, and had given her his
arm, and made her spring over the corpses,— an attempt
which would have succeeded, had it not been for the ferocious
pleasantry of the barber Charlot.

The Commune watched the Convention; the Evêché watched
the Commune. Cimourdain, naturally upright and detesting
intrigue, had broken more than one mysterious thread in the
hand of Pache, whom Beurnonville called " the black man."
Cimourdain at the Evêché was on confidential terms with all.
He was consulted by Dobsent and Momoro. He spoke
Spanish with Gusman, Italian with Pio, English with Arthur,
Flemish with Pereyra, German with the Austrian Proly, the
bastard of a prince. He created a harmony between these
discordances. Hence his position was obscure and strong.
Hébert feared him.

In these times and among these tragic groups, Cimourdain possessed the power of the inexorable. He was an im-
peccable, who believed himself infallible. No person had
ever seen him weep. He was Virtue inaccessible and glacial.
He was the terrible offspring of Justice.

There is no half-way possible to a priest in a revolution.
A priest can only give himself up to this wild and prodigious
chance either from the highest or the lowest motive; he must
be infamous or he must be sublime. Cimourdain was sublime, but in isolation, in rugged inaccessibility, in inhospitable
secretiveness, sublime amid a circle of precipices. Lofty
mountains possess this sinister freshness.

Cimourdain had the appearance of an ordinary man,
dressed in every-day garments, poor in aspect. When young,
he had been tonsured; as an old man he was bald. What
little hair he had left was grey. His forehead was broad,

and to the acute observer it revealed his character. Cimourdain had an abrupt way of speaking, which was passionate and solemn; his voice was quick, his accent peremptory, his mouth bitter and sad, his eye clear and profound, and over his whole countenance an indescribable indignant expression.

Such was Cimourdain.

No one to-day knows his name. History has many of these great Unknown.

CHAPTER III

A CORNER NOT DIPPED IN STYX

WAS such a man indeed a man? Could the servant of the human race know fondness? Was he not too entirely a soul to possess a heart? This widespread embrace, which included everything and everybody, could it narrow itself down to one. Could Cimourdain love? We answer, Yes.

When young, and tutor in an almost princely family, he had had a pupil whom he loved,— the son and heir of the house. It is so easy to love a child. What can one not pardon a child? One forgives him for being a lord, a prince, a king. The innocence of his age makes one forget the crime of race; the feebleness of the creature causes one to overlook the exaggeration of rank. He is so little that one forgives him for being great. The slave forgives him for being his master. The old negro idolizes the white nursling. Cimourdain had conceived a passion for his pupil. Childhood is so ineffable that one may unite all affections upon it. Cimourdain's whole power of loving prostrated itself, so to speak, before this boy; that sweet, innocent being became a sort of prey for that heart condemned to solitude. He loved with a mingling of all tendernesses,— as father, as brother, as friend, as maker. The child was his son, not of his flesh, but of his mind. He was not the father, and this was not his work; but he was the master, and this his masterpiece. Of this little lord he had made a man,— perhaps a great man; who knows? Such are dreams. Has one need of the permission of a family to create an intelligence, a will, an upright character. He had communicated to the young viscount, his scholar, all the advanced ideas which he held himself; he had inoculated him with the redoubtable virus of his virtue; he had infused into his veins his own convictions, his own conscience and ideal,— into this brain of an aristocrat he had poured the soul of the people.

The spirit suckles; the intelligence is a breast. There is an analogy between the nurse who gives her milk and the preceptor who gives his thought. Sometimes the tutor is more father than is the father, just as often the nurse is more mother than the mother.

This deep spiritual paternity bound Cimourdain to his pupil. The very sight of the child softened him.

Let us add this: to replace the father was easy,— the boy no longer had one. He was an orphan; his father and mother were both dead. To keep watch over him he had only a blind grandmother and an absent great-uncle. The grandmother died; the great-uncle, head of the family, a soldier of high rank, provided with appointments at Court, avoided the old family dungeon, lived at Versailles, went forth with the army, and left the orphan alone in the solitary castle. So the preceptor was master in every sense of the word.

Let us add still further: Cimourdain had seen the child born. The boy, while very little, was seized with a severe illness. In this peril of death Cimourdain watched day and night. It is the physician who prescribes, it is the nurse who saves; and Cimourdain saved the child. Not only did his pupil owe to him education, instruction, science, but he owed him also convalescence and health; not only did his pupil owe him the development of his mind, he owed him life itself. We worship those who owe us all; Cimourdain adored this child.

The natural separation came about at length. The education completed, Cimourdain was obliged to quit the boy, grown to a young man. With what cold and unconscionable cruelty these separations are insisted upon! How tranquilly families dismiss the preceptor, who leaves his spirit in a child, and the nurse, who leaves her heart's blood!

Cimourdain, paid and put aside, went out of the grand world and returned to the sphere below. The partition between the great and the little closed again. The young lord, an officer of birth, and made captain at the outset, departed for some garrison; the humble tutor (already at the bottom of his heart an unsubmissive priest, hastened to go down again into that obscure ground-floor of the Church occupied by the under clergy, and Cimourdain lost sight of his pupil.

The Revolution came on; the recollection of that being whom he had made a man brooded within him, hidden but not extinguished by the immensity of public affairs.

It is a beautiful thing to model a statue and give it life; to mould an intelligence and instil truth therein is still more beautiful. Cimourdain was the Pygmalion of a soul.

The spirit may own a child.

This pupil, this boy, this orphan, was the sole being on earth whom he loved.

But even in such an affection, would a man like this prove vulnerable?

We shall see.

BOOK II

THE PUBLIC HOUSE OF THE RUE DU PAON

CHAPTER I

MINOS, ÆACUS, AND RHADAMANTHUS

THERE was a public-house in the Rue du Paon which was called a café. This café had a back room, which is to-day historical. It was there that often, almost secretly, met certain men, so powerful and so constantly watched that they hesitated to speak with one another in public.

It was there that on the 23d of October, 1792, the Mountain and the Gironde exchanged their famous kiss. It was there that Garat, although he does not admit it in his Memoirs, came for information on that lugubrious night when, after having put Clavière in safety in the Rue de Beaune, he stopped his carriage on the Pont Royal to listen to the tocsin.

On the 28th of June, 1793, three men were seated about a table in this back chamber. Their chairs did not touch; they were placed one on either of the three sides of the table, leaving the fourth vacant. It was about eight o'clock in the evening; it was still light in the street, but dark in tne back room, and a lamp, hung from a hook in the ceiling,— a luxury there,— lighted the table.

The first of these three men was pale, young, grave, with

thin lips and a cold glance. He had a nervous movement
in his cheek, which must have made it difficult for him to
smile. He wore his hair powdered. He was gloved; his
light-blue coat, well brushed, was without a wrinkle, carefully buttoned. He wore nankeen breeches, white stockings,
a high cravat, a plaited shirt-frill, and shoes with silver
buckles.

Of the other two men, one was a species of giant, the
other a sort of dwarf. The tall one was untidily dressed in
a coat of scarlet cloth, his neck bare, his unknotted cravat
falling down over his shirt-frill, his vest gaping from lack
of buttons. He wore top-boots; his hair stood stiffly up and
was disarranged, though it still showed traces of powder;
his very peruke was like a mane. His face was marked with
small-pox; there was a choleric line between his brows; a
wrinkle that signified kindness at the corner of his mouth;
his lips were thick, the teeth large; he had the fist of a
porter and eyes that blazed. The little one was a yellow man,
who looked deformed when seated. He carried his head
thrown back; the eyes were injected with blood, there were
livid blotches on his face; he had a handkerchief knotted
about his greasy straight hair; he had no forehead; the
mouth was enormous and horrible. He wore pantaloons instead of knee-breeches, slippers, a waistcoat which seemed
originally to have been of white satin, and over this a loose
jacket, under whose folds a hard, straight line showed that
a poniard was hidden.

The first of these men was named Robespierre; the second,
Danton; the third, Marat.

They were alone in the room. Before Danton was set a
glass and a dusty wine-bottle, reminding one of Luther's
pint of beer; before Marat a cup of coffee; before Robespierre only papers.

Near the papers stood one of those heavy, round-ridged,
leaden ink-stands which will be remembered by men who were
school-boys at the beginning of this century. A pen was
thrown carelessly by the side of the ink-stand. On the papers

lay a great brass seal, on which could be read *Palloy fecit,* and which was a perfect miniature model of the Bastille.

A map of France was spread in the middle of the table. Outside the door was stationed Marat's " watch-dog,"— a certain Laurent Basse, porter of No. 18, Rue des Cordeliers, who, some fifteen days after this 28th of June, say the 13th of July, was to deal a blow with a chair on the head of a woman named Charlotte Corday, at this moment vaguely dreaming in Caen. Laurent Basse was the proof-carrier of the " Friend of the People." Brought this evening by his master to the café of the Rue du Paon, he had been ordered to keep the room closed where Marat, Danton, and Robespierre were seated, and to allow no person to enter unless it might be some member of the Committee of Public Safety, the Commune, or the Evêché.

Robespierre did not wish to shut the door against Saint-Just; Danton did not want it closed against Pache; Marat would not shut it against Gusman.

The conference had already lasted a long time. It was in reference to papers spread on the table, which Robespierre had read. The voices began to grow louder. Symptoms of anger arose between these three men. From without, eager words could be caught at moments. At that period the example of the public tribunals seemed to have created the right to listen at doors. It was the time when the copying-clerk of Fabricius Pâris looked through the keyhole at the proceedings of the Committee of Public Safety,— a feat which, be it said by the way, was not without its use; for it was this Pâris who warned Danton on the night before the 31st of March, 1794. Laurent Basse had his ear to the door of the back room where Danton, Marat, and Robespierre were. Laurent Basse served Marat, but he belonged to the Evêché.

CHAPTER II

MAGNA TESTANTUR VOCE PER UMBRAS

DANTON had just risen and pushed his chair hastily back.

"Listen!" he cried. "There is only one thing imminent, — the peril of the Republic. I only know one thing,— to deliver France from the enemy. To accomplish that, all means are fair,— all! all! all! When I have to deal with a combination of dangers, I have recourse to every or any expedient; when I fear all, I have all. My thought is a lioness. No half-measures. No squeamishness in resolution. Nemesis is not a conceited prude. Let us be terrible and useful. Does the elephant stop to look where he sets his foot? We must crush the enemy!"

Robespierre replied mildly,—

"I shall be very glad."

And he added,—

"The question is to know where the enemy is."

"It is outside, and I have chased it there," said Danton.

"It is within, and I watch it," said Robespierre.

"And I will continue to pursue it," resumed Danton.

"One does not drive away an internal enemy."

"What, then, do you do?"

"Exterminate it."

"I agree to that," said Danton in his turn.

Then he continued,—

"I tell you Robespierre, it is without."

"Danton, I tell you it is within."

"Robespierre, it is on the frontier."

"Danton, it is in Vendée."

"Calm yourselves," said a third voice. "It is everywhere, and you are lost."

It was Marat who spoke.

Robespierre looked at him and answered tranquilly:
" Truce to generalities. I particularize. Here are facts."

" Pedant! " grumbled Marat.

Robespierre laid his hand on the papers spread before
him, and continued,—

" I have just read you the dispatches from Prieur, of
the Marne. I have just communicated to you the information given by that Gélambre. Danton, listen! The foreign
war is nothing; the civil war is all. The foreign war is a
scratch that one gets on the elbow; civil war is the ulcer
which eats up the liver. This is the result of what I have
been reading: The Vendée, up to this day divided between
several chiefs, is concentrating herself. Henceforth she will
have one sole captain —"

" A central brigand," murmured Danton.

" Who is," pursued Robespierre, " the man that landed
near Pontorson on the 2d of June. You have seen who he
was. Remember this landing coincides with the arrest of
the acting Representatives, Prieur, of the Côte-d'Or, and
Romme, at Bayeux, by the traitorous district of Calvados,
the 2d of June,— the same day."

" And their transfer to the castle of Caen," said Danton.

Robespierre resumed,—

" I continue my summing up of the dispatches. The war
of the Woods is organizing on a vast scale. At the same
time, an English invasion is preparing,— Vendeans and
English; it is Briton with Breton. The Hurons of Finistère
speak the same language as the Topinambes of Cornwall. I
have shown you an intercepted letter from Puisaye, in which
it is said that ' twenty thousand red-coats distributed among
the insurgents will be the means of raising a hundred thousand
more.' When the peasant insurrection is prepared, the
English descent will be made. Look at the plan; follow it on
the map."

Robespierre put his finger on the chart and went on:

" The English have the choice of landing-place from
Cancale to Paimbol. Craig would prefer the Bay of Saint-

Brieuc; Cornwallis, the Bay of Saint-Cast.   That is mere detail.

The left bank of the Loire is guarded by the rebel Vendean army; and as to the twenty-eight leagues of open country between Ancenis and Pontorson, forty Norman parishes have promised their aid.   The descent will be made at three points,— Plérin, Iffiniac, and Pléneuf.   From Plérin they can go to Saint-Brieuc, and from Pléneuf to Lamballe. The second day they will reach Dinan, where there are nine hundred English prisoners, and at the same time they will occupy Saint-Jouan and Saint-Méen; they will leave cavalry there.   On the third day, two columns will march,— the one from Jouan on Bedée, the other from Dinan on Becheral, which is a natural fortress, and where they will establish two batteries.   The fourth day they will reach Rennes.   Rennes is the key of Brittany.   Whoever has Rennes has the whole.   Rennes captured, Châteauneuf and Saint-Malo will fall.   There are at Rennes a million of cartridges and fifty artillery field-pieces —"

" Which they will sweep off," murmured Danton.

Robespierre continued,—

" I conclude.   From Rennes three columns will fall,— the one on Fougères, the other on Vitré, the third on Redon.   As the bridges are cut, the enemy will furnish themselves — you have seen this fact particularly stated — with pontoons and planks, and they will have guides for the points fordable by the cavalry.   From Fougères they will radiate to Avranches; from Redon to Ancenis; from Vitré to Laval.   Nantes will capitulate.   Brest will yield.   Redon opens the whole extent of the Vilaine; Fougères gives them the route of Normandy; Vitré opens the route to Paris.   In fifteen days they will have an army of brigands numbering three hundred thousand men, and all Brittany will belong to the King of France."

" That is to say, the King of England," said Danton.

" No, to the King of France."

And Robespierre added,—

" The King of France is worse.   It needs fifteen days to

expel the stranger, and eighteen hundred years to eliminate monarchy."

Danton, who had reseated himself, leaned his elbows on the table, and rested his head in his hands in a thoughtful attitude.

"You see the peril," said Robespierre. "Vitré lays open to the English the road to Paris."

Danton raised his head and struck his two great clinched hands on the map as on an anvil.

"Robespierre, did not Verdun open the route to Paris to the Prussians?"

"Very well!"

"Very well, we will expel the English as we expelled the Prussians." And Danton rose again.

Robespierre laid his cold hand on the feverish fist of the other.

"Danton, Champagne was not for the Prussians, and Brittany is for the English. To retake Verdun was a foreign war; to retake Vitré will be civil war."

And Robespierre murmured in a chill, deep tone,—

"A serious difference."

He added aloud,—

"Sit down again, Danton, and look at the map instead of knocking it with your fist."

But Danton was wholly given up to his own idea.

"That is madness!" cried he,—" to look for the catastrophe in the west when it is in the east. Robespierre, I grant you that England is rising on the ocean; but Spain is rising among the Pyrenees; but Italy is rising among the Alps; but Germany is rising on the Rhine. And the great Russian bear is at the bottom. Robespierre, the danger is a circle, and we are within it. On the exterior, coalition; in the interior, treason. In the south, Servant half opens the door of France to the King of Spain. At the north, Dumouriez passes over to the enemy; for that matter, he always menaced Holland less than Paris. Neerwinden blots out Jemmapes and Valmy. The philosopher Rabaut Saint-Etienne, a traitor like

the Protestant he is, corresponds with the courtier Montes-
quiou. The army is destroyed. There is not a battalion
that has more than four hundred men remaining; the brave
regiment of Deux-Ponts is reduced to a hundred and fifty
men; the camp of Pamars has capitulated; there are only
five hundred sacks of flour left at Givet; we are falling back
on Landau; Wurmser presses Kléber; Mayence succumbs
bravely, Condé cowardly. Valenciennes also. But all that
does not prevent Chancel, who defends Valenciennes, and old
Féraud, who defends Condé, being heroes, as well as Meunier,
who defended Mayence. But all the rest are betraying us.
Dharville betrays us at Aix-la-Chapelle; Mouton at Brussels;
Valence at Bréda; Neuilly at Limbourg; Miranda at Maes-
tricht, Stingel, traitor: Lanoue, traitor; Ligonnier, traitor;
Menou, traitor; Dillon, traitor,— hideous coin of Dumouriez.
We must make examples. Custine's countermarches look suspicious to me. I suspect Custine of preferring the lucrative
prize of Frankfort to the useful capture of Coblentz. Frankfort can pay four millions of war tribute; so be it. What
would that be in comparison with crushing that nest of refugees? Treason, I say. Meunier died on the 13th of June.
Kléber is alone. In the meantime Brunswick strengthens and
advances. He plants the German flag on every French place
that he takes. The Margrave of Brandenburg is to-day the
arbiter of Europe; he pockets our provinces; he will adjudge
Belgium to himself,— you will see. One would say that we
were working for Berlin. If this continue, and we do not put
things in order, the French Revolution will have been for the
benefit of Potsdam; it will have accomplished for unique result the aggrandizement of the little State of Frederick II.,
and we shall have killed the King of France for the King of
Prussia's sake."

And Danton burst into a terrible laugh.

Danton's laugh made Marat smile.

"You have each one your hobby," said he. "Danton,
yours is Prussia; Robespierre, yours is the Vendée. I am going to state facts in my turn. You do not perceive the real

peril; it is this: The cafés and the gaming-houses. The Café Choiseul is Jacobin; the Café Pitou is Royalist; the Café Rendez-Vous attacks the National Guard; the Café of the Porte Saint Martin defends it; the Café Régence is against Brissot; the Café Corazza is for him; the Café Procope swears by Diderot; the Café of the Théâtre Français swears by Voltaire; at the Rotunde they tear up the assignats; the Cafés Saint Marceau are in a fury; the Café Manouri debates the question of flour; at the Café Foy uproars and fisticuffs; at the Perron the hornets of the finance buzz. These are the matters which are serious."

Danton laughed no longer. Marat continued to smile. The smile of a dwarf is worse than the laugh of a giant.

" Do you sneer at yourself, Marat? " growled Danton.

Marat gave that convulsive movement of his lip which was celebrated. His smile died.

" Ah, I recognize you, Citizen Danton! It is indeed you who in full Convention called me, ' the individual Marat.' Listen; I forgive you. We are playing the fool! Ah! *I* mock at myself! See what I have done! I denounced Chazot; I denounced Pétion; I denounced Kersaint; I denounced Moreton; I denounced Dufriche-Valazé; I denounced Ligonnier; I denounced Menou; I denounced Banneville; I denounced Gensonné; I denounced Biron; I denounced Lidon and Chambon. Was I mistaken? I smell treason in the traitor, and I find it best to denounce the criminal before he can commit his crime. I have the habit of saying in the evening that which you and others say on the following day. I am the man who proposed to the Assembly a perfect plan of criminal legislation. What have I done up to the present? I have asked for the instruction of the sections in order to discipline them for the Revolution; I have broken the seals of thirty-two boxes; I have reclaimed the diamonds deposited in the hands of Roland; I proved that the Brissotins gave to the Committee of the General Safety blank warrants; I noted the omissions in the report of Lindet upon the crimes of Capet; I voted the punishment of the tyrant in twenty-four hours; I defended the battalions

of Mauconseil and the Républicain; I prevented the reading
of the letter of Narbonne and of Malonet; I made a motion
in favour of the wounded soldiers; I caused the suppression of
the Commission of Six; I foresaw the treason of Dumouriez
in the affair of Mons; I demanded the taking of a hundred
thousand relatives of the refugees as hostages for the commissioners delivered to the enemy; I proposed to declare
traitor any Representative who should pass the barriers; I
unmasked the Roland faction in the troubles at Marseilles; I
insisted that a price should be set on the head of Egalité's
son; I defended Bouchotte; I called for a nominal appeal in
order to chase Isnard from the chair; I caused it to be declared that the Parisians had deserved well of the country.
That is why I am called a dancing-puppet by Louvet; that
is why Finistère demands my expulsion; why the city of Lou-
dun desires that I should be exiled, the city of Amiens that I
should be muzzled; why Coburg wishes me to be arrested, and
Lecointe Puiraveau proposes to the Convention to decree me
mad.   Ah, now, Citizen Danton, why did you ask me to come
to your little council if it were not to have my opinion?   Did
I ask to belong to it?   Far from that.   I have no taste for
dialogues with counter-revolutionists like Robespierre and you.
For that matter, I ought to have known that you would not
understand me,— you no more than Robespierre; Robespierre
no more than you.   So there is not a statesman here?   You
need to be taught to spell at politics; you must have the dot
put over the *i* for you.   What I said to you meant this: you
both deceive yourselves.   The danger is not in London as
Robespierre believes; nor in Berlin, as Danton believes: it is in
Paris.   It consists in the absence of unity; in the right of
each one to pull on his own side, commencing with you two;
in the binding of minds; in the anarchy of wills —"

"Anarchy!" interrupted Danton.   "Who causes that, if
not you?"

Marat did not pause.

"Robespierre, Danton, the danger is in this heap of cafés,
in this mass of gaming-houses, this crowd of clubs,— Clubs

of the Blacks, the Federals, the Women; the Club of the Im-
partials, which dates from Clermont-Tonnerre, and which was
the Monarchical Club of 1790, a social circle conceived by the
priest Claude Fauché; Club of the Woollen Caps, founded by
the gazetteer Prudhomme, *et cætera;* without counting your
Club of the Jacobins, Robespierre, and your club of the
Cordeliers, Danton. The danger lies in the famine which
caused the sack-porter Blin to hang up to the lamp of
the Hôtel de Ville the baker of the Market Palu, François Denis, and in the justice which hung the sack-porter Blin
for having hanged the baker Denis. The danger is in the
paper money, which the people depreciate. In the Rue du
Temple an assignat of a hundred francs fell to the ground,
and a passer-by, a man of the people, said, ' It is not worth
the pains of picking it up.' The stock-brokers and the
monopolists,— there is the danger. To have nailed the black
flag to the Hôtel de Ville,— a fine advance! You arrest
Baron Trenck; that is not sufficient. I want this old prison
intriguer's neck wrung. You believe that you have got out
of the difficulty because the President of the Convention puts
a civic crown on the head of Labertèche, who received forty-
one sabre cuts at Jemmapes, and of whom Chénier makes himself the elephant driver? Comedies and juggling! Ah, you
will not look at Paris! You seek the danger at a distance
when it is close at hand. What is the use of your police,
Robespierre? For you have your spies,— Payan at the Commune, Coffinhal at the Revolutionary Tribunal, David at the
Committee of General Security, Couthon at the Committee of
Public Safety. You see that I know all about it. Very well,
learn this: the danger is over your heads; the danger is under
your feet,— conspiracies! conspiracies! conspiracies! The
people in the streets read the newspapers to one another and
exchange nods; six thousand men, without civic papers, returned emigrants, Muscadins, and Mathevons, are hidden in
cellars and garrets and the wooden galleries of the Palais
Royal. People stand in a row at the bakers' shops, the women
stand in the doorways and clasp their hands, crying, ' When

shall we have peace?' You may shut yourselves up as close
as you please in the hall of the Executive Council, in order
to be alone; every word you speak is known; and as a proof,
Robespierre, here are the words you spoke last night to Saint-
Just: 'Barbaroux begins to show a fat paunch; it will be
a trouble to him in his flight.' Yes; the danger is everywhere,
and above all in the centre. In Paris the 'Retrogrades' plot,
while patrols go barefooted; the aristocrats arrested on the 9th
of March are already set at liberty; the fancy horses which
ought to be harnessed to the frontier-cannon spatter mud on
us in the streets; a loaf of bread weighing four pounds costs
three francs twelve sous; the theatres play indecent pieces;
and Robespierre will presently have Danton guillotined."

"Oh, there, there!" said Danton.

Robespierre attentively studied the map.

"What is needed," cried Marat, abruptly, "is a dictator.
Robespierre, you know that I want a dictator."

Robespierre raised his head.

"I know, Marat; you or me."

"Me or you," said Marat.

Danton grumbled between his teeth,—

"The dictatorship; only try it!"

Marat caught Danton's frown.

"Hold!" he began again; "one last effort. Let us get
some agreement. The situation is worth the trouble. Did we
not come to an agreement for the day of the 31st of May?
The entire question is a more serious one than that of Girond-
ism, which was a question of detail. There is truth in what
you say; but *the* truth, the whole truth, the real truth, is what
I say. In the south, Federalism; in the west, Royalism; in
Paris, the duel of the Convention and the Commune; on the
frontiers, the retreat of Custine and the treason of Dumouriez.
What does all this signify? Dismemberment. What is necessary for us? Unity. There is safety; but we must hasten
to reach it. Paris must assume the government of the Revolution. If we lose an hour, to-morrow the Vendeans may be at
Orleans, and the Prussians in Paris. I grant you this, Dan-

ton; I accord you that, Robespierre. So be it. Well, the conclusion is — a dictatorship. Let us seize the dictatorship, — we three who represent the Revolution. We are the three heads of Cerebus. Of these three heads, one talks,— that is you, Robespierre; one roars,— that is you, Danton —"

" The other bites," said Danton; " that is you, Marat."

" All three bite," said Robespierre.

There was a silence. Then the dialogue, full of dark threats, recommenced.

" Listen, Marat; before entering into a marriage, people must know each other. How did you learn what I said yesterday to Saint-Just? "

" That is my affair, Robespierre."

" Marat! "

" It is my duty to enlighten myself, and my business to inform myself."

" Marat! "

" I like to know things."

" Marat! "

" Robespierre, I know what you say to Saint-Just, as I know what Danton says to Lacroix; as I know what passes on the Quay of the Theatins, at the Hôtel Labriffe, the den where the nymphs of the emigration meet; as I know what happens in the house of the Thilles, near Gonesse, which belongs to Valmerange, former administrator of the post where Maury and Cazales went; where, since then, Sieyès and Vergniaud went, and where now some one goes once a week."

In saying " some one," Marat looked significantly at Danton.

Danton cried,—

" If I had two farthings' worth of power, this would be terrible."

Marat continued,—

" I know what I am saying to you, Robespierre, just as I knew what was going on in the Temple tower when they fattened Louis XVI. there, so well that the he-wolf, the she-wolf, and the cubs ate up eighty-six baskets of peaches in the month of September alone.   During that time the people were starving.   I know that, as I know that Roland was hidden in a lodging looking on a back court, in the Rue de la Harpe; as I know that six hundred of the pikes of July 14th were manufactured by Faure, the Duke of Orleans's locksmith; as I know what they do in the house of the Saint-Hilaire, the mistress of Sillery.   On the days when there is to be a ball, it is old Sillery himself who chalks the floor of the yellow saloon of the Rue Neuve des Mathurins; Buzot and Kersaint dined there.   Saladin dined there on the 27th, and with whom, Robespierre?   With your friend Lasource."

"Mere words!" muttered Robespierre.   "Lasource is not my friend."

And he added thoughtfully,—

"In the mean while there are in London eighteen manufactories of false assignats."

Marat went on in a voice still tranquil, though it had a slight tremulousness that was threatening,—

"You are the faction of the All-Importants!   Yes; I know everything, in spite of what Saint-Just calls 'the silence of State —'"

Marat emphasized these last words, looked at Robespierre, and continued,—

"I know what is said at your table the days when Lebas invites David to come and eat the dinner cooked by his betrothed, Elizabeth Duplay,— your future sister-in-law, Robespierre.   I am the far-seeing eye of the people, and from the bottom of my cave I watch.   Yes, I see; yes, I hear; yes, I know!   Little things content you.   You admire yourselves. Robespierre poses to be contemplated by his Madame de Chalabre, the daughter of that Marquis de Chalabre who played whist with Louis XV. the evening Damiens was executed.   Yes, yes; heads are carried high.   Saint-Just lives in a cravat.   Legendre's dress is scrupulously correct,— new frock-coat and white waistcoat, and a shirt-frill to make people forget his apron.   Robespierre imagines that history will be interested to know that he wore an olive-coloured frock-

coat *à la Constituante*, and a sky-blue dress-coat *à la Convention*. He has his portrait hanging on all the walls of his
chamber —"

Robespierre interrupted him in a voice even more composed
than Marat's own:—

" And you, Marat, have yours in all the sewers."

They continued this style of conversation, in which the
slowness of their voices emphasized the violence of the attacks
and retorts, and added a certain irony to menace.

" Robespierre, you have called those who desire the overthrow of thrones ' the Don Quixotes of the human race.' "

" And you, Marat, after the 4th of August, in No. 559 of
the ' Friend of the People ' (ah, I have remembered the number; it may be useful!), you demanded that the titles of the
nobility should be restored to them. You said, ' A duke is
always a duke.' "

" Robespierre, in the sitting of December 7th, you defended the woman Roland against Viard."

" Just as my brother defended you, Marat, when you were
attacked at the Jacobin Club. What does that prove?
Nothing! "

" Robespierre, we know the cabinet of the Tuileries where
you said to Garat: ' I am tired of the Revolution!' "

" Marat, it was here, in this public-house, that, on the 29th
of October, you embraced Barbaroux."

" Robespierre, you said to Buzot: ' The Republic!
What is that?' "

" Marat, it was also in this public-house that you invited
three Marseillais suspects to keep you company."

" Robespierre, you have yourself escorted by a stout fellow
from the market, armed with a club."

" And you, Marat, on the eve of the 10th of August you
asked Buzot to help you flee to Marseilles disguised as a
jockey."

" During the prosecutions of September you hid yourself,
Robespierre."

" And you, Marat — you showed yourself."

" Robespierre, you flung the red cap on the ground."

" Yes, when a traitor hoisted it. That which decorates Dumouriez sullies Robespierre."

" Robespierre, you refused to cover Louis XVI.'s head with a veil while soldiers of Chateauvieux were passing."

" I did better than veil his head: I cut it off."

Danton interposed, but it was like oil flung upon flames.

" Robespierre, Marat," said he; " calm yourselves."

Marat did not like being named the second. He turned about.

" With what does Danton meddle?" he asked.

Danton bounded.

" With what do I meddle? With this! That we must not have fratricide; that there must be no strife between two men who serve the people; that it is enough to have a foreign war; that it is enough to have a civil war; that it would be too much to have a domestic war; that it is I who have made the Revolution, and I will not permit it to be spoiled. Now you know what it is I meddle with!"

Marat replied, without raising his voice,—

" You had better meddle with getting your accounts ready."

" My accounts!" cried Danton. " Go ask for them in the defiles of Argonne, in Champagne delivered, in Belgium conquered, in the armies where I have already four times offered my breast to the musket-shots. Go demand them at the Place de la Revolution, at the scaffold of January 21st, from the throne flung to the ground, from the guillotine; that widow —"

Marat interrupted him,—

" The guillotine is a virgin Amazon; she does not give birth."

" Are you sure?" retorted Danton. " I tell you I will make her fruitful."

" We shall see," said Marat. He smiled.

Danton saw this smile.

" Marat," cried he, " you are the man that hides; I am the man of the open air and broad day. I hate the life of a reptile. It would not suit me to be a wood-house. You inhabit a cave; I live in the street. You hold communication with none; whosoever passes may see and speak with me."

"Pretty fellow! Will you mount up to where I live?" snarled Marat.

Then his smile disappeared, and he continued, in a peremptory tone,—

"Danton, give an account of the thirty-three thousand crowns, ready money, that Montmorin paid you in the king's name under pretext of indemnifying you for your post of solicitor at the Châtelet."

"I was of the 14th of July," said Danton, haughtily.

"And the Garde-Meuble, and the crown diamonds?"

"I was of the 6th of October."

"And the thefts of your *alter ego*, Lacroix, in Belgium?"

"I was of the 20th of June."

"And the loans to the Montansier?"

"I urged the people on to the return from Varennes."

"And the opera-house, built with money that you furnished?"

"I armed the sections of Paris."

"And the hundred thousand livres, secret funds of the Ministry of Justice?"

"I caused the 10th of August."

"And the two millions for the Assembly's secret expenses, of which you took the fourth?"

"I stopped the enemy on their march, and I barred the passage to the kings in coalition."

"Prostitute!" said Marat.

Danton was terrible as he rose to his full height.

"Yes!" cried he. "I am a harlot! I sold myself, but I saved the world!"

Robespierre had gone back to biting his nails. As for him, he could neither laugh nor smile. The laugh (the lightning) of Danton, and the smile (the sting) of Marat were both wanting to him.

Danton resumed,—

9

"I am like the ocean; I have my ebb and flow. At low water my shoals may be seen; at high tide you may see my waves."

"You foam," said Marat.

"My tempest," said Danton.

Marat had risen at the same moment as Danton. He also exploded. The snake became suddenly a dragon.

"Ah!" cried he. "Ah, Robespierre! Ah, Danton! You will not listen to me! Well, you are lost; I tell you so. Your policy ends in an impossibility to go farther; you have no longer an outlet; and you do things which shut every door against you,— except that of the tomb."

"That is our grandeur," said Danton.

He shrugged his shoulders.

Marat hurried on:—

"Danton, beware. Vergniaud has also a wide mouth, thick lips, and frowning eyebrows; Vergniaud is pitted, too, like Mirabeau and like thee; that did not prevent the 31st of May. Ah, you shrug your shoulders! Sometimes a shrug of the shoulders makes the head fall. Danton, I tell thee, that big voice, that loose cravat, those top-boots, those little suppers, those great pockets,— all those are things which concern Louisette."

Louisette was Marat's pet name for the guillotine.

He pursued:—

"And as for thee, Robespierre, thou art a Moderate, but that will serve nothing. Go on! powder thyself, dress thy hair, brush thy clothes, play the vulgar coxcomb, have clean linen, keep curled and frizzed and bedizened; none the less thou wilt go to the Place de Grève! Read Brunswick's proclamation. Thou wilt get a treatment no less than that of the regicide Damiens! Fine as thou art, thou wilt be dragged at the tails of four horses."

"Echo of Coblentz!" said Robespierre between his teeth.

"I am the echo of nothing; I am the cry of the whole, Robespierre! Ah, you are young, you! How old art thou, Danton? Four-and-thirty. How many are your years,

Robespierre? Thirty-three. Well, I — I have lived always! I am the old human suffering; I am six thousand years old."

"That is true," retorted Danton. "For six thousand years Cain has been preserved in hatred, like the toad in a rock; the rock breaks, Cain springs out among men, and is called Marat."

"Danton!" cried Marat, and a livid glare illuminated his eyes.

"Well, what?" asked Danton.

Thus these three terrible men conversed.

They were conflicting thunderbolts.

CHAPTER III

A STIRRING OF THE INMOST NERVES

THERE was a pause in the dialogue; these Titans withdrew for a moment each into his own reflections.

Lions dread hydras. Robespierre had grown very pale, and Danton very red. A shiver ran through the frames of both.

The wild-beast glare in Marat's eyes had died out; a calm, cold and imperious, settled again on the face of this man, dreaded by his formidable associates.

Danton felt himself conquered, but he would not yield. He resumed,—

"Marat talks very loud about the dictatorship and unity, but he has only one ability,— that of breaking to pieces."

Robespierre parted his thin lips, and said,—

"As for me, I am of the opinion of Anacharsis Cloots: I say, Neither Roland nor Marat."

"And I," replied Marat, "I say, Neither Danton or Robespierre."

He regarded both fixedly, and added,—

"Let me give you advice, Danton. You are in love, you think of marrying again; do not meddle any more with politics. Be wise."

And moving backward a step toward the door, as if to go out, he made them a menacing salute, and said,—

"Adieu, gentlemen."

Danton and Robespierre shuddered.

At this instant a voice rose from the bottom of the room, saying,—

"You are wrong, Marat."

All three turned about. During Marat's explosion some one had entered unperceived by the door at the end of the room.

"Is it you, Citizen Cimourdain?" asked Marat. "Goodday."

It was indeed Cimourdain.

"I say you are wrong, Marat," he repeated.

Marat turned green, which was his way of growing pale.

"You are useful, but Robespierre and Danton are necessary. Why threaten them? Union, union, citizens! The people expect unity."

This entrance acted like a dash of cold water, and had the effect that the arrival of a stranger does on a family quarrel, — it calmed the surface, if not the depths.

Cimourdain advanced toward the table.

Danton and Robespierre knew him. They had often remarked among the public tribunals of the Convention this obscure but powerful man, whom the people saluted. Nevertheless, Robespierre, always a stickler for forms, asked,—

"Citizen, how did you enter?"

"He belongs to the Evêché," replied Marat, in a voice in which a certain submission was perceptible.

Marat braved the Convention, led the Commune, and feared the Evêché. This is a law.

Mirabeau felt Robespierre stirring at some unknown depth below; Robespierre felt Marat stir; Marat left Hébert stir; Hébert, Babeuf. As long as the layers underneath are still, the politician can advance; but under the most revolutionary there must be some subsoil, and the boldest stop in dismay when they feel under their feet the earthquake they have created.

To be able to distinguish the movement which covetousness causes from that brought about by principle, to combat the one and second the other, is the genius and the virtue of great revolutionists.

Danton saw that Marat faltered.

"Oh, Citizen Cimourdain is not one too many," said he. And he held out his hand to the new-comer.

Then he said,—

"Zounds! explain the situation to Citizen Cimourdain. He appears just at the right moment. I represent the Mountain; Robespierre represents the Committee of Public Safety; Marat represents the Commune; Cimourdain represents the Evêché. He is come to give the casting vote."

"So be it," said Cimourdain, simply and gravely. "What is the matter in question?"

"The Vendée," replied Robespierre.

"The Vendée!" repeated Cimourdain.

Then he continued: "There is the great danger. If the Revolution perish, she will perish by the Vendée. One Vendée is more formidable than ten Germanys. In order that France may live, it is necessary to kill the Vendée."

These few words won him Robespierre.

Still Robespierre asked this question: "Were you not formerly a priest?"

Cimourdain's priestly air did not escape Robespierre. He recognized in another that which he had within himself.

Cimourdain replied,—

"Yes, citizen."

"What difference does that make?" cried Danton. "When priests are good fellows, they are worth more than others. In revolutionary times the priests melt into citizens, as the bells do into arms and cannon. Danjou is a priest; Daunou is a priest; Thomas Lindet is the Bishop of Evreux.

Robespierre, you sit in the Convention side by side with Massieu, Bishop of Beauvais. The Grand Vicar Vaugeois was a member of the Insurrection Committee of August 10th. Chabot is a Capuchin. It was Dom Gerle who devised the tennis-court oath; it was the Abbé Audran who caused the National Assembly to be declared superior to the king; it was the Abbé Goutte who demanded of the Legislature that the dais should be taken away from Louis XVI.'s armchair; it was the Abbé Grégoire who proposed the abolition of royalty."

" Seconded," sneered Marat, " by the actor Collot d'Herbois. Between them they did the work,— the priest overturned the throne; the comedian flung down the king."

" Let us get back to the Vendée," said Robespierre.

" Well, what is it? " demanded Cimourdain. " What is this Vendée doing now? "

Robespierre answered,—

" This: she has found a chief. She becomes terrible.

" Who is this chief, Citizen Robespierre? "

" A *ci-devant* Marquis de Lantenac, who styles himself a Breton prince."

Cimourdain made a movement.

" I know him," said he; " I was chaplain in his house."

He reflected for a moment, then added,—

" He was a man of gallantry before being a soldier."

" Like Biron, who was a Lauzun," said Danton.

And Cimourdain continued, thoughtfully: " Yes, an old man of pleasure. He must be terrible."

" Frightful," said Robespierre. " He burns the villages, kills the wounded, massacres the prisoners, shoots the women."

" The women! "

" Yes. Among others he had the mother of three children shot. Nobody knows what became of the little ones. He is really a captain; he understands war."

" Yes, in truth," replied Cimourdain. " He was in the Hanoverian war, and the soldiers said, ' Richelieu in appearance, Lantenac at the bottom.' Lantenac was the real general. Talk about him to your colleague Dussaulx."

Robespierre remained silent for a moment; then the dialogue began anew between him and Cimourdain.

"Well, Citizen Cimourdain, this man is in Vendée."

"Since when?"

"The last three weeks."

"He must be declared an outlaw."

"That is done."

"A price must be set on his head."

"It is done."

"A large reward must be offered to whoever will take him."

"That is done."

"Not in assignats."

"That is done."

"In gold."

"That is done."

"And he must be guillotined."

"That *will* be done."

"By whom?"

"By you."

"By me?"

"Yes; you will be delegated by the Committee of Public Safety with unlimited powers."

"I accept," said Cimourdain.

Robespierre made his choice of men rapidly,— the quality of a true statesman. He took from the portfolio before him a sheet of white paper, on which could be read this printed heading: "THE FRENCH REPUBLIC ONE AND INDIVISIBLE. — COMMITTEE OF PUBLIC SAFETY."

Cimourdain continued,—

"Yes, I accept. The terrible against the terrible. Lantenac is ferocious; I shall be so too. War to the death against this man. I will deliver the Republic from him, please God."

He checked himself; then resumed,—

"I am a priest; no matter; I believe in God."

"God has gone out of date," said Danton.

"I believe in God," said Cimourdain, unmoved.

Robespierre gave a sinister nod of approval.

Cimourdain asked,—

" To whom am I delegated? "

" The commandant of the exploring division sent against Lantenac.   Only,— I warn you,— he is a nobleman."

Danton cried out,—

" That is another thing which matters little.   A noble! Well, what then!   It is with the nobles as with the priests. When one of either class is good, he is excellent.   Nobility is a prejudice; but we should not have it in one sense more than the other,— no more against than in favour of it. Robespierre, is not Saint-Just a noble?   Florelle de Saint-Just, zounds!   Anacharsis Cloots is a baron.   Our friend Charles Hesse, who never misses a meeting of the Cordeliers, is a prince, and the brother of the reigning Landgrave of Hesse-Rothenburg.   Montaut, the intimate of Marat, is the Marquis de Montaut.   There is in the revolutionary tribunal a juror who is a priest,— Vilate; and a juror who is a noble-man,— Leroy, Marquis de Montflabert.   Both are tried men."

" And you forget," added Robespierre, " the foreman of the revolutionary jury."

"Antonelle? "

" Who is the Marquis Antonelle," said Robespierre.

Danton continued,—

" Dampierre was a nobleman,— the one who lately got himself killed before Condé for the Republic; and Beaurepaire was a noble,— he who blew his brains out rather than open the gates of Verdun to the Prussians."

" All of which," grumbled Marat, " does not alter the fact that on the day Condorcet said, ' the Gracchi were nobles,' Danton cried out, ' All nobles are traitors, beginning with Mirabeau and ending with thee.' "

Cimourdain's grave voice made itself heard:—

" Citizen Danton, Citizen Robespierre, you are perhaps right to have confidence, but the people distrusts them; and the people is not wrong in so doing.   When a priest is charged with the surveillance of a nobleman, the responsibility is doubled, and it is necessary for the priest to be inflexible."

"True," said Robespierre.

Cimourdain added,—

"And inexorable."

Robespierre replied,—

"It is well said, Citizen Cimourdain. You will have to deal with a young man. You will have the ascendency over him, being double his age. It will be necessary to direct him, but he must be carefully managed. It appears that he possesses military talent; all the reports are unanimous as to that. He belongs to a corps which has been detached from the Army of the Rhine to go into Vendée. He arrives from the frontier, where he was noticeable for intelligence and courage. He leads the exploring column in a superior way. For fifteen days he has held the old Marquis de Lantenac in check. He restrains and drives him before him. He will end by forcing him to the sea, and tumbling him into it headlong. Lantenac has the cunning of an old general, and the audacity of a youthful captain. This young man has already enemies, and those who are envious of him. The Adjutant-General Léchelle is jealous of him."

"That L'Echelle [1] wants to be commander-in-chief," interrupted Danton. "There is nothing in his favour but a pun: 'It needs a ladder to get on top of a cart.' All the same. Charette [2] beats him."

"And he is not willing," pursued Robespierre, "that anybody besides himself should beat Lantenac. The misfortune of the Vendean war is in such rivalries. Heroes badly commanded,— that is what our soldiers are. A simple captain of hussars, Chérin, enters Saumur with trumpets playing *Ça ira;* he takes Saumur; he could keep on and take Cholet but he has no orders, so he halts. All those commands of the Vendée must be remodelled. The head-quarters are scattered, the forces dispersed. A scattered army is an army paralyzed; it is a rock crumbled into dust. At the camp of Paramé there are only some tents. There are a hundred useless little companies posted between Tréguier and Dinan, of which a division

---

[1] A ladder.   [2] *Charrette.*— a cart.

might be formed that could guard the whole cost.   Léchelle, supported by Parrein, strips the northern coast under pretext of protecting the southern, and so opens France to the English.   A half million peasants in revolt and a descent of England upon France,— that is Lantenac's plan.   The young commander of the exploring column presses his sword against Lantenac's loins, keeps it there, and beats him without Léchelle's permission.   Now, Léchelle is his general, so Léchelle denounces him.   Opinions are divided in regard to this young man.   Léchelle wants to have him shot.   Prieur, of the Marne, wants to make him adjutant-general."

"This youth appears to me to possess great qualities," said Cimourdain.

"But he has one fault."   The interruption came from Marat.

"What is it?" demanded Cimourdain.

"Clemency," said Marat.

Then he added,—

"He is firm in battle, and weak afterward.   He shows indulgence; he pardons; he grants mercy; he protects devotees and nuns; he saves the wives and daughters of aristocrats; he releases prisoners; he sets priests free."

"A grave fault," murmured Cimourdain.

"A crime," said Marat.

"Sometimes," said Danton.

"Often," said Robespierre.

"Almost always," chimed in Marat.

"When one has to deal with the enemies of the country — always," said Cimourdain.

Marat turned toward him.

"And what, then, would you do with a republican chief who set a royalist chief at liberty?"

"I should be of Léchelle's opinion; I would have him shot."

"Or guillotined," said Marat.

"He might have his choice," said Cimourdain.

Danton began to laugh.

" I like one as well as the other."

" Thou art sure to have one or the other," growled Marat.
His glance left Danton and settled again on Cimourdain.

" So, Citizen Cimourdain, if a republican leader were to
flinch, you would cut off his head? "

" Within twenty-four hours."

" Well," retorted Marat, " I am of Robespierre's opinion;
Citizen Cimourdain ought to be sent as delegate of the Committee of Public Safety to the commandant of the exploring
division of the coast army. How is it you call this commandant? "

Robespierre answered,—

" He is a *ci-devant* noble."

He began to turn over the papers.

" Get the priest to guard the nobleman," said Danton. " I
distrust a priest when he is alone; I distrust a noble when
he is alone. When they are together, I do not fear them.
One watches the other, and they do well."

The indignant look always on Cimourdain's face grew
deeper, but without doubt finding the remark just at bottom,
he did not look at Danton, but said in his stern voice:—

" If the republican commander who is confided to me makes
one false step the penalty will be death."

Robespierre, with his eyes on the portfolio, said,—

" Here is the name, Citizen Cimourdain. The commandant,
in regard to whom full powers will be granted you, is a so-
called viscount; his name is Gauvain."

Cimourdain turned pale.

" Gauvain! " he cried.

Marat saw his sudden pallor.

" The Viscount Gauvain! " repeated Cimourdain.

" Yes," said Robespierre.

" Well," said Marat, with his eyes fixed on the priest.

There was a brief silence, which Marat broke.

" Citizen Cimourdain, on the conditions named by yourself,
do you accept the mission as commissioner delegate near the
Commandant Gauvain? Is it decided? "

"It is decided," replied Cimourdain.   He grew paler and paler.

Robespierre took the pen which lay near him, wrote in his slow, even hand four lines on the sheet of paper which bore the heading COMMITTEE OF PUBLIC SAFETY, signed them, and passed the sheet and the pen to Danton; Danton signed, and Marat, whose eyes had not left Cimourdain's livid face, signed after Danton.

Robespierre took the paper again, dated it, and gave it to Cimourdain, who read,—

YEAR II. OF THE REPUBLIC.

Full powers are granted to Citizen Cimourdain, delegated Commissioner of Public Safety to the Citizen Gauvain, commanding the Exploring Division of the Army of the Coasts.

ROBESPIERRE. DANTON. MARAT.

And beneath the signatures:—

June 28, 1793.

The revolutionary calendar, called the Civil Calendar, had no legal existence at this time, and was not adopted by the Convention, on the proposition of Romme, until October 5, 1793.

While Cimourdain read, Marat watched him.

He said in a half-voice, as if talking to himself,—

"It will be necessary to have all this formalized by a decree of the Convention, or a special warrant of the Committee of Public Safety.   There remains something yet to be done."

"Citizen Cimourdain, where do you live?" asked Robespierre.

"Court of Commerce."

"So do I, too," said Danton.   "You are my neighbour."

Robespierre resumed,—

"There is not a moment to lose.   To-morrow you will receive your commission in form, signed by all the members of the Committee of Public Safety.   This is a confirmation of the commission. It will accredit you in a special manner to the acting Representatives, Philippeaux, Prieur of the Marne, Lecointre, Alquier, and the others. We know you. Your powers are unlimited. You can make Gauvain a general or send him to the scaffold. You will receive your commission to-morrow at three o'clock. When shall you set out? "

" At four," said Cimourdain.

And they separated.

As he entered his house, Marat informed Simonne Evrard that he should go to the Convention on the morrow.

BOOK III

THE CONVENTION

CHAPTER I

WE approach the grand summit.
Behold the Convention!

The gaze grows steady in presence of this height.

Never has a more lofty spectacle appeared on the horizon of mankind.

There is one Himalaya, and there is one Convention.

The Convention is perhaps the culminating point of History.

During its lifetime — for it lived — men did not quite understand what it was. It was precisely the grandeur which escaped its contemporaries; they were too much scared to be dazzled. Everything grand possesses a sacred horror. It is easy to admire mediocrities and hills; but whatever is too lofty, whether it be a genius or a mountain,— an assembly as well as a masterpiece,— alarms when seen too near. An immense height appears an exaggeration. It is fatiguing to climb. One loses breath upon acclivities, one slips down declivities; one is hurt by sharp, rugged heights which are in themselves beautiful; torrents in their foaming reveal the precipices; clouds hide the mountain-tops; a sudden ascent terrifies as much as a fall. Hence there is a greater sensation of fright than admiration. What one feels is fantastic enough,— an aversion to the grand. One sees the abyss and loses sight of the sublimity; one sees the monster and does not perceive the marvel. Thus the Convention was at first judged. It was measured by the purblind,— it, which needed to be looked at by eagles.

To-day we see it in perspective, and it throws across the deep and distant heavens, against a background at once serene and tragic, the immense profile of the French Revolution.

CHAPTER II

THE 14th of July delivered.

The 10th of August blasted.

The 21st of September founded.

The 21st of September was the Equinox; was Equilibrium, — *Libra*, the balance. It was, according to the remark of Romme, under this sign of Equality and Justice that the Republic was proclaimed. A constellation heralded it.

The Convention is the first avatar of the peoples. It was by the Convention that the grand new page opened and the future of to-day commenced.

Every idea must have a visible enfolding; a habitation is necessary to any principle; a church is God between four walls; every dogma must have a temple. When the Convention became a fact, the first problem to be solved was how to lodge the Convention.

At first the Riding-school, then the Tuileries, was taken. A platform was raised, scenery arranged,— a great grey painting by David imitating bas-reliefs; benches were placed in order; there was a square tribune, parallel pilasters with plinths like blocks and long rectilinear stems; square enclosures, into which the spectators crowded, and which were called the public tribunes; a Roman velarium, Grecian draperies; and in these right-angles and these straight lines the Convention was installed,— the tempest confined within this geometrical

plan. On the tribune the Red Cap was painted in grey.
The royalists began by laughing at this grey red cap, this
theatrical hall, this monument of pasteboard, this sanctuary of
papier-maché, this Pantheon of mud and spittle. How
quickly it would disappear! The columns were made of the
staves from hogsheads, the arches were of deal boards, the bas-
reliefs of mastic, the entablatures were of pine, the statues of
plaster; the marbles were paint, the walls canvas; and of this
provisional shelter France has made an eternal dwelling.

When the Convention began to hold its sessions in the
Riding-school, the walls were covered with the placards which
sprouted over Paris at the period of the return from Varennes.

On one might be read: " The king returns. Any person
who cheers him shall be beaten; any person who insults him
shall be hanged." On another: " Peace! Hats on! He
is about to pass before his judges." On another: " The
king has aimed at the nation. He has hung fire; it is now
the nation's turn." On another: " The Law! The Law!"
It was within those walls that the Convention sat in judgment
on Louis XVI.

At the Tuileries, where the Convention began to sit on the
10th of May, 1793, and which was called the Palais-National,
the assembly-hall occupied the whole space between the Pavillon de l'Horloge, called the Pavilion of Unity, and the
Pavillon Marsan, then named Pavilion of Liberty. The Pavilion of Flora was called Pavillon Egalité. The hall was
reached by the grand staircase of Jean Bullant. The whole
ground-floor of the palace, beneath the story occupied by the
Assembly, was a kind of long guard-room, littered with bundles and camp-beds of the troops of all arms, who kept watch
about the Convention. The Assembly had a guard of honour
styled " the Grenadiers of the Convention."

A tricoloured ribbon separated the palace where the Assembly sat from the garden in which the people came and
went.

CHAPTER III

LET us finish the description of that sessions-hall. Everything in regard to this terrible place is interesting.

What first struck the sight of any one entering was a great statue of Liberty, placed between two wide windows. One hundred and forty feet in length, thirty-four feet in width, thirty-seven feet in height,— such were the dimensions of this room, which had been the king's theatre, and which became the theatre of the Revolution. The elegant and magnificent hall built by Vigarani for the courtiers was hidden by the rude timber-work which in '93 supported the weight of the people. This framework, whereon the public tribunes were erected, had (a detail deserving notice) one single post for its only point of support. This post was of one piece, ten metres [32 feet 6 inches] in circumference. Few caryatides have laboured like that beam; it supported for years the rude pressure of the Revolution. It sustained applause, enthusiasm, insolence, noise, tumult, riot,— the immense chaos of opposing rages. It did not give way. After the Convention it witnessed the Council of the Ancients. The 18th Brumaire relieved it.

Percier then replaced the wooden pillar by columns of marble, which did not last so well.

The ideal of architects is sometimes strange. The architect of the Rue de Rivoli had for his ideal the trajectory of a cannon-ball; the architect of Carlsruhe, a fan; a gigantic drawer would seem to have been the model of the architect who built the hall where the Convention began to sit on the 10th of May, 1793; it was long, high, and flat. At one of the sides of the parallelogram was a great semicircle; this amphitheatre contained the seats of the Representatives, but without tables or desks. Garan-Coulon, who wrote a great deal, held his paper on his knee. In front of the seats was the tribune; be-

10

fore the tribune, the bust of Lepelletier Saint-Fargeau; behind was the President's arm-chair.

The head of the bust passed a little beyond the ledge of the tribune, for which reason it was afterward moved away from that position.

The amphitheatre was composed of nineteen semicircular rows of benches, rising one behind the other, the supports of the seats prolonging the amphitheatre into the two corners.

Below, in the horse-shoe at the foot of the tribune, the ushers had their places.

On one side of the tribune a placard nine feet in length was fastened to the wall in a black wooden frame bearing on two leaves, separated by a sort of sceptre, the "Declaration of the Rights of Man;" on the other side was a vacant place, at a later period occupied by a similar frame, containing the Constitution of Year II., with the leaves divided by a sword. Above the tribune, over the head of the orator, from a deep *loge* with double compartments always filled with people, floated three immense tricoloured flags, almost horizontal, resting on an altar upon which could be read the word LAW. Behind this altar there arose, tall as a column, an enormous Roman fasces like the sentinel of free speech. Colossal statues, erect against the wall, faced the Representatives. The President had Lycurgus on his right hand and Solon on his left; Plato towered above the Mountain.

These statues had plain blocks of wood for pedestals, resting on a long cornice which encircled the hall, and separated the people from the Assembly. The spectators could lean their elbows on this cornice.

The black wooden frame of the proclamation of the "Rights of Man" reached to the cornice, and broke the regularity of the entablature,— an infraction of the straight line which caused Chabot to murmur: "It is ugly," he said to Vadier.

On the heads of the statues alternated crowns of oak-leaves and laurel. A green drapery, on which similar crowns were painted in deeper green, fell in heavy folds straight down from the cornice of the circumference, and covered the whole wall of the ground-floor occupied by the Assembly. Above this drapery the wall was white and naked. In it, as if hollowed out by a gigantic axe, without moulding or foliage, were two stories of public tribunes,— the lower ones square, the upper ones round. According to rule, for Vitruvius was not dethroned, the archivolts were superimposed upon the architraves. There were ten tribunes on each side of the hall, and two huge boxes at either end,— in all, twenty-four. There the crowds gathered thickly.

The spectators in the lower tribunes, overflowing their borders, grouped themselves along the reliefs of the cornice. A long iron bar, firmly fixed at a height to lean on, served as a safety rail to the upper tribunes, and guarded the spectators against the pressure of the throngs mounting the stairs. Nevertheless, a man was once thrown headlong into the Assembly; he fell partly upon Massieu, Bishop of Beauvais, and thus was not killed. He said "Hullo! Why, a bishop is really good for something!"

The hall of the Convention could hold two thousand persons comfortably; on the days of insurrection it held three.

The Convention held two sittings, one in the daytime and one in the evening.

The back of the President's chair was curved, and studded with gilt nails. The table was upheld by four winged monsters, with a single foot; one might have thought they had come out of the Apocalypse to assist at the Revolution. They seemed to have been unharnessed from Ezekiel's chariot to drag the dung-cart of Sanson.

On the President's table was a huge hand-bell almost large enough to have served for a church, a great copper inkstand, and a parchment folio, which was the book of official reports.

Many times freshly severed heads, borne aloft on the tops of pikes, sprinkled their blood-drops over this table.

The tribune was reached by a staircase of nine steps. These steps were high, steep, and hard to mount. One day Gensonné stumbled as he was going up. "It is a scaffold-

ladder," said he.   " Serve your apprenticeship," Carrier cried
out to him.

In the angles of the hall, where the wall had looked too
naked, the architect had put Roman fasces for decorations,
with the axe turned to the people.

At the right and left of the tribune were square blocks
supporting two candelabra twelve feet in height, having each
four pairs of lamp̈s.   There was a similar candelabrum in
each public box.

On the pedestals were carved circles, which the people called
guillotine-collars.

The benches of the Assembly reached almost to the cornice
of the tribunes; so that the Representatives and the spectators
could talk together.

The outlets from the tribunes led into a labyrinth of sombre
corridors, often filled with a savage din.

The Convention overcrowded the palace and flowed into
the neighbouring mansions,— the Hôtel de Longueville and
the Hôtel de Coigny.   It was to the Hôtel de Coigny, if one
may believe a letter of Lord Bradford's, that the royal
furniture was carried after the 10th of August.   It took two
months to empty the Tuileries.

The committees were lodged in the neighbourhood of the
hall: in the Pavillon Egalité were those of Legislation, Agri-
culture, and Commerce; in the Pavilion of Liberty were the
Marine, the Colonies, Finance, Assignats, and Public Safety;
the War Department was at the Pavilion of Unity.

The Committee of General Security communicated directly
with that of Public Safety by an obscure passage, lighted day
and night with a reflector-lamp, where the spies of all parties
came and went.   People spoke there in whispers.

The bar of the Convention was several times moved.   Generally it was at the right of the President.

At the far ends of the hall the vertical partitions which
closed the concentric semicircles of the amphitheatre left between them and the wall a couple of narrow, deep passages,
from which opened two dark square doors.

The Representatives entered directly into the hall by a door opening on the Terrace des Feuillants.,

This hall, dimly lighted during the day by deep-set windows, took a strange nocturnal aspect when, with the approach of twilight, it was badly illuminated by lamps. Their pale glare intensified the evening shadows, and the lamplight sessions were lugubrious.

It was impossible to see clearly; from the opposite ends of the hall, to the right and to the left, indistinct groups of faces insulted each other. People met without recognizing one another. One day Laignelot, hurrying toward the tribune, hit against some person in the sloping passage between the benches. " Pardon, Robespierre," said he. " For whom do you take me? " replied a hoarse voice. " Pardon, Marat," said Laignelot.

At the bottom, to the right and left of the President, were two reserved tribunes; for, strange to say, the Convention had its privileged spectators. These tribunes were the only ones that had draperies. In the middle of the architrave two gold tassels held up the curtains. The tribunes of the people were bare.

The whole surroundings were peculiar and savage, yet correct. Regularity in barbarism is rather a type of revolution. The hall of the Convention offered the most complete specimen of what artists have since called " architecture Messidor; " it was massive, and yet frail.

The builders of that time mistook symmetry for beauty. The last word of the Renaissance had been uttered under Louis XV., and a reaction followed. The noble was pushed to insipidity, and the pure to absurdity. Prudery may exist in architecture. After the dazzling orgies of form and colour of the eighteenth century, Art took to fasting, and only allowed herself the straight line. This species of progress ends in ugliness, and Art reduced to a skeleton is the phenomenon which results. The fault of this sort of wisdom and abstinence is, that the style is so severe that it becomes meagre.

Outside of all political emotion, there was something in the

very architecture of this hall which made one shiver.   One re-
called confusedly the ancient theatre with its garlanded boxes,
its blue and crimson ceiling, its prismed lustres, its girandoles
with diamond reflections, its brilliant hangings, its profusion
of Cupids and Nymphs on the curtain and draperies, the
whole royal and amorous idyll — painted, sculptured, gilded
— which had brightened this sombre spot with its smile, where
now one saw on every side hard rectilinear angles, cold and
sharp as steel; it was something like Boucher guillotined by
David.

CHAPTER IV

BUT when one saw the Assembly, the hall was forgotten.
    Whoever looked at the drama no longer remembered
the theatre.   Nothing more chaotic and more sublime.   A
crowd of heroes; a mob of cowards.   Fallow deer on a mountain; reptiles in a marsh.   Therein swarmed, elbowed one another, provoked one another, threatened, struggled, and lived,
all those combatants who are phantoms to-day.

A convocation of Titans.

To the right, the Gironde,— a legion of thinkers; to the
left, the Mountain,— a group of athletes.   On one side Brissot, who had received the keys of the Bastille; Barbaroux,
whom the Marseillais obeyed; Kervélégan, who had under his
hand the battalion of Brest, garrisoned in the Faubourg Saint
Marceau; Gensonné, who had established the supremacy of
the Representatives over the generals; the fatal Guadet, to
whom the queen one night, at the Tuileries, showed the sleeping Dauphin: Guadet kissed the forehead of the child, and
caused the head of the father to fall.   Salles, the crack-
brained denouncer of the intimacy between the Mountain and
Austria.   Sillery, the cripple of the Right, as Couthon was
the paralytic of the Left.   Lause-Duperret, who, having been
called a scoundrel by a journalist, invited him to dinner, say-

ing, " I know that by scoundrel you simply mean a man
who does not think like yourself." Rabaut Saint-Etienne,
who commenced his almanac for 1790 with this saying:
" The Revolution is ended." Quinette, one of those who over-
threw Louis XVI.; the Jansenist Camus, who drew up the
civil constitution of the clergy; believed in the miracles of the
Deacon Paris, and prostrated himself each night before a
figure of Christ seven feet high, which was nailed to the wall
of his chamber. Fauchet, a priest, who, with Camille Desmoulins, brought about the 14th of July; Isnard, who committed the crime of saying, " Paris will be destroyed," at the
same moment when Brunswick was saying, " Paris shall be
burned." Jacob Dupont, the first who cried, " I am an Atheist," and to whom Robespierre replied, " Atheism is aristo-
cratic." Lanjuinais, stern, sagacious, and valiant Breton;
Ducos, the Euryalus of Boyer-Fonfrède; Rebecqui, the
Pylades of Barbaroux (Rebecqui gave in his resignation because Robespierre had not yet been guillotined). Richaud,
who combated the permanency of the Sections. Lasource,
who had given utterance to the murderous apothegm, " Woe
to grateful nations!" and who was afterward to contradict
himself at the foot of the scaffold by this haughty sarcasm
flung at the Mountainists: " We die because the people
sleep; you will die because the people awake." Biroteau, who
caused the abolition of inviolability to be decreed; who was
also, without knowing it, the forger of the axe, and raised the
scaffold for himself. Charles Villatte, who sheltered his conscience behind this protest: " I will not vote under the
hatchet." Louvet, the author of " Faublas," who was to end
as a bookseller in the Palais Royal, with Lodoiska behind
the counter. Mercier, author of the " Picture of Paris," who
exclaimed, " On the 21st of January, all kings felt for the
backs of their necks!" Marec, whose anxiety was " the faction of the ancient limits." The journalist Carra, who said
to the headsman at the foot of the scaffold, " It bores me to
die. I would have liked to see the continuation." Vigée,
who called himself a grenadier in the second battalion of May-

enne and Loire, and who, when menaced by the public tribunals, cried, " I demand that at the first murmur of the
tribunals we all withdraw and march on Versailles, sabre in
hand! " Buzot, reserved for death by famine; Valazé destined to die by his own dagger; Condorcet, who was to perish
at Bourg-la-Reine (become Bourg-Egalité), betrayed by the
Horace which he had in his pocket; Pétion, whose destiny
was to be adored by the crowd in 1792 and devoured by wolves
in 1794: twenty others still,— Pontecoulant, Marboz, Lidon,
Saint-Martin, Dussaulx, the translator of Juvenal, who had
been in the Hanover campaign; Boileau, Bertrand, Lesterp-
Beauvais, Lesage, Gomaire, Gardien, Mainvelle, Duplentier,
Lacaze, Antiboul, and at their head a Barnave, who was styled
Vergniaud.

On the other side, Antoine Louis Léon Florelle de Saint-
Just, pale, with a low forehead, a regular profile, eye mysterious, a profound sadness, aged twenty-three. Merlin of
Thionville, whom the Germans called *Feuerteufel*,—" the fire-
devil." Merlin of Douai, the culpable author of the " Law
of the Suspected." Soubrany, whom the people of Paris at
the first Prairial demanded for general. The ancient priest
Lebon, holding a sabre in the hand which had sprinkled holy
water; Billaud Varennes, who foresaw the magistracy of the
future, without judges or arbiters; Fabre d'Eglantine, who
fell upon a delightful treasure-trove,— the Republican Calendar,— just as Rouget de Lisle had a single sublime in-
spiration,— the " Marseillaise; " neither one nor the other
ever produced a second. Manuel, the attorney of the Commune, who had said, " A dead king is not a man the less."
Goujon, who had entered Tripstadt, Neustadt, and Spires, and
had seen the Prussian army flee. Lacroix, a lawyer turned
into a general, named Chevalier of Saint Louis, six days before the 10th of August. Fréron Thersites, the son of Fréron
Zöilus. Ruth, the inexorable searcher of the iron cupboard,
predestined to a great republican suicide,— he was to kill
himself the day the Republic died. Fouché, with the soul of
a demon and the face of a corpse. Camboulas, the friend

of Father Duchesne, who said to Guillotin, " Thou belongest
to the Club of the Feuillants, but thy daughter belongs to the
Jacobin Club." Jagot, who to such as complained to him of
the nudity of the prisoners, replied by this savage saying, " A
prison is a dress of stone." Javogues, the terrible desecrator
of the tombs of Saint Denis. Osselin, a proscriber, who hid
one of the proscribed, Madame Charry, in his house. Benta-
bolle, who, when he was in the chair, made signs to the tribunes
to applaud or hoot. The journalist Robert, the husband of
Mademoiselle Kéralio, who wrote: " Neither Robespierre nor
Marat come to my house. Robespierre may come when he
wishes — Marat, never." Garan Coulon, who, when Spain in-
terfered in the trial of Louis XVI., haughtily demanded
that the Assembly should not deign to read the letter of a
king in behalf of a king. Grégoire, a bishop, at first worthy
of the Primitive Church, but who afterward, under the Empire, effaced Grégoire the republican beneath the Count Grégoire. Amar, who said: " The whole earth condemns Louis
XVI. To whom, then, appeal for judgment? To the
planets? " Rouyer, who, on the 21st of January, opposed
the firing of the cannon of Pont Neuf, saying, " A king's
head ought to make no more noise in falling than the head
of another man." Chénier, the brother of André; Vadier, one
of those who laid a pistol on the tribunes; Tanis, who said to
Momoro,—

" I wish Marat and Robespierre to embrace at my table."

" Where dost thou live? "

" At Charenton."

" Anywhere else would have astonished me," replied Momoro.

Legendre, who was the butcher of the French Revolution,
as Pride had been of the English. " Come, that I may knock
you down," he cried to Lanjuinais.

" First have it decreed that I am a bullock," replied Lanjuinais.

Collot d'Herbois, that lugubrious comedian who had the
face of the antique mask, with two mouths which said yes

and no, approving with one while he blamed with the other;
branding Carrier at Nantes and defying Châlier at Lyons;
sending Robespierre to the scaffold and Marat to the Pantheon. Génissieux, who demanded the penalty of death against
whomsoever should have upon him a medallion of " Louis
XVI. martyred." Léonard Bourdon, the schoolmaster, who
had offered his house to the old man of Mont Jura. Topsent,
sailor; Goupilleau, lawyer; Laurent Lecointre, merchant; Du-
hem, physician; Sergent, sculptor; David, painter; Joseph
Egalité, prince.

Others still: Lecointe Puiraveau, who asked that a decree
should be passed declaring Marat mad. Robert Lindet, the
disquieting creator of that devil-fish whose head was the Committee of General Surety, and which covered France with
its one-and-twenty thousand arms called revolutionary committees. Lebœuf, upon whom Girez-Dupré, in his " Christmas
of False Patriots," had made this epigram,—

" Lebœuf vit Legendre et beugla."

Thomas Payne, the clement American; Anacharsis Cloots,
German, baron, millionaire, atheist, Hébertist, candid. The
upright Lebas, the friend of the Duplays. Rovère, one of
those strange men who are wicked for wickedness' sake,— for
the art, from love of the art, exists more frequently than people believe. Charlier, who wished that " you " should be employed in addressing aristocrats. Tallien, elegiac and ferocious, who will bring about the 9th Thermidor from love.
Cambacérès, a lawyer, who will be a prince later. Carrier, an
attorney, who will become a tiger. Laplanche, who will one
day cry, " I demand priority for the alarm-gun." Thuriot,
who desired the vote of the revolutionary tribunal to be given
aloud. Bourdon of the Oise, who challenged Chambon to a
duel, denounced Payne, and was himself denounced by Hébert.
Fayau, who proposed the sending of " an army of incendi-
aries " into the Vendée. Tavaux, who, on the 13th of April,
was almost a mediator between the Gironde and the Mountain.
Vernier, who proposed that the chiefs of the Gironde and the
Mountain should be sent to serve as common soldiers. Rew-

bell, who shut himself up in Mayence. Bourbotte, who had his horse killed under him at the taking of Saumur. Guimberteau, who directed the army of the Cherbourg coast. Jard Panvilliers, who managed the army of the coasts of Rochelle. Lecarpentier, who led the squadron of Cancale. Roberjot, for whom the ambush of Rastadt was waiting. Prieur, of the Marne, who bore in camp his old rank of major. Levasseur of the Sarthe, who by a word decided Serrent, commandant of the battalion of Saint-Amand, to kill himself. Reverchon, Maure, Bernard de Saintes, Charles Richard, Lequinio, and at the summit of this group a Mirabeau, who was called Danton.

Outside the two camps, and keeping both in awe, rose the man Robespierre.

CHAPTER V

BELOW crouched Dismay, which may be noble; and Fear, which is base. Beneath passions, beneath heroisms, beneath devotion, beneath rage, was the gloomy cohort of the Anonymous. The shoals of the Assembly were called the Plain. There was everything there which floats; the men who doubt, who hesitate, who recoil, who adjourn, who wait, each one fearing somebody. The Mountain was made up of the Select; the Gironde of the Select; the Plain was a crowd. The Plain was summed up and condensed in Sieyès.

Sieyès, a profound man, who had grown chimerical. He had stopped at the Tiers-Etat, and had not been able to mount up to the people. Certain minds are made to rest half-way. Sieyès called Robespierre a tiger, and was called a mole by Robespierre. This metaphysician had stranded, not on wisdom, but prudence. He was the courtier, not the servitor, of the Revolution. He seized a shovel, and went with the people to work in the Champ de Mars, harnessed to the same cart as Alexander de Beauharnais. He counselled energy, but never showed it. He said to the Girondists, " Put the cannon on your side." There are thinkers who are wrestlers: those were, like Condorcet, with Vergniaud; or like Camille Desmoulins, with Danton. There are thinkers whose aim is to preserve their lives: such were with Sieyès.

The best working vats have their lees. Underneath the Plain even was the Marsh,— a hideous stagnation which exposed to view the transparencies of egotism. There shivered the fearful in dumb expectation. Nothing could be more abject,— a conglomeration of shames feeling no shame; hidden rage; revolt under servitude. They were afraid in a cynical fashion; they had all the desperation of cowardice; they preferred the Gironde and chose the Mountain; the final catastrophe depended upon them; they poured toward the successful side; they delivered Louis XVI. to Vergniaud, Vergniaud to Danton, Danton to Robespierre, Robespierre to Tallien. They put Marat in the pillory when living, and deified him when dead. They upheld everything up to the day when they overturned everything. They had the instinct to give the decisive push to whatever tottered. In their eyes — since they had undertaken to serve on condition that the basis was solid — to waver was to betray them. They were number; they were force; they were fear. From thence came the audacity of turpitude.

Thence came May 31st, the 11th Terminal, the 9th Thermidor,— tragedies knotted by giants and untied by dwarfs.

CHAPTER VI

AMONG these men full of passions were mingled men filled with dreams. Utopia was there under all its forms,— under its warlike form, which admitted the scaffold, and under its innocent form, which would abolish capital punishment; phantom as it faced thrones; angel as it regarded the people. Side by side with the spirits that fought were the spirits that brooded. These had war in their heads, those peace. One brain, Carnot, brought forth fourteen armies; another intellect, Jean Debry, meditated a universal democratic federation.

Amid this furious eloquence, among these shrieking and growling voices, there were fruitful silences. Lakanal remained voiceless, and combined in his thoughts the system of public national education; Lanthenas held his peace, and created the primary schools; Revellière Lépaux kept still, and dreamed of the elevation of Philosophy to the dignity of Religion. Others occupied themselves with questions of detail, smaller and more practical. Guyton Morveaux studied means for rendering the hospitals healthy; Maire, the abolition of existing servitudes; Jean Bon Saint-André, the suppression of imprisonment for debt and constraint of the person; Romme, the proposition of Chappe; Duboë, the putting the archives in order; Coren Fustier, the creation of the Cabinet of Anatomy and the Museum of Natural History; Guyomard, river navigation and the damming of the Scheldt. Art had its monomaniacs. On the 21st of January, while the head of monarchy was falling on the Place de la Revolution, Bézard, the Representative of the Oise, went to see a picture of Rubens, which had been found in a garret in the Rue Saint-Lazare. Artists, orators, prophets, men-giants like Danton, child-men like Cloots, gladiators and philosophers, all had the same goal,— progress. Nothing disconcerted them. The grandeur of the Convention was, the searching how much reality there is in what men call the impossible. At one extreme, Robespierre had his eye fixed on Law; at the other, Condorcet had his fixed on Duty.

Condorcet was a man of reverie and enlightenment. Robespierre was a man of execution; and sometimes, in the final crises of worn-out orders, execution means extermination. Revolutions have two currents,— an ebb and a flow; and on these float all seasons, from that of ice to flowers. Each zone of these currents produces men adapted to its climate, from those who live in the sun to those who dwell among the thunderbolts.

CHAPTER VII

PEOPLE showed each other the recess of the left-hand passage where Robespierre had uttered low in the ear of Garat, Clavière's friend, this terrible epigram: "Clavière has conspired wherever he has respired." In this same recess, convenient for words needed to be spoken aside and for half-voiced cholers, Fabre d'Eglantine had quarrelled with Romme, and reproached him for having disfigured his calendar by changing "Fervidor" into "Thermidor." So, too, was shown the angle where, elbow to elbow, sat the seven Representatives of the Haute-Garonne, who, first called to pronounce their verdict upon Louis XVI., thus responded, one after the other: Mailhe, "Death;" Delmas, "Death;" Projean, "Death;" Calès, "Death;" Ayral, "Death;" Julien, "Death;" Desaby, "Death,"— eternal reverberation which fills all history, and which, since human justice has existed, has always given an echo of the sepulchre to the wall of the tribunal. People pointed out with their fingers, among that group of stormy faces, all the men from whose mouths had come the uproar of tragic notes,— Paganel, who said: "Death! A king is only made useful by death." Millaud, who said: "To-day, if death did not exist it would be necessary to invent it." The old Raffon du Trouillet, who said: "Speedy death!" Goupilleau, who cried: "The scaffold at once. Delay aggravates dying." Sieyès, who said, with funereal brevity: "Death!" Thuriot, who had rejected the appeal to the people proposed by Buzot: "What! the primary assemblies! What! Forty-four thousand tribunals! A case without limit. The head of Louis XVI. would have time to whiten before it would fall." Augustin Bon Robespierre, who, after his brother, cried: "I know nothing of the humanity which slaughters the people and pardons despots. Death! To demand a reprieve is to substitute an appeal to tyrants for the appeal to the people." Foussedoire, the sub-

stitute of Bernardin de Saint-Pierre, who had said: "I have
a horror of human bloodshed, but the blood of a king is not a
man's blood. Death!" Jean Bon Saint-André, who said:
"No free people without a dead tyrant." Lavicomterie, who
proclaimed this formula: "So long as the tyrant breathes,
Liberty is suffocated! Death!" Châteauneuf Randon, who
had uttered this cry: "Death to the last Louis!" Guyar-
din, who had said: "Let the Barrière Renversée be executed." (The Barrière Renversée was the Barrière du
Trône.) Tellier, who had said: "Let there be forged, to
aim against the enemy, a cannon of the calibre of Louis XVI.'s
head. And the indulgents,— Gentil, who said: "I vote for
confinement. To make a Charles I. is to make a Cromwell."
Bancel, who said: "Exile. I want to see the first king of
the earth condemned to a trade in order to earn his liveli-
hood." Albouys, who said: "Banishment! Let this living
ghost go wander among the thrones." Zangiacomi, who said:
"Confinement. Let us keep Capet alive as a scarecrow."
Chaillon, who said: "Let him live. I do not wish to make
a dead man of whom Rome will make a saint."

While these sentences fell from those severe lips and dispersed themselves one after another into history, women in
low-necked dresses and decorated with gems sat in the tribunes, list in hand, counting the voices and pricking each
vote with a pin.

Where tragedy entered, horror and pity remain.

To see the Convention, no matter at what period of its
reign, was to see anew the trial of the last Capet. The
legend of the 21st of January seemed mingled with all its
acts; the formidable Assembly was full of those fatal breaths
which blew upon the old torch of monarchy, that had burned
for eighteen centuries, and extinguished it. The decisive
trials of all kings in that judgment pronounced upon one
king was like the point of departure in the great war made
against the Past. Whatever might be the sitting of the
Convention at which one was present, the shadow of Louis
XVI.'s scaffold was seen thrust forward within it. Specta-

tors recounted to one another the resignation of Kersaint, the resignation of Roland, Duchâtel, the deputy of the Deux-Sèvres, who, being ill, had himself carried to the Convention on his bed, and dying voted the king's life which caused Marat to laugh; and they sought with their eyes the Representative whom history has forgotten, he who, after that session of thirty-seven hours, fell back on his bench overcome by fatigue and sleep, and when roused by the usher as his turn to vote arrived, half opened his eyes, said " Death," and fell asleep again.

At the moment Louis XVI. was condemned to death, Robespierre had still eighteen months to live; Danton, fifteen months; Vergniaud, nine months; Marat, five months and three weeks; Lepelletier Saint-Fargeau, one day. Quick and terrible blast from human mouths!

CHAPTER VIII

THE people had a window opening on the Convention,— the public tribunes; and when the window was not sufficient, they opened the door, and the street entered the Assembly. These invasions of the crowd into that senate make one of the most astounding visions of history. Ordinarily those irruptions were amicable. The market-place fraternized with the curule chair; but it was a formidable cordiality,— that of a people who one day took within three hours the cannon of the Invalides and forty thousand muskets besides. At each instant a troop interrupted the deliberations; deputations presented at the bar petitions, homages, offerings. The pike of honour of the Faubourg Saint Antoine entered, borne by women. Certain English offered twenty thousand pairs of shoes for the naked feet of our soldiers. " The citizen Arnoux," announced the " Moniteur," " Curé of Aubignan, Commandant of the Battal-

ion of Drôme, asks to march to the frontiers, and desires that
his cure may be preserved for him."

Delegates from the Sections arrived, bringing on hand-
barrows, dishes, patens, chalices, monstrances, heaps of gold,
silver, and enamel, presented to the country by this multi-
tude in rags, who demanded for recompense the permission to
dance the Carmagnole before the Convention. Chenard, Narbonne, and Vallière came to sing couplets in honour of the
Mountain. The Section of Mont Blanc brought the bust of
Lepelletier, and a woman placed a red cap on the head of the
President, who embraced her. The citizenesses of the Section of the Mail " flung flowers " to the legislators. " The
pupils of the country " came, headed by music, to thank the
Convention for having prepared the prosperity of the century.
The women of the Section of the Gardes Françaises offered
roses; the women of the Champs Elysées Section gave a crown
of oak-leaves; the women of the Section of the Temple came to
the bar to swear " only to unite themselves with true Republicans." The Section of Molière presented a medal of Franklin,
which was suspended by decree to the crown of the statue of
Liberty. The Foundlings — declared the Children of the Republic — filed through, habited in the national uniform. The
young girls of the Section of Ninety-two arrived in long
white robes, and the " Moniteur " of the following morning
contained this line: " The President received a bouquet from
the innocent hands of a young beauty." The orators saluted
the crowds, sometimes flattered them: they said to the mul-
titude, " Thou art infallible; thou art irreproachable; thou
art sublime." The people have an infantile side: they like
those sugar-plums. Sometimes Riot traversed the Assembly:
entered furious and withdrew appeased, like the Rhone which
traverses Lake Leman, and is mud when it enters and pure
and azure when it pours out.

Sometimes the crowd was less pacific, and Henriot was
obliged to come with his furnaces for heating shot to the
entrance of the Tuileries.

11

CHAPTER IX

A T the same time that it threw off revolution, this Assembly produced civilization.   Furnace, but forge too.
In this caldron, where terror bubbled, progress fermented.
Out of this chaos of shadow, this tumultuous flight of clouds,
spread immense rays of light parallel to the eternal laws,
— rays that have remained on the horizon, visible forever in
the heaven of the peoples, and which are, one, Justice; another, Tolerance; another, Goodness; another, Right; another, Truth; another, Love.

The Convention promulgated this grand axiom: " The
liberty of each citizen ends where the liberty of another
citizen commences,"— which comprises in two lines all human social law.   It declared indigence sacred; it declared
infirmity sacred in the blind and the deaf and dumb, who
became wards of the State; maternity sacred in the girl-
mother, whom it consoled and lifted up; infancy sacred in
the orphan, whom it caused to be adopted by the country;
innocence sacred in the accused who was acquitted, whom
it indemnified.   It branded the slave-trade; it abolished
slavery.   It proclaimed civic joint responsiblity.   It decreed
gratuitous instruction.   It organized national education by
the normal school of Paris; central schools in the chief towns;
primary schools in the communes.   It created the academies
of music and the museums.   It decreed the unity of the Code,
the unity of weights and measures, and the unity of calculation by the decimal system.   It established the finances of
France, and caused public credit to succeed to the long monarchical bankruptcy.   It put the telegraph in operation.
To old age it gave endowed almshouses; to sickness, purified
hospitals; to instruction, the Polytechnic School; to science, the
Bureau of Longitudes; to human intellect, the Institute.   At
the same time that it was national it was cosmopolitan.   Of
the eleven thousand two hundred and ten decrees which

emanated from the Convention, a third had a political aim;
two thirds, a human aim. It declared universal morality the
basis of society, and universal conscience the basis of law.
And all that servitude abolished, fraternity proclaimed, humanity protected, human conscience rectified, the law of work
transformed into right, and from onerous made honourable,
— national riches consolidated, childhood instructed and
raised up, letters and sciences propagated, light illuminating all heights, aid to all sufferings, promulgation of all
principle,— the Convention accomplished, having in its bowels
that hydra, the Vendée; and upon its sholders that heap of
tigers, the kings.

CHAPTER X

IMMENSE place! All types were there,— human, inhuman, superhuman. Epic gathering of antagonisms,—
Guillotin avoiding David, Bazire insulting Chabot, Gaudet
mocking Saint-Just, Vergniaud disdaining Danton, Louvet
attacking Robespierre, Buzot denouncing Egalité, Chambon
branding Pache; all execrating Marat. And how many
names remain still to be registered! — Armonville, styled Bonnet Rouge, because he always attended the sittings in a
Phrygian cap, a friend of Robespierre, and wishing, " after
Louis XVI., to guillotine Robespierre in order to restore an
equilibrium; " Massieu, colleague and counterpart of that
good Lamourette, a bishop fitted to leave his name to a kiss;
Lehardy of the Mobihan, stigmatizing the priests of Brittany; Barère, the man of majorities, who presided when
Louis XVI. appeared at the bar, and who was to Paméla
what Louvet was to Lodoiska; the Oratorian Danou, who said,
" Let us gain time; " Dubois Crancé, close to whose ear
leaned Marat; the Marquis de Châteauneuf, Laclos, Hérault
of Séchelles, who recoiled before Henriot crying, " Gunners,
to your pieces; " Julien, who compared the Mountain to

Thermopylæ; Gamon, who desired a public tribune reserved
solely for women; Laloy, who adjudged the honours of the
séance to the Bishop Gobel coming into the Convention to
lay down his mitre and put on the red cap; Lecomte, who
exclaimed, " So the honours are for whosoever will unfrock
himself; " Féraud, whose head Boissy d'Anglas saluted, leaving this question to history " Did Boissy d'Anglas salute
the head,— that is to say the victim,— or the pike; that is
to say the assassins? " the two brothers Duprat, one a member
of the Mountain, the other of the Girondé, who hated each
other like the two brothers Chénier.

At this tribune were uttered those mysterious words which
sometimes possess unconsciously to those who pronounce them
the prophetic accent of revolutions, and in whose wake ma-
terial facts appear suddenly to assume an inexplicable dis-
content and passion, as if they had taken umbrage at the
things just heard; events seem angered by words: catastrophes follow furious, and as if exasperated by the speech of
men.   Thus a voice upon a mountain suffices to set the
avalanche in motion.   A word too much may be followed
by a landslip.   If no one had spoken, the catastrophe
would not have happened.   You might say sometimes that
events are irascible.

It was thus, by the hazard of an orator's ill-comprehended
word, that Madame Elizabeth's head fell.

At the Convention intemperance of language was a right.
Threats flew about and crossed one another like sparks in
a conflagration.

PÉTION: " Robespierre, come to the point."

ROBESPIERRE: " The point is yourself, Pétion; I shall
come to it, and you will see it."

A VOICE: " Death to Marat! "

MARAT: " The day Marat dies there will be no more Paris,
and the day that Paris expires there will be no longer a Republic."

Billaud Varennes rises, and says, " We wish —"

Barère interrupts him: " Thou speakest like a king."

Another day, Philippeaux, " A member has drawn his sword upon me."

AUDOUIN: " President, call the assassin to order."

THE PRESIDENT: " Wait."

PANIS: " President, I call you to order — I! "

There was rude laughter moreover.

LECOINTRE: " The Curé of Chant de Bout complains of Fauchet, his bishop, who forbids his marrying."

A VOICE: " I do not see why Fauchet, who has mistresses, should wish to hinder others from having wives."

A SECOND VOICE: " Priest, take a wife! "

The galleries joined in the conversation. They said " thee " and " thou " to the members. One day the Representative Ruamps mounted to the tribune. He had one hip very much larger than the other. A spectator, crying out, thus jeered him: " Turn that toward the Right, since thou hast a cheek *à la David*."

Such were the liberties the people took with the Convention. On one occasion, however, during the tumult of the 11th of April, 1793, the President commanded a disorderly person in the tribunes to be arrested.

One day when the session had for witness the old Buonarotti, Robespierre takes the floor and speaks for two hours, staring at Danton, sometimes straight in the face, which was serious; sometimes obliquely, which was worse. He thunders on to the end, however. He closes with an indignant outburst full of menacing words: " The conspirators are known, the corrupters and the corrupted are known; the traitors are known; they are in this assembly. They hear us; we see them, and we do not move our eyes from them. Let them look above their heads, and they will see the sword of the law; let them look into their conscience, and they will see their own infamy. Let them beware! " And when Robespierre has finished, Danton, with his face raised toward the ceiling, his eyes half closed, one arm hanging loosely down, throws himself back in his seat, and is heard to hum,—

"Cadet Roussel fait des discours,
Qui ne sont pas longs quand ils sont courts." [1]

Imprecations followed one another,— conspirator! assassin!
scoundrel! factionist! moderate! They denounced one another to the bust of Brutus that stood there,— apostrophes,
insults, challenges; furious glances from one side to the
other; fists shaken; pistols allowed to be seen; poniards half
drawn; terrible blazing forth in the tribune. Certain persons talked as if they were driven back against the guillotine;
heads wavered, frightened and awed. Mountainists, Girondists, Feuillantists, Moderates, Terrorists, Jacobins, Cordeliers,
eighteen regicide priests,— all these men a mass of vapours
driven wildly in every direction.

CHAPTER XI

SPIRITS which were a prey of the wind. But this was
a miracle-working wind. To be a member of the Convention was to be a wave of the ocean. This was true even of
the greatest there. The force of impulsion came from on
high. There was a Will in the Convention which was that
of all, and yet not that of any one person. This Will was
an Idea,— an idea indomitable and immeasurable, which
swept from the summit of heaven into the darkness below.
We call this Revolution. When that Idea passed, it beat
down one and raised up another; it scattered this man into
foam and dashed that one upon the reefs. This Idea knew
whither it was going, and drove the whirlpool before it. To
ascribe the Revolution to men is to ascribe the tide to the
waves.

The Revolution is a work of the Unknown. Call it good

[1] " Cadet Roussel doth make his speech
Quite short when it no length doth reach."

or bad, according as you yearn toward the future or the past, but leave it to the power which caused it. It seems the joint work of grand events and grand individualities mingled, but it is in reality the result of events. Events dispense, men suffer; events dictate, men sigh. The 14th of July is signed Camille Desmoulins; the 10th of August is signed Danton; the 2d of September is signed Marat; the 21st of September is signed Grégoire; the 21st of January is signed Robespierre; but Desmoulins, Danton, Marat, Grégoire, and Robespierre are mere scribes. The great and mysterious writer of these grand pages has a name,— God; and a mask, Destiny. Robespierre believed in God: yea, verily!

The Revolution is a form of the eternal phenomenon which presses upon us from every quarter, and which we call Necessity. Before this mysterious complication of benefits and sufferings arises the Wherefore of history. *Because:* this answer of him who knows nothing is equally the response of him who knows all.

In presence of these climacteric catastrophes which devastate and revivify civilization, one hesitates to judge their details. To blame or praise men on account of the result is almost like praising or blaming ciphers on account of the total. That which ought to happen happens; the blast which out to blow blows. The Eternal Serenity does not suffer from these north winds. Above revolutions Truth and Justice remain as the starry sky lies above and beyond tempests.

CHAPTER XII

SUCH was the unmeasured and immeasurable Convention, — a camp cut off from the human race, attacked by all the powers of darkness at once; the night-fires of the besieged army of Ideas; a vast bivouac of minds upon the edge of a precipice. There is nothing in history comparable to this group, at the same time senate and populace, conclave and street-crossing, Areopagus and public square, tribunal and the accused.

The Convention always bent to the wind; but that wind came from the mouth of the people, and was the breath of God.

And to-day, after eighty-four years have passed away, always when the Convention presents itself before the reflection of any man, whosoever he may be,— historian or philosopher,— that man pauses and meditates. It would be impossible not to remain thoughtfully attentive before this grand procession of shadows.

CHAPTER XIII

MARAT IN THE GREEN-ROOM.

MARAT, in accordance with his declaration to Simonne Evrard, went to the Convention the morning after that interview in the Rue du Paon. There was in the Convention a marquis who was a Maratist, Louis de Montaut, the same who afterward presented to the Convention a decimal clock surmounted by the bust of Marat. At the moment Marat entered, Chabot had approached De Montaut. He began: —

" *Ci-devant* —"

Montaut raised his eyes. " Why do you call me *ci-devant?* "

" Because you are so."

" I? "

" For you were a marquis."

" Never."

" Bah! "

" My father was a soldier; my grandfather was a weaver."

" What song is that you are singing, Montaut? "

" I do not call myself Montaut."

" What do you call yourself, then? "

" Maribon."

" In point of fact," said Chabot, " it is all the same to me." And he added between his teeth: " No marquis on any terms."

Marat paused in the corridor to the left and watched Montaut and Chabot. Whenever Marat entered, there was a buzz, but afar from him. About him people kept silence.

Marat paid no attention thereto. He disdained " the croaking of the mud-pool." In the gloomy obscurity of the lower row of seats, Compé of the Oise, Prunelle, Villars, a bishop who was afterward a member of the French Academy, Boutroue, Petit, Plaichard, Bonet, Thibaudeau, and Valdruche pointed him out to one another.

" See Marat! "

" Then he is not ill? "

" Yes, for he is here in a dressing-gown."

" In a dressing-gown! "

" Zounds, yes! "

" He takes liberties enough! "

" He dares to come like that into the Convention! "

" As he came one day crowned with laurels, he may certainly come in a dressing-gown."

" Face of brass and teeth of verdigris."

" His dressing-gown looks new."

" What is it made of? "

" Reps."

" Striped."

" Look at the lapels."

" They are fur."

" Tiger-skin."

" No; ermine."

" Imitation."

" He has stockings on! "

" That is odd."

" And shoes with buckles! "

" Of silver! "

" Camboula's sabots will not pardon that."

People in other seats affected not to see Marat. They talked of indifferent matters. Santhonax accosted Dussaulx,

" Have you heard, Dussaulx? "

" What? "

" The *ci-devant* Count de Brienne? "

" Who was in La Force with the *ci-devant* Duke de Villeroy? "

" Yes."

" I knew them both."

" Well? "

" They were so horribly frightened that they saluted all the red caps of all the turnkeys, and one day they refused to play a game of piquet because somebody offered them cards that had kings and queens among them."

" Well? "

" They were guillotined yesterday."

" The two of them? "

" Both."

" Indeed; how had they behaved in prison? "

" As cowards."

" And how did they show on the scaffold? "

" Intrepid."

Then Dussaulx ejaculated: " It is easier to die than to live! "

Barère was reading a report; it was in regard to the Vendée. Nine hundred men of Morbihan had started with cannon to assist Nantes. Redon was menaced by the peasants. Paimbœuf had been attacked. A fleet was cruising about Maindrin to prevent invasions. From Ingrande, as far as Maure, the entire left bank of the Loire was bristling with royalist batteries. Three thousand peasants were masters of Pornic. They cried, " Long live the English! " A letter from Santerre to the Convention, which Barère was reading, ended with these words: —

"Seven thousand peasants attacked Vannes. We repulsed them, and they have left in our hands four cannon —"

"And how many prisoners?" interrupted a voice.
Barère continued: "Postscript of the letter: —

"'We have no prisoners, because we no longer make any.'"[1]

Marat, standing motionless, did not listen; he appeared absorbed by a stern preoccupation. He held in his hand a paper, which he crumpled between his fingers; had any one unfolded it, he might have read these lines in Momoro's writing,— probably a response to some question he had been asked by Marat: —

"No opposition can be offered to the full powers of delegated commissioners, above all, those of the Committee of Public Safety. Genissieux in vain said, in the sitting of May 6th, 'Each Commissioner is more than a king; it had no effect. Life and death are in their hands. Massade at Angers; Trullard at Saint-Amand; Nyon with General Marcé; Parrein with the army of Sables; Millier with the army of Niort: they are all-powerful. The Club of the Jacobins has gone so far as to name Parrein brigadier-general. The circumstances excuse everything. A delegate from the Committee of Public Safety holds in check a commander-in-chief."

Marat ceased crumpling the paper, put it in his pocket, and walked slowly toward Montaut and Chabot, who continued to converse, and had not seen him enter.
Chabot was saying: "Maribon, or Montaut, listen to this: I have just come from the Committee of Public Safety."
"And what is being done there?"
"They are setting a priest to watch a noble."
"Ah!"
"A noble like yourself —"
"I am not a noble," interrupted Montaut.

[1] Moniteur, vol. xix. p. 81.

"To be watched by a priest —"

"Like you."

"I am not a priest," said Chabot.

They both began to laugh.

"Make your story explicit," resumed Montaut.

"Here it is then. A priest named Cimourdain is delegated with full powers to a viscount named Gauvain; this viscount commands the exploring column of the army of the coast. The question will be to keep the nobleman from trickery and the priest from treason."

"It is very simple," replied Montaut. "It is only necessary to bring death into the matter."

"I come for that," said Marat.

They looked up.

"Good-morning, Marat," said Chabot. "You rarely attend our meetings."

"My doctor has ordered me baths," answered Marat.

"One should beware of baths," returned Chabot. "Seneca died in one."

Marat smiled.

"Chabot, there is no Nero here."

"Yes, there is you," said a rude voice.

It was Danton who passed and ascended to his seat.

Marat did not turn round. He thrust his head in between Montaut and Chabot.

"Listen; I come about a serious matter. One of us three must propose to-day the draft of a decree to the Convention."

"Not I," said Montaut; "I am never listened to. I am a marquis."

"And I," said Chabot —"I am not listened to. I am a Capuchin."

"And I," said Marat —"I am not listened to. I am Marat."

There was a silence among them.

It was not safe to interrogate Marat when he appeared preoccupied, still Montaut hazarded a question.

" Marat, what is the decree that you wish passed? "

" A decree to punish with death any military chief who allows a rebel prisoner to escape."

Chabot interrupted,—

" The decree exists; it was passed in April."

" Then it is just the same as if it did not exist," said Marat. " Everywhere, all through Vendée, anybody who chooses helps prisoners to escape, and gives them an asylum with impunity."

" Marat, the fact is, the decree has fallen into disuse."

" Chabot, it must be put into force anew."

" Without doubt."

" And to do that, the Convention must be addressed."

" Marat, the Convention is not necessary; the Committee of Public Safety will suffice."

" The end will be gained," added Montaut, " if the Committee of Public Safety cause the decree to be placarded in all the communes of the Vendée, and make two or three good examples."

" Of men in high position," returned Chabot,—" of generals."

Marat grumbled: " In fact that will answer."

" Marat," resumed Chabot, " go yourself and say that to the Committee of Public Safety."

Marat stared straight into his eyes, which was not pleasant even for Chabot.

" The Committee of Public Safety," said he, " sits in Robespierre's house; I do not go there."

" I will go myself," said Montaut.

" Good! " said Marat.

The next morning an order from the Committee of Public Safety was sent in all directions among the towns and villages of Vendée, enjoining the publication and strict execution of the decree of death against any person conniving at the escape of brigands and captive insurgents. This decree proved only a first step: the Convention was to go further than that. A few months later, the 11th Brumaire, Year II.

(November, 1793), when Laval opened its gates to the Vendean fugitives, the Convention decreed that any city giving asylum to the rebels should be demolished and destroyed. On their side, the princes of Europe, in the manifesto of the Duke of Brunswick, conceived by the emigrants and drawn up by the Marquis de Linnon, intendant of the Duke of Orleans, had declared that every Frenchman taken with arms in his hand should be shot, and that, if a hair of the king's head fell, Paris should be razed to the ground.

Cruelty against barbarity.

PART III

LA VENDÉE

BOOK I

LA VENDÉE

CHAPTER I

THE FORESTS

THERE were at that time seven ill-famed forests in Brittany. The Vendean war was a revolt of priests. This revolt had the forests as auxiliaries. These spirits of darkness aid one another.

The seven Black Forests of Brittany were the forest of Fougères, which stopped the way between Dol and Avranches; the forest of Princé, which was eight leagues in circumference; the forest of Paimpol, full of ravines and brooks, almost inaccessible on the side toward Baignon, with an easy retreat upon Concornet, which was a royalist town; the forest of Rennes, from whence could be heard the tocsin of the republican parishes, always numerous in the neighbourhood of the cities (it was in this forest that Puysaye lost Focard); the forest of Machecoul, which had Charette for its wild beast; the forest of Garnache, which belonged to the Tré-

175

moilles, the Gauvains, and the Rohans; and the forest of Brocéliande, which belonged to the fairies.

One gentleman of Brittany bore the title of Lord of the Seven Forests: this was the Viscount de Fontenay, Breton Prince. For the Breton Prince existed distinct from the French Prince. The Rohans were Breton princes. Garnier de Saintes, in his report to the Convention of the 15th Nivose, Year II., thus distinguishes the Prince de Talmont: "This Capet of the brigands, Sovereign of Maine and of Normandy."

The record of the Breton forests from 1792 to 1800 would form a history of itself, mingling like a legend with the vast undertaking of the Vendée. History has its truth: Legend has hers. Legendary truth is wholly different from historic; legendary truth is invention that has reality for a result. Still history and legend have the same aim,— that of depicting the external type of humanity.

La Vendée can only be completely understood by adding legend to history; the latter is needed to describe its entirety, the former the details. We may say, too, that La Vendée is worth the pains. La Vendée was a prodigy.

This war of the Ignorant, so stupid and so splendid, so abject yet magnificent, was at once the desolation and the pride of France. La Vendée is a wound which is at the same time a glory.

At certain crises human society has its enigmas,— enigmas which resolve themselves into light for sages, but which the ignorant in their darkness translate into violence and barbarism. The philosopher is slow to accuse; he takes into consideration the agitation caused by these problems, which cannot pass without casting about them shadows dark as those of the storm-cloud.

If one wish to comprehend Vendée, one must picture to one's self this antagonism: on one side the French Revolution, on the other the Breton peasant. In face of these unparalleled events — an immense promise of all benefits at once, a fit of rage for civilization, an excess of maddened

progress, an improvement that exceeded measure and com-
prehension — must be placed this grave, strange, savage man,
with an eagle glance and flowing hair; living on milk and
chestnuts; his ideas bounded by his thatched roof, his hedge,
and his ditch, able to distinguish the sound of each village bell in the neighbourhood; using water only to drink;
wearing a leather jacket covered with silken arabesques, un-
cultivated but clad embroidered; tattooing his garments as
his ancestors the Celts had tattooed their faces; looking up
to a master in his executioner; speaking a dead language,
which was like forcing his thoughts to dwell in a tomb;
driving his bullocks, sharpening his scythe, winnowing his
black grain, kneading his buckwheat biscuit; venerating his
plough first, his grandmother next; believing in the Blessed
Virgin and the White Lady; devoted to the altar, but also
to the lofty mysterious stone standing in the midst of the
moor; a labourer in the plain, a fisher on the coast, a poacher
in the thicket; loving his kings, his lords, his priests, his
very lice; pensive, often immovable for entire hours upon
the great deserted sea-shore, a melancholy listener to the
sea.

Then ask yourself if it would have been possible for this
blind man to welcome that light.

CHAPTER II

THE PEASANTS

THE peasant had two points on which he leaned,— the
field which nourished him, the wood which concealed
him.

It is difficult to picture to one's self what those Breton
forests really were. They were towns. Nothing could be
more secret, more silent, and more savage than those inextri-

12

cable entanglements of thorns and branches; those vast thickets were the home of immobility and silence; no solitude could present an appearance more death-like and sepulchral. Yet if it had been possible to fell those trees at one blow, as by a flash of lightning, a swarm of men would have stood revealed in those shades. There were wells, round and narrow, masked by coverings of stones and branches, the interior at first vertical, then horizontal, spreading out underground like funnels, and ending in dark chambers. Cambyses found such in Egypt, and Westermann found the same in Brittany. There they were found in the desert, here in the forest; the caves of Egypt held dead men, the caves of Brittany were filled with the living. One of the wildest glades of the wood of Misdon, perforated by galleries and cells amid which came and went a mysterious society, was called "the great city." Another glade, not less deserted above ground and not less inhabited beneath, was styled "the place royal."

This subterranean life had existed in Brittany from time immemorial. From the the earliest days man had there hidden, flying from man. Hence those hiding-places, like the dens of reptiles, hollowed out below the trees. They dated from the era of the Druids, and certain of those crypts were as ancient as the cromlechs. The larvæ of legend and the monsters of history all passed across that shadowy land,— Toutates, Cæsar, Höel, Neomenes, Geoffrey of England, Alain of the iron glove, Pierre Manclerc; the French house of Blois, the English house of Montfort; kings and dukes, the nine barons of Brittany, the judges of the Great Days, the Counts of Nantes contesting with the Counts of Rennes; highwaymen, banditti, Free Lances; René II., Viscount de Rohan; the governors for the king; "the good Duke of Chaulnes," hanging the peasants under the windows of Madame de Sévigné; in the fifteenth century the butcheries by the nobles, in the sixteenth and seventeenth centuries the wars of religion, in the eighteenth century the thirty thousand dogs trained to hunt men. Beneath these pitiless tramplings the inhabitants made up their minds to disappear. Each in turn — the

Troglodytes to escape the Celts, the Celts to escape the
Romans, the Bretons to escape the Normans, the Huguenots
to escape the Roman Catholics, the smugglers to escape the
excise officers — took refuge first in the forest and then
underground, the resource of hunted animals.   It is this to
which tyranny reduces nations.   During two thousand years
despotism under all its forms — conquest, feudality, fanaticism, taxes — beset this wretched, distracted Brittany: a sort
of inexorable battue, which only ceased under one shape to
recommence under another.   Men hid underground.   When
the French Republic burst forth, Terror, which is a species of
rage, was already latent in human souls, and when the Republic burst forth, the dens were ready in the woods.   Brittany
revolted, finding itself oppressed by this forced deliverance,
— a mistake natural to slaves.

CHAPTER III

CONNIVANCE OF MEN AND FORESTS

THE gloomy Breton forests took up anew their ancient
rôle, and were the servants and accomplices of this rebellion, as they had been of all others.   The subsoil of every
forest was a sort of madrepore, pierced and traversed in all
directions by a secret highway of mines, cells, and galleries.
Each one of these blind cells could shelter five or six men.
There are in existence certain strange lists which enable one
to understand the powerful organization of that vast peasant
rebellion.   In Ille-et-Vilaine, in the forest of Pertre, the
refuge of the Prince de Talmont, not a breath was heard, not a
human trace to be found, yet there were collected six thousand men under Focard.   In the forest of Meulac, in Morbihan, not a soul was to be seen, yet it held eight thousand
men.   Still, these two forests, Pertre and Meulac, do not

count among the great Breton forests. If one trod there, the explosion was terrible. Those hypocritical copses, filled with fighters waiting in a sort of underground labyrinth, were like enormous black sponges whence, under the pressure of the gigantic foot of Revolution, civil war spurted out. Invisible battalions lay there in wait. These untrackable armies wound along beneath the republican troops; burst suddenly forth from the earth and sank into it again; sprang up in numberless force and vanished at will; gifted with a strange ubiquity and power of disappearance, an avalanche at one instant, gone like a cloud of dust at the next; colossal, yet able to become pygmies at will; giants in battle, dwarfs in ability to conceal themselves, jaguars with the habits of moles.

There were not only the forests, there were the woods. Just as below cities there are villages, below these forests there were woods and underwoods. The forests were united by the labyrinths (everywhere scattered) of the woods. The ancient castles, which were fortresses; the hamlets, which were camps; the farms, which were enclosures for ambushes and snares, traversed by ditches and palisaded by trees,— were the meshes of the net in which the republican armies were caught.

This whole formed what is called the " Bocage."

There was the wood of Misdon, which had a pond in its centre, and which was held by Jean Chouan. There was the wood of Gennes, which belonged to Taillefer. There was the wood of Huisserie, which belonged to Gouge-le-Bruant; the wood of Charnie, where lurked Courtillé-le-Batard, called Saint-Paul, chief of the camp of the Vache Noire; the wood of Burgault, which was held by that enigmatical Monsieur Jacques, reserved for a ·mysterious end in the vault of Juvardeil.

There was the wood of Charreau, where Pimousse and Petit-Prince, when attacked by the garrison of Château-neuf, rushed forward and seized the grenadiers in the republican ranks about the waist and carried them back prisoners; the wood of La Heureuserie, the witness of the rout of

the military post of Longue-Faye; the wood of Aulne, whence
the route between Rennes and Laval could be overlooked;
the wood of La Gravelle, which a prince of La Trémoille
had won at a game of bowls; the wood of Lorges, in
the Cotes-du-Nord, where Charles de Boishardy reigned after
Bernard de Villeneuve; the wood of Bagnard, near Fontenay,
where Lescure offered battle to Chalbos, who accepted the
challenge, although one against five; the wood of La Duron-
dais, which in old days had been disputed by Alain le Redru
and Hérispoux, the son of Charles the Bald; the wood of
Croqueloup, upon the edge of that moor where Coquereau
sheared the prisoners; the wood of Croix-Bataille, which witnessed the Homeric insults of Jambe d'Argent to Morière and
of Morière to Jambe d'Argent; the wood of La Saudraie,
which we have seen being searched by a Paris regiment. There
were many others besides.   In several of these forests and
woods there were not only subterranean villages grouped
about the burrow of the chief, but also actual hamlets of low
huts, hidden under the trees, sometimes so numerous that the
forest was filled with them.   Frequently they were betrayed
by the smoke.   Two of these hamlets of the wood of Misdon
have remained famous,— Lorrière, near Létang, and the
group of cabins called the Rue de Bau, on the side toward
Saint-Ouen-les-Toits.

The women lived in the huts, and the men in the cellars.
In carrying on the war they utilized the galleries of the
fairies and the old Celtic mines.   Food was carried to the
buried men.   Some were forgotten, and died of hunger; but
these were awkward fellows, who had not known how to open
the mouth of their well.   Usually the cover, made of moss
and branches, was so artistically fashioned that, although impossible on the outside to distinguish from the surrounding
turf, it was very easy to open and close on the inside.   These
hiding places were dug with care.   The earth taken out of
the well was flung into some neighbouring pond.   The sides
and the bottom were carpeted with ferns and moss.   These
nooks were called " lodges."   The men were as comfortable

there as could be expected, considering that they lacked light, fire, bread, and air.

It was a difficult matter to unbury themselves and come up among the living without great precaution. They might find themselves between the legs of an army on the march. These were formidable woods, snares with a double trap; the Blues dared not enter, the Whites dared not come out.

CHAPTER IV

THEIR LIFE UNDERGROUND

THE men grew weary of their wild-beast lairs. Sometimes in the night they came forth at any risk, and went to dance upon the neighbouring moor; else they prayed, in order to kill time. " Every day," says Bourdoiseau, " Jean Chouan made us count our rosaries."

It was almost impossible to keep those of the Bas-Maine from going out for the Fête de la Gerbe when the season came. Some of them had ideas peculiar to themselves. " Denys," says Tranche Montagne, " disguised himself as a woman, in order to go to the theatre at Laval, then went back into his hole." Suddenly they would rush forth in search of death, exchanging the dungeon for the sepulchre. Sometimes they raised the cover of their trench, and listened to hear if there were fighting in the distance; they followed the combat with their ears. The firing of the republicans was regular; the firing of the royalists, open and dropping,— this guided them. If the platoon-firing ceased suddenly, it was a sign that the royalists were defeated; if the irregular firing continued, and retreated toward the horizon, it was a sign that they had the advantage. The Whites always pursued; the Blues never, because they had the country against them.

These underground belligerents were kept perfectly informed of what was going on. Nothing could be more rapid, nothing more mysterious, than their means of communication. They had cut all the bridges, broken up all the wagons; yet they found means to tell each other everything, to give each other timely warning. Relays of emissaries were established from forest to forest, from village to village, from farm to farm, from cottage to cottage, from bush to bush. A peasant with a stupid air passed by: he carried dispatches in his hollow stick. An ancient constituent, Boétidoux, furnished them, to pass from one end of Brittany to the other, with republican passports according to the new form, with blanks for the names, of which this traitor had bundles. It was impossible to discover these emissaries. Says Puysaye: " The secrets confided to more than four hundred thousand individuals were religiously guarded."

It appeared that this quadrilateral — closed on the south by the line of the Sables to Thouars, on the east by the line of Thouars to Saumur and the river of Thoué, on the north by the Loire, and on the west by the ocean — possessed everywhere the same nervous activity, and not a single point of this soil could stir without shaking the whole. In the twinkling of an eye Luçon had information in regard to Noirmoutier, and the camp of La Loué knew what the camp of Croix-Morineau was doing. It seemed as if the very birds of the air carried tidings. The 7th Messidor, Year III., Hoche wrote: " One might believe that they have telegraphs." They were in clans, as in Scotland; each parish had its captain. In that war my father fought, and I can speak advisedly thereof.

CHAPTER V

THEIR LIFE IN WARFARE

MANY of them were only armed with pikes. Good fowl-ing-pieces were abundant. No marksmen could be more expert than the poachers of the Bocage and the smugglers of the Loroux. They were strange combatants, terrible and intrepid.

The decree for the levy of three hundred thousand men had been the signal for the tocsin to sound in six hundred villages. The blaze of the conflagration burst forth in all quarters at the same time. Poitou and Anjou exploded on one day. Let us add that a premonitory rumbling had made itself heard on the moor of Kerbader upon the 8th of July, 1792, a month before the 10th of August. Alain Redeler, to-day forgotten, was the precusor of La Rochejacquelein and Jean Chouan. The royalists forced all able-bodied men to march under pain of death. They requisitioned harnesses, carts, and provisions. At once Sapinaud had three thousand soldiers, Cathelineau ten thousand, Stofflet twenty thousand, and Charette was master of Noirmoutier. The Viscount de Scépeaux roused the Haut Anjou; the Chevalier de Dieuzie, the Entre Vilaine et Loire; Tristan l'Hermite, the Bas-Maine; the barber Gaston, the city of Guéménée; and Abbé Bernier all the rest.

It needed but little to rouse all those multitudes. In the altar of a priest who had taken the oath to the republic — a " priest swearer," as the people said — was placed a great black cat, which sprang suddenly out during Mass. " It is the devil!" cried the peasants, and a whole canton rose in revolt. A breath of fire issued from the confessionals. In order to attack the Blues and to leap the ravines, they had their poles fifteen feet in length, called *ferte*, an arm available for combat and for flight. In the thickest of the frays, when the peasants were attacking the republican squares if they ╵hanced to meet upon the battle-field a cross or a chapel, all fell upon their knees and said a prayer under the enemy's fire; the rosary counted, such as were still living sprang up again and rushed upon the foe! Alas, what giants! They loaded their guns as they ran; that was their peculiar talent. They were made to believe whatever their leaders chose. The priests showed them other priests whose necks had been reddened by means of a cord, and said to them, "These are the guillotined who have been brought back to life." They had their spasms of chivalry: they honoured Fesque, a republican standard-bearer, who allowed himself to be sabred without losing hold of his flag. The peasants had a vein of mockery: they called the republican and married priests "Des sans-calottes devenus sans-culottes!" ("The unpetticoated become the un-breeched.")

They began by being afraid of the cannon, then they dashed forward with their sticks and took them. They captured first a fine bronze cannon, which they baptized "The Missionary;" then another which dated from the Roman Catholic wars, upon which were engraved the arms of Riche-lieu and a head of the Virgin; this they named "Marie Jeanne." When they lost Fontenay they lost Marie Jeanne, about which six hundred peasants fell without flinching; then they retook Fontenay in order to recover Marie Jeanne: they brought it back beneath a *fleur-de-lis* embroidered banner, and covered with flowers, and forced the women who passed to kiss it. But two cannon were a small store. Stofflet had taken Marie Jeanne; Cathelineau, jealous of his success, started out of Pin-en-Mange, assaulted Jallais, and captured a third. Forest attacked Saint-Florent and took a fourth. Two other captains, Chouppes and Saint Pol, did better; they simu-lated cannon by the trunks of trees, gunners by mannikins, and with this artillery, about which they laughed heartily, made the Blues retreat to Mareuil. This was their great era. Later, when Chalbos routed La Marsonnière, the peasants left behind them on the dishonoured field of battle thirty-two can-non bearing the arms of England. England at that time paid the French princes, and as Nantiat wrote on the 10th of May,

1794, " sent funds to Monseigneur, because Pitt had been told that it was proper so to do."

Mellinet, in a report of the 31st of March, said, " Long live the English! " is the cry of the rebels. The peasants delayed themselves by pillage. These devotees were robbers. Savages have their vices. It is by these that civilization captures them later. Puysaye says: [1] " I several times preserved the burg of Phélan from pillage." And further on,[2] he recounts how he avoided entering Montfort: " I made a circuit in order to prevent the plundering of the Jacobins' houses."

They robbed Cholet; they sacked Challans. After having failed at Granville, they pillaged Ville-Dieu. They styled the " Jacobin herd " those of the country people who had joined the Blues, and exterminated such with more ferocity than other foes. They loved battle like soldiers, and massacre like brigands. To shoot the " clumsy fellows "— that is, the *bourgeois* — pleased them; they called that " breaking Lent."

At Fontenay, one of their priests, the Curé Barbotin, struck down an old man by a sabre stroke. At Saint-Germain-sur-Ille, one of their captains, a nobleman, shot the solicitor of the commune and took his watch. At Machecoul, for five weeks they shot republicans at the rate of thirty a day, setting them in a row, which was called " the rosary." Back of the line was a trench, into which some of the victims fell alive; they were buried all the same. We have seen a revival of such actions. Joubert, the President of the district, had his hands sawed off. They put sharp handcuffs, forged expressly, on the Blues whom they made prisoners. They massacred them in the public places, with the hunting cry, " In at the death! "

Charette, who signed " Fraternity, the Chevalier Charette," and who wore for head-covering a handkerchief knotted about his brows after Marat's fashion, burned the city of Pornic, and the inhabitants in their houses. During that time Carrier was horrible. Terror replied to terror. The Breton insurgent had almost the appearance of a Greek rebel, with his

[1] Vol. ii. p. 187.   [2] ibid., p. 434.

short jacket, his gun slung over his shoulder, his leggings, and large breeches similar to the fustanella. The peasant lad resembled the klepht.

Henri de la Rochejacquelein, at the age of one-and-twenty, set out for this war armed with a stick and a pair of pistols. The Vendean army counted a hundred and fifty-four divisions. They undertook regular sieges; they held Bressuire invested for three days. One Good Friday ten thousand peasants cannonaded the town of Sables with red-hot balls. They succeeded in a single day in destroying fourteen republican cantons, from Montigné to Courbeveilles. On the high wall of Thouars this dialogue was heard between La Rochejacquelein and a peasant lad as they stood below:—

" Charles ! "

" Here I am."

" Stand so that I can mount on your shoulders."

" Jump up."

" Your gun."

" Take it."

And Rochejacquelein leaped into the town, and the towers which Duguesclin had besieged were taken without the aid of ladders.

They preferred a cartridge to a gold louis. They wept when they lost sight of their village belfry. To run away seemed perfectly natural to them; at such times the leaders would cry: " Throw off your sabots, but keep your guns." When munitions were wanting, they counted their rosaries and rushed forth to seize the powder in the caissons of the republican artillery; later; D'Elbée demanded powder from the English. If they had wounded men among them, at the approach of the enemy they concealed these in the grain-fields or among the ferns, and went back in search of them when the fight was ended. They had no uniforms. Their garments were torn to bits. Peasants and nobles wrapped themselves in any rags they could find. Roger Mouliniers wore a turban and a pelisse taken from the wardrobe of the theatre of La Flèche; the Chevalier de Beauvilliers wore a barrister's gown, and set a woman's bonnet on his head over a woollen cap. All wore the white belt and a scarf; different grades were marked by the knots; Stofflet had a red knot; La Rochejacquelein had a black knot; Wimpfen, who was half a Girondist, and who for that matter never left Normandy, wore the leather jacket of the Carabots of Caen. They had women in their ranks,— Madame de Lescure, who became Madame de la Rochejacquelein; Thérèse de Mollien, the mistress of La Rouarie (she who burned the list of the chiefs of the parishes); Madame de la Rochefoucauld (beautiful, young), who, sabre in hand, rallied the peasants at the foot of the great tower of the castle of Puy Rousseau; and that Antoinette Adams, styled the Chevalier Adams, who was so brave that when captured she was shot standing, out of respect for her courage.

This epic period was a cruel one. Men were mad. Madame de Lescure made her horse tread upon the republicans stretched on the ground: *dead*, she averred,— only wounded perhaps. Sometimes the men proved traitors; the women never. Mademoiselle Fleury, of the Théâtre Français, went from La Rouarie to Marat; but it was for love. The captains were often as ignorant as the soldiers. Monsieur de Sapinaud could not spell; he was at fault in regard to the orthography of the commonest word. There was enmity among the leaders; the captains of the Marais cried, " Down with those of the High Country! " Their cavalry was not numerous, and difficult to form. Puysaye writes: " Many a man who would cheerfully give me his two sons grows lukewarm if I ask for one of his horses." Poles, pitchforks, reaping-hooks, guns, old and new, poachers' knives, spits, cudgels bound and studded with iron,— these were their arms; some of them carried slung round them crosses made of dead men's bones. They rushed to an attack with loud cries, springing up suddenly from every quarter, from the woods, the hills, the bushes, the hollows of the roads,— killing, exterminating, destroying; then were gone. When they marched through a republican town they cut down the liberty pole, set it on fire, and danced in circles about it as it burned. All their habits were nocturnal. The Vendean rule was always to appear unexpectedly. They would march fifteen leagues in silence, not so much as stirring a blade of grass as they went. When evening came, after the chiefs had settled what republican posts should be surprised on the morrow, the men loaded their guns, mumbled their prayers, pulled off their sabots, and filed in long columns through the woods, marching barefoot across the heath and moss, without a sound, without a word, without a breath. It was like the march of cats through the darkness.

CHAPTER VI

THE SPIRIT OF THE PLACE PASSES INTO THE MAN

THE Vendée in insurrection did not number less than five hundred thousand, counting men, women, and children. A half-million of combatants is the sum total given by Tuffin de la Rouarie.

The federalists helped them; the Vendée had the Gironde for accomplice. La Lozère sent thirty thousand men into the Bocage. Eight departments coalesced,— five in Brittany, three in Normandy. Evreux, which fraternized with Caen, was represented in the rebellion by Chaumont its mayor, and Gardembas a man of note. Buzot, Gorsas, and Barbaroux at Caen, Brissot at Moulins, Chassan at Lyons, Rabaut-Saint-Etienne at Nismes, Meillen and Duchâtel in Brittany,— all these mouths blew the furnace.

There were two Vendées,— the great, which carried on the war of the forests; and the little, which waged the war of the thickets. It is that shade which separates Charette from Jean Chouan. The little Vendée was honest, the great corrupt; the little was much better. Charette was made a marquis, lieutenant-general of the king's armies, and received the great cross of Saint Louis, Jean Chouan remained Jean Chouan.

Charette borders on the bandit; Jean Chouan on the paladin.

As to the magnanimous chiefs Bonchamps, Lescure, La Rochejacquelein,— they deceived themselves. The grand Catholic army was an insane attempt; disaster could not fail to follow it. Let any one imagine a tempest of peasants attacking Paris, a coalition of villages besieging the Pantheon, a troop of herdsmen flinging themselves upon a host governed by the light of intellect. Le Mans and Savenay chastised this madness. It was impossible for the Vendée to cross the Loire; she could do everything except that leap. Civil war does not conquer. To pass the Rhine establishes a Cæsar and strengthens a Napoleon; to cross the Loire killed La Rochejacquelein. The real strength of Vendée was Vendée at home; there she was invulnerable, unconquerable. The Vendean at home was smuggler, labourer, soldier, shepherd, poacher, sharp-shooter, goatherd, bell-ringer, peasant, spy, assassin, sacristan, wild beast of the wood.

La Rochejacquelein is only Achilles; Jean Chouan is Proteus.

The rebellion of the Vendée failed. Other revolts have succeeded,— that of Switzerland, for example. There is this difference between the mountain insurgent like the Swiss and the forest insurgent like the Vendean,— that almost always the one fights for an ideal, the other for a prejudice. The one soars, the other crawls; the one combats for humanity, the other for solitude; the one desires liberty, the other wishes isolation; the one defends the commune, the other the parish, — " Communes! Communes!" cried the heroes of Morat; the one has to deal with precipices, the other with quagmires; the one is the man of torrents and foaming streams, the other of stagnant puddles where pestilence lurks; the one has his head in the blue sky, the other in the thicket; the one is on a summit, the other in a shadow.

The education of heights and shallows is very different. The mountain is a citadel; the forest is an ambuscade: one inspires audacity, the other teaches trickery. Antiquity placed the gods on heights and the satyrs in copses. The satyr is the savage, half man, half brute. Free countries have Apennines, Alps, Pyrenees, and Olympus. Parnassus is a mountain. Mont Blanc is the colossal auxiliary of William Tell. Below and above those immense struggles of souls against the night which fills the poems of India, the Himalayas may be seen. Greece, Spain, Italy, Helvetia have for their likeness the mountain; Cimmeria, Germany, Brittany has the wood. The forest is barbarous.

The configuration of soil decides many of man's actions. The earth is more his accomplice than people believe. In presence of certain savage landscapes one is tempted to exonerate man and criminate creation. One feels a certain hidden provocation on the part of Nature; the desert is sometimes unhealthy for the conscience, especially for the conscience that is little illuminated. Conscience may be a giant, — then she produces a Socrates, a Christ; she may be a dwarf, — then she moulds Atreus and Judas. The narrow conscience becomes quickly reptile in its instincts: forests where twilight reigns; the bushes, the thorns, the marshes beneath the branches,— all have a fatal attraction for her; she undergoes the mysterious infiltration of evil persuasions. Optical illusions, unexplained mirages, the terrors of the hour or the scene, throw man into this sort of fright,— half religious, half bestial, which engenders superstition in ordinary times, and brutality at violent epochs. Hallucinations hold the torch which lights the road to murder. The brigand is dizzied by a vertigo. Nature in her immensity has a double meaning, which dazzles great minds and blinds savage souls. When man is ignorant, when his desert is peopled with visions, the obscurity of solitude adds itself to the obscurity of intelligence; hence come depths in the human soul, black and profound as an abyss. Certain rocks, certain ravines, certain thickets, certain wild openings in the trees through which night looks down, push men on to mad and atrocious actions. One might almost say that there are places which are the home of the spirit of evil. How many tragic sights have been watched by the sombre hill between Baignon and Phélan! Vast horizons lead the soul on to wide, general ideas; circumscribed horizons engender narrow, one-sided conceptions, which condemn great hearts to be little in point of soul. Jean Chouan was an example of this truth. Broad ideas are hated by partial ideas; this is in fact the struggle of progress.

Neighbourhood, country,— these two words sum up the whole of the Vendean war: a quarrel of the local idea against the universal; of the peasant against the patriot.

CHAPTER VII

LA VENDÉE ENDED BRITTANY

BRITTANY is an ancient rebel. Each time she revolted during two thousand years she was in the right; but the last time she was wrong. Still, at bottom (against the revolution as against monarchy, against the acting Representatives as against governing dukes and peers, against the rule of assignats as against the sway of excise officers, whosoever might be the men that fought, Nicolas Rapin, François de la Noue, Captain Pluviaut, the Lady of La Garnache or Stofflet, Coquereau, and Lechandelier de Pierreville; under De Rohan against the king, and under La Rochejacquelein for the king) it was always the same war that Brittany waged,— the war of the Local Spirit against the Central. Those ancient provinces were ponds; that stagnant water could not bear to flow; the wind which swept across did not revivify,— it irritated them.

Finistère formed the bounds of France: there the space given to man ended, and the march of generations stopped. "Halt!" the ocean cried to the land, to barbarism and to civilization. Each time that the centre — Paris — gives an impulse, whether that impulse come from royalty or republicanism, whether it be in the interest of despotism or liberty, it is something new, and Brittany bristles up against it.

"Leave us in peace! What is it they want of us?" The Marais seizes the pitchfork, the Bocage its carbine. All our attempts, our initiative movement in legislation and in education, our encyclopedias, our philosophies, our genius, our glories, all fail before the Houroux; the tocsin of Bazouges menaces the French Revolution, the moor of Faou rises in rebellion against the voice of our towns, and the bell of the Haut-des-Prés declares war against the Tower of the Louvre.

Terrible blindness! The Vendean insurrection was the result of a fatal misunderstanding.

A colossal scuffle, a jangling of Titans, an immeasurable rebellion, destined to leave in history only one word,— the Vendée,— word illustrious yet dark; committing suicide for the absent, devoted to egotism, passing its time in making to cowardice the offer of a boundless bravery; without calculation, without strategy, without tactics, without plan, without aim, without chief, without responsibility; showing to what extent Will can be impotent; chivalric and savage; absurdity at its climax, a building up a barrier of black shadows against the light; ignorance making a long resistance at once idiotic and superb against justice, right, reason, and deliverance; the terror of eight years, the rendering desolate fourteen departments, the devastation of fields, the destruction of harvests, the burning of villages, the ruin of cities, the pillage of houses, the massacre of women and children, the torch in the thatch, the sword in the heart, the terror of civilization, the hope of Mr. Pitt,— such was this war, the unreasoning effort of the parricide.

In short, by proving the necessity of perforating in every direction the old Breton shadows, and piercing this thicket with arrows of light from every quarter at once, the Vendée served Progress. The catastrophes had their uses.

13

BOOK II

THE THREE CHILDREN

CHAPTER I

PLUSQUAM CIVILIA BELLA

THE summer of 1792 had been very rainy; the summer of 1793 was dry and hot. In consequence of the civil war, there were no roads left, so to speak, in Brittany. Still it was possible to get about, thanks to the beauty of the season. Dry fields make an easy route.

At the close of a lovely July day, about an hour before sunset, a man on horseback, who came from the direction of Avranches, drew rein before the little inn called the Croix-Branchard, which stood at the entrance of Pontorson, and which for years past had borne this inscription on its sign: "Good cider on draught." It had been warm all day, but the wind was beginning now to rise.

The traveller was enveloped in an ample cloak which covered the back of his horse. He wore a broad hat with a tricoloured cockade, which was a sufficiently bold thing to do in this country of hedges and gunshots, where a cockade was a target. The cloak, fastened about his neck, was thrown back to leave his arms free, and beneath glimpses could be had of a tricoloured sash and two pistols thrust in it. A sabre hung down below the cloak.

At the sound of the horse's hoofs the door of the inn

opened and the landlord appeared, a lantern in his hand. It was the intermediate hour between day and night: still light along the highway, but dark in the house. The host looked at the cockade.

" Citizen," said he, " do you stop here? "

" No."

" Where are you going, then? "

" To Dol."

" In that case go back to Avranches or remain at Pontorson."

" Why? "

" Because there is fighting at Dol."

" Ah! " said the horseman.

Then he added,—

" Give my horse some oats."

The host brought the trough, emptied a measure of oats into it, and took the bridle off the horse, which began to snuff and eat.

The dialogue continued:—

" Citizen, has that horse been seized? "

" No."

" It belongs to you? "

" Yes. I bought and paid for it."

" Where do you come from? "

" Paris."

" Not direct? "

" No."

" I should think not! The roads are closed, but the post runs still."

" As far as Alençon. I left it there."

" Ah! Very soon there will be no longer any posts in France. There are no more horses. A horse worth three hundred livres costs six hundred, and fodder is beyond all price. I have been postmaster, and now I am keeper of a cookshop. Out of thirteen hundred and thirteen postmasters that there used to be, two hundred have resigned. Citizen, you travelled according to the new tariff? "

" That of the 1st of May — yes."

" Twenty sous a post for a carriage, twelve for a gig, five sous for a van.   You bought your horse at Alençon? "

" Yes."

" You have ridden all day? "

" Since dawn."

" And yesterday? "

" And the day before."

" I can see that.   You came by Domfront and Mortain."

" And Avranches."

" Take my advice, citizen; rest yourself.   You must be tired.   Your horse is certainly."

" Horses have a right to be tired; men have not."

The host again fixed his eyes on the traveller, whose face was grave, calm, and severe, and framed by grey hair.

The innkeeper cast a glance along the road, which was deserted as far as the eye could reach, and said,—

" And you travel alone in this fashion? "

" I have an escort."

" Where is it? "

" My sabre and pistols."

The innkeeper brought a bucket of water, and while the horse was drinking, studied the traveller, and said mentally: " All the same, he has the look of a priest."

The horseman resumed: " You say there is fighting at Dol? "

" Yes.   That ought to be about beginning."

" Who is fighting? "

" One *ci-devant* against another *ci-devant*."

" You said —"

" I say that an ex-noble who is for the Republic is fighting against another ex-noble who is for the king."

" But there is no longer a king."

" There is the little fellow!   The odd part of the business is that these two *ci-devants* are relations."

The horseman listened attentively.   The innkeeper continued:—

" One is young, the other old.   It is the grand-nephew who
fights the great-uncle.   The uncle is a royalist, the nephew a
patriot.   The uncle commands the Whites, the nephew commands the Blues.   Ah, they will show no quarter, I'll warrant
you.   It is a war to the death."

" Death? "

" Yes, citizen.   Hold! would you like to see the compliments
they fling at each other's heads?   Here is a notice the old
man finds means to placard everywhere, on all the houses and
all the trees, and that he has had stuck up on my very door."

The host held up his lantern to a square of paper fastened
on a panel of the double door, and as the placard was written
in large characters, the traveller could read it as he sat on his
horse:—

" The Marquis de Lantenac has the honour of informing his grand-
nephew, the Viscount Gauvain, that, if the Marquis has the good
fortune to seize his person, he will cause the Viscount to be decently
shot."

" Here," added the host, " is the reply."

He went forward, and threw the light of the lantern upon
a second placard placed on a level with the first upon the other
leaf of the door.   The traveller read:—

" Gauvain warns Lantenac that, if he take him, he will have him
shot."

" Yesterday," said the host, " the first placard was stuck on
my door, and this morning the second.   There was no waiting for the answer."

The traveller in a half-voice, and as if speaking to himself,
uttered these words, which the innkeeper heard without really
comprehending,—

" Yes; this is more than war in the country; it is war in
families.   It is necessary, and it is well.   The grand restora-
tion of the people must be bought at this price."

And the traveller raised his hand to his hat and saluted the
second placard, on which his eyes were still fixed.

The host continued:—

" So, citizen, you understand how the matter lies. In the cities and the large towns we are for the Revolution, in the country they are against it; that is to say, in the towns people are Frenchmen, and in the villages they are Bretons. It is a war of the townspeople against the peasants. They call us clowns, we call them boors. The nobles and the priests are with them."

" Not all," interrupted the horseman.

" Certainly not, citizen, since we have here a viscount against a marquis."

Then he added to himself: " And I feel sure I am speaking to a priest."

The horseman continued: " And which of the two has the best of it? "

" The viscount so far. But he has to work hard. The old man is a tough one. They belong to the Gauvain family,— nobles of these parts. It is a family with two branches: there is the great branch, whose chief is called the Marquis de Lantenac! and there is the lesser branch, whose head is called the Viscount Gauvain. To-day the two branches fight each other. One does not see that among trees, but one sees it among men. This Marquis de Lantenac is all-powerful in Brittany; the peasants consider him a prince. The very day he landed, eight thousand men joined him; in a week, three hundred parishes had risen. If he had been able to get foothold on the coast, the English would have landed. Luckily this Gauvain was at hand,— the other's grand-nephew: odd chance! He is the republican commander, and he has checkmated his grand-uncle. And then, as good luck would have it, when this Lantenac arrived, and was massacring a heap of prisoners, he had two women shot, one of whom had three children that had been adopted by a Paris battalion. And that made a terrible battalion; they call themselves the Battalion of the Bonnet Rouge. There are not many of those Parisians left, but they are furious bayonets. They have been incorporated into the division of Commandant Gauvain;

NINETY-THREE 199

nothing can stand against them. They mean to avenge the
women and retake the children. Nobody knows what the old
man has done with the little ones: that is what enraged the
Parisian grenadiers. Suppose those babies had not been mixed
up in the matter, the war would not be what it is. The viscount is a good, brave young man; but the old fellow is a
terrible marquis. The peasants call it the war of Saint
Michael against Beelzebub. You know, perhaps, that Saint
Michel is an angel of the district; there is a mountain named
after him out in the bay; they say he overcame the demon,
and buried him under another mountain near here, which is
called Tombelaine."

"Yes," murmured the horseman; "Tumba Beleni, the tomb
of Belenus,— Belus, Bel, Belial, Beelzebub."

"I see that you are well informed." And the host again
spoke to himself: "He understands Latin! Decidedly he is
a priest." Then he resumed: "Well, citizen, for the peasants it is that war beginning over again. For them the royalist general is Saint Michael, and Beelzebub is the republican
commander. But if there is a devil, it is certainly Lantenac;
and if there is an angel, it is Gauvain. You will take nothing, citizen?"

"I have my gourd and a bit of bread. But you do not tell
me what is passing at Dol!"

"This. Gauvain commands the exploring column of the
coast. Lantenac's aim was to rouse a general insurrection,
and sustain Lower Brittany by the aid of Lower Normandy,
open the door to Pitt, and give a shove forward to the Vendean
army, with twenty thousand English, and two hundred thousand peasants. Gauvain cut this plan short: he holds the
coast, and he drives Lantenac into the interior and the English into the sea. Lantenac was here, and Gauvain has dislodged him; has taken from him the Pont-au-Beau, has driven
him out of Avranches, chased him out of Villedieu, and kept
him from reaching Granville. He is manœuvring to shut him
up again in the forest of Fougères, and to surround him.
Yesterday everything was going well; Gauvain was here with

his division. All of a sudden, an alarm! the old man, who is skilful, made a point; information comes that he hás marched on Dol. If he takes Dol, and establishes a battery on Mount Dol (for he has cannon), then there will be a place on the coast where the English can land, and everything is lost. That is why, as there was not a minute to lose, that Gauvain, who is a man with a head, took counsel with nobody but himself, asked no orders and waited for none, but sounded the signal to saddle, put to his artillery, collected his troop, drew his sabre, and while Lantenac throws himself on Dol, Gauvain throws himself on Lantenac. It is at Dol that these two Breton heads will knock together. There will be a fine shock. They are at it now."

" How long does it take to get to Dol? "

" At least three hours for a troop with cannon; but they are there now."

The traveller listened, and said: " In fact, I think I hear cannon."

The host listened. " Yes, citizen; and the musketry. They have opened the ball. You would do well to pass the night here. There will be nothing good to catch over there."

" I cannot stop. I must keep on my road."

" You are wrong. I do not know your business; but the risk is great, and unless it concern what you hold dearest in the world —"

" In truth, it is that which is concerned," said the cavalier.

" Something like your son —"

" Very nearly that," said the cavalier.

The innkeeper raised his head, and said to himself.

" Still this citizen gives me the impression of being a priest." Then, after a little reflection: " All the same, a priest may have children."

" Put the bridle back on my horse," said the traveller. " How much do I owe you? " He paid the man.

The host set the trough and the bucket back against the wall, and returned toward the horseman. " Since you are determined to go, listen to my advice. It is clear that you are going to Saint Malo. Well, do not pass by Dol. There are two roads,— the road by Dol, and the road along the sea-shore. There is scarcely any difference in their length. The sea-shore road passes by Saint-Georges-de-Brehaigne, Cherrueix, and Hirèlle-Vivier. You leave Dol to the south and Cancale to the north. Citizen, at the end of the street you will find the branching off of the two routes; that of Dol is on the left, that of Saint-Georges-de-Brehaigne on the right. Listen well to me: if you go by Dol, you will fall into the middle of the massacre. That is why you must not take to the left, but to the right."

"Thanks," said the traveller. He spurred his horse forward. The obscurity was now complete; he hurried on into the night. The innkeeper lost sight of him.

When the traveller reached the end of the street where the two roads branched off, he heard the voice of the innkeeper calling to him from afar,—

"Take the right!"

He took the left.

CHAPTER II

DOL

DOL, a Spanish city of France in Brittany, as the guide-books style it, is not a town; it is a street,— a great old Gothic street, bordered all the way on the right and the left by houses with pillars, placed irregularly, so that they form nooks and elbows in the highway, which is nevertheless very wide. The rest of the town is only a network of lanes, attaching themselves to this great diametrical street, and pouring into it like brooks into a river. The city, without gates or walls, open, overlooked by Mount Dol, could not have sustained a siege; but the street might have sustained one. The promontories of houses, which were still to be seen fifty years back, and the two-pillared galleries which bordered the street, made a battle-ground that was very strong and capable of offering great resistance. Each house was a fortress in fact, and it would be necessary to take them one after another. The old market was very nearly in the middle of the street.

The innkeeper of the Croix-Branchard had spoken truly, — a mad conflict filled Dol at the moment he uttered the words. A nocturnal duel between the Whites, that morning arrived, and the Blues, who had come upon them in the evening, burst suddenly over the town. The forces were unequal: the Whites numbered six thousand; there were only fifteen hundred of the Blues. But there was equality in point of obstinate rage; strange to say, it was the fifteen hundred who had attacked the six thousand.

One one side a mob, on the other a phalanx. On one side six thousand peasants, with blessed medals on their leather vests, white ribbons on their round hats, Christian devices on their braces, chaplets at their belts, carrying more pitchforks than sabres, carbines without bayonets, dragging cannon with ropes; badly equipped, ill disciplined, poorly armed, but frantic. In opposition to them were fifteen hundred soldiers, wearing three-cornered hats, coats with large tails and wide lapels, shoulder-belts crossed, copper-hilted swords, and carrying guns with long bayonets. They were trained, skilled; docile, yet fierce; obeying like men who would know how to command: volunteers also, shoeless and in rags too, but volunteers for their country. On the side of Monarchy, peasants who were paladins; for the Revolution, barefooted heroes, and each troop possessing a soul in its leader: the royalists having an old man, the republicans a young one. On this side, Lantenac; on the other, Gauvain.

The Revolution, side by side with its faces of youthful giants like those of Danton, Saint-Just, and Robespierre, has faces of ideal youth, like those of Hoche and Marceau. Gauvain was one of these.

He was thirty years old; he had a Herculean bust, the

solemn eye of a prophet, and the laugh of a child. He did
not smoke, he did not drink, he did not swear. He carried a
dressing-case through the whole war; he took care of his nails,
his teeth, and his hair, which was dark and luxuriant. During halts he himself shook in the wind his military coat, riddled
with bullets and white with dust. Though always rushing
headlong into an affray, he had never been wounded. His
singularly sweet voice had at command the abrupt imperi-
ousness needed by a leader. He set the example of sleeping
on the ground, in the wind, the rain, and the snow, rolled in
his cloak and with his noble head pillowed on a stone. His
was a heroic and innocent soul. The sabre in his hand transfigured him. He had that effeminate air which in battle turns
into something formidable. With all that, a thinker and a
philosopher, a youthful sage,— Alcibiades in appearance,
Socrates in speech.

In that immense improvisation of the French Revolution
this young man had become at once a leader. His division,
formed by himself, was like a Roman legion, a kind of complete little army. It was composed of infantry and cavalry;
it had its scouts, its pioneers, its sappers, pontoniers; and as
a Roman legion had its catapults, this one had its cannon.
Three pieces, well mounted, rendered the column strong,
while leaving it easy to guide.

Lantenac was also a thorough soldier,— a more consummate
one. He was at the same time wary and hardy. Old heroes
have more cold determination than young ones, because they
are far removed from the warmth of life's morning; more
audacity, because they are near death. What have they to
lose? So very little. Hence the manœuvres of Lantenac
were at once rash and skilful. But in the main, and almost
always, in this dogged hand-to-hand conflict between the old
man and the young, Gauvain gained the advantage. It was
rather the work of fortune than anything else. All good
luck — even successes which are in themselves terrible — go to
youth. Victory is somewhat of a woman.

Lantenac was exasperated against Gauvain,— justly, because Gauvain fought against him; in the second place, because he was of his kindred.   What did he mean by turning Jacobin,— this Gauvain, this mischievous dog! his heir (for the marquis had no children), his grand-nephew, almost his grandson!   " Ah," said this quasi-grandfather, " if I put my hand on him, I will kill him like a dog! "

For that matter, the Revolution was right to disquiet itself in regard to this Marquis de Lantenac.   An earthquake followed his landing.   His name spread through the Vendean insurrection like a train of powder, and Lantenac at once became the centre.   In a revolt of that nature, where each is jealous of the other, and each has his thicket or ravine, the arrival of a superior rallies the scattered leaders who have been equals among themselves.   Nearly all the forest captains had joined Lantenac, and, whether near or far off, they obeyed him.   One man alone had departed; it was the first who had joined him,— Gavard.   Wherefore?   Because he had been a man of trust.   Gavard had known all the secrets and adopted all the plans of the ancient system of civil war; Lantenac appeared to replace and supplant him.   One does not inherit from a man of trust; the shoe of La Ronain did not fit Lantenac.   Gavard departed to join Bonchamp.

Lantenac, as a military man, belonged to the school of Frederick II.; he understood combining the great war with the little.   He would have neither a " confused mass " (like the great Catholic and Royal army), a crowd destined to be crushed, nor a troop of guerillas scattered among the hedges and copses,— good to harass, impotent to destroy.   Guerilla warfare finishes nothing, or finishes ill; it begins by attacking a republic and ends by rifling a diligence.   Lantenac did not comprehend this Breton war as the other chiefs had done,— neither as La Rochejacquelin, who was all for open country campaigns; nor as Jean Chouan, all for the forest.   He would have neither Vendée nor Chouannerie; he wanted real warfare: he would make use of the peasant, but he meant to depend on the soldier.   He wanted bands for strategy and regiments for tactics.   He found these village armies admirable for attack, for ambush and surprise, quickly gathered, quickly dispersed; but he felt that they lacked solidity,— they were like water in his hand. He wanted to create a solid base in this floating and diffused war; he wanted to join to the savage army of the forests regularly drilled troops that would make a pivot about which he could manœuvre the peasants. It was a profound and terrible conception; if it had succeeded, the Vendée would have been unconquerable.

But where find regular troops? Where look for soldiers, where seek for regiments, where discover an army ready made? In England. Hence Lantenac's determined idea,— to land the English. Thus the conscience of parties compromises with itself. The white cockade hid the red uniform from Lantenac's sight. He had only one thought,— to get possession of some point on the coast, and deliver it up to Pitt. That was why, seeing Dol defenceless, he flung himself upon it; the taking of the town would give him Mount Dol, and Mount Dol the coast.

The place was well chosen. The cannon of Mount Dol would sweep the Fresnois on one side and Saint-Brelade on the other; would keep the cruisers of Cancale at a distance, and leave the whole beach, from Raz-sur-Couesnon to Saint-Mêloir-des-Oudes, clear for an invasion. For the carrying out of this decisive attempt, Lantenac had brought with him only a little over six thousand men, the flower of the bands which he had at his disposal, and all his artillery,— ten sixteen-pound culverins, a demi-culverin, and a four-pounder. His idea was to establish a strong battery on Mount Dol, upon the principle that a thousand shots fired from ten cannon do more execution than fifteen hundred fired with five. Success appeared certain. They were six thousand men. Toward Avranches, they had only Gauvain and his fifteen hundred men to fear, and Léchelle in the direction of Dinan. It was true that Léchelle had twenty-five thousand men, but he was twenty leagues away. So Lantenac felt confidence! on Léchelle's side he put the great distance against the great numbers; with Gauvain, the size of the force against their propinquity. Let us add that Léchelle was an idiot, who later on allowed his twenty-five thousand men to be exterminated in the *landes* of the Croix-Bataille,— a blunder which he attoned for by suicide.

So Lantenac felt perfect security. His entrance into Dol was sudden and stern. The Marquis de Lantenac had a stern reputation; he was known to be without pity. No resistance was attempted. The terrified inhabitants barricaded themselves in their houses. The six thousand Vendeans installed themselves in the town with rustic confusion; it was almost like a fair-ground, without quartermasters, without allotted camp, bivouacking at hazard, cooking in the open air, scattering themselves among the churches, forsaking their guns for their rosaries. Lantenac went in haste with some artillery officers to reconnoitre Mount Dol, leaving the command to Gouge-le-Bruant, whom he had appointed field-sergeant.

This Gouge-le-Bruant has left a vague trace in history. He had two nicknames, Brise-bleu, on account of his massacre of patriots, and Imânus, because he had in him a something that was indescribably horrible. Imânus, derived from *imanis*, is an old bas-Norman word which expresses superhuman ugliness, something almost divine in its awfulness,— a demon, a satyr, an ogre. An ancient manuscript says, " With my two eyes I saw Imânus." The old people of the Bocage no longer know to-day who Gouge-le-Bruant was, nor what Brisebleu signifies; but they know, confusedly, Imânus. Imânus is mingled with the local superstitions; they talk of him still at Trémorel and at Plumaugat, two villages where Gouge-le-Bruant has left the trace of his sinister course. In the Vendée the others were savages; Gourge-le-Bruant was the barbarian. He was a species of cacique, tattooed with Christian crosses and *fleur-de-lis;* he had on his face the hideous, almost supernatural glare of a soul which no other human soul resembled. He was infernally brave in combat; atrocious afterward. His was a heart full of tortuous intricacies, capable of all forms of devotion, inclined to all madnesses. Did he reason? Yes; but as serpents crawl, in a twisted fashion.

He started from heroism to reach murder. It was impossible to divine whence his resolves came to him; they were sometimes grand from their very monstrosity. He was capable of every possible unexpected horror; his ferocity was epic. Hence his mysterious nickname, Imânus. The Marquis de Lantenac had confidence in his cruelty. It was true that Imânus excelled in cruelty, but in strategy and in tactics he was less clever, and perhaps the marquis erred in making him his field-sergeant. However that might be, he left Imânus behind him with instructions to replace him and look after everything. Gouge-le-Bruant, a man more of a fighter than a soldier, was fitter to cut the throats of a clan than to guard a town. Still he posted main-guards.

When evening came, as the Marquis de Lantenac was returning toward Dol, after having decided upon the ground for his battery, he suddenly heard the report of cannon. He looked forward. A red smoke was rising from the principal street. There had been surprise, invasion, assault; they were fighting in the town. Although very difficult to astonish, he was stupefied. He had not been prepared for anything of the sort. Who could it be? Evidently it was not Gauvain. No man would attack a force that numbered four to his one. Was it Léchelle? But could he have made such a forced march? Léchelle was improbable; Gauvain impossible.

Lantenac urged on his horse; as he rode forward he encountered the flying inhabitants; he questioned them. They were mad with terror; they cried, " The Blues! the Blues! " When he arrived, the situation was a bad one. This is what had happened.

CHAPTER III

SMALL ARMIES AND GREAT BATTLES

AS we have just seen, the peasants, on arriving at Dol, dispersed themselves through the town, each man following his own fancy, as happens when troops " obey from friendship," a favourite expression with the Vendeans,— a species of obedience which makes heroes, but not troopers. They thrust the artillery out of the way along with the baggage, under the arches of the old market-hall. They were weary; they ate, drank, counted their rosaries, and lay down pell-mell across the principal street, which was encumbered rather than guarded.

As night came on, the greater portion fell asleep, with their heads on their knapsacks, some having their wives beside them, for the peasant women often followed their husbands, and the robust ones acted as spies. It was a mild July evening; the constellation glittered in the deep purple of the sky. The entire bivouac, which resembled rather the halt of a caravan than an army encamped, gave itself up to repose. Suddenly, amid the dull gleams of twilight, such as had not yet closed their eyes saw three pieces of ordnance pointed at the entrance of the street. It was Gauvain's artillery. He had surprised the main-guard. He was in the town, and his column held the top of the street.

A peasant started up, crying, " Who goes there? " and fired his musket; a cannon-shot replied. Then a furious discharge of musketry burst forth. The whole drowsy crowd sprang up with a start. A rude shock,— to fall asleep under the stars and wake under a volley of grape-shot.

The first moments were terrific. There is nothing so tragic as the aimless swarming of a thunderstricken crowd. They flung themselves on their arms; they yelled, they ran; many fell. The assaulted peasants no longer knew what they were

about, and blindly shot one another. The townspeople,
stunned with fright, rushed in and out of their houses, and
wandered frantically amid the hubbub. Families shrieked to
one another. A dismal combat ensued, in which women and
children were mingled. The balls, as they whistled overhead,
streaked the darkness with rays of light. A fusilade poured
from every dark corner. There was nothing but smoke and
tumult. The entanglement of the baggage-wagons and the
cannon-carriages was added to the confusion. The horses became unmanageable; the wounded were trampled under foot.
The groans of the poor wretches, helpless on the ground, filled
the air. Horror here, stupefaction there. Soldiers and officers sought for one another. In the midst of all this could be
seen creatures made indifferent to the awful scene by personal
preoccupations. A woman sat nursing her new-born babe,
seated on a bit of wall, against which her husband leaned with
his leg broken; and he, while his blood was flowing, tranquilly
loaded his rifle and fired at random, straight before him into
the darkness. Men lying flat on the ground fired across the
spokes of the wagon-wheels. At moments there rose a hideous
din of clamours, then the great voices of the cannon drowned
all. It was awful. It was like a felling of trees; they dropped
one upon another. Gauvain poured out a deadly fire from his
ambush, and suffered little loss.

Still the peasants, courageous amid their disorder, ended
by putting themselves on the defensive; they retreated into
the market,— a vast, obscure redoubt, a forest of stone pillars. There they again made a stand; anything which resembled a wood gave them confidence. Imânus supplied the
absence of Lantenac as best he could. They had cannon, but
to the great astonishment of Gauvain they did not make use
of it; that was owing to the fact that the artillery officers had
gone with the marquis to reconnoitre Mount Dol, and the
peasants did not know how to manage the culverins and demi-
culverins. But they riddled with balls the Blues who cannonaded them; they replied to the grape-shot by volleys of
musketry. It was now they who were sheltered. They had

14

heaped together the drays, the tumbrels, the casks, all the litter of the old market, and improvised a lofty barricade, with openings through which they could pass their carbines. From these holes their fusilade was murderous. The whole was quickly arranged. In a quarter of an hour the market presented an impregnable front.

This became a serious matter for Gauvain. This market suddenly transformed into a citadel was unexpected. The peasants were inside it, massed and solid. Gauvain's surprise had succeeded, but he ran the risk of defeat. He got down from his saddle. He stood attentively studying the darkness, his arms folded, clutching his sword in one hand, erect, in the glare of a torch which lighted his battery. The gleam, falling on his tall figure, made him visible to the men behind the barricade. He became an aim for them, but he did not notice it. The shower of balls sent out from the barricade fell about him as he stood there, lost in thought. But he could oppose cannon to all these carbines, and cannon always ends by getting the advantage. Victory rests with him who has the artillery. His battery, well manned, insured him the superiority.

Suddenly a lightning-flash burst from the shadowy market; there was a sound like a peal of thunder, and a ball broke through a house above Gauvain's head. The barricade was replying to the cannon with its own voice. What had happened? Something new had occurred. The artillery was no longer confined to one side. A second ball followed the first and buried itself in the wall close to Gauvain. A third knocked his hat off on the ground. These balls were of a heavy calibre. It was a sixteen-pounder that fired.

" They are aiming at you, commandant," cried the artillerymen.

They extinguished the torch. Gauvain, as if in a reverie, picked up his hat. Some one had in fact aimed at Gauvain: it was Lantenac. The marquis had just arrived within the barricade from the opposite side. Imânus had hurried to meet him.

"Monseigneur, we are surprised!"

"By whom?"

"I do not know."

"Is the route to Dinan free?"

"I think so."

"We must begin a retreat."

"It has commenced. A good many have run away."

"We must not run; we must fall back. Why are you not making use of this artillery?"

"The men lost their heads; besides, the officers were not here."

"I am come."

"Monseigneur, I have sent toward Fougères all I could of the baggage, the women, everything useless. What is to be done with the three little prisoners?"

"Ah, those children!"

"Yes."

"They are our hostages. Have them taken to La Tourgue."

This said, the marquis rushed to the barricade. With the arrival of the chief the whole face of affairs changed. The barricade was ill-constructed for artillery; there was only room for two cannon; the marquis put in position a couple of sixteen-pounders, for which loop-holes were made. As he leaned over one of the guns, watching the enemy's battery through the opening, he perceived Gauvain.

"It is he!" cried the marquis.

Then he took the swab and rammer himself, loaded the piece, sighted it, and fired. Thrice he aimed at Guavain and missed. The third time he only succeeded in knocking his hat off.

"Numbskull!" muttered Lantenac; "a little lower, and I should have taken his head." Suddenly the torch went out, and he had only darkness before him. "So be it!" said he. Then turning toward the peasant gunners, he cried: "Now let them have it!"

Gauvain, on his side, was not less in earnest. The seriousness of the situation increased. A new phase of the combat developed itself. The barricade had begun to use cannon. Who could tell if it were not about to pass from the defensive to the offensive? He had before him, after deducting the killed and fugitives, at least five thousand combatants, and he had left only twelve hundred serviceable men. What would happen to the republicans if the enemy perceived their paucity of numbers? The rôles were reversed. He had been the assailant,— he would become the assailed. If the barricade were to make a sortie, everything might be lost. What was to be done? He could no longer think of attacking the barricade in front; an attempt at main force would be foolhardy: twelve hundred men cannot dislodge five thousand. To rush upon them was impossible; to wait would be fatal. He must make an end. But how?

Gauvain belonged to the neighbourhood; he was acquainted with the town; he knew that the old market-house where the Vendeans were intrenched was backed by a labyrinth of narrow and crooked streets. He turned towards his lieutenant, who was that valiant Captain Guéchamp, afterward famous for clearing out the forest of Concise, where Jean Chouan was born, and for preventing the capture of Bourgneuf by holding the dike of La Chaîne against the rebels.

" Guéchamp," said he, " I leave you in command. Fire as fast as you can. Riddle the barricade with cannon-balls. Keep all those fellows over yonder busy."

" I understand," said Guéchamp.

" Mass the whole column with their guns loaded, and hold them ready to make an onslaught." He added a few words in Guéchamp's ear.

" I hear," said Guéchamp.

Gauvain resumed: " Are all our drummers on foot? "

" Yes."

" We have nine. Keep two and give me seven."

The seven drummers ranged themselves in silence in front of Gauvain. Then he said: " Battalion of the Bonnet Rouge! "

Twelve men, of whom one was a sergeant, stepped out from the main body of the troop.

"I demand the whole battalion," said Gauvain.

"Here it is," replied the sergeant.

"You are twelve!"

"There are twelve of us left."

"It is well," said Gauvain.

This sergeant was the good, rough trooper Radoub, who had adopted, in the name of the battalion, the three children they had encountered in the wood of La Saudraie. It will be remembered that only a demi-battalion had been exterminated at Herbe-en-Pail, and Radoub was fortunate enough not to have been among the number.

There was a forage-wagon standing near; Gauvain pointed toward it with his finger. "Sergeant, order your men to make some straw ropes and twist them about their guns, so that there will be no noise if they knock together."

A minute passed; the order was silently executed in the darkness.

"It is done," said the sergeant.

"Soldiers, take off your shoes," commanded Gauvain.

"We have none," returned the sergeant.

They numbered, counting the drummers, nineteen men; Gauvain made the twentieth. He cried: "Follow me! Single file! The drummers next to me, the battalion behind them. Sergeant, you will command the battalion."

He put himself at the head of the column, and while the firing on both sides continued, these twenty men, gliding along like shadows, plunged into the deserted lanes. The line marched thus for some time, twisting along the fronts of the houses. The whole town seemed dead; the citizens were hidden in their cellars. Every door was barred; every shutter closed; no light to be seen anywhere. Amid this silence the principal street kept up its din; the cannonading continued; the republican battery and the royalist barricade spit forth their volleys with undiminished fury.

After twenty minutes of this tortuous march, Gauvain,

who kept his way unerringly through the darkness, reached the end of a lane which led into the broad street, but on the other side of the market-house. The position was turned. In this direction there was no intrenchment, according to the eternal imprudence of barricade builders; the market was open, and the entrance free among the pillars where some baggage-wagons stood ready to depart. Gauvain and his nineteen men had the five thousand Vendeans before them, but their backs instead of their faces.

Gauvain spoke in a low voice to the sergeant; the soldiers untwisted the straw from their guns; the twelve grenadiers posted themselves in line behind the angle of the lane, and the seven drummers waited with their drumsticks lifted. The artillery firing was intermittent. Suddenly, in a pause between the discharges, Gauvain waved his sword, and cried in a voice which rang like a trumpet through the silence: " Two hundred men to the right; two hundred men to the left; all the rest in the centre! "

The twelve muskets fired, and the seven drums beat.

Gauvain uttered the formidable battle-cry of the Blues: " To your bayonets! Down upon them! "

The effect was prodigious. This whole peasant mass felt itself surprised in the rear, and believed that it had a fresh army at its back. At the same instant, on hearing the drums, the column which Guéchamp commanded at the head of the street began to move, sounding the charge in its turn, and flung itself at a run on the barricade. The peasants found themselves between two fires. Panic magnifies: a pistol-shot sounds like the report of a cannon; in moments of terror the imagination heightens every noise; the barking of a dog sounds like the roar of a lion. Add to this the fact that the peasant catches fright as easily as thatch catches fire, and as quickly as a blazing thatch becomes a conflagration, a panic among peasants becomes a rout. An indescribably confused flight ensued.

In a few instants the market-hall was empty; the terrified rustics broke away in all directions; the officers were power-

less; Imânus uselessly killed two or three fugitives; nothing
was to be heard but the cry, " Save yourselves! "   The army
poured through the streets of the town like water through
the holes of a sieve, and dispersed into the open country
with the rapidity of a cloud carried along by a whirlwind.
Some fled toward Châteauneuf, some toward Plerguer, others
toward Antrain.

The Marquis de Lantenac watched this stampede. He
spiked the guns with his own hands and then retreated,—
the last of all, slowly, composedly, saying to himself, " Decidedly, the peasants will not stand. We must have the
English."

CHAPTER IV

" IT IS THE SECOND TIME "

THE victory was complete. Gauvain turned toward the
men of the Bonnet Rouge battalion, and said: " You
are twelve, but you are equal to a thousand." Praise from
a chief was the cross of honour of those times.

Guéchamp, dispatched beyond the town by Gauvain, pursued the fugitives and captured a great number. Torches
were lighted and the town was searched. All who could not
escape surrendered. They illuminated the principal street
with fire-pots. It was strewn with dead and dying. The root
of a combat must always be torn out; a few desperate groups
here and there still resisted; they were surrounded, and threw
down their arms.

Gauvain had remarked, amid the frantic pell-mell of the
retreat, an intrepid man, a sort of agile and robust form,
who protected the flight of others, but had not himself fled.
This peasant had used his gun so energetically — the barrel
for firing, the butt-end for knocking down — that he had
had broken it; now he grasped a pistol in one hand — and a

sabre in the other. No one dared approach him. **Suddenly**
Gauvain saw him reel and support himself against a pillar of
the broad street. The man had just been wounded; but he
still clutched the sabre and pistol in his fists. Gauvain put
his sword under his arm and went up to him. " Surrender! "
said he.

The man looked steadily at him. The blood ran through
his clothing from a wound which he had received, and made
a pool at his feet.

" You are my prisoner," added Gauvain. The man remained silent. " What is your name? "

The man answered, " I am called the Shadow-dancer."

" You are a brave man," said Gauvain. And he held out
his hand.

The man cried, " Long live the king! " Gathering up all
his remaining strength, he raised both arms at once, fired his
pistol at Gauvain's heart, and dealt a blow at his head with
the sabre.

He did it with the swiftness of a tiger; but some one else
had been still more prompt. This was a man on horseback,
who had arrived unobserved a few minutes before. This man,
seeing the Vendean raise the sabre and pistol, rushed between
him and Gauvain. But for this interposition, Gauvain would
have been killed.

The horse received the pistol-shot, the man received the
sabre-stroke, and both fell. It all happened in the time it
would have needed to utter a cry.

The Vendean sank on his side upon the pavement. The
sabre had struck the man full in the face; he lay senseless on
the stones. The horse was killed.

Gauvain approached. " Who is this man? " said he. He
studied him. The blood from the gash inundated the wounded
man, and spread a red mask over his face. It was impossible
to distinguish his features, but one could see that his hair
was grey. " This man has saved my life," continued Gauvain. " Does any one here know him? "

" Commandant," said a soldier, " he came into the town a

few minutes ago.   I saw him enter; he came by the road from
Pontorson."

The chief surgeon hurried up with his instrument-case.   The
wounded man was still insensible.   The surgeon examined him
and said: " A simple gash.   It is nothing.   It can be sewed
up.   In eight days he will be on his feet again.   It was a
beautiful sabre-stroke! "

The sufferer wore a cloak, a tricoloured sash, pistols, and
a sabre.   He was laid on a litter.   They undressed him.   A
bucket of fresh water was brought: the surgeon washed the
cut: the face began to be visible.   Gauvain studied it with
profound attention.

" Has he any papers on him? " he asked.

The surgeon felt in the stranger's side-pocket and drew
out a pocket-book, which he handed to Gauvain.   The
wounded man, restored by the cold water, began to come to
himself.   His eyelids moved slightly.

Gauvain examined the pocket-book; he found in it a sheet
of paper, folded four times; he opened this and read: —

"Committee of Public Safety.   The Citizen Cimourdain."

He uttered a cry: " Cimourdain! "

The wounded man opened his eyes at this exclamation.

Gauvain was astounded.   " Cimourdain!   It is you!   This
is the second time you have saved my life."

Cimourdain looked at him.   A gleam of ineffable joy
lighted his bleeding face.

Gauvain fell on his knees beside him, crying, " My master! "

" Thy father," said Cimourdain.

CHAPTER V

THE DROP OF COLD WATER

THEY had not met for many years, but their hearts had never been parted; they recognized each other as if they had separated the evening before.

An ambulance had been improvised in the town-hall of Dol. Cimourdain was placed on a bed in a little room next the great common chamber of the other wounded. The surgeon sewed up the cut and put an end to the demonstrations of affection between the two men, judging that Cimourdain ought to be left to sleep. Besides, Gauvain was claimed by the thousand occupations which are the duties and cares of victory.

Cimourdain remained alone, but he did not sleep: he was consumed by two fevers,— that of his wound and that of his joy. He did not sleep, and still it did not seem to himself that he was awake. Could it be possible that his dream was realized? Cimourdain had long ceased to believe in luck, yet here it was. He had refound Gauvain. He had left him a child, he found him a man; he found him great, formidable, intrepid. He found him triumphant, and triumphing for the people. Gauvain was the real support of the Revolution in Vendée; and it was he, Cimourdain, who had given this tower of strength to the Republic. This victor was his pupil. The light which he saw illuminating this youthful face (reserved perhaps for the Republican Pantheon) was his own thought,— his, Cimourdain's. His disciple — the child of his spirit — was from henceforth a hero, and before long would be a glory. It seemed to Cimourdain that he saw the apotheosis of his own soul. He had just seen how Gauvain made war; he was like Chiron, who had watched Achilles fight. There was a mysterious analogy between the priest and the centaur, for the priest is only half man.

All the chances of this adventure, mingled with the sleeplessness caused by his wound, filled Cimourdain with a sort of mysterious intoxication. He saw a glorious youthful destiny rising; and what added to his profound joy was the possession of full power over this destiny. Another success like that which he had just witnessed, and Cimourdain would only need to speak a single word to induce the Republic to confide an army to Gauvain. Nothing dazzles like the astonishment of complete victory. It was an era when each man had his military dream; each one wanted to make a general. Danton wished to appoint Westermann; Marat wished to appoint Rossignol; Hébert wished to appoint Ronsin; Robespierre wished to put these all aside. Why not Gauvain, asked Cimourdain of himself; and he dreamed. All possibilities were before him: he passed from one hypothesis to another; all obstacles vanished. When a man puts his foot on that ladder, he does not stop, it is an infinite ascent: one starts from earth and one reaches the stars. A great general is only a leader of armies; a great captain is at the same time a leader of ideas. Cimourdain dreamed of Gauvain as a great captain. He seemed to see — for reverie travels swiftly — Gauvain on the ocean, chasing the English; on the Rhine, chastising the Northern kings; on the Pyrenees, repulsing Spain; on the Alps, making a signal to Rome to rouse itself. There were two men in Cimourdain,— one tender, the other stern; both were satisfied, for the inexorable was his ideal; and at the same time that he saw Gauvain noble, he saw him terrible. Cimourdain thought of all that it was necessary to destroy before beginning to build up, and said to himself: "Verily, this is no time for tendernesses. Gauvain will be ' up to the mark,' " an expression of the period. Cimourdain pictured Gauvain spurning the shadows with his foot, with a breastplate of light, a meteor-glare on his brow, rising on the grand ideal wings of Justice, Reason, and Progress, but with a sword in his hand: an angel,— a destroyer likewise.

In the height of this reverie, which was almost an ecstasy, he heard through the half-open door a conversation in the great hall of the ambulance which was next his chamber. He recognized Gauvain's voice; through all those years of separation that voice had rung ever in his ear, and the voice of the man had still a tone of the childish voice he had loved. He listened. There was a sound of soldiers' footsteps; one of the men said: —

" Commandant, this is the man who fired at you. While nobody was watching, he dragged himself into a cellar. We found him. Here he is."

Then Cimourdain heard this dialogue between Gauvain and the prisoner: —

" You are wounded? "

" I am well enough to be shot."

" Lay that man on a bed. Dress his wounds; take care of him; cure him."

" I wish to die."

" You must live. You tried to kill me in the king's name; I show you mercy in the name of the Republic."

A shadow passed across Cimourdain's forehead. He was like a man waking up with a start, and he murmured with a sort of sinister dejection: " In truth, he is one of the merciful."

CHAPTER VI

A HEALED BREAST; A BLEEDING HEART

A CUT heals quickly; but there was in a certain place a person more seriously wounded than Cimourdain. It was the woman who had been shot, whom the beggar Tellmarch had picked up out of the great lake of blood at the farm of Herbe-en-Pail.

Michelle Fléchard was even in a more critical situation than Tellmarch had believed. There was a wound in the shoulder-blade corresponding to the wound above the breast; at the same time that the ball broke her collar-bone, another ball traversed her shoulder, but, as the lungs were not touched, she might recover. Tellmarch was a " philospoher,"— a peasant phrase which means a little of a doctor, a little of a surgeon, and a little of a sorcerer. He carried the wounded woman to his forest lair, laid her upon his sea-weed bed, and treated her by the aid of those mysterious things called " simples; " and thanks to him she lived. The collar-bone knitted together, the wounds in the breast and shoulder closed; after a few weeks she was convalescent. One morning she was able to walk out of the carnichot, leaning on Tellmarch, and seat herself beneath the trees in the sunshine. Tellmarch knew little about her; wounds in the breast demand silence, and during the almost death-like agony which had preceded her recovery she had scarcely spoken a word. When she tried to speak, Tellmarch stopped her, but she kept up an obstinate reverie; he could see in her eyes the sombre going and coming of poignant thoughts. But this morning she was quite strong; she could almost walk alone; a cure is a paternity, and Tellmarch watched her with delight. The good old man began to smile. He said to her: —

" We are upon our feet again; we have no more wounds."

" Except in the heart," said she. She added, presently: " Then you have no idea where they are."

" Who are ' they? ' " demanded Tellmarch.

" My children."

This " then " expressed a whole world of thoughts; it signified: " Since you do not talk to me, since you have been so many days beside me without opening your mouth, since you stop me each time I attempt to break the silence, since you seem to fear that I shall speak, it is because you have nothing to tell me." Often in her fever, in her wanderings, her delirium, she had called her children, and had seen clearly (for delirium makes its observations) that the old man did not reply to her.

The truth was, Tellmarch did not know what to say to her. It is not easy to tell a mother that her children are lost. And then, what did he know? Nothing. He knew that a mother

had been shot; that this mother had been found on the ground
by himself; that when he had taken her up she was almost a
corpse; that this quasi-corpse had three children; and that
Lantenac, after having had the mother shot, carried off the
little ones. All his information ended there. What had become of the children? Were they even living? He knew,
because he had inquired, that there were two boys and a little
girl, barely weaned. Nothing more. He asked himself a
host of questions concerning this unfortunate group, but could
answer none of them. The people of the neighbourhood whom
he had interrogated contented themselves with shaking their
heads. The Marquis de Lantenac was a man of whom they
did not willingly talk. They did not willinglly talk *of* De
Lantenac, and they did not willingly talk *to* Tellmarch.
Peasants have a species of suspicion peculiar to themselves.
They did not like Tellmarch. Tellmarch the Caimand was
a puzzling man. Why was he always studying the sky?
What was he doing and what was he thinking in his long hours
of stillness? Yes, indeed, he was odd! In this district in
full warfare, in full conflagration, in high tumult; where all
men had only one business,— devastation; and one work,—
carnage; where whosoever could burned a house, cut the throats
of a family, massacred an outpost, sacked a village; where
nobody thought of anything but laying ambushes for one
another, drawing one another into snares, killing one another,
— this solitary, absorbed in Nature, as if submerged in the
immense peacefulness of its beauties, gathering herbs and
plants, occupied solely with the flowers, the birds, and the
stars, was evidently a dangerous man. Plainly he was not in
possession of his reason; he did not lie in wait behind thickets;
he did not fire a shot at any one. Hence he created a certain
dread about him. " That man is mad," said the passers-by.

Tellmarch was more than an isolated man,— he was
shunned. People asked him no questions and gave him few
answers; so he had not been able to inform himself as he could
have wished. The war had drifted eleswhere; the armies had
gone to fight farther off; the Marquis de Lantenac had dis-

appeared from the horizon, and in Tellmarch's state of mind
for him to be conscious there was a war it was necessary for
it to set its foot on him.

After that cry, " My children," Tellmarch ceased to smile,
and the woman went back to her thoughts. What was passing
in that soul? It was as if she looked out from the depths of
a gulf. Suddenly she turned toward Tellmarch, and cried
anew, almost with an accent of rage: " My children!"

Tellmarch drooped his head like one guilty. He was thinking of this Marquis de Lantenac, who certainly was not thinking of him, and who probably no longer remembered that he
existed. He accounted for this to himself, saying, " A lord,
when he is in danger, he knows you; when he is once out of
it, he does not know you any longer." And he asked himself:
" But why, then, did I save this lord?" And he answered
his own question: " Because he was a man." Thereupon he
remained thoughtful for some time, then began again mentally: " Am I very sure of that?" He repeated his bitter
words: " If I had known!"

This whole adventure overwhelmed him, for in that which
he had done he perceived a sort of enigma. He meditated
dolorously. A good action might sometimes be evil. He who
saves the wolf kills the sheep. He who sets the vulture's
wing is responsible for his talons. He felt himself in truth
guilty. The unreasoning anger of this mother was just.
Still, to have saved her consoled him for having saved the
marquis. But the children?

The mother meditated also. The reflections of these two
went on side by side; and, perhaps, though without speech,
met one another amid the shadows of reverie. The woman's
eyes, with a night-like gloom in their depths, fixed themselves
anew on Tellmarch. " Nevertheless, that cannot be allowed to
pass in this way," said she.

" Hush!" returned Tellmarch, laying his finger on his lips.

She continued: " You did wrong to save me, and I am
angry with you for it. I would rather be dead, because I am
sure I should see them then. I should know where they are.

They would not see me, but I should be near them. The dead, — they ought to have power to protect."

He took her arm and felt her pulse. " Calm yourself; you are bringing back your fever."

She asked him almost harshly, " When can I go away from here? "

" Go away? "

" Yes. Walk."

" Never, if you are not reasonable. To-morrow, if you are wise."

" What do you call being wise? "

" Having confidence in God."

" God! What has he done with my children? " Her mind seemed wandering. Her voice became very sweet. " You understand," she said to him, " I cannot rest like this. You have never had any children, but I have. That makes a difference. One cannot judge of a thing when one does not know what it is. You never had any children, had you? "

" No," replied Tellmarch.

" And I — I had nothing besides them. What am I without my children? I should like to have somebody explain to me why I have not my children. I feel that things happen, but I do not understand. They killed my husband; they shot me: all the same, I do not understand it."

" Come," said Tellmarch, " there is the fever taking you again. Do not talk any more."

She looked at him and relapsed into silence. From this day she spoke no more. Tellmarch was obeyed more absolutely than he liked. She spent long hours of stupefaction, crouched at the foot of an old tree. She dreamed, and held her peace. Silence makes an impenetrable refuge for simple souls that have been down into the innermost depths of suffering. She seemed to relinquish all effort to understand. To a certain extent despair is unintelligible to the despairing.

Tellmarch studied her with sympathetic interest. In presence of this anguish the old man had thoughts such as might have come to a woman. " Oh, yes," he said to himself, " her lips do not speak, but her eyes talk. I know well what is the matter,— what her one idea is. To have been a mother, and to be one no longer! To have been a nurse, and to be so no more! She cannot resign herself. She thinks about the tiniest child of all, that she was nursing not long ago. She thinks of it; thinks, thinks. In truth, it must be so sweet to feel a little rosy mouth that draws your very soul out of your body, and who, with the life that is yours, makes a life for itself." He kept silence on his side, comprehending the impotency of speech in face of an absorption like this. The persistence of an all-absorbing idea is terrible. And how to make a mother thus beset hear reason? Maternity is inexplicable; you cannot argue with it. That it is which renders a mother sublime; she becomes unreasoning; the maternal instinct is divinely animal. The mother is no longer a woman, she is a wild creature; her children are her cubs. Hence in the mother there is something at once inferior and superior to argument. A mother has an unerring instinct. The immense mysterious Will of creation is within her and guides her. Hers is a blindness superhumanly enlightened.

Now Tellmarch desired to make this unhappy creature speak; he did not succeed. On one occasion he said to her: "As ill-luck will have it, I am old, and I cannot walk any longer. At the end of a quarter of an hour my strength is exhausted, and I am obliged to rest; if it were not for that I would accompany you. After all, perhaps it is fortunate that I cannot. I should be rather a burden than useful to you. I am tolerated here; but the Blues are suspicious of me, as being a peasant; and the peasants suspect me of being a wizard."

He waited for her to reply. She did not even raise her eyes. A fixed idea ends in madness or heroism. But of what heroism is a poor peasant woman capable? None. She can be a mother, and that is all. Each day she buried herself deeper in her reverie. Tellmarch watched her. He tried to give her occupation; he brought her needles and thread and a thimble, and at length, to the satisfaction of the poor Caimand,

15

she began some sewing. She dreamed, but she worked,— a sign of health; her energy was returning little by little. She mended her linen, her garments, her shoes; but her eyes looked cold and glassy as ever. As she bent over her needle, she sang unearthly melodies in a low voice. She murmured names, — probably the names of children,— but not distinctly enough for Tellmarch to catch them. She would break off abruptly and listen to the birds, as if she thought they might have brought her tidings. She watched the weather. Her lips would move,— she was speaking low to herself. She made a bag and filled it with chestnuts. One morning Tellmarch saw her preparing to set forth, her eyes gazing away into the depths of the forest.

"Where are you going?" he asked.

She replied, "I am going to look for them."

He did not attempt to detain her.

CHAPTER VII

THE TWO POLES OF THE TRUTH

AT the end of a few weeks, which had been filled with the vicissitudes of civil war, the district of Fougères could talk of nothing but the two men who were opposed to each other, and yet were occupied in the same work; that is, fighting side by side the great revolutionary combat.

The savage Vendean duel continued, but the Vendée was losing ground. In Ille-et-Vilaine in particular, thanks to the young commander who had at Dol so opportunely replied to the audacity of six thousand royalists by the audacity of fifteen hundred patriots, the insurrection, if not quelled, was at least greatly weakened and circumscribed. Several lucky hits had followed that one, and out of these successes had grown a new position of affairs. Matters had changed their face, but a singular complication had arisen.

In all this portion of the Vendée the Republic had the
upper hand,— that was beyond a doubt. But which republic?
In the triumph which was opening out, two forms of republic
made themselves felt,— the republic of terror, and the republic of clemency; the one desirous to conquer by rigour, and
the other by mildness. Which would prevail? These two
forms — the conciliating and the implacable — were represented by two men, each of whom possessed his special influence
and authority: the one a military commander, the other a civil
delegate. Which of them would prevail?

One of the two, the delegate, had a formidable basis of
support; he had arrived bearing the threatening watchword
of the Paris Commune to the battalions of Santerre: "No
mercy; no quarter!" He had, in order to put everything
under his control, the decree of the Convention, ordaining
" death to whomsoever should set at liberty and help a captive
rebel chief to escape." He had full powers, emanating from
the Committee of Public Safety, and an injunction commanding obedience to him as delegate, signed ROBESPIERRE, DAN-
TON, MARAT. The other, the soldier, had on his side only
this strength,— pity. He had only his own arm, which chastised the enemy; and his heart, which pardoned them. A conqueror, he believed that he had the right to spare the conquered.

Hence arose a conflict, hidden but deep, between these two
men. The two stood in different atmospheres; both combat-
ing the rebellion, and each having his own thunderbolt,— that
of the one, victory; that of the other, terror.

Throughout all the Bocage nothing was talked of but them;
and what added to the anxiety of those who watched them from
every quarter was the fact that these two men so diametrically
opposed were at the same time closely united. These two an-
tagonists were friends. Never sympathy loftier and more
profound joined two hearts; the stern had saved the life of
the clement, and bore on his face the wound received in the
effort. These two men were the incarnation,— the one of life,
the other of death; the one was the principle of destruction,

the other of peace, and they loved each other. **Strange problem!** Imagine Orestes merciful and Pylades pitiless. Picture Arimanes the brother of Ormus!

Let us add that the one of the pair who was called " the ferocious " was, at the same time, the most brotherly of men. He dressed the wounded, cared for the sick, passed his days and nights in the ambulance and hospitals, was touched by the sight of barefooted children, had nothing for himself, gave all to the poor. He was present at all the battles; he marched at the head of the columns and in the thickest of the fight, armed,— for he had in his belt a sabre and two pistols,— yet disarmed, because no one had ever seen him draw his sabre or touch his pistols. He faced blows, and did not return them. It was said that he had been a priest.

One of these men was Gauvain; the other was Cimourdain. There was friendship between the two men, but hatred between the two principles; this hidden war could not fail to burst forth. One morning the battle began.

Cimourdain said to Gauvain: " What have we accomplished? "

Gauvain replied: " You know as well as I. I have dispersed Lantenac's bands. He has only a few men left. Then he is driven back to the forest of Fougères. In eight days he will be surrounded."

" And in fifteen days? "

" He will be taken."

" And then? "

" You have read my notice? "

" Yes. Well? "

" He will be shot."

" More clemency! He must be guillotined."

" As for me," said Gauvain, " I am for a military death."

" And I," replied Cimourdain, " for a revolutionary death." He looked Gauvain in the face, and added: " Why did you set at liberty those nuns of the convent of Saint Marc-le-Blanc? "

" I do not make war on women," answered Gauvain.

"Those women hate the people; and where hate is concerned, one woman outweighs ten men.   Why did you refuse to send to the revolutionary tribunal all that herd of old fanatical priests who were taken at Louvigné?"

"I do not make war on old men."

"An old priest is worse than a young one.   Rebellion is more dangerous preached by white hairs.   Men have faith in wrinkles.   No false pity, Gauvain!   The regicides are liberators.   Keep your eye fixed on the tower of the Temple."

"The Temple tower!   I would bring the Dauphin out of it.   I do not make war on children."

Cimourdain's eyes grew stern.   "Gauvain, learn that it is necessary to make war on a woman when she calls herself Marie Antoinette, on an old man when he is named Pius VI. and Pope, and upon a child when he is named Louis Capet."

"My master, I am not a politician."

"Try not to be a dangerous man.   Why, at the attack on the post of Cossé, when the rebel Jean Treton, driven back and lost, flung himself alone, sabre in hand, against the whole column, didst thou cry, 'Open the ranks!   Let him pass?'"

"Because one does not set fifteen hundred to kill a single man."

"Why, at the Cailleterie d'Astillé, when you saw your soldiers about to kill the Vendean Joseph Bézier, who was wounded and dragging himself along, did you exclaim, 'Go on before!   This is my affair!' and then fire your pistol in the air?"

"Because one does not kill a man on the ground."

"And you were wrong.   Both are to-day chiefs of bands. Joseph Bézier is Mustache, and Jean Treton is Jambe d'Argent.   In saving those two men you gave two enemies to the Republic."

"Certainly I could wish to give her friends, and not enemies."

"Why, after the victory of Landéan, did you not shoot your three hundred peasant prisoners?"

"Because Bonchamp had shown mercy to the republican

prisoners, and I wanted it said that the Republic showed mercy
to the royalist prisoners."

" But, then, if you take Lantenac you will pardon him? "

" No."

" Why?   Since you showed mercy to the three hundred
peasants? "

" The peasants are ignorant men; Lantenac knows what
he does."

" But Lantenac is your kinsman."

" France is the nearest."

" Lantenac is an old man."

" Lantenac is a stranger.   Lantenac has no age.   Lantenac
summons the English.   Lantenac is invasion.   Lantenac is
the enemy of the country.   The duel between him and me can
only finish by his death or mine."

" Gauvain, remember this vow."

" It is sworn."

There was silence, and the two looked at each other.

Then Gauvain resumed: " It will be a bloody date, this
year '93 in which we live."

" Take care!" cried Cimourdain.   " Terrible duties exist.
Do not accuse that which is not accusable.   Since when is it
that the illness is the fault of the physician?   Yes, the char-
acteristic of this tremendous year is its pitilessness.   Why?
Because it is the grand revolutionary year.   This year in
which we live is the incarnation of the Revolution.   The Revolution has an enemy,— the old world,— and it is without pity
for it; just as the surgeon has an enemy,— gangrene,— and
is without pity for it.   The Revolution extirpates royalty in
the king, aristocracy in the noble, despotism in the soldier,
superstition in the priest, barbarism in the judge; in a word,
everything which is tyranny, in all which is the tyrant.   The
operation is fearful; the Revolution performs it with a sure
hand.   As to the amount of sound flesh which it sacrifices, demand of Boerhaave what he thinks in regard to that.   What
tumour does not cause a loss of blood in its cutting away?
Does not the extinguishing of a conflagration ·demand an

energy as fierce as that of the fire itself? These formidable necessities are the very condition of success. A surgeon resembles a butcher; a healer may have the appearance of an executioner. The Revolution devotes itself to its fatal work. It mutilates, but it saves. What! you demand pity for the virus? You wish it to be merciful to that which is poisonous? It will not listen. It holds the post,— it will exterminate it. It makes a deep wound in civilization, from whence will spring health to the human race. You suffer? Without doubt. How long will it last? The time necessary for the operation. After that you will live. The Revolution amputates the world. Hence this hæmorrhage,—'93."

" The surgeon is calm," said Gauvain, " and the men that I see are violent."

" The Revolution," replied Cimourdain, " needs savage workmen to aid it! It pushes aside every hand that trembles. It has only faith in the inexorables. Danton is the terrible, Robespierre is the inflexible; Saint-Just is the immovable, Marat is the implacable. Take care, Gauvain! these names are necessary. They are worth as much as armies to us; they will terrify Europe."

" And perhaps the future also," said Gauvain. He checked himself, and resumed: " For that matter, my master, you err. I accuse no one. According to me, the true point of view of the Revolution is its irresponsibility. Nobody is innocent, nobody is guilty. Louis XVI. is a sheep thrown among lions: he wishes to escape, he tries to flee, he seeks to defend himself; he would bite if he could. But one is not a lion at will; his craze to be one passes for crime. This enraged sheep shows his teeth: ' The traitor!' cry the lions; and they eat him. That done, they fight among themselves."

" The sheep is a brute."

" And the lions, what are they? "

This retort set Cimourdain thinking. He raised his head, and answered: " These lions are consciences. These lions are ideas. These lions are principles."

" They produce the reign of Terror."

"One day, the Revolution will be the justification of this Terror."

"Beware lest the Terror become the calumny of the Revolution." Gauvain continued: "Liberty, Equality, Fraternity,— these are the dogmas of peace and harmony. Why give them an alarming aspect? What is it we want? To bring the peoples to a universal republic. Well, do not let us make them afraid. What can intimidation serve? The people can no more be attracted by a scarecrow than birds can. One must not do evil to bring about good; one does not overturn the throne in order to leave the gibbet standing. Death to kings, and life to nations! Strike off the crowns; spare the heads! The Revolution is concord, not fright. Clement ideas are ill served by cruel men. Amnesty is to me the most beautiful word in human language. I will only shed blood in risking my own. Besides, I simply know how to fight; I am nothing but a soldier. But if I may not pardon, victory is not worth the trouble it costs. During battle let us be the enemies of our enemies, and after the victory their brothers."

"Take care!" repeated Cimourdain, for the third time. "Gauvain, you are more to me than a son; take care!" Then he added thoughtfully: "In a period like ours, pity may become one of the forms of treason."

Any one listening to the talk of these two men might have fancied he heard a dialogue between the sword and the axe.

CHAPTER VIII

DOLOROSA

IN the mean while the mother was seeking her little ones. She went straight forward. How did she live? It is impossible to say; she did not know herself. She walked day and night; she begged, she ate herbs, she lay on the ground, she slept in the open air, in the thickets, under the stars, sometimes in the rain and wind. She wandered from village to village, from farm to farm, seeking a clew. She stopped on the thresholds of the peasants' cots. Her dress was in rags. Sometimes she was welcomed, sometimes she was driven away; when she could not get into the houses, she went into the woods. She did not know the district; she was ignorant of everything except Siscoignard and the parish of Azé. She had no route marked out; she retraced her steps, travelled roads already gone over, made useless journeys; sometimes she followed the highway, sometimes a cart-track, as often the paths among the copses. In these aimless wanderings she had worn out her miserable garments; she had shoes at first, then she walked barefoot, then with her feet bleeding. She crossed the track of warfare, among gun-shots, hearing nothing, seeing nothing, avoiding nothing,— seeking her children. Revolt was everywhere; there were no more gendarmes, no more mayors, no authorities of any sort. She had only to deal with chance passers. She spoke to them, she asked,—

" Have you seen three little children anywhere? "

Those she addressed would look at her.

" Two boys and a girl," she would say. Then she would name them: " René-Jean, Gros-Alain, Georgette. You have not seen them? "

She would ramble on thus: " The eldest is four years and a half old; the little girl is twenty months." Then would come the cry: " Do you know where they are? They have been taken from me."

The listeners would stare at her, and that was all.

When she saw that she was not understood, she would say: " It is because they belong to me,— that is why."

The people would pass on their way. Then she would stand still, uttering no further word, but digging at her breast with her nails.

However, one day, a peasant listened to her. The good man set himself to thinking. " Wait, now," said he. " Three children? "

" Yes."

" Two boys —"

" And a girl."

" You are hunting for them? "

" Yes."

" I have heard talk of a lord who had taken three little children, and had them with him."

" Where is this man? " she cried.   " Where are they? "

The peasant replied: " Go to La Tourgue."

" Shall I find my children there? "

" It may easily be."

" You say —"

" La Tourgue."

" What is that,— La Tourgue? "

" It is a place."

" Is it a village, a castle, a farm? "

" I never was there."

" Is it far? "

" It is not near."

" In which direction? "

" Toward Fougères."

" Which way must I go? "

" You are at Ventortes," said the peasant; " you must leave Ernée to the left and Coxelles to the right; you will pass by Lorchamps and cross the Leroux."   He pointed his finger to the west.   " Always straight before you and toward the sunset."

Ere the peasant had dropped his arm, she was hurrying on.

He cried after her: " But take care.   They are fighting over there."

She did not answer or turn round; on she went, straight before her.

CHAPTER IX

A PROVINCIAL BASTILE

1. *La Tourgue.*

FORTY years ago, a traveller who entered the forest of Fougères from the side of Laignelet, and left it toward Parigné, was met on the border of this vast old wood by a sinister spectacle. As he came out of the thickets, La Tourgue rose abruptly before him. Not La Tourgue living, but La Tourgue dead,— La Tourgue cracked, battered, seamed, dismantled.

The ruin of an edifice is as much its ghost as a phantom is that of man. No more lugubrious vision could strike the gaze than that of La Tourgue. What the traveller had before his eyes was a lofty round tower, standing alone at the corner of the wood like a malefactor. This tower, rising from a perpendicular rock, was so severe and solid that it looked almost like a bit of Roman architecture, and the frowning mass gave the idea of strength even amid its ruin. It was Roman in a way, since it was Romanic. Begun in the ninth century, it had been finished in the twelfth, after the third Crusade. The peculiar ornaments of the mouldings told its age. On ascending the height, one perceived a breach in the wall; if one ventured to enter, he found himself within the tower,— it was empty. It resembled somewhat the inside of a stone trumpet set upright on the ground,— from top to bottom no partitions, no ceilings, no floors. There were places where arches and chimneys had been torn away; falconet embrasures were seen; at different heights, rows of granite corbels and a few transverse beams marked where the different stories had been: these beams were covered with the ordure of night-birds. The colossal wall was fifteen feet in thickness at the base and twelve at the summit; here and there were chinks and holes which had been doors, through which one caught glimpses of staircases in the shadowy interior of the wall. The passer-by who penetrated there at evening heard the cry of the wood-owl, the goat-suckers, and the bats, and saw beneath his feet brambles, stones, reptiles, and above his head, across a black circle which looked like the mouth of an enormous well, he could perceive the stars.

The neighbourhood kept a tradition that in the upper stories of this tower there were secret doors formed like those in the tombs of the kings of Judah, of great stones turning on pivots, opening by a spring, and forming part of the wall when closed,— an architectural mystery which the Crusaders had brought from the East along with the pointed arch. When these doors were shut, it was impossible to discover them, so accurately were they fitted into the other stones. At this day such doors may still be seen in those mysterious cities of the Anti-Libanus which escaped the burial of the twelve towns in the time of Tiberius.

2. *The Breach.*

THE breach by which one entered the ruin had been the opening of a mine. For a connoisseur, familiar with Errard, Sardi, and Pagan, this mine had been skilfully planned. The fire-chamber, shaped like a mitre, was proportioned to the strength of the keep it had been intended to disembowel; it must have held at least two hundredweight of powder. The channel was serpentine, which does better service than a straight one. The crumbling of the mine left naked among the broken stones the saucisse which had the requisite diameter, that of a hen's egg. The explosion had left a deep rent in the wall by which the besiegers could enter.

This tower had evidently sustained at different periods real sieges conducted according to rule. It was scarred with balls, and these balls were not all of the same epoch. Each projectile has its peculiar way of marking a rampart; and those of every sort had left their traces on this keep, from the stone

balls of the fourteenth century to the iron ones of the
eighteenth. The breach gave admittance into what must have
been the ground-floor. In the wall of the tower opposite the
breach there opened the gateway of a crypt cut in the rock,
and stretching among the foundations of the tower under the
whole extent of the ground-floor hall. This crypt, three
fourths filled up, was cleared out in 1855 under the direction
of Monsieur Auguste le Prévost, the antiquary of Bernay.

3. *The Oubliette.*

THIS crypt was the oubliette. Every keep had one. This
crypt, like many penal prisons of that era, had two stories.
The upper floor, which was entered by the wicket, was a
vaulted chamber of considerable size, on a level with the
ground-floor hall. On the walls could be seen two parallel
and vertical furrows, extending from one side to the other,
and passing along the vault of the roof, in which they had
left deep ruts like old wheel-tracks. It was what they were
in fact; these two furrows had been hollowed by two wheels.
Formerly, in feudal days, victims were torn limb from limb
in this chamber by a method less noisy than dragging them
at the tails of horses. There had been two wheels, so immense that they touched the walls and an arch. To each of
these wheels an arm and a leg of the victim were attached;
then the wheels were turned in the inverse direction, which
crushed the man. It required great force; hence the furrows
which the wheels had worn in the wall as they grazed it. A
chamber of this kind may still be seen at Vianden.

Below this room there was another. That was the real
dungeon. It was not entered by a door; one penetrated into
it by a hole. The victim, stripped naked, was let down by
means of a rope placed under his armpits into the dungeon,
through an opening left in the centre of the flagging of the
upper chamber. If he persisted in living, food was flung to
him through this aperture. A hole of this sort may yet be
seen at Bouillon. The wind swept up through this opening.

The lower room, dug out beneath the ground-floor hall, was a well rather than a chamber. It had water at the bottom, and an icy wind filled it. This wind, which killed the prisoner in the depths, preserved the life of the captive in the room above; it rendered his prison respirable. The captive above, groping about beneath his vault, only got air by this hole. For the rest, whatever entered or fell there could not get out again. It was for the prisoner to be cautious in the darkness. A false step might make the prisoner in the upper room a prisoner in the dungeon below. That was his affair. If he clung to life, this hole was a peril; if he wished to be rid of it, this hole was his resource. The upper floor was the dungeon; the lower, the tomb, a superposition which resembled society at that period. It was what our ancestors called a moat-dungeon. The thing having disappeared, the name has no longer any significance in our ears. Thanks to the Revolution, we hear the words pronounced with indifference.

Outside the tower, above the breach, which forty years since was the only means of ingress, might be seen an opening larger than the other loophole, from which hung an iron grating bent and loosened.

4. *The Bridge-Castle.*

On the opposite side from the breach a stone bridge was connected with the tower, having three arches still in almost perfect preservation. This bridge had supported a building of which some fragments remained. It had evidently been destroyed by fire; there were left only portions of the framework, between whose blackened ribs the daylight peeped, as it rose beside the tower like a skeleton beside a phantom. This ruin is to-day completely demolished,— not a trace of it is left. It only needs one day and a single peasant to destroy that which it took many centuries and many kings to build.

La Tourgue is a rustic abbreviation for La Tour-Gauvain, just as *La Jupelle* stands for La Jupellière, and *Pinson-le-Tort*, the nickname of a hunchbacked leader, is put for Pin-

son-le-Tortu. La Tourgue, which forty years since was a
ruin, and which is to-day a shadow, was a fortress in 1793.
It was the old bastile of the Gauvains; toward the west guarding the entrance to the forest of Fougères,— a forest which
is itself now hardly a grove. This citadel had been built on
one of the great blocks of slate which abound between Mayenne
and Dinan, scattered everywhere among the thickets and
heaths, like missiles that had been flung in some conflict between Titans. The tower made up the entire fortress; beneath the tower was the rock, and at the foot of the rock one
of those water-courses which the month of January turns into
a torrent, and which the month of June dries up.

Thus protected, this fortress was in the Middle Ages almost
impregnable. The bridge alone weakened it. The Gothic
Gauvains had built without bridge. They got into it by one
of those swinging foot-bridges which a blow of an axe sufficed to break away. As long as the Gauvains remained vis-
counts they contented themselves with this; but when they
became marquises and left the cavern for the court, they flung
three arches across the torrent, and made themselves accessible
on the side of the plain just as they had made themselves
accessible to the king. The marquises of the seventeenth century and the marquises of the eighteenth no longer wished
to be impregnable. An imitation of Versailles replaced the
traditions of their ancestors.

Facing the tower, on the western side, was a high plateau
which ended in two plains; this plateau almost touched the
tower, only separated from it by a very deep ravine, through
which ran the water-course, which was a tributary of the
Couesnon. The bridge which joined the fortress and the
plateau was built up high on piers; and on these piers was
constructed, as at Chenonceaux, an edifice in the Mansard
style, more habitable than the tower. But customs were still
very rude; the lords continued to occupy chambers in the keep
which were like dungeons. The building on the bridge,
which was a sort of small castle, was made into a long corridor, that served as an entrance, and was called the hall of

the guards; above this hall of the guards, which was a kind of entresol, a library was built; above the library, a granary. Long windows, with small panes in Bohemian glass; pilasters between the windows; medallions sculptured on the wall; three stories: below, bartizans and muskets; in the middle, books; on high, sacks of oats,— the whole at once somewhat savage and very princely.

The tower rose gloomy and stern at the side. It overlooked this coquettish building with all its lugubrious height. From its platform one could destroy the bridge.

The two edifices — the one rude, the other elegant — clashed rather than contrasted. The two styles had nothing in keeping with each other. Although it should seem that two semi-circles ought to be identical, nothing can be less alike than a Romanic arch and the classic archivault. That tower, in keeping with the forests, made a stronger neighbour for that bridge, worthy of Versailles. Imagine Alain Barte- Torte giving his arm to Louis XIV. The juxtaposition was sinister. These two majesties thus mingled made up a whole which had something inexpressibly menacing in it.

From a military point of view, the bridge (we must insist upon this) was a traitor to the tower. It embellished, but disarmed; in gaining ornament, the fortress lost strength. The bridge put it on a level with the plateau. Still impregnable on the side toward the forest, it became vulnerable toward the plain. Formerly it commanded the plateau; now it was commanded thereby. An enemy installed there would speedily become master of the bridge. The library and the granary would be for the assailant and against the citadel. A library and a granary resemble each other in the fact that both books and straw are combustible. For an assailant who serves himself by fire, to burn Homer or to burn a bundle of straw, provided it make a flame, is all the same; the French proved this to the Germans by burning the library at Heidelburg, and the Germans proved it to the French by burning the library of Strasburg. This bridge, added to the Tourgue, was, therefore, strategically an error; but in the seventeenth century, under Colbert and Louvois, the Gauvain princes no more considered themselves besiegable than did the princes of Rohan or the prinees of La Trémoille. Still, the builders of the bridge had used certain precautions. In the first place they had foreseen the possibility of conflagration: below the three casements that looked down the stream they had fastened transversely to cramp-irons, which could still be seen half a century back, a strong ladder, whose length equalled the height of the two stories of the bridge,— a height which surpassed that of the three ordinary stories. Secondly, they had guarded against assault,— they had cut off the bridge by means of a low, heavy iron door. This door was arched; it was locked by a great key, which was hidden in a place known to the master alone, and, once closed, this door could defy a battering-ram and almost brave a cannon-ball. It was necessary to cross the bridge in order to reach this door, and to pass through the door in order to enter the tower. There was no other entrance.

5. *The Iron Door.*

The second story of the castle on the bridge was raised by the arches, so that it corresponded with the second story of the tower. It was at this height, for greater security, that the iron door had been placed. The iron door opened toward the library on the bridge side, and toward a grand vaulted hall, with a pillar in the centre, on the side to the tower.

This hall, as has already been said, was the second story of the keep. It was circular, like the tower; a long loop-hole, looking out on the fields, lighted it. The rude wall was naked, and nothing hid the stones, which were however symmetrically laid. This hall was reached by a winding staircase built in the wall,— a very simple thing when walls are fifteen feet in thickness. In the Middle Ages a town had to be taken street by street; a street, house by house; a house, room by room. A fortress was besieged story by story. In this respect La Tourgue was very skilfully disposed, and was very intractable

16

and difficult. A spiral staircase, at first very steep, led from one floor to the other. The doors were askew, and were not of the height of a man. To pass through, it was necessary to bow the head; now, a head bowed was a head cut off, and at each door the besieged awaited the besiegers.

Below the circular hall with the pillar were two similar chambers, which made the first and the ground floor; and above were three. Upon these six chambers, placed one upon another, the tower was closed by a lid of stone, which was the platform, and which could only be reached by a narrow watch-tower. The fifteen feet thickness of wall which it had been necessary to pierce in order to place the iron door, and in the middle of which it was set, embedded it in a long arch; so that the door when closed was, both on the side toward the tower and on that toward the bridge, under a porch six or seven feet deep; when it was open, these two porches joined and made the entrance-arch.

In the thickness of the wall of the porch toward the bridge opened the low gate of Saint Gille's screw-stairway, which led into the corridor of the first story beneath the library. This offered another difficulty to besiegers. The small castle of the bridge showed, on the side toward the plateau, only a perpendicular wall; and the bridge was cut there. A draw-bridge put the besieged in communication with the plateau; and this draw-bridge (on account of the height of the plateau, never lowered except at an inclined plane) allowed access to the long corridor, called the guard-room. Once masters of this corridor, besiegers, in order to reach the iron door, would have been obliged to carry by main force the winding stair-case which led to the second story.

6. *The Library.*

As for the library, it was an oblong room, the width and length of the bridge, with a single door,— the iron one. A false leaf-door hung with green cloth, which it was only neces-sary to push, masked in the interior the entrance-arch of the tower. The library wall from floor to ceiling was filled with glazed book-cases, in the beautiful style of the seventeenth-century cabinet-work. Six great windows, three on either side, one above each arch, lighted this library. Through these windows the interior could be seen from the height of the plateau. In the spaces between these windows stood six marble busts on pedestals of sculptured oak,— Hermolaüs, of Byzantium; Athenæus, the grammarian of Naucratis; Suidas; Casaubon; Clovis, King of France; and his chancellor, Anachalus, who for that matter was no more chancellor than Clovis was king.

There were books of various sorts in this library. One has remained famous. It was an old quarto with prints, having for title " Saint Bartholomew," in great letters; and for second title, " Gospel according to Saint Bartholomew, preceded by a dissertation by Pantœnus, Christian philosopher, as to whether this gospel ought to be considered apocryphal, and whether Saint Bartholomew was the same as Nathaniel." This book, considered a unique copy, was placed on a reading-desk in the middle of the library. In the last century, people came to see it as a curiosity.

7. The Granary.

As for the granary, which took, like the library, the oblong form of the bridge, it was simply the space beneath the wood-work of the roof. It was a great room filled with straw and hay, and lighted by six Mansard windows. There was no ornament except a figure of Saint Bartholomew carved on the door, with this line beneath,—

"Barnabus sanctus falcem jubet ire per herbam."

Thus it was a lofty, wide tower of six stories, pierced here and there with loop-holes, having for entrance and egress a single door of iron leading to a bridge-castle closed by a draw-bridge; behind the tower a forest; in front a plateau of heath, higher than the bridge, lower than the tower; beneath the bridge a deep, narrow ravine full of brushwood,— a torrent in winter, a brook in spring-time, a stony moat in summer.

This was the Tower Gauvain, called La Tourgue.

CHAPTER X

THE HOSTAGES

JULY passed; August came. A blast, fierce and heroic, swept over France. Two spectres had just passed beyond the horizon,— Marat with a dagger in his heart, Charlotte Corday headless. Affairs everywhere were waxing formidable.

As to the Vendée, beaten in grand strategic schemes, she took refuge in little ones,— more redoubtable, we have already said. This war was now an immense fight, scattered about among the woods. The disasters of the large army, called the Catholic and Royal, had commenced. The army from Mayence had been ordered into the Vendée. Eight thousand Vendeans had fallen at Ancenis; they had been repulsed from Nantes, dislodged from Montaigu, expelled from Thouars, chased from Noirmoutier, flung headlong out of Cholet, Mortagne, and Saumur; they had evacuated Parthenay, abandoned Clisson, fallen back from Châtillon, lost a flag at Saint-Hilaire; they had been beaten at Pornic, at the Sables, at Fontenay, at Doué, at the Château d'Eau, at the Ponts-de-Cé; they were kept in check at Luçon, were retreating from the Chataigneraye, and were routed at the Roche-sur-Yon. But on the one hand they were menacing Rochelle; and on the other an English fleet in the Guernsey waters, commanded by General Craig, and bearing several English regiments and some of the best officers of the French navy, only waited a signal from the Marquis de Lantenac to land. This landing might make the royalist revolt again victorious.

Pitt was in truth a State malefactor. Policy has treasons sure as an assassin's dagger. Pitt stabbed our country and betrayed his own: to dishonour his country was to betray it. Under him and through him England waged a Punic war; she spied, she cheated, she hid. Poacher and forger, she stopped at nothing; she descended to the very minutiæ of hatred. She monopolized tallow, which cost five francs a pound. An Englishman was taken at Lille on whom was found a letter from Prigent, Pitt's agent in Vendée, which contained these lines: —

"I beg you to spare no money. We hope that the assassinations will be committed with prudence; disguised priests and women are the persons most fit for this duty. Send sixty thousand francs to Rouen and fifty thousand to Caen."

This letter was read in the Convention on the first of August by Barère. The cruelties of Parrein, and later the atrocities of Carrier, replied to these perfidies. The republicans of Metz and the republicans of the South were eager to march against the rebels. A decree ordered the formation of eighty companies of pioneers for burning the copses and thickets of the Bocage. It was an unheard-of crisis. The war only ceased on one footing to begin on another. " No mercy! No prisoners! " was the cry of both parties. The history of that time is black with awful shadows.

During this month of August, La Tourgue was besieged. One evening, just as the stars were rising amid the calm twilight of the dog-days, when not a leaf stirred in the forest, not a blade of grass trembled on the plain, across the stillness of the night swept the sound of a horn. This horn was blown from the top of the tower. The peal was answered by the voice of a clarion from below. On the summit of the tower stood an armed man; at the foot, a camp spread out in the shadow.

In the obscurity about the Tower Gauvain could be distinguished a moving mass of black shapes. It was a bivouac. A few fires began to blaze beneath the trees of the forest and

among the heaths of the plateau, pricking the darkness here
and there with luminous points, as if the earth were studding
itself with stars at the same instant as the sky; but they were
the sinister stars of war.   On the side toward the plateau the
bivouac stretched out to the plains, and on the forest side extended into the thicket.   La Tourgue was invested.

The outstretch of the besiegers' bivouac indicated a numerous force.   The camp tightly clasped the fortress, coming
close up to the rock on the side toward the tower, and close
to the ravine on the bridge side.

There was a second sound of the horn, followed by another
peal from the clarion.   This time the horn questioned, and
the trumpet replied.   It was the demand of the tower to the
camp: "Can we speak to you?"   The clarion was the
answer for the camp; "Yes."

At this period the Vendeans, not being considered belligerents by the Convention, and a decree having forbidden the
exchange of flags of truce with "the brigands," the armies
supplemented as they could the means of communication which
the law of nations authorizes in ordinary war and interdicts
in civil strife.   Hence on occasion a certain understanding
between the peasant's horn and the military trumpet.   The
first call was only to attract attention; the second put the
question, "Will you listen?"   If on this second summons
the clarion kept silent, it was a refusal; if the clarion replied,
it was a consent.   It signified, "Truce for a few moments."

The clarion having answered the second appeal, the man
on the top of the tower spoke, and these words could be
heard : —

"Men, who listen to me, I am Gouge le-Bruant, surnamed Brise-Bleu because I have exterminated many of yours;
surnamed also Imânus, because I mean to kill still more than
I have already done.   My finger was cut off by a blow from
a sabre on the barrel of my gun in the attack of Granville; at
Laval you guillotined my father, my mother, and my sister
Jacqueline, aged eighteen.   This is who I am.   I speak to you
in the name of my lord Marquis Gauvain de Lantenac, Vis-

count de Fontenay, Breton prince, lord of the Seven Forests,
— my master.

"Learn, first, that Monseigneur the Marquis, before shutting himself in this tower where you hold him blockaded, distributed the command among six chiefs, his lieutenants. He gave to Delière the district between the road to Brest and the road to Ernée; to Tréton, the district between Roë and Laval; to Jacquet, called Taillefer, the border of the Haut-Maine; to Gaulier, named Grand Pierre, Château Gontier; to Lecomte, Craon; to Dubois Guy, Fougères; and to De Rochambeau, all of Mayenne. So the taking of this fortress will not end matters for you; and even if Monseigneur the Marquis should die, the Vendée of God and the king will still live. That which I say — know this — is to warn you. Monseigneur is here by my side; I am the mouth through which his words pass. You who are besieging us, keep silence. This is what it is important for you to hear: —

"Do not forget that the war you are making against us is without justice. We are men inhabiting our own country, and we fight honestly; we are simple and pure,— beneath the will of God, as the grass is beneath the dew. It is the Republic which has attacked us; she comes to trouble us in our fields; she has burned our houses, our harvests, and ruined our farms, while our women and children were forced to wander with naked feet among the woods when the winter robin was still singing. You who are down there and who hear me, you have enclosed us in the forest and surrounded us in this tower; you have killed or dispersed those who joined us; you have cannon; you have added to your troop the garrisons and posts of Mortain, of Barenton, of Teilleul, of Landivy, of Evran, of Tinteniac, and of Vitré — by which means you are four thousand five hundred soldiers who attack us; and we — we are nineteen men who defend ourselves. You have provisions and munitions. You have succeeded in mining and blowing up a corner of our rock and a bit of our wall. That has made a gap at the foot of the tower, and this gap is a breach by which you can enter, although

it is not open to the sky; and the tower, still upright and
strong, makes an arch above it.   Now, you are preparing the
assault; and we,— first, Monseigneur the Marquis, who is
Prince of Brittany, and secular Prior of the Abbey of Saint
Marie de Lantenac, where a daily Mass was established by
Queen Jeanne; and, next to him, the other defenders of the
tower, who are the Abbé Turmeau, whose military name is
Grand Francœur; my comrade Guinoiseau, who is captain of
Camp Vert; my comrade Chante-en-Hiver, who is captain of
Camp Avoine; my comrade Musette, who is captain of Camp
Fourmis; and I, peasant, born in the town of Daon, through
which runs the brook Moriandre,— we all, all have one thing
to say to you.   Men, who are at the bottom of this tower, lis-
ten!

"We have on our hands three prisoners, who are three
children.   These children were adopted by one of your regiments, and they belong to you.   We offer to surrender these
three children to you, on one condition; it is that we shall
depart freely.   If you refuse, listen well.   You can only attack us in one of two ways,— by the breach, on the side of
the forest; or by the bridge, on the side of the plateau.   The
building on the bridge has three stories; in the lower story,
I, Imânus — I who speak to you — have put six hogsheads
of tar and a hundred fascines of dried heath; in the top story
there is straw; in the middle story there are books and papers.
The iron door which communicates between the bridge and
the tower is closed, and Monseigneur carries the key; I have
myself made a hole under the door, and through this hole
passes a sulphur slow-match, one end of which is in the tar
and the other within reach of my hand, inside the tower.   I
can fire it when I choose.   If you refuse to let us go out, the
three children will be placed in the second floor of the bridge,
between the story where the sulphur-match touches the tar
and the floor where the straw is, and the iron door will be
shut on them.   If you attack by the bridge, it will be you who
set the building on fire; if you attack by the breach it will be
we; if you attack by the breach and the bridge at the same

time, the fire will be kindled at the same instant by us both, and, in any case, the three children will perish.

"Now, accept or refuse. If you accept, we come out. If you refuse, the children die. I have spoken."

The man speaking from the top of the tower became silent. A voice from below cried: "We refuse!"

This voice was abrupt and severe. Another voice, less harsh, though firm, added: "We give you four-and-twenty hours to surrender at discretion." There was a silence, then the same voice continued: "To-morrow, at this hour, if you have not surrendered, we commence the assault."

And the first voice resumed: "And then no quarter!"

To this savage voice another replied from the top of the tower! Between the two battlements a lofty figure bent forward, and in the starlight the stern face of the Marquis de Lantenac could be distinguished; his sombre glance shot down into the obscurity and seemed to look for some one; and he cried: "Hold, it is thou, priest!"

"Yes, traitor; it is I," replied the stern voice from below.

CHAPTER XI

TERRIBLE AS THE ANTIQUE

THE implacable voice was, in truth, that of Cimourdain: the younger and less imperative that of Gauvain.

The Marquis de Lantenac did not deceive himself in fancying that he recognized Cimourdain. As we know, a few weeks in this district, made bloody by civil war, had rendered Cimourdain famous; there was no notoriety more darkly sinister than his. People said: Marat at Paris, Châlier at Lyons, Cimourdain in Vendée. They stripped the Abbé Cimourdain of all the respect which he had formerly commanded; that is the consequence of a priest's unfrocking himself. Cimourdain inspired horror. The severe are unfortunate; those who note their acts condemn them, though perhaps, if their consciences could be seen, they would stand absolved. A Lycurgus misunderstood appears a Tiberius. Those two men, the Marquis de Lantenac and the Abbé Cimourdain, were equally poised in the balance of hatred. The maledictions of the royalists against Cimourdain made a counterpoise to the execrations of the republicans against Lantenac. Each of these men was a monster to the opposing camp; so far did this equality go, that while Prieur, of the Marne, was setting a price on the head of Lantenac, Charette at Noirmoutiers set a price on the head of Cimourdain. Let us add, these two men — the marquis and the priest — were up to a certain point the same man. The bronze mask of civil war has two profiles,— the one turned toward the past, the other set toward the future; but both equally tragic. Lantenac was the first of these profiles, Cimourdain the second; only, the bitter sneer of Lantenac was full of shadow and night, and on the fatal brow of Cimourdain shone a gleam from the morning.

And now the besieged of La Tourgue had a respite. Thanks to the intervention of Gauvain, a sort of truce for twenty-four hours had been agreed upon.

Imânus had, indeed, been well informed. Through the requisitions of Cimourdain, Gauvain had now four thousand five hundred men under his command, part national guards, part troops of the Line; with these he had surrounded Lantenac in La Tourgue, and was able to level twelve cannon at the fortress,— a masked battery of six pieces on the edge of the forest toward the tower, and an open battery of six on the plateau, toward the bridge. He had succeeded in springing the mine and making a breach at the foot of the tower.

Thus, when the twenty-four hours' truce was ended, the attack would begin under these conditions: On the plateau and in the forest were four thousand five hundred men. In the tower nineteen! History might find the names of those besieged nineteen in the list of outlaws. We shall perhaps encounter them.

As commander of these four thousand five hundred men, which almost made an army, Cimourdain had wished Gauvain to allow himself to be made adjutant-general. Gauvain refused, saying, "When Lantenac is taken, we will see. As yet, I have merited nothing." Those great commands, with low regimental rank, were, for that matter, a custom among the republicans. Bonaparte was, after this, at the same time colonel of artillery and general-in-chief of the army of Italy.

The Tower Gauvain had a strange destiny,—a Gauvain attacked, a Gauvain defended it. From that fact rose a certain reserve in the attack, but not in the defence; for Lantenac was a man who spared nothing. Moreover, he had always lived at Versailles, and had no personal associations with La Tourgue, which he scarcely knew indeed. He had sought refuge there because he had no other asylum,— that was all; he would have demolished it without scruple. Gauvain had more respect for the place.

The weak point of the fortress was the bridge; but in the library, which was on the bridge, were the family archives. If the assault took place on that side, the burning of the bridge would be inevitable. To burn the archives seemed to Gauvain like attacking his forefathers. La Tourgue was the ancestral dwelling of the Gauvains; in this tower centred all their fiefs of Brittany, just as all the fiefs of France centred in the tower of the Louvre. The home associations of Gauvain were there; he had been born within those walls. The tortuous fatalities of life forced him, a man, to attack this venerable pile which had sheltered him when a child. Could he be guilty of the impiety of reducing this dwelling to ashes? Perhaps his very cradle was stored in some corner of the granary above the library. Certain reflections are emotions. Gauvain felt himself moved in the presence of this ancient house of his family. That was why he had spared the bridge. He had confined himself to making any sally or escape impossible by this outlet, and had guarded the bridge by a battery, and chosen the opposite side for the attack. Hence the mining and sapping at the foot of the tower.

Cimourdain had allowed him to take his own way. He reproached himself for it; his stern spirit revolted against all these Gothic relics, and he no more believed in pity for buildings than for men. Sparing a castle was a beginning of clemency. Now, clemency was Gauvain's weak point. Cimourdain, as we have seen, watched him,— drew him back from this, in his eyes, fatal weakness. Still, he himself, though he felt a sort of rage in being forced to admit it to his soul, had not revisited La Tourgue without a secret shock; he felt himself softened at the sight of that study where were still the first books he had made Gauvain read. He had been the priest of the neighbouring village, Parigné; he, Cimourdain, had dwelt in the attic of the bridge-castle; it was in the library that he had held Gauvain between his knees as a child, and taught him to lisp out the alphabet; it was within those four old walls that he had seen grow this well-beloved pupil, the son of his soul, increase physically and strengthen in mind. This library, this small castle, these walls full of his blessings upon the child,— was he about to overturn and burn them? He had shown them mercy,— not without remorse. He had allowed Gauvain to open the siege from the opposite point. La Tourgue had its savage side, the tower, and its civilized side, the library. Cimourdain had allowed Gauvain to batter a breach in the savage side alone.

In truth, attacked by a Gauvain, defended by a Gauvain this old dwelling returned in the height of the Fernch Revolution to feudal customs. Wars between kinsmen make up the history of the Middle Ages: the Eteocles and Polynices are Gothic as well as Grecian, and Hamlet does at Elsinore what Orestes did in Argos.

CHAPTER XII

POSSIBLE ESCAPE

THE whole night was consumed in preparations on the one side and the other. As soon as the sombre parley which we have just heard had ended, Gauvain's first act was to call his lieutenant.

Guéchamp, of whom it will be necessary to know somewhat, was a man of second-rate, honest, intrepid, mediocre; a better soldier than leader; rigorously intelligent up to the point where it ceases to be a duty to understand; never softened; inaccessible to corruption of any sort,— whether of venality, which corrupts the conscience; or of pity, which corrupts justice. He had on soul and heart those two shades, — discipline and the countersign, as a horse has his blinkers on both eyes; and he walked unflinchingly in the space thus left visible to him. His way was straight, but narrow. A man to be depended on; rigid in command, exact in obedience.

Gauvain spoke rapidly to him. "Guéchamp, a ladder."

"Commandant, we have none."

"One must be had."

"For scaling?"

"No, for escape."

Guéchamp reflected an instant, then answered: "I understand. But for what you want, it must be very high."

"At least three stories."

"Yes, Commandant, that is pretty nearly the height."

"It must even go beyond that, for we must be certain of success."

"Without doubt."

"How does it happen that you have no ladder?"

"Commandant, you did not think best to besiege La Tourgue by the plateau; you contented yourself with blockading it on this side. You wished to attack, not by the bridge, but the tower; so we only busied ourselves with the mine, and the escalade was given up.   That is why we have no ladders."

" Have one made immediately."

" A ladder three stories high cannot be improvised."

" Have several short ladders joined together."

" One must have them in order to do that."

" Find them."

" There are none to be found.   All through the country the peasants destroy the ladders, just as they break up the carts and cut the bridges."

" It is true; they try to paralyze the Republic."

" They want to manage so that we can neither transport baggage, cross a river, nor escalade a wall."

" Still, I must have a ladder."

" I just remember, Commandant, at Javené, near Fougères, there is a large carpenter's shop.   They might have one there."

" There is not a minute to lose."

" When do you want the ladder? "

" To-morrow at this hour, at the latest."

" I will send an express full speed to Javené.   He can take a requisition.   There is a post of cavalry at Javené which will furnish an escort.   The ladder can be here to-morrow before sunset."

" It is well; that will answer," said Gauvain.   " Act quickly; go."

Ten minutes after, Guéchamp came back and said to Gauvain: " Commandant, the express has started for Javené."

Gauvain ascended the plateau and remained for a long time with his eyes fixed on the bridge-castle across the ravine. The gable of the building, without other means of access than the low entrance closed by the raising of the draw-bridge, faced the escarpment of the ravine.   In order to reach the arches of the bridge from the plateau, it was neces-sary to descend this escarpment,— a feat possible to ac-complish by clinging to the brushwood.   But once in the moat, the assailants would be exposed to all the projectiles that might rain from the three stories.

Gauvain finished by convincing himself that at the point which the siege had reached, the veritable attack ought to be by the breach of the tower. He took every measure to render any escape out of the question; he increased the strictness of the investment; drew closer the ranks of his battalions, so that nothing could pass between. Gauvain and Cimourdain divided the investment of the fortress between them. Gauvain reserved the forest side for himself, and gave Cimourdain the side of the plateau. It was agreed that while Gauvain, seconded by Guéchamp, conducted the assault through the mine, Cimourdain should guard the bridge and ravine, with every match of the open battery lighted.

CHAPTER XIII

WHAT THE MARQUIS WAS DOING

WHILE without every preparation for the attack was going on, within everything was preparing for resistance.

It is not without a real analogy that a tower is called a " douve; " and sometimes a tower is breached by a mine, as a cask is bored by an auger. The wall opens like a bung-hole. This was what had happened at La Tourgue. The great blast of two or three hundredweight of powder had burst the mighty wall through and through. This breach started from the foot of the tower, traversed the wall in its thickest part, and made a sort of shapeless arch in the ground-floor of the fortress. On the outside the besiegers, in order to render this gap practicable for assault, had enlarged and finished it off by cannon-shots.

The ground-floor which this breach penetrated was a great

round hall, entirely empty, with a central pillar which supported the keystone of the vaulted roof.   This chamber, the
largest in the whole keep, was not less than forty feet in
diameter.   Each story of the tower was composed of a similar
room, but smaller, with guards to the embrasures of the
loop-holes.   The ground-floor chamber had neither loop-holes
nor air-holes; there was about as much air and light as in
a tomb.   The door of the dungeon, made more of iron than
wood, was in this ground-floor room.   Another door opened
upon a staircase which led to the upper chambers.   All the
staircases were contrived in the interior of the wall.   It was
into this lower room that the besiegers could arrive by the
breach they had made.   This hall taken, there would still be
the tower to take.   It had always been impossible to breathe
in that hall for any length of time.   Nobody ever passed
twenty-four hours there without suffocating.   Now, thanks
to the breach, one could exist there.   That was why the besieged had not closed the breach.   Besides, of what service
would it have been?   The cannon would have re-opened it.
They stuck an iron torch-holder into the wall, and put a
torch in it, which lighted the ground-floor.

Now, how to defend themselves?   To wall up the hole
would be easy, but useless.   A retirade would be of more
service.   A retirade is an intrenchment with a re-entering
angle,— a sort of rafted barricade, which admits of converg-
ing the fire upon the assailants, and while leaving the breach
open exteriorly blocks it on the inside.   Materials were not
lacking.   They constructed a retirade with fissures for the
passage of the gun-barrels.   The angle was supported by
the central pillar; the wings touched the wall on either side.

The marquis directed everything.   Inspirer, commander,
guide, and master,— a terrible spirit.   Lantenac belonged
to that race of warriors of the eighteenth century, who at
eighty years saved cities.   He resembled that Count d'Alberg
who, almost a centenarian, drove the King of Poland from
Riga.   " Courage, friends," said the marquis; " at the com-
mencement of this century, in 1713, at Bender, Charles XII..

shut up in a house with three hundred Swedes, held his own against twenty thousand Turks."

They barricaded the two lower floors, fortified the chambers, battlemented the alcoves, supported the doors with joists driven in by blows from a mallet; and thus formed a sort of buttress. It was necessary to leave free the spiral staircase which joined the different floors, for they must be able to get up and down, and to stop it against the besiegers would have been to close it against themselves. The defence of any place has thus always some weak side.

The marquis, indefatigable, robust as a young man, set an example,— lifted beams, carried stones, put his hand to the work, commanded, aided, fraternized, laughed with this ferocious clan, but remained always the noble still,— haughty, familiar, elegant, savage. He permitted no reply to his orders. He had said: "If the half of you should revolt, I would have them shot by the other half, and defend the place with those that were left." Such things make a leader adored.

CHAPTER XIV

WHAT IMÂNUS WAS DOING

WHILE the marquis occupied himself with the breach and the tower, Imânus was busy with the bridge. At the beginning of the siege, the escape-ladder which hung transversely below the windows of the second story had been removed by the marquis's orders, and Imânus had put it in the library. (It was, perhaps, the loss of this ladder which Gauvain wished to supply.) The windows of the lower floor, called the guard-room, were defended by a triple bracing of iron bars set in the stone, so that neither ingress nor egress was possible by them. The library windows had no bars, but they were very high.

17

Imânus took three men with him, who, like himself, possessed capabilities and resolution that would carry them through anything: these men were Hoisnard, called Branche d'Or, and the two brothers Pique-en-Bois. Imânus, carrying a dark lantern, opened the iron door and carefully visited the three stories of the bridge-castle. Branche d'Or was implacable as Imânus, having had a brother killed by the Republicans. Imânus examined the upper room filled with hay and straw, and the ground-floor, where he had several fire-pots added to the tuns of tar; he placed the heap of fascines so that they touched the casks, and assured himself of the good condition of the sulphur-match, of which one end was in the bridge and the other in the tower. He spread over the floor, under the tuns and fascines, a pool of tar, in which he dipped the end of the sulphur-match. Then he brought into the library, between the ground-floor where the tar was and the garret filled with straw, the three cribs in which lay René-Jean, Gros-Alain, and Georgette, buried in deep sleep. They carried the cradles very gently in order not to awaken the little ones. They were simple village cribs, a sort of low osier-basket, which stood on the floor so that a child could get out unaided. Near each cradle Imânus placed a porringer of soup, with a wooden spoon. The escape-ladder, unhooked from its cramping-irons, had been set on the floor against the wall; Imânus arranged the three cribs, end to end, in front of the ladder. Then, thinking that a current of air might be useful, he opened wide the six windows of the library; the summer night was warm and starlight. He sent the brothers Pique-en-Bois to open the windows of the upper and lower stories. He had noticed on the eastern façade of the building a great dried old ivy, the colour of tinder, which covered one whole side of the bridge from top to bottom, and framed in the windows of the three stories. He thought this ivy might be left.

Imânus took a last watchful glance at everything; that done, the four men left the châtelet and returned to the tower. Imânus double-locked the heavy iron door, studied attentively the enormous bolts, and nodded his head in a satisfied way at the sulphur-match which passed through the hole he had drilled, and was now the sole communication between the tower and the bridge. This train or wick started from the round chamber, passed beneath the iron door, entered under the arch, twisted like a snake down the spiral stair-case leading to the lower story of the bridge, crept over the floor, and ended in the heap of dried fascines laid on the pool of tar. Imânus had calculated that it would take about a quarter of an hour for this wick, when lighted in the interior of the tower, to set fire to the pool of tar under the library. These arrangements all concluded, and every work carefully inspected, he carried the key of the iron door back to the marquis, who put it in his pocket.

It was important that every movement of the besiegers should be watched. Imânus, with his cowherd's horn in his belt, posted himself as sentinel on the watch-tower of the platform at the top of the tower. While keeping a constant look-out, one eye on the forest and one on the plateau, he worked at making cartridges, having near him, in the embrasure of the watch-tower window, a powder-horn, a canvas-bag full of good-sized balls, and some old newspapers, which he tore up for wadding.

When the sun rose it lighted in the forest eight battalions, with sabres at their sides, knapsacks on their backs, and guns with fixed bayonets, ready for the assault; on the plateau, a battery with caissons, cartridges, and boxes of case-shot; within the fortress, nineteen men loading several guns, muskets, blunderbusses, and pistols,— and three children sleeping in their cradles.

BOOK III

THE MASSACRE OF SAINT BARTHOLOMEW

CHAPTER I

THE children woke. The little girl was the first to open her eyes. The waking of children is like the unclosing of flowers,— a perfume seems to exhale from those fresh young souls.

Georgette, twenty months old, the youngest of the three who was still a nursing baby in the month of May, raised her little head, sat up in her cradle, looked at her feet, and began to chatter. A ray of the morning fell across her crib; it would have been difficult to decide which was the rosiest,— Georgette's foot or Aurora. The other two still slept; the slumber of boys is heavier. Georgette, gay and happy, began to chatter. René-Jean's hair was brown, Gros-Alain's was auburn, Georgette's blond. These tints would change later in life. René-Jean had the look of an infant Hercules; he slept lying on his stomach, with his two fists in his eyes. Gros-Alain had thrust his legs outside his little bed.

All three were in rags. The garments given them by the battalion of the Bonnet Rouge had worn to shreds; they had not even a shirt between them. The two boys were almost naked; Georgette was muffled in a rag which had once been a petticoat, but was now little more than a jacket. Who had taken care of these children? Impossible to say. Not a mother. These savage peasant fighters, who dragged them

along from forest to forest, had given them their portion
of soup. That was all. The little ones lived as they could.
They had everybody for master, and nobody for father.
But even about the rags of childhood there hangs a halo.
These three tiny creatures were lovely.

Georgette prattled. A bird sings, a child prattles; but
it is the same hymn,— hymn indistinct, inarticulate, but full
of profound meaning. The child, unlike the bird, has the
sombre destiny of humanity before it: this thought saddens
any man who listens to the joyous song of a child. The
most sublime psalm that can be heard on this earth is the
lisping of a human soul from the lips of childhood. This
confused murmur of thought which is as yet only instinct,
holds a strange unreasoning appeal to eternal justice; perchance it is a protest against life while standing on its
threshold,— a protest unconscious, yet heart-rending. This
ignorance, smiling at infinity, lays upon all creation the burden of the destiny which shall be offered to this feeble, unarmed creature; if unhappiness comes, it seems like a be-
trayal of confidence. The babble of an infant is more and
less than speech: it is not measured, and yet it is a song;
not syllables, and yet a language,— a murmur that began in
heaven, and will not finish on earth; it commenced before human birth, and will continue in the sphere beyond! These
lispings are the echo of what the child said when he was an
angel, and of what he will say when he enters eternity. The
cradle has a yesterday, just as the grave has a to-morrow:
this morrow and this yesterday join their double mystery in
that incomprehensible warbling; and there is no such proof
of God, of eternity, and the duality of destiny, as in this awe-
inspiring shadow flung across that flower-like soul.

There was nothing saddening in Georgette's prattle; her
whole lovely face was a smile. Her mouth smiled, her eyes
smiled, the dimples in her cheeks smiled. There was a serene
acceptance of the morning in this smile. The soul has faith
in the sunlight. The sky was blue, warm, beautiful. This
frail creature, who knew nothing, who comprehended noth-

ing, softly cradled in a dream which was not thought, felt herself in safety amidst the loveliness of Nature,— these sturdy trees, this pure verdure, this landscape fair and peaceful, with its noises of birds, brooks, insects, leaves, above which glowed the brightness of the sun.

After Georgette, René-Jean, the eldest, who was past four, awoke. He sat up, jumped in a manly way over the side of his cradle, found out the porringer, considered that quite natural, and so sat down on the floor and began to eat his soup.

Georgette's prattle had not awakened Gros-Alain, but at the sound of the spoon in the porringer he turned over with a start, and opened his eyes. Gros-Alain was the one three years old. He saw his bowl; he had only to stretch out his arm and take it. So, without leaving his bed, he followed René-Jean's example, seized the spoon in his little fists, and began to eat, holding the bowl on his knees.

Georgette did not hear them; the modulations of her voice seemed measured by the cradling of a dream. Her great eyes, gazing upward, were divine. No matter how dark the ceiling in the vault above the child's head, heaven is reflected in its eyes.

When René-Jean had finished his portion, he scraped the bottom of the bowl with his spoon, sighed, and said with dignity, " I have eaten my soup."

This roused Georgette from her reverie. " Thoup! " said she. Seeing that René-Jean had eaten, and that Gros-Alain was eating, she took the porringer which was placed by her cradle, and began to eat in her turn,— not without carrying the spoon to her ear much oftener than to her mouth. From time to time she renounced civilization, and ate with her fingers.

When Gros-Alain had scraped the bottom of his porringer too, he leaped out of bed and joined his brother.

NINETY-THREE

A **263**

CHAPTER II

SUDDENLY from without, down below, on the side of the forest, came the stern, loud ring of a trumpet. To this clarion-blast a horn from the top of the tower replied. This time it was the clarion which called, and the horn which made answer. The clarion blew a second summons, and the horn again replied. Then from the edge of the forest rose a voice, distant but clear, which cried thus: —

"Brigands, a summons! If at sunset you have not surrendered at discretion, we commence the attack."

A voice, which sounded like the roar of a wild animal, responded from the summit of the tower: "Attack!"

The voice from below resumed: "A cannon will be fired, as a last warning, half an hour before the assault."

The voice from on high repeated: "Attack!"

These voices did not reach the children, but the trumpet and the horn rose loud and clear. At the first sound of the clarion, Georgette lifted her head, and stopped eating; at the sound of the horn, she dropped her spoon into the porringer; at the second blast of the trumpet, she lifted the little forefinger of her right hand, and, raising and depressing it in turn, marked the cadences of the flourish which prolonged the blast. When the trumpet and the horn ceased, she remained with her finger pensively lifted, and murmured, in a half voice, "Muthic." We suppose that she wished to say, "Music."

The two elders, René-Jean and Gros-Alain, had paid no attention to the trumpet and horn; they were absorbed by something else: a wood-louse was just making a journey across the library floor.

Gros-Alain perceived it, and cried: "There is a little creature!" René-Jean ran up. Gros-Alain continued: "It stings."

"Do not hurt it," said René-Jean.

And both remained watching the traveller.

Georgette proceeded to finish her soup; that done, she looked about for her brothers. René-Jean and Gros-Alain were in the recess of one of the windows, gravely stooping over the wood-louse,— their foreheads touching, their curls mingling. They held their breath in wonder, and examined the insect, which had stopped, and did not attempt to move, though not appreciating the admiration it received.

Georgette seeing that her brothers were watching something, must needs know what it was. It was not an easy matter to reach them; still, she undertook the journey. The way was full of difficulties. There were things scattered over the floor. There were footstools overturned, heaps of old papers, packing-cases forced open and empty, trunks, rubbish of all sorts, in and out of which it was necessary to sail,— a whole archipelago of reefs; but Georgette risked it. The first task was to get out of her crib; then she entered the chain of reefs, twisted herself through the straits, — pushed a footstool aside, crept between two coffers, got over a heap of papers, climbing up one side and rolling down the other, regardless of the exposure to her poor little naked legs, and succeeded in reaching what a sailor would have called an open sea,— that is, a sufficiently wide space of the floor which was not littered over, and where there were no more perils; then she bounded forward, traversed this space, which was the whole width of the room, on all fours with the agility of a kitten, and got near to the window. There a fresh and formidable obstacle encountered her: the great ladder lying along the wall reached to this window, the end of it passing a little beyond the corner of the recess; it formed between Georgette and her brothers a sort of cape, which must be crossed. She stopped and meditated; her internal monologue ended, she came to a decision. She resolutely twisted her rosy fingers about one of the rungs, which were vertical, as the ladder lay along its side; she tried to raise herself on her feet, and fell back; she began again, and fell a second time; the third effort was successful. Then,

,tanding up, she caught hold of the rounds in succession, and walked the length of the ladder. When she reached the extremity there was nothing more to support her; she tottered, but seizing in her two hands the end of one of the great poles, which held the rungs, she rose again, doubled the promontory, looked at René-Jean and Gros-Alain, and began to laugh.

CHAPTER III

AT that instant, René-Jean, satisfied with the result of his investigations of the wood-louse, raised his head, and announced, " 'T is a she-creature."

Georgette's laughter made René-Jean laugh, and René-Jean's laughter made Gros-Alain laugh. Georgette seated herself beside her brothers, the recess forming a sort of little reception chamber; but their guest, the wood-louse had disappeared. He had taken advantage of Georgette's laughter to hide himself in a crack of the floor.

Other incidents followed the wood-louse's visit. First, a flock of swallows passed. They probably had their nests under the edge of the overhanging roof. They flew close to the window, a little startled by the sight of the children, describing great circles in the air, and uttering their melodious spring song. The sound made the three little ones look up, and the wood-louse was forgotten.

Georgette pointed her finger toward the swallows, and cried, " Chicks! "

René-Jean reprimanded her. " Miss, you must not say ' chicks; ' they are birds."

" Birz," repeated Georgette.

And all three sat and watched the swallows.

Then a bee entered. There is nothing so like a soul as a bee. It goes from flower to flower as a soul from star to star, and gathers honey as the soul does light. This visitor made a great noise as it came in; it buzzed at the top of its voice, seeming to . say, " I have come! I have first been to see the roses, now I come to see the children. What is going on here? " A bee is a house-wife; its song is a grumble. The children did not take their eyes off the new comer as long as it stayed with them. The bee explored the library, rummaged in the corners, fluttered about with the air of being at home in a hive, and wandered, winged and melodious, from book-case to book-case, examining the titles of the volumes through the glass doors as if it had an intellect. Its explorations finished, it departed.

" She is going to her own house," said René-Jean.

" It is a beast," said Gros-Alain.

" No," replied René-Jean, " it is a fly."

" A f'y," said Georgette.

Thereupon Gros-Alain, who had just found on the floor a cord with a knot in one end, took the opposite extremity between his thumb and forefinger, and made a sort of windmill of the string, watching its whirls with profound attention.

On her side, Georgette, having turned into a quadruped again, and recommenced her capricious course back and forward across the floor, discovered a venerable tapestry-covered armchair, so eaten by moths that the horse-hair stuck out in several places. She stopped before this seat. She enlarged the holes, and diligently pulled out the long hairs. Suddenly she lifted one finger; that meant, " Listen! "

The two brothers turned their heads. A vague, distant noise surged up from without: it was probably the attacking camp executing some strategic manœuvre in the forest, horses neighed, drums beat, caissons rolled, chains clanked, military calls and responses,— a confusion of savage sounds, whose mingling formed a sort of harmony. The children listened in delight.

" It is the good God who does that," said René-Jean.

CHAPTER IV

THE noise ceased. René-Jean remained lost in a dream.
How do ideas vanish and reform themselves in the
brains of those little ones? What is the mysterious motive
of those memories at once so troubled and so brief? There
was in that sweet, pensive little soul a mingling of ideas of
the good God, of prayer, of joined hands, the light of a
tender smile it had formerly known and knew no longer;
and René-Jean murmured, half aloud, " Mamma!"

" Mamma!" repeated Gros-Alain.

" Mamma!" cried Georgette.

Then René-Jean began to leap. Seeing this, Gros-Alain
leaped too. Gros-Alain repeated every movement and gesture of his brother. Three years copies four years; but
twenty months keeps its independence.

Georgette remained seated, uttering a word from time to
time. Georgette could not yet manage sentences. She was
a thinker; she spoke in apothegms; she was monosyllabic.
Still, after a little, example proved infectious and she ended by
trying to imitate her brothers; and these three little pairs of
naked feet began to dance, to run, to totter amidst the dust of
the old polished oak floor, beneath the grave aspects of the
marble busts toward which Georgette from time time cast an
unquiet glance, murmuring " Momommes." Probably in
Georgette's language this signified something which looked
like a man, but yet was not one,— perhaps the first glim-
mering of an idea in regard to phantoms. Georgette, oscillating rather than walking, followed her brothers, but her
favourite mode of locomotion was on all fours.

Suddenly René-Jean, who had gone near a window, lifted
his head, then dropped it, and hastened to hide himself in a
corner of the wall made by the projecting window recess.
He had just caught sight of a man looking at him. It
was a soldier, from the encampment of Blues on the plateau,

who profiting by the truce, and perhaps infringing it a little, had ventured to the very edge of the escarpment, whence the interior of the library was visible. Seeing René-Jean hide himself, Gros-Alain hid too; he crouched down beside his brother, and Georgette hurried to hide herself behind them. So they remained, silent, motionless, Georgette pressing her finger against her lips. After a few instants, René-Jean ventured to thrust out his head; the soldier was there still. René-Jean retreated quickly, and the three little ones dared not even breathe. This suspense lasted for some time. Finally the fear began to bore Georgette; she gathered courage to look out. The soldier had disappeared. They began again to run about and play.

Gros-Alain, although the imitator and admirer of René-Jean, had a specialty,— that of discoveries. His brother and sister saw him suddenly galloping wildly about, dragging after him a little cart, which he had unearthed behind some box. This doll's wagon had lain forgotten for years among the dust, living amicably in the neighbourhood of the printed works of genius and the busts of sages. It was, perhaps, one of the toys that Gauvain had played with when a child.

Gros-Alain had made a whip of his string, and cracked it loudly; he was very proud. Such are discoverers. The child discovers a little wagon; the man, an America: the spirit of adventure is the same.

But it was necessary to share the godsend. René-Jean wished to harness himself to the carriage, and Georgette wished to ride in it. She succeeded in seating herself. René-Jean was the horse. Gros-Alain was the coachman. But the coachman did not understand his business; the horse began to teach him. René-Jean shouted, " Say ' Whoa!' "

" Whoa! " repeated Gros-Alain.

The carriage upset. Georgette rolled out. Child-angels can shriek; Georgette did so. Then she had a vague wish to weep.

" Miss," said René-Jean, " you are too big."

NINETY-THREE 269

"Me big!" stammered Georgette. And her size consoled her for her fall.

The cornice of entablature outside the windows was very broad; the dust blowing from the plain of heath had collected there; the rains had hardened it into soil, the wind had brought seeds; a blackberry-bush had profited by the shallow bed to grow up there. This bush belonged to the species called fox blackberry. It was August now, and the bush was covered with berries; a branch passed in by the window, and hung down nearly to the floor. Gros-Alain, after having discovered the cord and the wagon, discovered this bramble. He went up to it. He gathered a berry and ate.

"I am hungry," said René-Jean.

Georgette arrived, galloping up on her hands and knees. The three between them stripped the branch, and ate all the berries. They stained their faces and hands with the purple juice till the trio of little seraphs was changed into a knot of little fauns, which would have shocked Dante and charmed Virgil. They shrieked with laughter. From time to time the thorns pricked their fingers. There is always a pain attached to every pleasure. Georgette held out her finger to René-Jean, on which showed a tiny drop of blood, and pointing to the bush, said, "P'icks."

Gros-Alain, who had suffered also, looked suspiciously at the branch and said: "It is a beast."

"No," replied René-Jean; "it is a stick."

"Then a stick is wicked," retorted Gros-Alain.

Again Georgette, though she had a mind to cry, burst out laughing.

CHAPTER V

IN the mean time René-Jean, perhaps jealous of the discoveries made by his younger brother, had conceived a grand project. For some minutes past, while busy eating the berries and pricking his fingers, his eyes turned frequently toward the chorister's desk mounted on a pivot and isolated like a monument in the centre of the library. On this desk lay the celebrated volume of " Saint Bartholomew." It was in truth a magnificent and priceless folio. It had been published at Cologne by the famous publisher of the edition of the Bible of 1682, Blœuw, or, in Latin, Cœsius. It was printed, not on Dutch paper, but upon that beautiful Arabian paper so much admired by Edrisi, which was made of silk and cotton and never grew yellow; the binding was of gilt leather, and the clasps of silver; the boards were of that parchment which the parchment sellers of Paris took an oath to buy at the Hall Saint Mathurin, " and nowhere else." The volume was full of engravings on wood and copper, with geographical maps of many countries; it had on a fly-leaf a protest of the printers, paper-makers, and publishers against the edict of 1635, which set a tax on " leather, fur, cloven-footed animals, sea-fish, and paper; " and at the back of the frontispiece could be read a dedication to the Gryphes, who were to Lyons what the Elzevirs were to Amsterdam. These combinations resulted in a famous copy almost as rare as the " Apostol " at Moscow.

The book was beautiful; it was for that reason René-Jean looked at it, too long perhaps. The volume chanced to be open at a great print representing Saint Bartholomew carrying his skin over his arm. He could see this print where he stood. When the berries were all eaten, René-Jean watched it with a feverish longing, and Georgette, following the direction of her brother's eyes, perceived the engraving, and said " Pic'sure."

This exclamation seemed to decide René-Jean. Then, to the utter stupefaction of Gros-Alain, an extraordinary thing happened. A great oaken chair stood in one corner of the library; René-Jean marched toward it, seized and dragged it unaided up to the desk. Then he mounted thereon and laid his two hands on the volume. Arrived at this summit, he felt a necessity for being magnificently generous; he took hold of the upper end of the " pic'sure " and tore it carefully down. The tear went diagonally over the saint, but that was not the fault of René-Jean; it left in the book the left side, one eye, and a bit of the halo of the old apocryphal evangelist. He offered Georgette the other half of the saint and all his skin. Georgette took the saint, and observed, " Momommes."

" And I! " cried Gros-Alain.

The tearing of the first page of a book by children is like the shedding of the first drop of blood by men,— it decides the carnage. René-Jean turned the leaf; next to the saint came the Commentator Pantœnus. René-Jean bestowed Pantœnus upon Gros-Alain. Meanwhile Georgette tore her large piece into two little morsels, then the two into four, and continued her work till history might have noted that Saint Bartholomew, after having been flayed in Armenia, was torn limb from limb in Brittany.

CHAPTER VI

THE quartering completed, Georgette held out her hand to René-Jean, and said, " More! " After the saint and the commentator followed portraits of frowning glossarists. The first in the procession was Gavantus: René-Jean tore him out and put Gavantus into Georgette's hand. The whole group of Saint Bartholomew's commentators met the same fate in turn.

There is a sense of superiority in giving. René-Jean kept
nothing for himself. Gros-Alain and Georgette were watching him,— he was satisfied with that; the admiration of his
public was reward enough. René-Jean, inexhaustible in his
magnanimity, offered Frabricio Pignatelli to Gros-Alain,
and Father Stilting to Georgette; he followed these by the
bestowal of Alphonse Tostat on Gros-Alain, and Cornelius a
Lapide upon Georgette. Then Gros-Alain received Henry,
Hammond, and Georgette received Father Roberti, together
with a view of the city of Douai, where that father was born,
in 1619. Gros-Alain received the protest of the stationers,
and Georgette obtained the dedication to the Gryphes. Then
it was the turn of the maps. René-Jean proceeded to dis-
tribute them. He gave Gros-Alain Ethiopia, and Lycaonia
fell to Georgette. This done he tumbled the book upon the
floor.

This was a terrible moment. With mingled ectasy and
fright Gros-Alain and Georgette saw René-Jean wrinkle his
brows, stiffen his legs, clinch his fists, and push the massive
folio off the stand. The majestic old tome was fairly a
tragic spectacle. Pushed from its resting-place, it hung
for an instant on the edge of the desk,— seemed to hesitate,
trying to balance itself,— then crashed down, and broken,
crumpled, torn, ripped from its bindings, its clasps fractured, flattened itself miserably upon the floor. Fortunately
it did not fall on the children; they were only bewildered,
not crushed. Victories do not always finish so well. Like
all glories it made a great noise, and left a cloud of dust.

Having flung the book on the ground, René-Jean descended from the chair. There was a moment of silence and
fright; victory has its terrors. The three children seized
one another's hands and stood at a distance, looking toward
the vast dismantled tome. But after a brief reverie Gros-
Alain approached it quickly and gave it a kick. Nothing
more was needed. The appetite for destruction grows rapidly. René-Jean kicked it, Georgette dealt a blow with her
little foot which overset her, though she fell in a sitting

position, by which she profited to fling herself on Saint Bartholomew. The spell was completely broken. René-Jean pounced upon the saint, Gros-Alain dashed upon him, and joyous, distracted, triumphant, pitiless, tearing the prints, slashing the leaves, pulling out the markers, scratching the binding, ungluing the gilded leather, breaking off the nails from the silver corners, ruining the parchment, making mince-meat of the august test, working with feet, hands, nails, teeth,— rosy, laughing, ferocious, the three angels of prey demolished the defenceless evangelist. They annihilated Armenia, Judea, Benevento, where rest the relics of the saint; Nathaniel, who is perhaps the same as Bartholomew; the Pope Gelasius, who declared the Gospel of Saint Bartholomew (Nathaniel, apocryphal; all the portraits, all the maps; and the inexorable massacre of the old book absorbed them so entirely that a mouse ran past without their perceiving it. It was an extermination. To tear in pieces history, legend, science, miracles, whether true or false, the Latin of the Church, superstitions, fanaticisms, mysteries,— to rend a whole religion from top to bottom would be a work for three giants; but the three children completed it. Hours passed in the labour, but they reached the end; nothing remained of Saint Bartholomew.

When they had finished, when the last page was loosened, the last print lying on the ground, when nothing was left of the book but the edges of the text and pictures in the skeleton of the binding, René-Jean sprang to his feet, looked at the floor covered with scattered leaves, and clapped his hands. Gros-Alain clapped his hands likewise. Georgette took one of the pages in her hand, rose, leaned against the window-sill, which was on a level with her chin, and commenced to tear the great leaf into tiny bits, and scatter them out of the casement. Seeing this, René-Jean and Gros-Alain began the same work. They picked up and tore into small bits, picked up again and tore, and flung the pieces out of the window, as Georgette had done, page by

18

page. Rent by these little desperate fingers, the entire ancient volume almost flew down the wind.

Georgette thoughtfully watched these swarms of little white papers dispersed by the breeze, and said: " Butterf'ies ! "

So the massacre ended with these tiny ghosts vanishing in the blue of heaven!

CHAPTER VII

THUS was Saint Bartholomew for the second time made a martyr,— he who had been the first time sacrificed in the year of our Lord 49.

Then the evening came on; the heat increased; there was sleep in the air. Georgette's eyes began to close; René-Jean went to his crib, pulled out the straw sack which served instead of a mattress, dragged it to the window stretched himself thereon, and said, " Let us go to bed." Gros-Alain laid his head against René-Jean, Georgette placed hers on Gros-Alain, and the three malefactors fell asleep.

The warm breeze entered by the open windows, the perfume of wild flowers from the ravines and hills mingled with the breath of evening. Nature was calm and pitiful; everything beamed, was at peace, full of love; the sun gave its caress, which is light, to all creation; everywhere could be heard and felt that harmony which is thrown off from the infinite sweetness of inanimate things. There is a motherhood in the infinite,— she perfects her grandeur by her goodness; creation is a miracle in full bloom. It seemed as if one could feel some invisible Being take those mysterious precautions which in the formidable conflict of opposing elements of life protect the weak against the strong; at the same time there was beauty everywhere,— the splendour equalled the gentleness. The landscape that seemed asleep had those lovely hazy effects which the changings of light and shadow produce on the fields and rivers; the mists mounted toward the clouds like reveries changing into dreams; the birds circled noisily about La Tourgue; the swallows looked in through the windows, as if they wished to be certain that the children slept well.

They were prettily grouped upon one another, motionless, half-naked, posed like little Cupids; they were adorable and pure; the united ages of the three did not make nine years. They were dreaming dreams of paradise, which were reflected on their lips in vague smiles. Perchance God whispered in their ears. They were of those whom all human languages call the weak and blessed; they were made majestic by innocence. All was silence about them, as if the breath from their tender bosoms was the care of the universe, and listened to by the whole creation; the leaves did not rustle, the grass did not stir. It seemed as if the vast starry world held its breath for fear of disturbing these three humble angelic sleepers, and nothing could have been so sublime as that reverent respect of Nature in presence of this littleness.

The sun was near its setting; it almost touched the horizon. Suddenly, across this profound peace burst a lightning-like glare, which came from the forest; then a savage noise. A cannon had just been fired. The echoes seized upon this thundering, and repeated it with an infernal din; the prolonged growling from hill to hill was terrible. It woke Georgette. She raised her head slightly, lifted her little finger, and said: "Boom!" The noise died away; the silence swept back; Georgette laid her head on Gros-Alain, and fell asleep once more.

BOOK VI

THE MOTHER

CHAPTER I

DEATH PASSES

WHEN this evening came, the mother whom we saw wandering almost at random had walked the whole day. This was indeed the history of all her days,— to go straight before her without stopping. For her slumbers of exhaustion, given in to in any corner that chanced to be nearest, were no more rest than the morsels she ate here and there (as the birds pick up crumbs) were nourishment. She ate and slept just what was absolutely necessary to keep her from falling down dead. She had passed the previous night in an empty barn; civil wars leave many such. She had found in a bare field four walls, an open door, a little straw beneath the ruins of a roof; and she had slept on the straw under the rafters, feeling the rats slip about beneath, and watching the stars rise through the gaping wreck above. She slept for several hours; then she woke in the middle of the night and set out again in order to get over as much road as possible before the great heat of the day should set in. For any one who travels on foot in the summer, midnight is more fitting than noon.

She had followed to the best of her ability the brief itinerary the peasant of Vautortes had marked out for her: she had gone as straight as possible toward the west. Had there

been any one near, he might have heard her ceaselessly murmur, half aloud, "La Tourgue." Except the names of her
children, this word was all she knew. As she walked, she
dreamed. She thought of the adventures with which she
had met; she thought of all she had suffered, all which she
had accepted,— of the meetings, the indignities, the terms
offered; the bargains proposed and submitted to,— now for
a shelter, now for a morsel of bread, sometimes simply to
obtain from some one information as to her route. A
wretched woman is more unfortunate than a wretched man,
for she may be a prey to lust. Frightful wandering march!
But nothing mattered to her, provided she could discover her
children.

Her first encounter this day had been a village. The
dawn was beginning to break; everything was still tinged
with the gloom of night. A few doors were already half
open in the principal streets, and curious faces looked out of
the windows; the inhabitants were agitated like a disturbed
bee-hive: this arose from a noise of wheels and chains which
had been heard. On the church square a frightened group
with their heads raised, watched something descend a high
hill along the road toward the village. It was a four-
wheeled wagon drawn by five horses, harnessed with chains.
On this wagon could be distinguished a heap like a pile of
long joists, in the middle of which lay some shapeless object, covered with a large canvas resembling a pall. Ten
horseman rode in front of the wagon, and ten others behind;
these men wore three-cornered hats, and above their shoulders
rose what seemed to be the points of naked sabres. This
whole cortége, advancing slowly showed black and distinct
against the horizon, the wagon looked black, the harness
looked black, the horsemen looked black. Behind them
gleamed the pallor of the morning. They entered the village and moved toward the square. Daylight had come on
while the wagon was going down the hill, and the cortége
could be distinctly seen; it was like watching a procession of
shadows, for not a man in the party uttered a word. The

horsemen were gendarmes; they did in truth carry drawn sabres. The cover was black.

The wretched wandering mother entered the village from the opposite side, and approached the mob of peasants at the moment the gendarmes and the wagon reached the square. Among the crowd, voices whispered questions and replies: —

" What is it? "

" The guillotine."

" Whence does it come? "

" From Fougères."

" Where is it going? "

" I do not know. They say to a castle in the neighbourhood of Parigné."

" Parigné."

" Let it go where it likes, provided it does not stop here."

This great cart, with its lading hidden by a sort of shroud; this team, these gendarmes, the noise of the chains, the silence of the men, the grey dawn,— all made up a whole that was spectral. The group traversed the square and passed out of the village. The hamlet lay in a hollow between two hills: at the end of a quarter of an hour, the peasants, who had stood still as if petrified, saw the lugubrious procession reappear on the summit of the western hill; the heavy wheels jolted along the ruts, the chains clanked in the morning wind, the sabres shone in the rising sun,— then the road turned off, and the cortége disappeared.

It was the very moment when Georgette woke in the library by the side of her still sleeping brothers, and wished her rosy feet good-morning.

CHAPTER II

DEATH SPEAKS

THE mother watched this mysterious procession, but neither comprehended nor sought to understand; her eyes were busy with another vision,— her children, lost amidst the darkness. She went out of the village also, a little after the cortége which had filed past, and followed the same route at some distance behind the second squad of gendarmes. Suddenly the word " guillotine " recurred to her. " Guillotine! " she said to herself. This rude peasant, Michelle Fléchard, did not know what that was, but instinct warned her. She shivered without being able to tell wherefore; it seemed horrible to her to walk behind this thing and she turned to the left, quitted the high-road, and passed into a wood, which was the forest of Fougères. After wandering for some time, she perceived a belfry and some roofs; it was one of the villages scattered along the edge of the forest. She went toward it; she was hungry. It was one of the villages in which the republicans had established military posts. She passed on to the square in front of the mayoralty.

In this village there was also fright and anxiety. A crowd pressed up to the flight of steps. On the top step stood a man, escorted by soldiers; he held in his hand a great open placard; at his right was stationed a drummer, at his left a bill-sticker, carrying a paste-pot and brush. Upon the balcony over the door appeared the mayor, wearing a tricoloured scarf over his peasant dress. The man with the placard was a public crier. He wore his shoulder-belt, with a small wallet hanging from it,— a sign that he was going from village to village, and had something to publish throughout the district. At the moment Michelle Fléchard approached, he had unfolded the placard, and was beginning to read. He read in a loud voice: —

" THE FRENCH REPUBLIC: ONE AND INDIVISIBLE."

The drum beat. There was a sort of movement among the
assembly. A few took off their caps; others pulled their hats
closer over their heads. At that time and in that country one
could almost recognize the political opinions of a man by his
head-gear: hats were royalists; caps republican. The confused murmur of voices ceased; everybody listened; the crier
read: —

"In virtue of the orders we have received, and the authority delegated to us by the Committee of Public Safety —"

The drum beat the second time. The crier continued: —

"And in execution of the decree of the National Convention, which
puts beyond the law all rebels taken with arms in their hands, and
which ordains capital punishment to whomsoever shall give them shelter
or help them to escape —"

A peasant asked, in a low voice of his neighbour: "What
is that,— capital punishment?"
His neighbour replied: "I do not know."
The crier fluttered the placard: —

"In accordance with Article 17th of the law of April 30, which
gives full power to delegates and sub-delegates against rebels, we declare outlaws —"

He made a pause, and resumed: —

"The individuals known under the names and surnames which follow —"

The whole assemblage listened intently. The crier's voice
sounded like thunder. He read: —

"Lantenac, brigand —"

"That is Monseigneur," murmured a peasant. And
through the whole crowd went the whisper: "It is Monseigneur." The crier resumed: —

"**Lantenac,** *ci-devant* marquis, brigand. Imânus, brigand —"

Two peasants glanced sideways at each other.
" That is Gouge-le-Bruant."
" Yes; it is Brise-Bleu."
The crier continued to read the list: —

" Grand Francœur, brigand —"

The assembly murmured,—
" He is a priest."
" Yes; the Abbé Turmeau."
" Yes; he is curé somewhere in the neighbourhood of the wood of Chapelle."
" And brigand," said a man in a cap.
The crier read: —

" Boisnouveau, brigand. The two brothers, Pique-en-Bois, brigands. Houzard, brigand —"

" That is Monsieur de Quelen," said a peasant.

" Panier, brigand —"

" That is Monsieur Sepher."

" Place Nette, brigand —"

" That is Monsieur Jamois."
The crier continued his reading without noticing these commentaries: —

" Guinoiseau, brigand. Chatenay, styled Robi, brigand —"

A peasant whispered: " Guinoiseau is the same as Le Blond; Chatenay is from Saint Ouen."

" Hoisnard, brigand —" pursued the crier.

Among the crowd could be heard,—
" He is from Ruillé."
" Yes; it is Branche d'Or."
" His brother was killed in the attack on Pontorson."
" Yes; Hoisnard Malonnière."

" A fine young chap of nineteen."

" Attention!" said the crier. " Listen to the last of the list : —

" Belle Vigue, brigand. La Musette, brigand. Sabretout, brigand. Brin d'Amour —"

A lad nudged the elbow of a young girl. The girl smiled. The crier continued : —

" Chante-en-Hiver, brigand. Le Chat, brigand —"

A peasant said, " That is Moulard."

" Tabouze, brigand —"

Another peasant said: " That is Gauffre."

" There are two of the Gauffres," added a woman.

" Both good fellows," grumbled a lad.

The crier shook the placard, and the drum beat. The crier resumed his reading : —

" The above-named, in whatsoever place taken, and their identity established, shall be immediately put to death."

There was a movement among the crowd. The crier went on : —

" Any one affording them shelter or aiding their escape, will be brought before a court-martial and put to death. Signed —"

The silence grew profound.

" The Delegate of the Committee of Public Safety,

" Cimourdain.

" A priest," said a peasant.

" The former curé of Parigné," said another.

A townsman added, " Turmeau and Cimourdain — A Blue priest and a White."

" Both black," said another townsman.

The mayor, who was on the balcony lifted his hat, and cried: " Long live the Republic!"

A roll of the drum announced that the crier had not finished.

He was making a sign with his hand. " Attention! " said he. " Listen to the last four lines of the Government proclamation. They are signed by the Chief of the exploring column of the North Coasts, Commandant Gauvain."

" Listen! " exclaimed the voices of the crowd. And the crier read: —

" Under pain of death —"

All were silent.

" It is forbidden, in pursuance of the above order, to give aid or succour to the nineteen rebels above named, at this time shut up and surrounded in La Tourgue."

" What? " cried a voice. It was the voice of a woman; of the mother.

CHAPTER III

MUTTERINGS AMONG THE PEASANTS

MICHELLE FLECHARD had mingled with the crowd. She had listened to nothing, but one hears certain things without listening. She caught the words " La Tourgue." She raised her head. " What? " she repeated " La Tourgue! "

People stared at her. She appeared out of her mind. She was in rags. Voices murmured, " She looks like a brigand." A peasant woman, who carried a basket of buckwheat biscuits, drew near, and said to her in a low voice: " Hold your tongue! "

Michelle Fléchard gazed stupidly at the woman. Again she understood nothing. The name La Tourgue had passed through her mind like a flash of lightning and the darkness closed anew behind it. Had she not a right to ask information? What had she done that they should stare at her in this way?

But the drum had beat for the last time; the bill-sticker posted up the placard; the mayor retired into the house; the crier set out for some other village, and the mob dispersed. A group remained before the placard; Michelle Fléchard joined this knot of people. They were commenting on the names of the men declared outlaws. There were peasants and townsmen among them; that is to say, Whites and Blues.

A peasant said: " After all, they have not caught everybody. Nineteen are only nineteen. They have not got Riou, they have not got Benjamin Moulins, nor Goupil of the parish of Andouillé."

" Nor Lorieul of Monjean," said another.

Others added,—

" Nor Brice Denys."

" Nor François Dudouet."

" Yes, him of Laval."

" Nor Huet of Launey, Villiers."

" Nor Grégis."

" Nor Pilon."

" Nor Filleul."

" Nor Ménicent."

" Nor Guéharrée."

" Nor the three brothers Logerais."

" Nor Monsieur Lechandelier de Pierreville."

" Idiots! " said a stern-faced, white-haired old man. " They have all if they have Lantenac."

" They have not got him yet," murmured one of the young men.

The old man added: " Lantenac taken, the soul is taken. Lantenac dead, La Vendée is slain."

" Who, then, is this Lantenac? " asked a townsman.

A townsman replied: " He is a *ci-devant*."

Another added: " He is one of those who shoot women."

Michelle Fléchard heard and said: " It is true."

They turned toward her.

She went on: " For he shot me."

It was a strange speech; it was like hearing a living woman declare herself dead. People began to look at her a little suspiciously. She was indeed a startling object; trembling at everything, scared, quaking, showing a sort of wild-animal trouble, so frightened that she was frightful. There is always something terrible in the feebleness of a despairing woman; she is a creature who has reached the furthest limits of destiny. But peasants have not a habit of noticing details. One of them muttered, " She might easily be a spy."

" Hold your tongue and get away from here," the good woman who had already spoken to her said in a low tone. Michelle Fléchard replied: " I am doing no harm. I am looking for my children."

The good woman glanced at those who were staring at Michelle, touched her forehead with one finger and winked, saying: " She is a simpleton." Then she took her aside and gave her a biscuit. Michelle Fléchard, without thanking her, began to eat greedily.

" Yes," said the peasants, " she eats like an animal; she is an idiot." So the tail of the mob dwindled away. They all went away, one after another.

When Michelle Fléchard had devoured her biscuit, she said to the peasant woman: " Good! I have eaten. Now where is La Tourgue? "

" It is taking her again! " cried the peasant.

" I must go to La Tourgue! Show me the way to La Tourgue! "

" Never! " exclaimed the peasant. " Do you want to get yourself killed, eh? Besides, I don't know. Oh, see here! You are really crazy! Listen, poor woman, you look tired. Will you come to my house and rest yourself? "

" I never rest," said the mother.

" And her feet are torn to pieces! " murmured the peasant.

Michelle Fléchard resumed: " Don't I tell you that they have stolen my children? — a little girl and two boys. I come from the carnichot in the forest. You can ask Tellmarch the Caimand about me, and the man I met in the field down yonder. It was the Caimand who cured me; it seems I had something broken. All that is what happened to me. Then there is Sergeant Radoub besides,— you can ask him, he will tell thee. Why, he was the one we met in the wood. Three,— I tell you three children! even the oldest one's name, — René-Jean. I can prove all that. The other's name is Gros-Alain, and the little girl's is Georgette. My husband is dead,— they killed him; he was the farmer at Siscoignard. You look like a good woman,— show me the road! I am not crazy; I am a mother! I have lost my children; I am trying to find them,— that is all. I don't know exactly which way I have come. I slept last night in a barn on the straw. La Tourgue, that is where I am going. I am not a thief. You must see that I am telling the truth; you ought to help me find my children. I do not belong to the neighbourhood. I was shot, but I do not know where."

The peasant shook her head, and said: " Listen, traveller. In times of revolution you mustn't say things that cannot be understood; you may get yourself taken up in that way."

" But La Tourgue! " cried the mother. " Madame, for the love of the Child Jesus and the Blessed Virgin up in Paradise, I beg you, madame, I entreat you, I conjure you, tell me which way I must go to get to La Tourgue! "

The peasant woman went into a passion. " I do not know! And if I knew I would not tell! It is a bad place. People do not go there."

" But I am going," said the mother. And she set forth again.

The woman watched her depart, muttering, " Still, she must have something to eat." She ran after Michelle Fléchard and put a roll of black bread in her hand: " There is for your supper."

Michelle Fléchard took the buckwheat bread, did not answer, did not turn her head, but walked on. She went out of the village. As she reached the last houses she met three ragged, barefooted little children. She approached them, and said:

" These are two girls and a boy."   Noticing that they looked
at the bread, she gave it to them.   The children took the
bread, then grew frightened.   She plunged into the forest.

CHAPTER IV

A MISTAKE

ON the same morning, before the dawn appeared, this
happened amidst the obscurity of the forest, along the
crossroad which goes from Javené to Lécousse.

All the roads of the Breage are between high banks; but of
all the routes, that leading from Javené to Parigné by the way
of Lécousse is the most deeply embedded.   Besides that, it is
winding; it is a ravine rather than a road.   This road comes
from Vitré, and had the honour of jolting Madame de
Sévigné's carriage.   It is, as it were, walled in to the right
and left by hedges.   There could be no better place for an
ambush.

On this morning, an hour before Michelle Fléchard from
another point of the forest reached the first village where she
had seen the sepulchral apparition of the wagon escorted by
gendarmes, a crowd of men filled the copses where the Javené
road crosses the bridge over the Couesnon.   The branches
hid them.   These men were peasants, all wearing jackets of
skins, which the kings of Brittany wore in the sixth century
and the peasants in the eighteenth.   The men were armed,—
some with guns, others with axes.   Those who carried axes
had just prepared in an open space a sort of pyre of dried
fagots and billets, which only remained to be set on fire;
those who had guns were stationed at the two sides of the
road in watchful positions.   Anybody who could have looked
through the leaves would have seen everywhere fingers on
triggers, and guns aimed toward the openings left by the

interlacing branches. These men were on the watch   All
the guns converged toward the road, which the first gleams
of day had begun to whiten.   In this twilight low voices held
converse :—

" Are you sure of that? "

" Well, they say so."

" *She* is about to pass? "

" They say she is in the neighbourhood."

" She must not go out."

" She must be burned."

" We are three villages who have come out for that."

" Yes; but the escort? "

" The escort will be killed."

" But will she pass by this road? "

" They say so."

" Then she comes from Vitré? "

" Why not? "

" But somebody said she was coming from Fougères."

" Whether she comes from Fougères or Vitré, she comes
from the devil."

" Yes."

" And must go back to him."

" Yes."

" So she is going to Parigné? "

" It appears so."

" She will not go."

" No."

" No, no, no! "

" Attention."

" It became prudent now to be silent, for the day was
breaking. Suddenly these ambushed men held their breath;
they caught a sound of wheels and horses' feet. They peered
through the branches, and could perceive indistinctly a long
wagon, an escort on horseback, and something on the wagon,
coming toward them along the high-banked road.

" There she is," said one, who appeared to be the leader.

" Yes," said one of the scouts; " with the escort."

" How many men? "

" Twelve."

" We were told they were twenty."

" Twelve or twenty, *we* must kill the whole."

" Wait until they get within sure aim."

A little later, the wagon and its escort appeared at a turn in the road. " Long live the king! " cried the chief peasant. A hundred guns were fired at the same instant.

When the smoke scattered, the escort was scattered also. Seven horsemen had fallen; five had fled. The peasants rushed up to the wagon.

" Hold! " cried the chief; " it is not the guillotine! It is a ladder."

A long ladder was, in fact, all the wagon carried. The two horses had fallen wounded; the driver had been killed, but not intentionally.

" All the same," said the chief; " a ladder with an escort looks suspicious. It was going toward Parigné. It was for the escalade of La Tourgue, very sure."

" Let us burn the ladder! " cried the peasants.

And they burned the ladder. As for the funereal wagon for which they had been waiting, it was pursuing another road, and was already two leagues off, in the village where Michelle Fléchard saw it pass at sunrise.

CHAPTER V

VOX IN DESERTO

WHEN Michelle Fléchard left the three children to whom she had given her bread, she took her way at random through the wood. Since nobody would point out the road, she must find it out for herself. Now and then she sat down, then rose, then reseated herself again. She was borne down by that terrible fatigue which first attacks the muscles, then

19

passes into the bones,— weariness like that of a slave. She was a slave in truth,— the slave of her lost children. She must find them; each instant that elapsed might be to their hurt. Whoso has a duty like this woman's has no rights; it is forbidden even to stop to take breath. But she was very tired. In the extreme of exhaustion which she had reached, another step became a question,— Can one make it? She had walked all the day, encountering no other village, not even a house. She took first the right path, then a wrong one, ending by losing herself amidst leafy labyrinths, resembling one another precisely. Was she approaching her goal? Was she nearing the term of her Passion? She was in the Via Dolorosa, and felt the overwhelming of the last station. Was she about to fall in the road, and die there? There came a moment when to advance farther seemed impossible to her. The sun was declining, the forest growing dark; the paths were hidden beneath the grass, and she was helpless. She had nothing left but God. She began to call; no voice answered.

She looked about; she perceived an opening in the branches turned in that direction, and found herself suddenly on the edge of the wood. She had before her a valley, narrow as a trench, at the bottom of which a clear streamlet ran along over the stones. She discovered then she was burning with thirst; she went down to the stream, knelt by it, and drank. She took advantage of her kneeling position to say her prayers.

When she rose she tried to decide upon a course. She crossed the brook. Beyond the little valley stretched, as far as the eye could reach, a plateau covered with short underbrush, which, starting from the brook, ascended in an inclined plain, and filed the whole horizon. The forest had been a solitude; this plain was a desert. Behind every bush of the forest she might meet some one; on the plateau, as far as she could see, nothing met her gaze. A few birds, which seemed frightened, were flying away over the heath. Then, in the midst of this awful abandonment, feeling her knees give way under her, and as if gone suddenly mad, the distracted mother flung forth this strange cry into the silence: " Is there any one here? "

She waited for an answer. It came. A low, deep voice burst forth; it proceeded from the verge of the horizon, was borne forward from echo to echo; it was either a peal of thunder or a cannon, and it seemed as if the voice replied to the mother's question, and that it said, " Yes." Then the silence closed in anew.

The mother rose, animated with fresh life. There was some one; it seemed to her as if she had now some person with whom she could speak. She had just drank and prayed; her strength came back; she began to ascend the plateau in the direction whence she had heard that vast and far-off voice. Suddenly she saw a lofty tower start up on the extreme edge of the horizon. It was the only object visible amidst the savage landscape; a ray from the setting sun crimsoned its summit. It was more than a league away. Behind the tower spread a great sweep of scattered verdure lost in the midst: it was the forest of Fougères. This tower appeared to her to be the point whence came the thundering which had sounded like a summons in her ear. Was it that which had given the answer to her cry?

Michelle Fléchard reached the top of the plateau; she had nothing but the plain before her. She walked toward the tower.

CHAPTER VI

THE SITUATION

THE moment had come. The inexorable held the pitiless. Cimourdain had Lantenac in his hand.

The old royalist rebel was taken in his form; it was evident that he could not escape, and Cimourdain meant that the mar-

quis should be beheaded here,— upon his own territory, his
own lands,— on this very spot, in sight of his ancestral dwell-
ing-place, that the feudal stronghold might see the head of
the feudal lord fall, and the example thus be made memorable.
It was with this intention that he had sent to Fougères for the
guillotine, which we lately saw upon its road. To kill Lantenac, was to slay the Vendée; to slay the Vendée was to save
France. Cimourdain did not hesitate. The conscience of
this man was quiet; he was urged to ferocity by a sense of
duty.

The marquis appeared lost; as far as that went, Cimourdain
was tranquil. But there was a consideration which troubled
him. The struggle must inevitably be a terrible one. Gauvain would direct it, and perhaps would wish to take part.
This young chief was a soldier at heart; he was just the man
to fling himself into the thick of this pugilistic combat. If
he should be killed,— Gauvain, his child! the unique affection
he possessed on earth! So far fortune had protected the
youth; but fortune might grow weary. Cimourdain trembled. His strange destiny had placed him here between these
two Gauvains,— for one of whom he wished death, for the
other life.

The cannon-shot which had roused Georgette in her cradle
and summoned the mother in the depths of her solitude had
done more than that. Either by accident, or owing to the
intention of the man who fired the piece, the ball, although
only meant as a warning, had struck the guard of iron bars
which protected the great loop-hole of the first floor of the
tower, broken it and half wrenched it away. The besieged
had not had time to repair this damage.

The besieged had been boastful, but they had very little
ammunition. Their situation, indeed, was much more critical
than the besiegers supposed. If they had had powder enough
they would have blown up La Tourgue when they and the
enemy should be together within it; this had been their dream.
But their reserves were exhausted; they had not more than
thirty charges left for each man. They had plenty of guns,

blunderbusses, and pistols, but few cartridges. They had loaded all the weapons in order to keep up a steady fire; but how long could this steady firing last? They must lavishly exhaust the resources which they required to husband. That was the difficulty. Fortunately (sinister fortune) the struggle would be mostly man to man; sabre and poniard would be more needed than firearms. The conflict would be rather a duel with knives than a battle with guns. This was the hope of the besieged.

The interior of the tower seemed impregnable. In the lower hall, which the mine had breached, the retirade so skilfully constructed guarded the entrance. Behind the retirade was a long table covered with loaded weapons, blunderbusses, carbines, and muskets; sabres, axes, and poniards. Since they had no powder to blow up the tower, the crypt of the oubliettes could not be utilized; therefore the marquis had closed the door of the dungeon. Above the ground-floor hall was the round chamber which could only be reached by the narrow, winding staircase. This chamber (in which there also set a table covered with loaded weapons ready to the hand) was lighted by the great loop-hole, the grating of which had just been broken by the cannon-ball. From this chamber the spiral staircase ascended to the circular room on the second floor, in which was the iron door communicating with the bridge-castle. This chamber was called indifferently the " room with the iron door," or the " mirror-room," from numerous small looking-glasses hung to rusty old nails on the naked stones of the wall,— a fantastic mingling of elegance and savage desolation. Since the apartments on the upper floor could not be successfully defended, this mirror-room became what Manesson Mallet, the law-giver in regard to fortified places, calls " the last post where the besieged can capitulate." The struggle, as we have already said, would be to keep the assailants from reaching this room. This second-floor round chamber was lighted by loop-holes; still, a torch burned there. This torch, in an iron holder like the one in the hall below, had been kindled by Imânus, and the end of the sulphur-match placed near it. Terrible carefulness! At the end of the ground-floor hall was a board placed upon trestles, which held food, like the arrangement in a Homeric cavern; great dishes of rice, furmety of black grain, hashed veal, hotchpotch, biscuits, stewed fruit, and jugs of cider. Whoever wished could eat and drink.

The cannon-shot set them all on the watch. Not more than a half hour of quiet remained to them. From the top of the tower Imânus watched the approach of the besiegers.

Lantenac had ordered his men not to fire as the assailants came forward. He said: " They are four thousand five hundred. To kill outside is useless. When they try to enter, we are as strong as they." Then he laughed, and added: " Equality, Fraternity."

It had been agreed that Imânus should sound a warning on his horn when the enemy began to advance. The little troop, posted behind the retirade or on the stairs, waited with one hand on their muskets, the other on their rosaries.

This was what the situation had resolved itself into: For the assailants a breach to mount, a barricade to force, three rooms (one above the other) to take in succession by main strength, two winding staircases to be carried step by step under a storm of bullets. For the besieged — to die!

CHAPTER VII

PRELIMINARIES

GAUVAIN on his side arranged the order of attack. He gave his last instructions to Cimourdain, whose part in the action, it will be remembered, was to guard the plateau, and to Guéchamp, who was to wait with the main body of the army in the forest camp. It was understood that neither the masked battery of the wood nor the open battery of the plateau would fire unless there should be a sortie or an attempt at escape on the part of the besieged. Gauvain had reserved for himself the command of the storming column. It was that which troubled Cimourdain.

The sun had just set. A tower in an open country resembles a ship in open sea. It must be attacked in the same manner: it is a boarding rather than an assault. No cannon; nothing useless attempted. What would be the good of cannonading walls fifteen feet thick? A port-hole; men forcing it on the one side, men guarding it on the other; axes, knives, pistols, fists, and teeth,— that is the undertaking.

Gauvain felt that there was no other way of carrying La Tourgue. Nothing can be more murderous than a conflict so close that the combatants look into one another's eyes. He had lived in this tower when a child, and knew its formidable recesses by heart. He meditated profoundly.

A few paces from him his lieutenant, Guéchamp, stood with a spy-glass in his hand, examining the horizon in the direction of Parigné. Suddenly he cried " Ah! at last! "

This exclamation aroused Gauvain from his reverie. " What is it, Guéchamp? "

" Commandant, the ladder is coming."

" The escape-ladder? "

" Yes."

" How? It has not yet got here? "

" No, Commandant. And I was troubled. The express that I sent to Javené came back."

" I know it."

" He told me that he had found at the carpenter's shop in Javené a ladder of the requisite dimensions; he took it; he had it put on a cart; he demanded an escort of twelve horsemen, and he saw them set out from Parigné,— the cart, the escort, and the ladder. Then he rode back full speed, and made his report; and he added that the horses being good and the departure having taken place about two o'clock in the morning the wagon would be here before sunset."

" I know all that. Well? "

" Well, Commandant, the sun has just set, and the wagon which brings the ladder has not yet arrived."

" Is it possible? Still, we must commence the attack. The hour has come. If we were to wait, the besieged would think we hesitated."

" Commandant, the attack can commence."

" But the escape-ladder is necessary."

" Without doubt."

" But we have not got it."

" We have it."

" How? "

" It was that which made me say, ' Ah! at last! ' The wagon did not arrive; I took my telescope, and examined the route from Parigné to La Tourgue, and, Commandant, I am satisfied. The wagon and the escort are coming down yonder; they are descending a hill. You can see them."

Gauvain took the glass and looked. " Yes; there it is. There is not light enough to distinguish very clearly. But I can see the escort,— it is certainly that. Only the escort appears to me more numerous than you said, Guéchamp."

" And to me also."

" They are about a quarter of a league off."

" Commandant, the escape-ladder will be here in a quarter of an hour."

" We can attack."

It was indeed a wagon which they saw approaching, but not the one they believed. As Gauvain turned he saw Sergeant Radoub standing behind him, upright, his eyes downcast, in the attitude of military salute.

" What is it, Sergeant Radoub? "

" Citizen commandant, we, the men of the Battalion of the Bonnet Rouge, have a favour to ask of you."

" What? "

" To have us killed."

" Ah! " said Gauvain.

" Will you have that kindness? "

" But — that is according to circumstances," said Gauvain.

" Listen, Commandant. Since the affair of Dol, you are careful of us. We are still twelve."

" Well? "

" That humiliates us."

" You are the reserve."

" We would rather be the advance-guard."

" But I need you to decide success at the close of the engagement. I keep you back for that."

" Too much."

" No. You are in the column. You march."

" In the rear. Paris has a right to march in front."

" I will think of it, Sergeant Radoub."

" Think of it to-day, my commandant. There is an opportunity. There are going to be hard blows to give or to take. It will be lively. La Tourgue will burn the fingers of those that touch her. We demand the favour of being in the party." The sergeant paused, twisted his moustache, and added, in an altered voice: " Besides, look you, my commandant, our little ones are in this tower. Our children are there, — the children of the battalion,— our three children. That abominable beast called Brise-Bleu and Imânus, this Gouge-le-Bruant, this Bouge-le-Gruant, this Fouge-le-Truant, this thunder-clap of the devil, threatens our children. Our children,— our pets, Commandant. If all the earthquakes should mix in the business, we cannot have any misfortune happen to them. Do you hear that — authority? We will have none of it. A little while ago I took advantage of the truce, and mounted the plateau, and looked at them through a window; yes, they are certainly there,— you can see them from the edge of the ravine. I did see them, and they were afraid of me, the darlings. Commandant, if a single hair of their little cherub pates should fall, I swear by the thousand names of everything sacred,— I, Sergeant Radoub,— that I will have revenge out of somebody. And that is what all the battalion: either we want the babies saved, or we want to be all killed. It is our right: yes— all killed. And now, salute and respect."

Gauvain held out his hand to Radoub, and said: "You are brave men. You shall have a place in the attacking column. I will divide you into two parties. I will put six of you in the vanguard to make sure that the troops advance, and six in the rear-guard to make sure that nobody retreats."

"Shall I command the twelve, as usual?"

"Certainly."

"Then, my commandant, thanks. For I am of the vanguard."

Radoub made another military salute, and went back to his company.

Gauvain drew out his watch, spoke a few words in Guéchamp's ear, and the storming column began to form.

CHAPTER VIII

THE WORD AND THE ROAR

NOW, Cimourdain, who had not yet gone to his post on the plateau, approached a trumpeter. "Sound your trumpet!" said he.

The clarion sounded; the horn replied. Again the trumpet and the horn exchanged a blast.

"What does that mean?" Gauvain asked Guéchamp. "What is it Cimourdain wants?"

Cimourdain advanced toward the tower, holding a white handkerchief in his hand. He spoke in a loud voice: "Men who are in the tower, do you know me?"

A voice — the voice of Imânus — replied from the summit: "Yes."

The following dialogue between the two voices reached the ears of those about:—

"I am the Envoy of the Republic."

"You are the late Curé of Parigné."

"I am the delegate of the Committee of Public Safety."

"You are a priest."

"I am the representative of the law."

"You are a renegade."

"I am the commissioner of the Revolution."

"You are an apostate."

"I am Cimourdain."

"You are the demon."

"Do you know me?"

"We hate you."

"Would you be content if you had me in your power?"

"We are here eighteen, who would give our heads to have yours."

"Very well! I come to deliver myself up to you."

From the top of the tower rang a burst of savage laughter, and this cry: "Come!"

The camp waited in the breathless silence of expectancy.

Cimourdain resumed: "On one condition."

"What?"

"Listen."

"Speak."

"You hate me?"

"Yes."

"And I love you. I am your brother."

The voice from the top of the tower replied: "Yes, Cain."

Cimourdain went on in a singular tone, at once loud and sweet: "Insult me; but listen. I come here under a flag of truce. Yes, you are my brothers. You are poor mistaken creatures. I am your friend. I am the light, and I speak to ignorance. Light is always brotherhood. Besides, have we not all the same mother,— our country? Well, listen to me: you will know hereafter, or your children will know, or your children's children will know, that what is done in this moment is brought about by the law above, and that the Revolution is the work of God. While awaiting the time when all consciences, even yours, shall understand this; when all fanaticisms, even yours, shall vanish,— while waiting for this great light to spread, will no one have pity on your darkness? I come to you. I offer you my head. I do more,— I hold out my hand to you. I demand of you the favour to destroy me in order to save yourselves. I have unlimited authority, and that which I say I can do. This is a supreme insant. I make a last effort. Yes, he who speaks to you is a citizen and in this citizen — yes — there is a priest. The citizen defies you, but the priest implores you. Listen to me. Many among you have wives and children. I am defending your children and your wives,— defending them against yourselves. Oh, my brothers —"

" Go on! Preach!" sneered Imânus.

" My brothers, do not let the terrible horn sound. Throats are to be cut. Many among us who are here before you will not see to-morrow's sun; yes, many of us will perish, and you — you are all going to die. Show mercy to yourselves. Why shed all this blood, when it is useless? Why kill so many men, when it would suffice to kill two? "

" Two? " repeated Imânus.

" Yes. Two."

" Who? "

" Lantenac and myself." Cimourdain spoke more loudly. " Two men are too many. Lantenac for us; I for you. This is what I propose to you, and you will all have your lives safe. Give us Lantenac, and take me. Lantenac will be guillotined, and you shall do what you choose with me."

" Priest," howled Imânus, " if we had thee we would roast thee at a slow fire! "

" I consent," said Cimourdain. He went on: " You, the condemned who are in this tower, you can all in an hour be living and free. I bring you safety. Do you accept? "

Imânus burst forth: " You are not only a villain, you are a madman. Ah, why do you come here to disturb us. Who begged you to come and speak to us? We give up Monseigneur? What is it you want? "

" His head. And I offer —"

" Your skin. Oh, we would flay you like a dog, Curé

Cimourdain! Well, no; your skin is not worth his head. Get away with you!"

"The massacre will be horrible. For the last time — reflect."

Night had come on during this strange colloquy, which could be heard without and within the tower. The Marquis de Lantenac kept silence, and allowed events to take their course. Leaders possess such sinister egotism; it is one of the rights of responsibility.

Imânus sent his voice beyond Cimourdain; he shouted: "Men, who attack us, we have submitted our propositions to you: they are settled; we have nothing to change in them. Accept them, else woe to all! Do you consent? We will give you up the three children, and you will allow liberty and life to us all!"

"To all, yes," replied Cimourdain, "except one."

"And that?"

"Lantenac."

"Monseigneur! Give up Monseigneur? Never!"

"We can only treat with you on that condition."

"Then begin."

Silence fell. Imânus descended after having sounded the signal on his horn; the marquis took his sword in his hand; the nineteen besieged grouped themselves in silence behind the retirade of the lower hall and sank upon their knees. They could hear the measured tread of the column as it advanced toward the tower in the gloom. The sound came nearer; suddenly they heard it close to them, at the very mouth of the breach. Then all, kneeling, aimed their guns and blunderbusses accross the openings of the barricade, and one of them — Grand Francœur, who was the priest Turmeau — raised himself, with a naked sabre in his right hand and a crucifix in his left, saying, in a solemn voice,—

"In the name of the Father, of the Son, and of the Holy Ghost!"

All fired at the same time, and the battle began.

CHAPTER IX

TITANS AGAINST GIANTS

THE encounter was frightful. This hand-to-hand contest went beyond the power of fancy in its awfulness. To find anything similar, it would be necessary to go back to the great duels of Æschylus or the ancient feudal butcheries; to " those attacks with short-arms " which lasted down to the seventeenth century, when men penetrated into fortified places be concealed breaches, tragic assaults, where, says the old sergeant of the province of Alentejo, " when the mines had done their work, the besiegers advanced bearing planks covered with sheets of tin, and, armed with round shields and furnished with grenades, they forced those who held the intrenchments or retirades to abandon them; and thus become masters, they vigorously drove in the besieged."

The place of attack was terrible; it was what in military language is called " a covered breach,"— that is to say, a crevice traversing the wall through and through, and not an extended fracture open to the sky. The powder had acted like an auger. The effect of the explosion had been so violent that the tower was cracked for more than forty feet above the chamber of the mine. But this was only a crack; the practicable rent which served as a breach, and which gave admittance into the lower hall, resembled a thrust from a lance which pierces, rather than a blow from an axe which gashes. It was a puncture in the flank of the tower; a long cut, something like the mouth of a well; a passage, twisting and mounting like an intestine along the wall fifteen feet in thickness; a misshapen cylinder, encumbered with obstacles, traps, stones broken by the explosion, where any one entering struck his head against the granite rock, his feet against the rubbish, while the darkness blinded him.

The assailants saw before them this black gap, the mouth

of a gulf, which had for upper and lower jaws all the stones of the jagged wall: a shark's mouth has not more teeth than had this frightful opening. It was necessary to enter this gap and to get out of it. Within was the wall; without rose the retirade,— without; that is to say, in the hall of the ground-floor.

The encounters of sappers in covered galleries when the countermine succeeds in cutting the mine, the butcheries in the gun-decks of vessels boarded in a naval engagement, alone have this ferocity. To fight in the bottom of a grave, — it is the supreme degree of horror; it is frightful for men to meet in the death-struggle in such narrow bounds. At the instant when the first rush of besiegers entered, the whole retirade blazed with lightnings; it was like a thunder-bolt bursting under-ground. The thunder of the assailants replied to that of the ambuscade; the detonations answered one another. Gauvain's voice was heard shouting, " Drive them back! " Then Lantenac's cry, " Hold firm against the enemy! " Then Imânus's yell, " Here, you men of the Main! " Then the clash of sabres against sabres, and echo after echo of terrible discharges that killed right and left. The torch fastened against the wall dimly lighted the horrible scene. It was impossible clearly to distinguish anything; the combatants struggled amidst a lurid night; whoever entered was suddenly struck deaf and blind,— deafened by the noise, blinded by the smoke. The combatants trod upon the corpses; they lacerated the wounds of the injured men lying helpless amidst the rubbish, stamped recklessly upon limbs already broken; the sufferers uttered awful groans; the dying fastened their teeth in the feet of their unconscious tormentors. Then for an instant would come a silence more dreadful than the tumult: the foes collared each other; the hissing sound of their breath could be heard; the gnashing of teeth, death-groans, curses,— then the thunder would recommence. A stream of blood flowed out from the tower through the breach and spread away across the darkness, and formed smoking pools upon the grass. One might have said that the tower had been wounded, and that the giantess was bleeding.

Strange thing! scarcely a sound of the struggle could be, heard without. The night was very black, and a sort of funereal calm reigned in plain and forest about the beleaguered fortress. Hell was within, the sepulchre without. This shock of men exterminating one another amidst the darkness, these musket volleys, these clamours, these shouts of rage,— all that din expired beneath that mass of walls and arches; air was lacking, and suffocation added itself to the carnage. Scarcely a sound reached those outside the tower. The little children slept.

The desperate strife grew madder. The retirade held firm. Nothing more difficult than to force a barricade with a re-entering angle. If the besieged had numbers against them, they had at least the position in their favour. The storming-column lost many men. Stretched in a long line outside the tower, it forced its way slowly in through the opening of the breach like a snake twisting itself into its den.

Gauvain, with the natural imprudence of a youthful leader, was in the hall in the thickest of the *mêlée*, with the bullets flying in every direction about his head. Besides the imprudence of his age, he had the assurance of a man who has never been wounded. As he turned about to give an order, the glare of a volley of musketry lighted up a face close beside him. "Cimourdain!" he cried. "What are you doing here?"

It was indeed Cimourdain. He replied: "I have come to be near you."

"But you will be killed!"

"Very well: you — what are you doing, then?"

"I am necessary here; you are not."

"Since you are here, I must be here too."

"No, my master!"

"Yes, my child!"

And Cimourdain remained near Gauvain.

The dead lay in heaps on the pavement of the hall. Although the retirade was not yet carried, numbers would evidently conquer at last. The assailants were sheltered, and the assailed under cover; ten besiegers fell to one among the besieged, but the besiegers were constantly renewed; the assailants increased, and the assailed grew less. The nineteen besieged were all behind the retirade, because the attack was made there. They had dead and wounded among them; not more than fifteen could fight now. One of the most furious, Chante-en-Hiver, had been horribly mutilated. He was a stubby, woolly-haired Breton, little and active; he had an eye shot out, and his jaw broken. He could walk still; he dragged himself up the spiral staircase, and reached the chamber of the first floor, hoping to be able to say a prayer there and die. He backed himself against the wall near the loop-hole in order to breathe a little fresh air.

Beneath, in front of the barricade, the butchery became more and more horrible. In a pause between the answering discharges, Cimourdain raised his voice: " Besieged! " cried he. " Why let any more blood flow? You are beaten. Surrender! Think! we are four thousand five hundred men against nineteen,— that is to say, more than two hundred against one. Surrender! "

" Let us stop these babblings," retorted the Marquis de Lantenac; and twenty balls answered Cimourdain.

The retirade did not reach to the arched roof; this space permitted the besieged to fire upon the barricade, but it also gave the besiegers an opportunity to scale it.

" Assault the retirade! " cried Gauvain. " Is there any man willing to scale the retirade? "

" I! " said Sergeant Radoub.
20

CHAPTER X

RADOUB

THEN a sort of stupor seized the assailants. Radoub had entered the breach at the head of the column, and of those men of the Parisian battalion of which he made the sixth, four had already fallen. After he had uttered that shout, " I ! " he was seen to recoil instead of advance. Stooping, bending forward, almost creeping between the legs of the combatants, he regained the opening of the breach and rushed out. Was it a flight? A man like this to fly! What did it mean?

When he was outside, Radoub, still blinded by the smoke, rubbed his eyes as if to clear them from the horror of the cavernous night he had just left, and studied the wall of the tower by the starlight. He nodded his head, as if to say, " I was not mistaken."

Radoub had noticed that the deep crack made by the explosion of the mine extended above the breach to the loophole of the upper story, whose iron grating had been shattered, and by a ball. The net-work of broken bars hung loosely down, so that a man could enter. A man could enter, but could he climb up? By the crevice it might have been possible for a cat to mount. That was what Radoub was. He belonged to the race which Pindar calls " the agile athletes." One may be an old soldier and a young man. Radoub, who had belonged to the French guards, was not yet forty; he was a nimble Hercules.

Radoub threw his musket on the ground, took off his shoulder-belts, laid aside his coat and jacket, guarding his two pistols, which he thrust in his trousers' belt, and his naked sabre, which he held between his teeth; the butt-ends of the pistols protruded above his belt. Thus lightened of everything useless, and followed in the obscurity by the eyes of all such of the attacking column as had not yet entered the breach, he began to climb the stones of the cracked wall as if they had been the steps of a staircase. Having no shoes was an advantage; nothing can cling like a naked foot. He twisted his toes into the holes of the stones; he hoisted himself with his fists, and bore his weight on his knees. The ascent was a hazardous one; it was somewhat like climbing along the teeth of a gigantic saw. "Luckily," thought he, "there is nobody in the chamber of the first story, else I should not be allowed to climb up like this."

Radoub had not more than forty feet left to mount. He was somewhat encumbered by the projecting butt-ends of his pistols; and, as he climbed, the crevice narrowed, rendering the ascent more and more difficult, so that the danger of falling increased as he went on. At last he reached the frame of the loop-hole and pushed aside the twisted and broken grating so that he had space enough to pass through. He raised himself for a last powerful effort, rested his knee on the cornice of the ledge, seized with one hand a bar of the grating at the left, with the other a bar at the right, lifted half his body in front of the embrasure of the loop-hole, and, sabre between his teeth, hung thus suspended by his two fists over the abyss. It only needed one spring more to land him in the chamber of the first floor.

But a face appeared in a loop-hole. Radoub saw a frightful spectacle rise suddenly before him in the gloom,— an eye torn out, a jaw fractured, a bloody mask. This mask, which had only one eye left, was watching him. This mask had two hands; these two hands thrust themselves out of the darkness of this loop-hole and clutched at Radoub; one of them seized the two pistols in his belt, the other snatched the sword from between his teeth. Radoub was disarmed. His knee slipped upon the inclined plane of the cornice; his two fists, cramped about the bars of the grating, barely sufficed to support him, and beneath was a sheer descent of forty feet.

This mask and these hands belonged to Chante-en-Hiver. Suffocated by the smoke which rose from the room below,

Chante-en-Hiver had succeeded in entering the embrasure of the loop-hole: the air from without had revived him; the freshness of the night had congealed the blood, and his strength had in a measure come back. Suddenly he perceived the torso of Radoub rise in front of the embrasure. Radoub, having his hands twisted about the bars, had no choice but to let himself fall or allow himself to be disarmed; so Chante-en-Hiver, with a horrible tranquillity, had taken the two pistols out of his belt and the sabre from between his teeth.

Then commenced an unheard-of duel,— a duel between the disarmed and the wounded. Evidently the dying man had the victory in his own hands. A single shot would suffice to hurl Radoub into the yawning gulf beneath his feet. Luckily for Radoub, Chante-en-Hiver held both pistols in the same hand, so that he could not fire either, and was forced to make use of the sabre. He struck Radoub a blow on the shoulder with the point. The sabre-stroke wounded Radoub, but saved his life. The soldier was unarmed, but in full possession of his strength. Regardless of his wound, which indeed was only a flesh-cut, he swung his body vigorously forward, loosed his hold of the bars, and bounded through the loop-hole. There he found himself face to face with Chante-en-Hiver, who had thrown the sabre behind him and was clutching a pistol in either hand. Chante-en-Hiver had Radoub close to the muzzle as he took aim upon his knees, but his enfeebled arm trembled, and he did not fire at once.

Radoub took advantage of this respite to burst out laughing. " I say, ugly face! " cried he, " do you suppose you frighten me with your bloody bullock's jaws? Thunder and Mars, how they have shattered your features! "

Chante-en-Hiver took aim.

Radoub continued: " It is not polite to mention it, but the grape-shot has dotted your mug very neatly. Bellona has disturbed your physiognomy, my lad. Come, come; spit out your little pistol-shot, my good fellow! "

Chante-en-Hiver fired; the ball passed so close to Radoub's head that it carried away part of his ear. His foe raised the second pistol in his other hand.

Radoub did not give him time to take aim. "It is enough to lose one ear!" cried he. "You have wounded me twice. It is my turn now."

He flung himself on Chante-en-Hiver, knocked aside his arm with such force that the pistol went off and the ball whizzed against the ceiling. He seized his enemy's broken jaw in both hands and twisted it about. Chante-en-Hiver uttered a howl of pain and fainted. Radoub stepped across his body and left him lying in the embrasure of the loop-hole.

"Now that I have announced my ultimatum, don't you stir again," said he. "Lie there, you ugly crawling snake! You may fancy that I am not going to amuse myself by massacring you. Crawl about on the ground at your ease,— under foot is the place for you. Die,— you can't get rid of that! In a little while you will learn what nonsense your priest has talked to you. Away with you into the great mystery, peasant!" And he hurried forward into the room. "One cannot see an inch before one's nose," grumbled he.

Chante-en-Hiver began to writhe convulsively upon the floor, and uttered fresh moans of agony.

Radoub turned back. "Hold your tongue! Do me the favour to be silent, citizen, without knowing it. I cannot trouble myself further with you; I should scorn to make an end of you. Just let me have quiet."

Then he thrust his hands into his hair as he stood watching Chante-en-Hiver. "But here, what am I to do now? It is all very fine, but I am disarmed. I had two shots to fire, and you have robbed me of them, animal! and with all that, a smoke that would blind a dog!"

Then his hand touched his wounded ear. "Aïe!" he said.

Then he went on: "You have gained a great deal by confiscating one of my ears! However, I would rather have one less of them than anything else: an ear is only an ornament. You have scratched my shoulder, too; but that is nothing. Expire, villager! I forgive you."

He listened. The din from the lower room was fearful. The combat had grown more furious than ever. "Things are going well down there;" he muttered. "How they howl 'Live the king!' One must admit that they die bravely."

His foot struck against the sabre. He picked it up, and said to Chante-en-Hiver, who no longer stirred, and who might indeed be dead: "See here, man of the woods, I will take my sabre; you have left me that, anyway. But I needed my pistols. The devil fly away with you, savage! Oh, there, what am I to do? I am no good whatever here."

He advanced into the hall trying to guide his steps in the gloom. Suddenly, in the shadow behind the central pillar, he perceived a long table upon which something gleamed faintly. He felt the objects. They were blunderbusses, carbines, pistols, a whole row of firearms laid out in order to his hand; it was the reserve of weapons the besieged had provided in this chamber, which would be their second place of stand, a whole arsenal.

"A sideboard!" cried Radoub; and he clutched them right and left, dizzy with joy. Thus armed, he became formidable.

He could see back of the table the door of the staircase, which communicated with the rooms above and below, standing wide open. Radoub seized two pistols, and fired them at random through the doorway; then he snatched a blunderbuss, and fired that,— then a blunderbuss loaded with buckshot, and discharged it. The blunderbuss, vomiting forth its fifteen balls, sounded like a volley of grape-shot. He got his breath back, and shouted down the staircase, in a voice of thunder, "Long live Paris!" Then seizing a second blunderbuss, still bigger than the first, he aimed it toward the staircase and waited.

The confusion in the lower hall was indescribable. This unexpected attack from behind paralyzed the besieged with astonishment. Two balls from Radoub's triple fire had taken effect: one had killed the elder of the brothers Pique-en-Bois; the other had killed De Quélen, nicknamed Houzard.

" They are on the floor above! " cried the marquis.

At this cry the men abandoned the retirade,— a flock of birds could not have fled more quickly; they plunged madly toward the staircase.

The marquis encouraged the flight. " Quick, quick! " he exclaimed. " There is most courage now in escape. Let us all get up to the second floor. We will begin again there." He left the retirade the last. This brave act saved his life.

Radoub, ambushed at the top of the stairs, watched the retreat, finger on trigger. The first who appeared at the turn of the spiral steps received the discharge of his gun full in their faces, and fell. Had the marquis been among them, he would have been killed. Before Radoub had time to seize another weapon, the others passed him,— the marquis behind all the rest, and moving more slowly.

Believing the first-floor chambers filled with the besiegers, the men did not pause there, but rushed on and gained the room above, which was the hall of the mirrors. There was the iron door; there was the sulphur-match; it was there they must capitulate or die.

Gauvain had been as much astounded as the besieged by the detonations from the staircase, and was unable to understand how aid could have reached him in that quarter; but he took advantage without waiting to comprehend. He leaped over the retirade, followed by his men, and pursued the fugitives up to the first floor. There he found Radoub.

The sergeant saluted, and said: " One minute, my commandant. I did that. I remembered Dol; I followed your plan: I took the enemy between two fires."

" A good scholar," answered Gauvain, with a smile.

After one has been a certain length of time in the darkness, the eyes become accustomed to the obscurity like those of a night-bird. Gauvain perceived that Radoub was covered with blood. "But you are wounded, comrade!" he exclaimed.

"Never mind that, my commandant! What difference does it make,— an ear more or less? I got a sabre-thrust, too, but it is nothing. One always cuts one's self a little in breaking a window; it is only losing a little blood."

The besiegers made a halt in the first-floor chamber, which had been conquered by Radoub. A lantern was brought. Cimourdain rejoined Gauvain. They held a council. It was time to reflect, indeed. The besiegers were not in the secrets of their foes; they were unaware of the lack of munitions; they did not know that the defenders of the tower were short of powder, that the second floor must be the last post where a stand could be made; the assailants could not tell but the staircase might be mined. One thing was certain,— the enemy could not escape. Those who had not been killed were as safe as if under lock and key. Lantenac was in the trap.

Certain of this, the besiegers could afford to give themselves time to choose the best means of bringing about the end. Numbers among them had been killed already. The thing now was to spare the men as much as possible in this last assault. The risk of this final attack would be great. The first fire would without doubt be a hot one. The combat was interrupted. The besiegers, masters of the ground and first floors, waited the orders of the commander-in-chief to renew the conflict. Gauvain and Cimourdain were holding counsel.

Radoub assisted in silence at their deliberation. At length he timidly hazarded another military salute. "Commandant!"

"What is it, Radoub?"

"Have I a right to a little recompense?"

"Yes, indeed. Ask what you like."

"I ask permission to mount the first."

It was impossible to refuse him; indeed, he would have done it without permission.

CHAPTER XI

DESPERATE

WHILE this consultation took place on the first floor, the besieged were barricading the second. Success is a fury; defeat is a madness. The encounter between the foes would be frenzied. To be close on victory intoxicates. The men below were inspired by hope, which would be the most powerful of human incentives if despair did not exist. Despair was above,— a calm, cold sinister despair.

When the besieged reached the hall of refuge, beyond which they had no resource, no hope, their first care had been to bar the entrance. To lock the door was useless; it was necessary to block the staircase. In a position like theirs, an obstacle across which they could see, and over which they could fight, was worth more than a closed door. The torch which Imânus had planted in the wall near the sulphur-match lighted the room. There was in the chamber one of those great, heavy oak chests which were used to hold clothes and linen before the invention of chests of drawers. They dragged this chest out, and stood it on end in the door-way of the staircase. It fitted solidly and closed the entrance, leaving open at the top a narrow space by which a man could pass; but it was scarcely probable that the assailants would run the risk of being killed one after another by any attempt to pass the barrier in single file.

This obstruction of the entrance afforded the besieged a respite. They numbered their company. Out of the nineteen only seven remained, of whom Imânus made one. With the exception of Imânus and the marquis, they were all wounded. The five wounded men (active still, for in the heat of combat any wound less than mortal leaves a man able to move about) were Chatenay (called Robi), Guinoiseau, Hoisnard (Branche d'Or), Brin d'Amour, and Grand

Francœur. All the others were dead. They had no munitions left; the cartridge-boxes were almost empty: they
counted the cartridges. How many shots were there left for
the seven to fire? Four! They had reached the pass where
nothing remained but to fall. They had retreated to the precipice; it yawned black and terrible; they stood upon the
very edge. Still, the attack was about to recommence,—
slowly, and all the more surely on that account. They
could hear the butt-end of the muskets sound along the staircase step by step, as the besiegers advanced. No means of
escape. By the library? On the plateau bristled six cannon with every match lighted. By the upper chambers? To
what end? They gaze on the platform: the only resource
when that was reached would be to fling themselves from
the top of the tower.

The seven survivors of this Homeric band found themselves inexorably enclosed and held fast by that thick wall
which at once protected and betrayed them. They were not
yet taken, but they were already prisoners.

The marquis spoke: " My friends, all is finished." Then
after a silence, he added: " Grand Francœur, become again
the Abbé Turmeau."

All knelt, rosary in hand. The measured stroke of the
muskets sounded nearer. Grand Francœur covered with
blood from a wound which had grazed his skull and torn
away his leather cap, raised the crucifix in his right hand.
The marquis, a sceptic at bottom, bent his knee to the
ground.

" Let each one confess his faults aloud," said Grand
Francœur. " Monseigneur, speak."

The marquis answered, " I have killed."

" I have killed," said Hoisnard.

" I have killed," said Guinoiseau.

" I have killed," said Brin d'Amour.

" I have killed," said Chatenay

" I have killed," said Imânus.

And Grand Francœur replied: " In the name of the most

Holy Trinity I absolve you. May your souls depart in peace!"

"Amen," replied all the voices.

The marquis raised himself. "Now let us die," he said. "And kill," added Imânus.

The blows from the butt-end of the besiegers' muskets began to shake the chest which barred the door.

"Think of God," said the priest; "earth no longer exists for you."

"It is true," replied the marquis; "we are in the tomb."

All bowed their heads and smote their breasts. The marquis and the priest were alone standing. The priest prayed, keeping his eyes cast down; the peasants prayed; the marquis reflected. The coffer echoed dismally, as if under the stroke of hammers.

At this instant a rapid, strong voice sounded suddenly behind him, exclaiming: "Did I not tell you so, monseigneur?"

All turned their heads in stupefied wonder. A gap had just opened in the wall. A stone, perfectly fitted into the others, but not cemented, and having a pivot above and a pivot below, had just revolved like a turnstile, leaving the wall open. The stone having revolved on its axis, the opening was double, and offered two means of exit,— one to the right and one to the left; narrow, but leaving space enough to allow a man to pass. Beyond this door, so unexpectedly opened, could be seen the first steps of a spiral staircase. A face appeared in the opening. The marquis recognized Halmalo.

CHAPTER XII

DELIVERANCE

" "IS it you, Halmalo? "
     " It is I, monseigneur. You see there are stones that turn; they really exist; you can get out of here. I am just in time; but come quickly. In ten minutes you will be in the heart of the forest."

" God is great," said the priest.

" Save yourself, monseigneur! " cried the men in concert.

" All of you go first," said the marquis.

" You must go first, monseigneur," returned the Abbé Turmeau. " I go the last."

And the marquis added, in a severe tone: " No struggle of generosity; we have no time to be magnanimous. You are wounded; I order you to live and to fly. Quick! Take advantage of this outlet. Thanks, Halmalo."

" Marquis, must we separate? " asked the Abbé Turmeau.

" Below, without doubt. We can only escape one by one."

" Does Monseigneur assign us a rendezvous? "

" Yes; a glade in the forest,— La Pierre Gauvain. Do you know the place? "

" We all know it."

" I shall be there to-morrow at noon. Let all those who can walk meet me at that time."

" Every man will be there."

" And we will begin the war anew," said the marquis.

As Halmalo pushed against the turning-stone, he found that it did not stir. The aperture could not be closed again.

" Monseigneur," he said, " we must hasten. The stone will not move. I was able to open the passage, but I cannot shut it."

The stone, in fact, had become deadened, as it were, on

its hinges from long disuse. It was impossible to make it revolve back into its place.

"Monseigneur," resumed Halmalo, "I had hoped to close the passage, so that the Blues, when they got in and found no one, would think you must have flown off in the smoke. But the stone will not budge. The enemy will see the outlet open, and can follow. At least, do not let us lose a second. Quick! everybody make for the staircase!"

Imânus laid his hand on Halmalo's shoulder. "Comrade, how much time will it take to get from here to the forest and to safety?"

"Is there any one seriously wounded?" asked Halmalo. They answered, "Nobody."

"In that case a quarter of an hour will be enough."

"Go," said Imânus; "if the enemy can be kept out of here for a quarter of an hour —"

"They may follow; they cannot overtake us."

"But," said the marquis, "they will be here in five minutes; that old chest cannot hold out against them any longer. A few blows from their muskets will end the business. A quarter of an hour! Who can keep them back for a quarter of an hour?"

"I," said Imânus.

"You, Gouge-le-Bruant?"

"I, monseigneur. Listen. Five out of six of you are wounded. I have not a scratch."

"Nor I," said the marquis.

"You are the chief, monseigneur. I am a soldier. Chief and soldier are two.

"I know we have each a different duty."

"No, monseigneur, we have, you and I, the same duty; it is to save you."

Imânus turned toward his companions. "Comrades, the thing necessary to be done is to hold the enemy in check and retard the pursuit as long as possible. Listen. I am in possession of my full strength; I have not lost a drop of blood; not being wounded, I can hold out longer than any of the others. Fly, all of you! Leave me your weapons; I will make good use of them. I take it on myself to stop the enemy for a good half hour. How many loaded pistols are there?"

"Four."

"Lay them on the floor." His command was obeyed. "It is well. I stay here. They will find somebody to talk with. Now, quick! get away."

Life and death hung in the balance; there was no time for thanks,— scarcely time for those nearest to grasp his hand.

"We shall meet soon," the marquis said to him.

"No, monseigneur; I hope not,— not soon; for I am going to die."

They got through the opening one after another and passed down the stairs, the wounded going first. While the men were escaping, the marquis took a pencil out of a notebook which he carried in his pocket and wrote a few words on the stone, which, remaining motionless, left the passage gaping open.

"Come, monseigneur, they are all gone but you," said Halmalo. And the sailor began to descend the stairs. The marquis followed.

Imânus remained alone.

CHAPTER XIII

THE EXECUTIONER

THE four pistols had been laid on the flags, for the chamber had no flooring. Imânus grasped a pistol in either hand. He moved obliquely toward the entrance to the staircase which the chest obstructed and masked.

The assailants evidently feared some surprise,— one of

NINETY-THREE 319

those final explosions which involve conqueror and conquered in the same catastrophe. This last attack was as slow and prudent as the first had been impetuous. They had not been able to push the chest backward into the chamber,— perhaps would not have done it if they could. They had broken the bottom with blows from their muskets, and pierced the top with bayonet holes; by these holes they were trying to see into the hall before entering. The light from the lanterns with which they had illuminated the staircase shone through these chinks.

Imânus perceived an eye regarding him through one of the holes. He aimed his pistol quickly at the place, and pulled the trigger. To his joy, a horrible cry followed the report. The ball had entered the eye and passed through the brain of the soldier, who fell backward down the stairs.

The assailants had broken two large holes in the cover; Imânus thrust his pistol through one of these and fired at random into the mass of besiegers. The ball must have rebounded, for he heard several cries, as if three or four were killed or wounded; then there was a great tramping and tumult as the men fell back. Imânus threw down the two pistols which he had just fired, and, taking the two which still remained, peered out through the holes in the chest. He was able to see what execution his shots had done.

The assailants had descended the stairs. The twisting of the spiral staircase only allowed him to look down three or four steps; the men he had shot lay writhing there in the death agony. Imânus waited. " It is so much time gained," thought he. Then he saw a man flat on his stomach creeping up the stairs; at the same instant the head of another soldier appeared lower down from behind the pillar about which the spiral wound. Imânus aimed at this head and fired. A cry followed, the soldier fell; and Imânus, while watching, threw away the empty pistol, and changed the loaded one from his left hand to his right. As he did so he felt a horrible pain, and, in his turn, uttered a yell of agony. A sabre had traversed his bowels. A fist (the fist of the man who had crept up the stairs) had just been thrust through the second hole in the bottom of the chest, and this first had plunged a sabre into Imânus's body. The wound was frightful; the abdomen was pierced through and through.

Imânus did not fall. He set his teeth together and muttered, "Good!" Then he dragged himself, tottering along, and retreated to the iron door, at the side of which the torch was still burning. He laid his pistol on the stones and seized the torch, and while with his left hand he held together the terrible wound through which his intestines protruded, with the right he lowered the torch till it touched the sulphur-match. It caught fire instantaneously; the wick blazed.

Imânus dropped the torch; it lay on the ground still burning. He seized his pistol anew, dropped forward upon the flags, and with what breath he had left blew the wick. The flame ran along it, passed beneath the iron door, and reached the bridge-castle. Then seeing that his execrable exploit had succeeded,— prouder, perhaps, of this crime than of the courage he had before shown,— this man, who had just proved himself a hero, only to sink into an assassin, smiled as he stretched himself out to die, and muttered: "They will remember me. I take vengeance on their little ones for the fate of our little one,— the king shut up in the Temple!"

CHAPTER XIV

IMÂNUS ALSO ESCAPES

AT this moment there was a great noise; the chest was hurled violently back into the hall, and gave passage to a man who rushed forward, sabre in hand, crying,—

"It is I — Radoub! What are you going to do? It

bores me to wait. I have risked it. Anyway I have just disembowelled one. Now I attack the whole of you. Whether the rest follow me or don't follow me, here I am. How many are there of you?"

It was indeed Radoub, and he was alone!

After the massacre Imânus had caused upon the stairs, Gauvain, fearing some secret mine, had drawn back his men and consulted with Cimourdain. Radoub, standing sabre in hand upon the threshold, sent his voice anew into the obscurity of the chamber across which the nearly extinguished torch cast a faint gleam, and repeated his question, "I am one. How many are you?"

There was no answer. He stepped forward. One of those sudden jets of light which an expiring fire sometimes sends out, and which seem like its dying throes, burst from the torch and illuminated the entire chamber. Radoub caught sight of himself in one of the mirrors hanging against the wall,— approached it, and examined his bleeding face and wounded ear. "Horrible mutilation!" said he.

Then he turned about, and, to his utter stupefaction, perceived that the hall was empty. "Nobody here!" he exclaimed. "Not a creature!"

Then he saw the revolving stone, and the staircase beyond the opening. "Ah! I understand! The key to the fields. Come up, all of you!" he shouted. "Comrades, come up! They have run away! They have filed off, dissolved, evaporated, cut their lucky! This old jug of a tower has a crack in it. There is the hole they got out by, the beggars! How is anybody to get the better of Pitt and Coburg while they are able to play such comedies as this? The very devil himself came to their rescue. There is nobody here!"

The report of a pistol cut his words short: a ball grazed his elbow and flattened itself against the wall.

"Aha!" said he. "So there is somebody left. Who was good enough to show me that little politeness?"

"I," answered a voice.

21

Radoub looked about, and caught sight of Imânus in the gloom. "Ah!" cried he. "I have got one at all events. The others have escaped, but you will not, I promise you."

"Do you believe it?" retorted Imânus.

Radoub made a step forward and paused. "Hey, you, lying on the ground there! Who are you?"

"I am a man who laughs at you who are standing up."

"What is it you are holding in your right hand?"

"A pistol."

"And in your left hand?"

"My entrails."

"You are my prisoner."

"I defy you!"

Imânus bowed his head over the burning wick, spent his last breath in stirring the flame, and expired.

A few seconds after, Gauvain and Cimourdain, followed by the whole troop of soldiers, were in the hall. They all saw the opening. They searched the corners of the room and explored the staircase; it had a passage at the bottom which led to the ravine. The besieged had escaped. They raised Imânus,— he was dead. Gauvain, lantern in hand, examined the stone which had afforded an outlet to the fugitives: he had heard of the turning-stone, but he too had always disbelieved the legend. As he looked he saw some lines written in pencil on the massive block; he held the lantern closer, and read these words: —

> "*Au revoir, Viscount.*
> "Lantenac."

Guéchamp was standing by his commandant. Pursuit was utterly useless; the fugitives had the whole country to aid them,— thickets, ravines, copses, the inhabitants. Doubtless they were already far away. There would be no possiblity of discovering them; they had the entire forest of Fougères, with its countless hiding-places, for a refuge. What was to be done? The whole struggle must begin anew.

Gauvain and Guéchamp exchanged conjectures and expressions of disappointment.

Cimourdain listened gravely, but did not utter a word.

" And the ladder, Guéchamp? " said Gauvain.

" Commandant, it has not come."

" But we saw a wagon escorted by gendarmes."

Guéchamp only replied: " It did not bring the ladder."

" What did it bring, then? "

" The guillotine," said Cimourdain.

CHAPTER XV

NEVER PUT A WATCH AND A KEY IN THE SAME POCKET

THE Marquis de Lantenac was not so far away as they believed. But he was none the less in safety, and completely out of their reach. He had followed Halmalo.

The staircase by which they descended in the wake of the other fugitives ended in a narrow vaulted passage close to the ravine and the arches of the bridge. This passage opened upon a deep natural fissure, which led into the ravine on one side and into the forest on the other. The windings of the path were completely hidden among the thickets; it would have been impossible to discover a man concealed there. A fugitive, once arrived at this point, had only to twist away like a snake. The opening from the staircase into the secret passage was so completely obstructed by brambles that the builders of the passage had not thought it necessary to close the way in any other manner.

The marquis had only to go forward now. He was not placed in any difficulty by lack of a disguise. He had not thrown aside his peasant's dress since coming to Brittany, thinking it more in character.

When Halmalo and the marquis passed out of the passage into the cleft, the five other men — Guinoiseau, Hoisnard (Branche d'Or), Brin d'Amour, Chatenay, and the Abbé Turmeau — were no longer there.

"They did not take much time to get away," said Hal-malo.

"Follow their example," returned the marquis.

"Must I leave, monseigneur?"

"Without doubt. I have already told you so. Each must escape alone to be safe. One man passes where two cannot. We should attract attention if we were together. You would lose my life and I yours."

"Does Monseigneur know the district?"

"Yes."

"Monseigneur still gives the rendezvous for the Pierre Gauvain?"

"To-morrow, — at noon."

"I shall be there. We shall all be there." Then Halmalo burst out: "Ah, monseigneur! When I think that we were together in the open sea, that we were alone, that I wanted to kill you, that you were my master, that you could have told me so, and that you did not speak! What a man you are!"

The marquis replied: "England! There is no other resource. In fifteen days the English must be in France."

"I have much to tell monseigneur. I obeyed his orders."

"We will talk of all that to-morrow."

"Farewell till to-morrow, monseigneur."

"By-the-way, are you hungry?"

"Perhaps I am, monseigneur. I was in such a hurry to get here that I am not sure whether I have eaten to-day."

The marquis took a cake of chocolate from his pocket, broke it in half, gave one piece to Halmalo, and began to eat the other himself.

"Monseigneur," said Halmalo, "at your right is the ravine; at your left, the forest."

"Very good. Leave me. Go your own way."

Halmalo obeyed. He hurried off through the darkness.

For a few instants the marquis could hear the crackling of the underbrush, then all was still. By that time it would have been impossible to track Halmalo. This forest of the Bocage was the fugitive's auxiliary. He did not flee,— he vanished. It was this facility for disappearance which made our armies hesitate before this ever-retreating Vendée, so formidable as it fled.

The marquis remained motionless. He was a man who forced himself to feel nothing; but he could not restrain his emotion on breathing this free air, after having been so long stifled in blood and carnage. To feel himself completely at liberty after having seemed so utterly lost; after having seen the grave so close, to be swept so suddenly beyond its reach; to come out of death back into life,— it was a shock even to a man like Lantenac. Familiar as he was with danger, in spite of all the vicissitudes he had passed through he could not at first steady his soul under this. He acknowledged to himself that he was content. But he quickly subdued this emotion, which was more like joy than any feeling he had known for years. He drew out his watch and struck the hour. What time was it?

To his great astonishment, the marquis found that it was only ten o'clock. When one has just passed through some terrible convulsion of existence in which every hope and life itself were at stake, one is always astounded to find that those awful minutes were no longer than ordinary ones. The warning cannon had been fired a little before sunset, and La Tourgue attacked by the storming-party half an hour later, between seven and eight o'clock,— just as night was falling. The colossal combat, begun at eight o'clock, had ended at ten. This whole *épopée* had only taken a hundred and twenty minutes to enact. Sometimes catastrophes sweep on with the rapidity of lightning,— the climax is overwhelming from its suddenness. On reflection, the astonishing thing was that the struggle could have lasted so long. A resistance for two hours of so small a number against so large a force was extraordinary; and certainly it had not been short or quickly finished, this battle of nineteen against **four** thousand.

But it was time he should be gone. Halmalo must be far away, and the marquis judged that it would not be necessary to wait there longer. He put his watch back into his waiscoat, but not into the same pocket; for he discovered that the key of the iron door given him by Imânus was there, and the crystal might be broken against the key. Then he moved toward the forest in his turn. As he turned to the left, it seemed to him that a faint gleam of light penetrated the darkness where he stood. He walked back, and across the underbrush, clearly outlined against a red background and become visible in their tiniest outlines, he perceived a great glare in the ravine; only a few paces separated him from it. He hurried forward,— then stopped, remembering what folly it was to expose himself in that light. Whatever might have happened, after all it did not concern him. Again he set out in the direction Halmalo had indicated, and walked a little way toward the forest.

Suddenly, deep as he was hidden among the brambles, he heard a terrible cry echo over his head. This cry seemed to proceed from the very edge of the plateau which stretched above the ravine. The marquis raised his eyes and stood still.

BOOK V

IN DÆMONE DEUS

CHAPTER I

FOUND, BUT LOST

AT the moment Michelle Fléchard caught sight of the
tower, she was more than a league away. She, who
could scarcely take a step, did not hesitate before these miles
which must be traversed. The woman was weak, but the
mother found strength. She walked on.

The sun set; the twilight came, then the night. Always
pressing on, Michelle heard a bell afar off, hidden by the
darkness, strike eight o'clock, then nine. The peal probably
came from the belfry of Parigné. From time to time she
paused to listen to strange sounds like the deadened echo of
blows, which might perhaps be the wind in the distance. She
walked straight on, breaking the furze and the sharp heath-
stems beneath her bleeding feet. She was guided by a faint
light which shone from the distant tower, defining its outlines against the night, and giving a mysterious glow to the
tower amidst the surrounding gloom. This light became
more distinct when the noise sounded louder, then faded suddenly.

The vast plateau across which Michelle Fléchard journeyed
was covered with grass and heath; not a house, not a tree
appeared. It rose gradually, and, as far as the eye could
reached, stretched in a straight hard line against the sombre

horizon where a few stars gleamed. She had always the
tower before her eyes; the sight kept her strength from failing. She saw the massive pile grow slowly as she walked on.

We have just said the smothered reports and the pale
gleams of light starting from the tower were intermittent;
they stopped, then began anew, offering an enigma full of
agony to the wretched mother. Suddenly they ceased; noise
and gleams of light both died. There was a moment of
complete silence,— an ominous tranquillity.

It was just at this moment that Michelle Fléchard reached
the edge of the plateau. She saw at her feet a ravine, whose
bottom was lost in the wan indistinctness of the night; also
at a little distance, on the top of the pleateau, an entanglement of wheels, metal, and harness, which was a battery;
and before her, confusedly lighted by the matches of the
cannon, an enormous edifice that seemed built of shadows
blacker than the shadows which surrounded it. This mass
of buildings was composed of a bridge whose arches were embedded in the ravine, and of a sort of castle which rose upon
the bridge; both bridge and castle were supported against a
lofty circular shadow,— the tower toward which this mother
had journeyed from so far. She could see lights come and
go in the loop-holes of the tower, and from the noise which
surged up she divined that it was filled with a crowd of men;
indeed, now and then their gigantic shadows were flung out
on the night. Near the battery was a camp, whose outposts
she might have perceived through the gloom and the underbrush, but she had as yet noticed nothing. She went close
to the edge of the plateau, so near the bridge that it seemed
to her she could almost touch it with her hand. The depth
of the ravine alone kept her from reaching it. She could
make out in the gloom the three stories of the bridge-castle.

How long she stood there Michelle Fléchard could not have
told, for her mind, absorbed in her mute contemplation of
this gaping ravine and this shadowy edifice, took no note
of time. What was this building? What was going on
within? Was it La Tourgue? A strange dizziness seized

her; in her confusion she could not tell if this were the goal she had been seeking on the starting-point of a terrible journey. She asked herself why she was there. She looked; she listened.

Suddenly a great blackness shut out every object. A cloud of smoke swept up between Michelle and the pile she was watching; a sharp report forced her to close her eyes. Scarcely had she done so, when a great light reddened the lids. She opened them again. It was no longer the night she had before her; it was the day,— but a fearful day! the day born of fire! She was watching the beginning of a conflagration. From black the smoke had become scarlet, filled with a mighty flame, which appeared and disappeared, writhing and twisting in serpentine coils. The flame burst out like a tongue from something which resembled blazing jaws; it was the embrasure of a window filled with fire. This window, covered by iron bars, already reddening in the heat, was a casement in the lower story of the bridge-castle. Nothing of the edifice was visible except this window. The smoke covered even the plateau, leaving only the mouth of the ravine black against the vermilion flames.

Michelle Fléchard stared in dumb wonder. It was like a dream; she could no longer tell where reality ended, and the confused fancies of her poor troubled brain began. Ought she to fly? Should she remain? There was nothing real enough for any definite decision to steady her mind. A wind swept up and burst the curtain of smoke; in the opening the frowning bastile rose suddenly in view,— donjon, bridge, châtelet,— dazzling in the terrible gilding of conflagration which framed it from top to bottom.

The appalling illumination showed Michelle Fléchard every detail of the ancient keep. The lowest story of the castle built on the bridge was burning. Above rose the other two stories, still untouched, but as it were supported on a corbel of flames. From the edge of the plateau where Michelle Fléchard stood, she could catch broken glimpses of the interior between the clouds of smoke and fire. The windows

were all open. Through the great casements of the second
story she could make out the cupboards stretched along
the walls, which looked to her full of books, and by one of
the windows could see a little group lying on the floor, in
the shadow, indistinct and massed together like birds in a
nest, which at times she fancied she saw move. She looked
fixedly in this direction. What was that little group lying
there in the shadow? Sometimes it flashed across her mind
that those were living forms; but she had fever; she had
eaten nothing since morning; she had walked without inter-
mission; she was utterly exhausted. She felt herself giving way to a sort of hallucination, which she had still reason
enough to struggle against. Still, her eyes fixed themselves
ever more steadily upon that one point; she could not look
away from that little heap upon the floor,— a mass of inanimate objects, doubtless, that had been left in that room
below which the flames roared and billowed.

Suddenly the fire, as if animated by a will and purpose,
flung downward a jet of flame toward the great dead ivy
which covered the façade whereat Michelle Fléchard was gazing. It seemed as if the fire had just discovered this out-
work of dried branches; a spark darted greedily upon it,
and a line of flame spread upward from twig to twig with
frightful rapidity. In the twinkling of an eye it reached
the second story. As they rose, the flames illuminated the
chamber of the first floor, and the awful glare threw out
in bold relief the three little creatures lying asleep upon
the floor. A lovely, statuesque group of legs and arms
interlaced, closed eyes, and angelic, smiling faces.

The mother recognized her children! She uttered a terrible cry. That cry of indescribable agony is only given
to mothers. No sound is at once so savage and so touching.
When a woman utters it, you seem to hear the yell of a sea-
wolf; when the sea-wolf cries thus, you seem to hear the
voice of a woman. This cry of Michelle Fléchard was a
howl. Hecuba howled, says Homer.

It was this cry which reached the Marquis de Lantenac.

When he heard it he stood still. The marquis was between the outlet of the passage through which he had been guided by Halmalo and the ravine. Across the brambles which enclosed him he saw the bridge in flames, and La Tourgue red with the reflection. Looking upward through the opening which the branches left above his head, he perceived close to the edge of the plateau on the opposite side of the gulf, in front of the burning castle, in the full light of the conflagration, the haggard, anguish-stricken face of a woman bending over the depth. It was this woman who had uttered that cry.

The face was no longer that of Michelle Fléchard; it was a Gorgon's. She was appalling in her agony; the peasant woman was transformed into one of the Eumenides; this unknown villager, vulgar, ignorant, unreasoning, had risen suddenly to the epic grandeur of despair. Great sufferings swell the soul to gigantic proportions. This was no longer a simple mother,— all maternity's voice cried out through hers: whatever sums up and becomes a type of humanity grows superhuman. There she towered on the edge of that ravine, in front of that conflagration, in presence of that crime, like a power from beyond the grave; she moaned like a wild beast, but her attitude was that of a goddess; the mouth, which uttered imprecations, was set in a flaming mask. Nothing could have been more regal than her eyes shooting lightnings through her tears. Her look blasted the conflagration.

The marquis listened. The mother's voice flung its echoes down upon his head,— inarticulate, heart-rending; sobs rather than words: —

"Ah, my God, my children! Those are my children! Help! Fire! fire! fire! O you brigands! Is there no one here? My children are burning up! Georgette! My babies! Gros-Alain! René-Jean! What does it mean? Who put my children there? They are asleep. Oh, I am mad! It is impossible! Help, help!"

A great bustle of movement was apparent in La Tourgue

and upon the plateau. The whole camp rushed out to the fire which had just burst forth. The besiegers, after meeting the grape-shot, had now to deal with the conflagration. Gauvain, Cimourdain, and Guéchamp were giving orders. What was to be done? Only a few buckets of water could be drained from the half-dried brook of the ravine. The consternation increased. The whole edge of the plateau was covered with men whose troubled faces watched the progress of the flames. What they saw was terrible: they gazed, and could do nothing.

The flames had spread along the ivy and reached the topmost story, leaping greedily upon the straw with which it was filled. The entire granary was burning now. The flames wreathed and danced as if in fiendish joy. A cruel breeze fanned the pyre. One could fancy the evil spirit of Imânus urging on the fire, and rejoicing in the destruction which had been his last earthly crime. The library, though between the two burning stories, was not yet on fire; the height of its ceiling and the thickness of the walls retarded the fatal moment; but it was fast approaching. The flames from below licked the stones; the flames from above whirled down to caress them with the awful embrace of death: beneath, a cave of lava; above, an arch of embers. If the floor fell first, the children would be flung into the lava stream; if the ceiling gave way, they would be buried beneath burning coals.

The little ones slept still; across the sheets of flame and smoke which now hid, now exposed the casements, the children were visible in that fiery grotto, within that meteoric glare, peaceful, lovely, motionless, like three confident cherubs slumbering in a hell. A tiger might have wept to see those angels in that furnace, those cradles in that tomb.

And the mother was wringing her hands: "Fire! I say, fire! Are they all deaf, that nobody comes? They are burning my children! Come, come, you men that I see yonder. Oh, the days and days that I have hunted,— and this is where I find them! Fire! Help! Three angels,—

to think of three angels burning there! What have they done, the innocents? They shot me; they are burning my little ones! Who is it does such things? Help! save my children! Do you not hear me? A dog,— one would have pity on a dog! My children! my children! They are asleep. O Georgette,— I see her face! René-Jean, Gros-Alain,— those are their names: you may know I am their mother. Oh, it is horrible! I have travelled days and nights! Why, this very morning I talked of them with a woman! Help, help! Where are those monsters? Horror, horror! The eldest not five years old, the youngest not two. I can see their little bare legs. They are asleep, Holy Virgin! Heaven gave them to me, and devils snatch them away. To think how far I have journeyed! My children, that I nourished with my milk! I, who thought myself wretched because I could not find them,— have pity on me! I want my children; I must have my children! And there they are in the fire! See, how my poor feet bleed! Help! It is not possible, if there are men on the earth, that my little ones will be left to die like this. Help! Murder! Oh, such a thing was never seen! O assassins! What is that dreadful house there? They stole my children from me in order to kill them. God of mercy, give me my children! They shall not die! Help! help! help! Oh, I shall curse Heaven itself, if they die like that!"

While the mother's awful supplications rang out, other voices rose upon the plateau and in the ravine.

" A ladder!"

" There is no ladder!"

" Water!"

" There is no water!"

" Up yonder, in the tower, on the second story, there is a door."

" It is iron."

" Break it in!"

" Impossible!"

And the mother, redoubling her agonized appeals: " Fire!

Help! Hurry, I say, if you will not kill me! My children, my children! Oh, the horrible fire! Take them out of it, or throw me in!"

In the interval between these clamours the triumphant crackling of the flames could be heard.

The marquis put his hand in his pocket and touched the key of the iron door. Then, stooping again beneath the vault through which he had escaped, he turned back into the passage from whence he had just emerged.

CHAPTER II

FROM THE DOOR OF STONE TO THE IRON DOOR

A WHOLE army distracted by the impossibility of giving aid; four thousand men unable to succour three children,— such was the situation. Not even a ladder to be had; that sent from Javené had not arrived. The flaming space widened like a crater that opens. To attempt the staying of the fire by means of the half-dried brook would have been mad folly,— like flinging a glass of water on a volcano.

Cimourdain, Guéchamp, and Radoub had descended into the ravine; Gauvain remounted to the room in the second story of the tower, where were the stone that turned, the secret passage, and the iron door leading into the library. It was there that the sulphur-match had been lighted by Imânus; from these the conflagration had started. Gauvain took with him twenty sappers. There was no possible resource except to break open the iron door; its fastenings were terribly secure. They began by blows with axes. The axes broke. A sapper said: " Steel snaps like glass against that iron." The door was made of double sheets of wrought-iron, bolted together; each sheet three fingers in thickness. They took iron bars and tried to shake the door beneath their blows; the bars broke "like matches!" said one of the sappers.

Gauvain murmured gloomily: "Nothing but a ball could open that door. If we could only get a cannon up here!"

"But how to do it?" answered the sapper.

There was a moment of consternation. Those powerless arms ceased their efforts. Mute, conquered, dismayed, these men stood staring at the immovable door. A red reflection crept from beneath it; behind, the conflagration was each instant increasing. The frightful corpse of Imânus lay on the floor,— a demoniac victor. Only a few moments more and the whole bridge-castle might fall in. What could be done? There was not a hope left.

Gauvain, with his eyes fixed on the turning-stone and the secret passage, cried furiously: "It was by that the Marquis de Lantenac escaped."

"And returns," said a voice.

The face of a white-haired man appeared in the stone frame of the secret opening. It was the marquis! Many years had passed since Gauvain had seen that face so near. He recoiled. The rest all stood petrified with astonishment.

The marquis held a large key in his hand; he cast a haughty glance upon the sappers standing before him, walked straight to the iron door, bent beneath the arch, and put the key in the lock. The iron creaked, the door opened, revealing a gulf of flame; the marquis entered it. He entered with a firm step, his head erect. The lookers-on followed him with their eyes. The marquis had scarcely moved half a dozen paces down the blazing hall when the floor, undermined by the fire, gave way beneath his feet and opened a precipice between him and the door. He did not even turn his head,— he walked steadily on. He disappeared in the smoke. Nothing more could be seen.

Had the marquis been able to advance farther? Had a new gulf of fire opened beneath his feet? Had he only succeeded in destroying himself? They could not tell. They had before them only a wall of smoke and flame. The marquis was beyond that, living or dead.

CHAPTER III

THE little ones opened their eyes at last. The conflagration had not yet entered the library, but it cast a rosy glow across the ceiling. The children had never seen an aurora like that; they watched it. Georgette was in ecstasies.

The conflagration unfurled all its splendours; the black hydra and the scarlet dragon appeared amidst the wreathing smoke in awful darkness and gorgeous vermilion. Long streaks of flame shot far out and illuminated the shadows, like opposing comets pursuing one another. Fire is recklessly prodigal with its treasures; its furnaces are filled with gems which it flings to the winds; it is not for nothing that charcoal is identical with the diamond. Fissures had opened in the wall of the upper story, through which the embers poured like cascades of jewels; the heaps of straw and oats burning in the granary began to stream out of the windows in an avalanche of golden rain, the oats turning to amethyst and the straw to carbuncles.

" Pretty ! " said Georgette.

They all three raised themselves.

" Ah ! " cried the mother. " They have awakened ! "

René-Jean got up, then Gros-Alain, and Georgette followed. René-Jean stretched his arms toward the window and said, " I am warm."

" Me warm," cooed Georgette.

The mother shrieked: " My children ! René ! Alain ! Georgette ! "

The little ones looked about. They strove to comprehend. When men are frightened, children are only curious. He who is easily astonished is difficult to alarm; ignorance is intrepidity. Children have so little claim to purgatory that if they saw it they would admire.

The mother repeated: " René! Alain! Georgette! "

René-Jean turned his head; that voice roused him from his reverie. Children have short memories, but their recollections are swift; the whole past is yesterday to them. René-Jean saw his mother; found that perfectly natural; and feeling a vague want of support in the midst of those strange surroundings, he called " Mamma! "

" Mamma! " said Gros-Alain.

" M'ma! " said Georgette. And she held out her little arms.

" My children! " shrieked the mother.

All three went close to the window-ledge; fortunately the fire was not on that side.

" I am too warm," said René-Jean. He added, " It burns." Then his eyes sought the mother. " Come here, mamma! " he cried.

" Tum, m'ma," repeated Georgette.

The mother, with her hair streaming about her face, her garments torn, her feet and hands bleeding, let herself roll from bush to bush down into the ravine. Cimourdain and Guéchamp were there, as powerless as Gauvain was above. The soldiers, desperate at being able to do nothing, swarmed about. The heat was unsupportable, but nobody felt it. They looked at the bridge, the height of the arches, the different stories of the castle,— the inaccessible windows. Help to be of any avail must come at once. Three stories to climb; no way of doing it!

Radoub, wounded, with a sabre-cut on his shoulder and one ear torn off, rushed forward dripping with sweat and blood. He saw Michelle Fléchard. " Hold! " cried he. " The woman that was shot! So you have come to life again? "

" My children! " groaned the mother.

" You are right," answered Radoub, " we have no time to occupy ourselves about ghosts." He attempted to climb the bridge, but in vain; he dug his nails in between the stones

22

and clung there for a few seconds, but the layers were as smoothly joined as if the wall had been new; Radoub fell back.

The conflagration swept on, each instant growing more terrible. They could see the heads of the three children framed in the red light of the window. In his frenzy Radoub shook his clinched hand at the sky, and shouted, " Is there no mercy yonder? "

The mother on her knees, clung to one of the piers, crying, " Mercy, mercy! "

The hollow sound of cracking timbers rose above the roar of the flames. The panes of glass in the book-cases of the library cracked and fell with a crash. It was evident that the timber-work had given way. Human strength could do nothing. Another moment and the whole would fall. The soldiers only waited for the final catastrophe. They could hear the little voices repeat, " Mamma! mamma! " The whole crowd was paralyzed with horror!

Suddenly, at the casement near that where the children stood, a tall form appeared against the crimson background of the flames. Every head was raised, every eye fixed. A man was above there,— a man in the library, in the furnace! The face showed black against the flames, but they could see the white hair; they recognized the Marquis de Lantenac. He disappeared, then appeared again. The indomitable old man stood in the window shoving out an enormous ladder. It was the escape ladder deposited in the library; he had seen it lying upon the floor and dragged it to the window. He held it by one end; with the marvellous agility of an athlete he slipped it out of the casement, and slid it along the wall down into the ravine.

Radoub folded his arms about the ladder as it descended within his reach, crying, " Long live the Republic! "

The marquis shouted, " Long live the King! "

Radoub muttered: " You may cry what you like, and talk nonsense if you please, you are an angel of mercy all the same."

The ladder was settled in place, and communication established between the burning floor and the ground. Twenty men rushed up, Radoub at their head, and in the twinkling of an eye they were hanging to the rungs from the top to the bottom, making a human ladder. He had his face turned toward the conflagration. The little army scattered among the heath and along the sides of the ravine pressed forward, overcome by contending emotions, upon the plateau, into the ravine, out on the platform of the tower.

The marquis disappeared again, then reappeared bearing a child in his arms. There was a tremendous clapping of hands. The marquis had seized the first little one that he found within reach. It was Gros-Alain.

Gros-Alain cried, " I am afraid."

The marquis gave the boy to Radoub; Radoub passed him on to the soldier behind, who passed him to another; and just as Gros-Alain, greatly frightened and sobbing loudly, was given from hand to hand to the bottom of the ladder, the marquis, who had been absent for a moment, returned to the window with René-Jean, who struggled and wept and beat Radoub with his little fists as the marquis passed him on to the sergeant.

The marquis went back into the chamber that was now filled with flames. Georgette was there alone. He went up to her. She smiled. This man of granite felt his eyelids grow moist. He asked, " What is your name? "

" Orgette," said she.

He took her in his arms; she was still smiling, and at the instant he handed her to Radoub, that conscience, so lofty and yet so darkened, was dazzled by the beauty of innocence: the old man kissed the child.

" It is the little girl! " said the soldiers; and Georgette in her turn descended from arm to arm till she reached the ground, amidst cries of exultation. They clapped their hands; they leaped; the old grenadiers sobbed, and she smiled at them.

The mother stood at the foot of the ladder breathless, mad,

intoxicated by this change,— flung, without transition, **from**
hell into paradise. Excess of joy lacerates the heart in **its**
own way. She extended her arms; she received first Gros-
Alain, then René-Jean, then Georgette. She covered them
with frantic kisses, then burst into a wild laugh and fainted.

A great cry rose: " They are all saved."

All were indeed saved, except the old man. But no one
thought of him,— not even he himself, perhaps. He remained for a few instants leaning against the window-ledge
lost in a reverie, as if he wished to leave the gulf of flames
time to make a decision. Then, without the least haste, slowly
indeed and proudly, he stepped over the window-sill, and erect,
upright, his shoulders against the rungs, having the conflagration at his back, the depth before him, he began to descend the ladder in silence, with the majesty of a phantom.

The men who were on the ladder sprang off; every witness
shuddered. About this man thus descending from that
height there was a sacred horror as about a vision; but he
plunged calmly into the darkness before him. They recoiled; he drew nearer them. The marble pallor of his face
showed no emotion; his haughty eyes were calm and cold. At
each step he made toward those men whose wondering eyes
gazed upon him out of the darkness, he seemed to tower
higher; the ladder shook and echoed under his firm tread: one
might have thought him the statue of the " Commendatore "
descending anew into his sepulchre.

As the marquis reached the bottom, and his foot left the
last rung and planted itself on the ground, a hand seized his
shoulder. He turned about.

" I arrest you," said Cimourdain.

" I approve of what you do," said Lantenac.

BOOK VI

AFTER THE VICTORY THE COMBAT BEGINS

CHAPTER I

LANTENAC TAKEN

THE marquis had indeed descended into the tomb. He was led away.

The crypt dungeon of the ground-floor of La Tourgue was immediately opened under Cimourdain's lynx-eyed superintendence. A lamp was placed within, a jug of water and a loaf of soldier's bread; a bundle of straw was flung on the ground, and in less than a quarter of an hour from the instant when the priest's hand seized Lantenac the door of the dungeon closed upon him. This done, Cimourdain went to find Gauvain; at that instant eleven o'clock sounded from the distant church-clock of Parigné.

Cimourdain said to his former pupil: " I am going to convoke a court-martial; you will not be there. You are a Gauvain, and Lantenac is a Gauvain. You are too near a kinsman to be his judge; I blame Egalité for having voted upon Capet's sentence. The court-martial will be composed of three judges,— an officer, Captain Guéchamp; a non-commissioned officer, Sergeant Radoub; and myself. I shall preside. Nothing of all this concerns you any longer. We will conform to the decree of the Convention; we will confine ourselves to proving the identity of the *ci-devant* Marquis de

Lantenac.   To-morrow the court-martial; day after to-morrow the guillotine.   The Vendée is dead."

Gauvain did not answer a word, and Cimourdain, preoccupied by the final task which remained for him to fulfil, left the young man alone.   Cimourdain had to decide upon the hour, and choose the place.   He had — like Lequinio at Granville, like Tallien at Bordeaux, like Châlier at Lyons, like Saint-Just at Strasbourg — the habit of assisting personally at executions; it was considered a good example for the judge to come and see the headsman do his work,— a custom borrowed by the Terror of '93 from the parliaments of France and the Inquisition of Spain.

Gauvain also was preoccupied.   A cold wind moaned up from the forest.   Gauvain left Guéchamp to give the necessary orders, went to his tent in the meadow which stretched along the edge of the wood at the foot of La Tourgue, took his hooded cloak and enveloped himself therein.   This cloak was bordered with the simple galoon which, according to the republican custom (chary of ornament), designated the commander-in-chief.   He began to walk about in this bloody field where the attack had begun.   He was alone there.   The fire still continued, but no one any longer paid attention to it. Radoub was beside the children and their mother, almost as maternal as she.   The bridge-castle was nearly consumed; the sappers hastened the destruction.   The soldiers were digging trenches in order to bury the dead; the wounded were being cared for; the retirade had been demolished; the chambers and stairs disencumbered of the dead; the soldiers were cleansing the scene of carnage, sweeping away the terrible rubbish of the victory,— with true military rapidity setting everything in order after the battle.

Gauvain saw nothing of all this.   So profound was his reverie that he scarcely cast a glance toward the guard about the tower, doubled by the orders of Cimourdain.   He could distinguish the breach through the obscurity, perhaps two hundred feet away from the corner of the field where he had taken refuge.   He could see the black opening.   It was there the attack had begun three hours before; it was by this dark gap that he (Gauvain) had penetrated into the tower; there was the ground-floor where the retirade had stood; it was on that same floor that the door of the marquis's prison opened. The guard at the breach watched this dungeon. While his eyes were absently fixed upon the heath, in his ear rang confusedly, like the echo of a knell, these words: "To-morrow the court-martial; day after to-morrow, the guillotine."

The conflagration, which had been isolated, and upon which the sappers had thrown all the water that could be procured, did not die away without resistance; it still cast out intermittent flames. At moments the cracking of the ceilings could be heard, and the crash one upon another of the different stories as they fell in a common ruin; then a whirlwind of sparks would fly through the air, as if a gigantic torch had been shaken; a glare like lightning illuminated the farthest verge of the horizon, and the shadow of La Tourgue, growing suddenly colossal, spread out to the edge of the forest.

Gauvain walked slowly to and fro amidst the gloom in front of the breach. At intervals he clasped his two hands at the back of his head, covered with his soldier's hood. He was thinking.

CHAPTER II

GAUVAIN'S SELF-QUESTIONING

HIS reverie was fathomless. A seemingly impossible change had taken place. The Marquis de Lantenac had been transfigured.

Gauvain had been a witness of this transfiguration. He would never have believed that such a state of affairs would arrive from any complication of events, whatever they might be. Never would he have imagined, even in a dream, that anything similar would be possible. The unexpected — that inexplicable power which plays with man at will — had seized Gauvain, and held him fast. He had before him the impossible become a reality, visible, palpable, inevitable, inexorable. What did he think of it — he, Gauvain? There was no chance of evasion; the decision must be made. A question was put to him; he could not avoid it. Put by whom? By events. And not alone by events; for when events, which are mutable, address a question to our souls, Justice, which is unchangeable, summons us to reply. Above the cloud which casts its shadow upon us is the star that sends toward us its light. We can no more escape from the light than from the shadow.

Gauvain was undergoing an interrogatory. He had been arraigned before a judge: before a terrible judge,— his conscience. Gauvain felt every power of his soul vacillate. His resolutions the most solid, his promises the most piously uttered, his decisions the most irrevocable, all tottered in this terrible overwhelming of his will. There are moral earthquakes. The more he reflected upon that which he had lately seen, the more confused he became. Gauvain, republican, believed himself, and was, just. A higher justice had revealed itself. Above the justice of revolutions is that of humanity. What had happened could not be eluded; the case was grave; Gauvain made part of it; he could not withdraw himself; and although Cimourdain had said, " It concerns you no further," he felt within his soul the pang which a tree may feel when torn upward from its roots.

Every man has a basis; a disturbance of this base causes a profound trouble; it was what Gauvain now felt. He pressed his head between his two hands, searching for the truth. To state clearly a situation like his is not easy; nothing could be more painful. He had before him the formidable ciphers which he must sum up into a total; to judge a human destiny by mathematical rules. His head whirled. He tried;

he endeavoured to consider the matter; he forced himself to collect his ideas, to discipline the resistance which he felt within himself, and to recapitulate the facts. He set them all before his mind.

To whom has it not arrived to make such a report, and to interrogate himself in some supreme circumstances upon the route which must be followed,— whether to advance or retreat?

Gauvain had just been witness of a miracle. Before the earthly combat had fairly ended, there came a celestial struggle,— the conflict of good against evil. A heart of adamant had been conquered. Given the man with all that he had of evil within him, violence, error, blindness, unwholesome obstinacy, pride, egotism,— Gauvain had just witnessed a miracle: the victory of humanity over the man. Humanity had conquered the inhuman. And by what means; in what manner? How had it been able to overthrow that colossus of wrath and hatred? What arms had it employed; what implement of war? The cradle!

Gauvain had been dazzled. In the midst of social war, in the very blaze of all hatreds and all vengeances, at the darkest and most furious moment of the tumult, at the hour when crime gave all its fires, and hate all its blackness,— at that instant of conflict, when every sentiment becomes a projectile; when the *mêlée* is so fierce that one no longer knows what is justice, honesty, or truth,— suddenly the Unknown (mysterious warner of *souls*) sent the grand rays of eternal truth resplendent across human light and darkness. Above that sombre duel between the false and the relatively true, there, in the depths, the face of truth itself abruptly appeared. Suddenly the force of the feeble had interposed. He had seen three poor creatures, almost new born, unreasoning, abandoned, orphans, alone, lisping, smiling; having against them civil war, retaliation, the horrible logic of reprisals, murder, carnage, fratricide, rage, hatred, all the Gorgons,— he had seen them triumph against those powers. He had seen the defeat and extinction of a horrible conflagra-

tion that had been charged to commit a crime; he had seen
atrocious premeditations disconcerted and brought to naught;
he had seen ancient feudal ferocity, inexorable disdain, pro-
fessed experiences of the necessities of war, reasons of State,
all the arrogant resolves of a savage old age, vanish before
the clear gaze of those who had not yet lived. And this was
natural; for he who has not yet lived has done no evil: he is
justice, truth, purity; and the highest angels of heaven hover
about those souls of little children.

A useful spectacle, a counsel, a lesson. The maddened,
merciless combatants, in face of all the projects, all the out-
rages of war, fanaticism, assassination, revenge kindling the
fagots, death coming torch in hand, had suddenly seen all-
powerful Innocence raise itself above this enormous legion
of crimes. And Innocence had conquered. One could say:
No, civil war does not exist; barbarism does not exist; hatred
does not exist; crime does not exist; darkness does not exist.
To scatter these spectres it only needed that divine aurora,—
innocence. Never in any conflict had Satan and God been
more plainly visible.

This conflict had a human conscience for its arena. The
conscience of Lantenac. Now the battle began again — more
desperate, more decisive still perhaps — in another conscience,
— the conscience of Gauvain.

What a battle-ground is the soul of man! We are given
up to those gods, those monsters, those giants,— our thoughts.
Often these terrible belligerents trample our very souls down
in their mad conflict.

Gauvain meditated. The Marquis de Lantenac, surrounded,
doomed, condemned, outlawed; shut in like the wild beast in
the circus, held like a nail in the pincers, enclosed in his refuge
become his prison, bound on every side by a wall of iron and
fire,— had succeeded in stealing away. He had performed
a miracle in escaping; he had accomplished that masterpiece,
— the most difficult of all in such a war,— flight. He had
again taken possession of the forest, to intrench himself therein; of the district, to fight there; of the shadow, to disappear

within it. He had once more become the formidable, the dangerous wanderer, the captain of the invincibles, the chief of the underground forces, the master of the woods. Gauvain had the victory, but Lantenac had his liberty. Henceforth Lantenac had security before him, limitless freedom, an inexhaustible choice of asylums. He was indiscernible, unapproachable, inaccessible. The lion had been taken in the snare, and had broken through.

Well, he had re-entered it. The Marquis de Lantenac had voluntarily, spontaneously, by his own free act, left the forest, the shadow, security, liberty, to return to that horrible peril: intrepid when Gauvain saw him the first time plunge into the conflagration at the risk of being engulfed therein; intrepid a second time, when he descended that ladder which delivered him to his enemies,— a ladder of escape to others, of perdition to him. And why had he thus acted? To save three children. And now what was it they were about to do to this man? Guillotine him. Had these three children been his own? No. Of his family? No. Of his rank? No. For three little beggars — chance children, foundlings, unknown, ragged, barefooted — this noble, this prince, this old man, free, safe, triumphant (for evasion is a triumph), had risked all, compromised all, lost all; and at the same time he restored the babes, had proudly brought his own head,— and this head, hitherto terrible, but now august, he offered to his foes. And what were they about to do? Accept the sacrifice.

The Marquis de Lantenac had had the choice between the life of others and his own: in this superb option he had chosen death. And it was to be granted him; he was to be killed. What a reward for heroism! Respond to a generous act by a barbarous one! What a degrading of the Revolution, what a belittling of the Republic! As this man of prejudice and servitude, suddenly transformed, returned into the circle of humanity, the men who strove for deliverance and freedom elected to cling to the horrors of civil war, to the routine of blood, to fratricide! The divine law of forgiveness, abnegation, redemption, sacrifice, existed for the combatants of error, and did not exist for the soldiers of truth! What! Not to make a struggle in magnanimity: resign themselves to this defeat? They, the stronger, to show themselves the weaker; they, victorious, to become assassins, and cause it to be said that there were those on the side of monarchy who saved children, and those on the side of the Republic who slew old men?

The world would see this great soldier, this powerful octogenarian, this disarmed warrior,— stolen rather than captured, seized in the performance of a good action; seized by his own permission, with the sweat of a noble devotion still upon his brow,— mount the steps of the scaffold as he would mount to the grandeur of an apotheosis! And they would put beneath the knife that head about which would circle, as suppliants, the souls of the three little angels he had saved! And before this punishment — infamous for the butchers — a smile would be seen on the face of that man, and the blush of shame on the face of the Republic! And this would be accomplished in the presence of Gauvain, the chief. And he who might hinder this would abstain. He would rest content under that haughty absolution, " This concerns thee no longer." And he was not even to say to himself that in such a case abdication of authority was complicity! He was not to perceive that of two men engaged in an action so hideous, he who permits the thing is worse than the man who does the work, because he is the coward!

But this death,— had he, Gauvain, not promised it? Had not he, the merciful, declared that Lantenac should have no mercy; that he would himself deliver Lantenac to Cimourdain? That head,— he owed it. Well, he would pay the debt; so be it. But it was, indeed, the same head.

Hitherto Gauvain had seen in Lantenac only the barbarous warrior, the fanatic of royalty and feudalism, the slaughterer of prisoners, an assassin whom war had let loose, a man of blood. That man he had not feared; he had proscribed that proscriber: the implacable would have found him inexorable.

Nothing more simple; the road was marked out and terribly plain to follow; everything foreseen: those who killed must be killed; the path of horror was clear and straight. Unexpectedly that straight line had been broken; a sudden turn in the way revealed a new horizon; a metamorphosis had taken place. An unknown Lantenac entered upon the scene. A hero sprang up from the monster: more than a hero,— a man; more than a soul,— a heart. It was no longer a murderer that Gauvain had before him, but a saviour. Gauvain was flung to the earth by a flood of celestial radiance. Lantenac had struck him with the thunder-bolt of generosity.

And Lantenac transfigured could not transfigure Gauvain! What! Was this stroke of light to produce no counterstroke? Was the man of the Past to push on in front, and the man of the Future to fall back? Was the man of barbarism and superstition suddenly to unfold angel pinions, and soar aloft to watch the man of the ideal crawl beneath him in the mire and the night? Gauvain to lie wallowing in the blood-stained rut of the past, while Lantenac rose to a new existence in the sublime future?

Another thing still. Their family! This blood which he was about to spill,— for to let it be spilled was to spill it himself,— was not this his blood, his, Gauvain's? His grandfather was dead, but his grand-uncle lived, and this grand-uncle was the Marquis de Lantenac. Would not that ancestor who had gone to the grave rise to prevent his brother from being forced into it? Would he not command his grandson henceforth to respect that crown of white hairs, become pure as his own angelic halo? Did not a spectre loom with indignant eyes between him, Gauvain, and Lantenac? Was, then, the aim of the Revolution to denaturalize man? Had she been born to break the ties of family and to stifle the instincts of humanity? Far from it. It was to affirm these glorious realities, not to deny them, that '89 had risen. To overturn the bastiles was to deliver humanity; to abolish feudality was to found families. The author being the point from whence authority sets out, and authority being included in

the author, there can be no other authority than paternity:
hence the legitimacy of the queen-bee who creates her people,
and who, being mother, is queen; hence the absurdity of the
king-man, who not being father, cannot be master. Hence
the suppression of the king; hence the Republic that comes
from all this! Family, humanity, revolution. Revolution
is the accession of the peoples; and, at the bottom, the People
is Man. The thing to decide was, whether when Lantenac
returned into humanity, Gauvain should return to his family.
The thing to decide was, whether the uncle and nephew should
meet again in a higher light, or whether the nephew's recoil
should reply to the uncle's progress. The question in this
pathetic debate between Gauvain and his conscience had resolved itself into this; and the answer seemed to come of itself,— he must save Lantenac.

Yes; but France?. Here the dizzying problem suddenly
changed its face. What! France at bay? France betrayed,
flung open, dismantled? Having no longer a moat. Germany would cross the Rhine; no longer a wall, Italy would
leap the Alps, and Spain the Pyrenees. There would remain
to France that great abyss, the ocean. She had for her the
gulf; she could back herself against it, and, giantess, supported by the entire sea, could combat the whole earth,— a
position, after all, impregnable. Yet no; this position would
fail her. The ocean no longer belonged to her. In this ocean
was England. True, England was at a loss how to traverse
it. Well, a man would fling her a bridge; a man would ex-
tend his hand to her; a man would go to Pitt, to Craig, to
Cornwallis, to Dundas, to the piraies, and say, " Come! " A
man would cry, " England, seize France! " And this man
was the Marquis de Lantenac. This man was now held fast.
After three months of chase, of pursuit, of frenzy, he had at
last been taken. The hand of the Revolution had just closed
upon the accursed one; the clinched fist of '93 had seized this
royalist murderer by the throat. Through that mysterious
premeditation from on high which mixes itself in human affairs, it was in the dungeon belonging to his family that this

parricide awaited his punishment. The feudal lord was in
the feudal oubliette. The stones of his own castle rose against
him and shut him in, and he who had sought to betray his
country had been betrayed by his own dwelling. God had
visibly arranged all this; the hour had sounded; the Revolution had taken prisoner this public enemy; he could no longer
fight, he could no longer struggle, he could no longer harm.
In this Vendée, which owned so many arms, his was the sole
brain; with his extinction, civil war would be extinct. He
was held fast,— tragic and fortunate conclusion! After so
many massacres, so much carnage, he was a captive, this man
who had slain so pitilessly; and it was his turn to die.

And if some one should be found to save him! Cimourdain,
that is to say, '93, held Lantenac, that is to say, Monarchy;
and could any one be found to snatch its prey from that hand
of bronze? Lantenac, the man in whom concentrated that
sheaf of scourges called the Past,— the Marquis de Lantenac,
— was in the tomb; the heavy eternal door had closed upon
him; would some one come from without to draw back the
bolt? This social malefactor was dead, and with him died revolt, fratricidal contest, bestial war; and would any one be
found to resuscitate him? Oh, how that death's-head would
laugh! That spectre would say, " It is well; I live again,—
the idiots! " How he would once more set himself at his
hideous work. How joyously and implacably this Lantenac
would plunge anew into the gulf of war and hatred, and on
the morrow would be seen again houses burning, prisoners
massacred, the wounded slain, women shot!

And, after all, did not Gauvain exaggerate this action
which had fascinated him? Three children were lost; Lantenac saved them. But who had flung them into that peril?
Was it not Lantenac? Who had set those three cradles in
the heart of the conflagration? Was it not Imânus? Who
was Imânus? The lieutenant of the marquis. The one responsible is the chief. Hence the incendiary and the assassin
was Lantenac. What had he done so admirable? He had
not persisted,— that was all. After having conceived the

crime, he had recoiled before it. He had become horrified at
himself. That mother's cry had awakened in him those remains of human mercy which exist in all souls, even the most
hardened; at this cry he had returned upon his steps. Out
of the night where he had buried himself, he hastened toward
the day; after having brought about the crime, he caused its
defeat. His whole merit consisted in this,— not to have been
a monster to the end.

And in return for so little, to restore him all. To give
him freedom, the fields, the plains, air, day; restore to him
the forest, which he would employ to shelter his bandits; restore him liberty, which he would use to bring about slavery;
restore life, which he would devote to death. As for trying to
come to an understanding with him; attempting to treat with
that arrogant soul; propose his deliverance under certain conditions; demand if he would consent, were his life spared,
henceforth to abstain from all hostilities and all revolt,— what
an error such an offer would be! what an advantage it would
give him! against what scorn would the proposer wound himself! how he would freeze the questioner by his response,
" Keep such shame for yourself: kill me! "

There was, in short, nothing to do with this man but to
slay or set him free. He was ever ready to soar or to sacrifice himself; his strange soul held at once the eagle and the
abyss. To slay him,— what a pang! To set him free,—
what a responsibility! Lantenac saved, all was to begin anew
with the Vendée,— like a struggle with a hydra whose heads
had not been severed. In the twinkling of an eye, with the
rapidity of a meteor, the flame extinguished by this man's
disappearance would blaze up again. Lantenac would never
stop to rest until he had carried out that execrable plan,—
to fling, like the cover of a tomb, Monarchy upon the Republic, and England upon France. To save Lantenac was to
sacrifice France. Life to Lantenac was death to a host of
innocent beings,— men, women, children, caught anew in that
domestic war; it was the landing of the English, the recoil
of the Revolution; it was the sacking of the villages, the rend-

ing of the people, the mangling of Brittany; it was flinging
the prey back into the tiger's claw. And Gauvain, in the
midst of uncertain gleams and rays of introverted light, beheld, vaguely sketched across his reverie, this problem rise,—
the setting the tiger at liberty.

And then the question reappeared under its first aspect;
the stone of Sisyphus, which is nothing other than the combat of man with himself, fell back. Was Lantenac that
tiger? Perhaps he had been; but was he still?

Gauvain was dizzy beneath the whirl and conflict in his
soul; his thoughts turned and circled upon themselves with
serpentine swiftness. After the closest examination, could
any one deny Lantenac's devotion; his stoical self-abnegation,
his superb disinterestedness? What! to attest his humanity
in the presence of the open jaws of civil war! What! in this
contest of inferior truths, to bring the highest truth of all!
What! to prove that above royalties, above revolutions, above
earthly questions, is the grand tenderness of the human soul,
— the recognition of the protection due to the feeble from
the strong, the safety due to those who are perishing from
those who are saved, the paternity due to all little children
from all old men! To prove these magnificent truths by the
gift of his head! to be a general, and renounce strategy, battle, revenge! What! to be a royalist, and to take a balance
and put in one scale the King of France, a monarchy
of fifteen centuries, old laws to re-establish, ancient society to restore, and in the other three little unknown peasants,
and to find the king, the throne, the sceptre, and fifteen centuries of monarchy too light to weigh against these three
innocent creatures! What! was all that nothing? What!
could he who had done this remain a tiger! Ought he to be
treated like a wild beast? No, no, no! The man who had
just illuminated the abyss of civil war by the light of a divine
action was not a monster. The sword-bearer was metamor-
phosed into the angel of day. The infernal Satan had again
become the celestial Lucifer. Lantenac had atoned for all his
barbarities by one act of sacrifice; in losing himself materially

23

he had saved himself morally; he had become innocent again, he had signed his own pardon. Does not the right of self-forgiveness exist? Henceforth he was venerable.

Lantenac had just shown himself almost superhuman; it was now Gauvain's turn. Gauvain was called upon to answer him. The struggle of good and evil passions made the world a chaos at this epoch: Lantenac, dominating the chaos, had just brought humanity out of it; it now remained for Gauvain to bring forth their family therefrom.

What was he about to do? Was Gauvain about to betray the trust Providence had shown in him? No; and he murmured within himself, "Let us save Lantenac." And a voice answered, "It is well. Go on; aid the English; desert; pass over to the enemy. Save Lantenac and betray France!" And Gauvain shuddered. "Thy solution is no solution, O dreamer!" Gauvain saw the Sphinx smile bitterly in the shadow.

This situation was a sort of formidable meeting-ground where hostile truths confronted one another, and where the three highest ideas of man — humanity, family, country — looked in one another's faces. Each of these voices took up the word in its turn, and each uttered truth. Each in its turn seemed to find the point where wisdom and justice met, and said, "Do this!" Was that the thing he ought to do? Yes: no. Reasoning said one thing, and feeling another: the two counsels were in direct opposition. Reasoning is only reason; feeling is often conscience. The one comes from man himself, the other from a higher source; hence it is that feeling has less clearness and more power. Still, what force stern reason possesses!

Gauvain hesitated. Maddening perplexity! Two abysses opened before him. Should he let the marquis perish? Should he save him? He must plunge into one depth or the other. Toward which of the two gulfs did Duty point?

CHAPTER III

THE COMMANDANT'S MANTLE

IT was, after all, with Duty that these victors had to deal.
Duty raised herself,— stern to Cimourdain's eyes; terrible to those of Gauvain. Simple before the one; complex,
diverse, tortuous, before the other.

Midnight sounded; then one o'clock. Without being conscious of it, Gauvain had gradually approached the entrance
to the breach. The expiring conflagration only flung out intermittent gleams; the plateau on the other side of the tower
caught the reflection and became visible for an instant, then
disappeared from view as the smoke swept over the flames.
This glare, reviving in jets and cut by sudden shadows, disproportioned objects, and made the sentinels look like phantoms. Lost in his reverie, Gauvain mechanically watched the
strife between the flame and smoke. These appearances and
disappearances of the light before his eyes had a strange,
subtle analogy with the revealing and concealment of truth
in his soul.

Suddenly, between two clouds of smoke, a long streak of
flame, shot out from the dying brazier, illuminated vividly
the summit of the plateau, and brought out the skeleton of a
wagon against the vermilion background. Gauvain stared at
this wagon. It was surrounded by horsemen wearing gendarmes' hats; it seemed to him the wagon which he had looked
at through Guéchamp's glass several hours before, when the
sun was setting and the wagon away off on the verge of the
horizon. Some men were mounted on the cart and appeared
to be unloading it; that which they took off seemed to be
heavy, and now and then gave out the sound of clanking iron.
It would have been difficult to tell what it was; it looked like
beams for a frame-work. Two of the men lifted between

them and set upon the ground a box, which, as well as he could judge by the shape, contained a triangular object.

The flame sank; all was again buried in darkness. Gauvain stood with fixed eyes lost in thought upon that which the darkness hid. Lanterns were lighted, men came and went on the plateau; but the forms of those moving about were confused, and, moreover, Gauvain was below and on the other side of the ravine, and therefore could see little of what was passing.

Voices spoke, but he could not catch the words. Now and then came a sound like the shock of timbers striking together. He could hear also a strange metallic creaking, like the sharpening of a scythe.

Two o'clock struck. Slowly, and like one who strove to retreat and yet was forced by some invisible power to advance, Gauvain approached the breach. As he came near, the sentinel recognized in the shadow the cloak and braided hood of the commandant, and presented arms. Gauvain entered the hall of the ground-floor, which had been transformed into a guard-room. A lantern hung from the roof; it cast just light enough so that one could cross the hall without treading upon the soldiers who lay, most of them asleep, upon the straw. There they lay; they had been fighting a few hours before; the grape-shot, partially swept away, scattered its grains of iron and lead over the floor and troubled their repose somewhat, but they were weary, and so slept. This hall had been the battle-ground, the scene of frenzied attack; there men had groaned, howled, ground their teeth, struck out blindly in their death-agony, and expired. Many of these sleepers' companions had fallen dead upon this floor, where they now lay down in their weariness; the straw which served them for a pillow had drunk the blood of their comrades. Now all was ended; the blood had ceased to flow, the sabres were dried; the dead were dead; these sleepers slumbered peacefully. Such is war. And then, perhaps to-morrow, the slumber of all will be the same.

At Gauvain's entrance a few of the men rose,— among

others, the officers in command. Gauvain pointed to the door
of the dungeon. " Open it," he said to the officer. The bolts
were drawn back; the door opened. Gauvain entered the dungeon. The door closed behind him.

BOOK VII

FEUDALITY AND REVOLUTION

CHAPTER I

THE ANCESTOR

A LAMP was placed on the flags of the crypt at the side of the air-hole in the oubliette. There could also be seen on the stones a jug of water, a loaf of army bread, and a truss of straw. The crypt being cut out in the rock, the prisoner who had conceived the idea of setting fire to the straw would have done it to his own hurt,— no risk of conflagration to the prison, certainty of suffocation to the prisoner.

At the instant the door turned on its hinges the marquis was walking to and fro in his dungeon,— that mechanical pacing natural to wild animals in a cage. At the noise of the opening and shutting of the door he raised his head, and the lamp which set on the floor between Gauvain and the marquis struck full upon the faces of both men. They looked at each other, and something in the glance of either kept the two motionless.

At length the marquis burst out laughing, and exclaimed: " Good-evening, sir. It is a long time since I have had the pleasure of meeting you. You do me the favour of paying me a visit; I thank you. I ask nothing better than to converse a little; I was beginning to bore myself. Your friends lose a great deal of time; proofs of identity, court-martials, — all those ceremonies take a long while; I could go much

quicker at need. Here I am in my house; take the trouble
to enter. Well, what do you say of all that is happening?
Original, is it not? Once on a time there was a king and a
queen: the king was the king; the queen was — France. They
cut the king's head off, and married the queen to Robespierre; this gentleman and that lady have a daughter named
Guillotine, with whom it appears I am to make acquaintance
to-morrow morning. I shall be delighted — as I am to see
you. Did you come about that? Have you risen in rank?
Shall you be the headsman? If it is a simple visit of friendship, I am touched. Perhaps, Viscount, you no longer know
what a nobleman is; well, you see one,— it is I. Look at the
specimen. It is an odd race; it believes in God, it believes in
tradition, it believes in family, it believes in its ancestors, it
believes in the example of its father,— in fidelity, loyalty,
duty toward its prince, respect to ancient laws, virtue, justice;
and it would shoot you with pleasure. Have the goodness to
sit down, I pray you,— on the stones, it must be, it is true,
for I have no armchair in my salon; but he who lives in the
mire can sit on the ground. I do not say that to offend you,
for what we call the ' mire ' you call the ' nation.' I fancy
that you do not insist I shall shout ' Liberty, Equality, Fraternity '? This is an ancient chamber of my house: formerly
the lords imprisoned clowns here; now clowns imprison the
lords. These stupidities are called a Revolution. It appears
that my head is to be cut off in thirty-six hours. I see nothing inconvenient in that; still, if my captors had been polite,
they would have sent me my snuff-box: it is up in the chamber
of the mirrors, where you used to play when you were a
child, where I used to dance you on my knees. Sir, let me
tell you one thing: You call yourself Gauvain, and, strange
to say, you have noble blood in your veins,— yes, by Heaven!
the same that runs in mine; yet the blood that made me a
man of honour makes you a rascal. Such are personal
idiosyncrasies! You will tell me it is not your fault that you
are a rascal; nor is it mine that I am a gentleman. Zounds!
one is a malefactor without knowing it: it comes from the air

one breathes.   In times like these of ours one is not responsible for what one does; the Revolution is guilty for the whole
world, and all your great criminals are great innocents.
What blockheads!   To begin with yourself.   Permit me to
admire you.   Yes, I admire a youth like you, who, a man of
quality, well placed in the State, having noble blood to shed
in a noble cause, Viscount of this Tower-Gauvain, Prince of
Brittany, able to be duke by right, and peer of France by
heritage,— which is about all a man of good sense could desire here below,— amuses himself, being what he is, to be what
you are; playing his part so well that he produces upon his
enemies the effect of a villain, and on his friends of an idiot.
By the way, give my compliments to the Abbé Cimourdain."

The marquis spoke perfectly at his ease, quietly, emphasiz-
ing nothing, in his polite society voice, his eyes clear and
tranquil, his hand in his waistcoat-pocket.   He broke off, drew
a long breath, and resumed: " I do not conceal from you
that I have done what I could to kill you.   Such as you
see me, I have myself, in person, three times aimed a cannon
at you.   A discourteous proceeding,— I admit it; but it
would be giving rise to a bad example to suppose that in war
your enemy tries to make himself agreeable to you.   For we
are in war, monsieur my nephew; everything is put to fire
and sword.   Into the bargain, it is true that they have killed
the king.   A pretty century!"

He checked himself again, and again resumed: " When
one thinks that none of these things would have happened if
Voltaire had been hanged and Rousseau sent to the galleys!
Ah, those men of mind,— what scourges!   But there, what
is it you reproach that monarchy with?   It is true that the
Abbé Pucelle was sent to his Abbey of Portigny with as much
time as he pleased for the journey; and as for your Monsieur
Titon, who had been, begging your pardon, a terrible de-
bauchee, and had gone the rounds of the loose women before
hunting after the miracles of the Deacon Paris, he was trans-
ferred from the Castle of Vincennes to the Castle of Ham in
Picardy, which is, I confess, a sufficiently ugly place.   There

are wrongs for you! I recollect: I cried out also in my day; I was as stupid as you."

The marquis felt in his pocket as if seeking his snuff-box, then continued: "But not so wicked. We talked just for talk's sake. There was also the mutiny of demands and petitions; and then up came those gentlemen the philosophers, and their writings were burned instead of the authors. The Court cabals mixed themselves in the matter; there were all those stupid fellows. Turgot, Quesnay, Malesherbes, the physiocratists, and so forth,— and the quarrel began. The whole came from the scribblers and the rhymesters. The Encyclopedia; Diderot D'Alembert,— ah, the wicked scoundrels! To think of a well-born man like the King of Prussia joining them! I would have suppressed all those paper-scratchers. Ah, we were justiciaries, our family; you may see there on the wall the marks of the quartering-wheel. We did not jest. No, no; no scribblers! While there are Arouets, there will be Marats; as long as there are fellows who scribble there will be scoundrels who assassinate; as long as there is ink, there will be black stains; as long as men's claws hold a goose's feather, frivolous stupidities will engender atrocious ones. Books cause crimes. The word ' chimera ' has two meanings,— it signifies dream, and it signifies monster. How dearly one pays for idle trash! What is that you sing to us about your rights? The rights of man! rights of the people! — is that empty enough, stupid enough, visionary enough, sufficiently void of sense? When I say Havoise, the sister of Conan II., brought the county of Brittany to Hoel Count of Nantes and Cornouailles, who left the throne to Alain Fergant the uncle of Bertha, who espoused Alain-le-noir Lord of Rosche-sur-Yon, and bore him Conan the Little, grandfather of Guy, or Gauvain de Thouars, our ancestor,— I state a thing that is clear, and there is a right. But your scoundrels, your rascals, your wretches, what do they call their rights? Deicide and regicide! Is it not hideous? Oh, the clowns! I am sorry for you, sir, but you belong to this proud Brittany blood; you and I had Gauvain de Thouars

for our ancestor; we had for another that great Duke of
Montbazon who was peer of France and honoured with the
Grand Collar of the Orders, who attacked the suburb of Tours,
and was wounded at the Battle of Arques, and died Grand
Huntsman of France, in his house of Couzières in Touraine,
aged eighty-six. I could tell you still further of the Duke
de Laudunois, son of the Lady of Garnache; of Claude de
Lorraine, Duke de Chevreuse and of Henri de Lenoncourt, and
of Françoise de Laval-Boisdauphin,— but to what purpose?
Monsieur has the honour of being an idiot, and considers himself the equal of my groom. Learn this: I was an old man
while you were still a brat; I remain as much your superior
as I was then. As you grew up you found means to belittle
yourself. Since we ceased to see each other each has gone
his own way: I followed honesty, you went in the opposite
direction. Ah, I do not know how all that will finish: those
gentlemen, your friends, are full-blown wretches! Verily, it
is fine, I grant you, a marvellous step gained in the cause of
progress,— to have suppressed in the army the punishment
of the pint of water inflicted on the drunken soldier for three
consecutive days; to have the Maximum, the Convention, the
Bishop Gobel, Monsieur Chaumette, and Monsieur Hébert;
to have exterminated the Past in one mass from the Bastille
to the peerage! They replace the saints by vegetables! So
be it, citizens! you are masters; reign, take your ease, do
what you like, stop at nothing! All this does not hinder the
fact that religion is religion, that royalty fills fifteen hundred
years of our history, and that the old French nobility are
loftier than you, even with their heads off. As for your cavil-
ling over the historic rights of royal races, we shrug our
shoulders at that. Chilperic, in reality, was only a monk
named Daniel; it was Rainfroi who invented Chilperic, in
order to annoy Charles Martel: we know those things just
as well as you do. The question does not lie there; the
question is this: To be a great kingdom, to be the ancient
France, to be a country perfectly ordered, wherein were to
be considered, first, the sacred person of its monarchs, abso-

lute lords of the State; then the princes; then the officers of the crown for the armies on land and sea, for the artillery, for the direction and superintendence of the finances; after that the officers of justice, great and small, those for the management of taxes and general receipts; and, lastly, the police of the kingdom in its three orders. All this was fine and nobly regulated; you have destroyed it. You have destroyed the provinces, like the lamentably ignorant creatures you are, without even suspecting what the provinces really were. The genius of France held the genius of the entire continent; each province of France represented a virtue of Europe: the frankness of Germany was in Picardy; the generosity of Sweden, in Champagne; the industry of Holland, in Burgundy; the activity of Poland, in Languedoc; the gravity of Spain, in Gascony; the wisdom of Italy, in Provence; the subtlety of Greece, in Normandy; the fidelity of Switzerland, in Dauphiny. You knew nothing of all that; you have broken, shattered, ruined, demolished; you have shown yourselves simply idiotic brutes. Ah, you will no longer have nobles? Well, you *shall* have none! Get your mourning ready: you shall have no more paladins, no more heroes; say good-night to the ancient grandeurs; find me a D'Assas at present! You are all of you afraid for your skins. You will have no more the chivalry of Fontenoy, who saluted before killing one another; you will have no more combatants like those in silk stockings at the siege of Lérida; you will have no more plumes floating past like meteors: you are a people finished, come to an end. You will suffer the outrage of invasion. If Alaric II. could return, he would no longer find himself confronted by Clovis; if Abderaman could come back, he would no longer find himself face to face with Charles Martel; if the Saxons, they would no longer find Pepin before them. You will have no more Agnadel, Rocroy, Lens, Staffarde, Neerwinden, Steinkirke, La Marsaille, Rancoux, Lawfeld, Mahon; you will have no Marignan, with Francis I.; you will have no Bouvines, with Philip Augustus taking prisoner with one hand Renaud Count of Boulogne, and with the other, Ferrand Count of Flanders; you will have Agincourt, but you will have no more the Sieur de Bacqueville, grand bearer of the oriflamme, enveloping himself in his banner to die. Go on, go on; do your work! Be the new men! become dwarfs!"

The marquis was silent for an instant, then began again: "But leave us great. Kill the kings, kill the nobles, kill the priests; tear down, ruin, massacre; trample under foot, crush ancient laws beneath your heels; overthrow the throne; stamp upon the altar of God, dash it in pieces, dance above it! On with you to the end! You are traitors and cowards, incapable of devotion or sacrifice. I have spoken; now have me guillotined, monsieur the viscount. I have the honour to be your very humble servant."

Then he added: "Ah, I do not hesitate to set the truth plainly before you. What difference can it make to me? I am dead."

"You are free," said Gauvain. He unfastened his commandant's cloak, advanced toward the marquis, threw it about his shoulders, and drew the hood close down over his eyes. The two men were of the same height.

"Well, what are you doing?" the marquis asked.

Gauvain raised his voice, and cried: "Lieutenant, open to me."

The door opened.

Gauvain exclaimed: "Close the door carefully behind me!" And he pushed the stupefied marquis across the threshold.

The hall turned into a guard-room was lighted, it will be remembered, by a horn lantern, whose faint rays only broke the shadows here and there. Such of the soldiers as were not asleep saw dimly a man of lofty stature, wrapped in the mantle and hood of the commander-in-chief, pass through the midst of them and move toward the entrance. They made a military salute, and the man passed on.

The marquis slowly traversed the guard-room, the breach (not without hitting his head more than once), and went out.

The sentinel, believing that he saw Gauvain, presented arms. When he was outside, having the grass of the fields under his feet, within two hundred paces of the forest, and before him space, night, liberty, life,— he paused, and stood motionless for an instant like a man who has allowed himself to be pushed on; who has yielded to surprise, and who, having taken advantage of an open door, asks himself if he has done well or ill, hesitates to go farther, and gives audience to a last reflection. After a few seconds' deep reverie he raised his right hand, snapped his thumb and middle finger, and said, " My faith! " And he hurried on.

The door of the dungeon had closed again. Gauvain was within.

CHAPTER II

THE COURT-MARTIAL

AT that period all courts-martial were very nearly discretionary. Dumas had offered in the Assembly a rough plan of military legislation, improved later by Talot in the Council of the Five Hundred; but the definitive code of war-councils was only drawn up under the Empire. Let us add in parenthesis, that from the Empire dates the law imposed on military tribunals to begin receiving the votes by the lowest grade. Under the Revolution this law did not exist. In 1793 the president of a military tribunal was almost the tribunal in himself. He chose the members, classed the order of grades, regulated the manner of voting,— was at once master and judge.

Cimourdain had selected for the hall of the court-martial that very room on the ground-floor where the retirade had been erected, and where the guard was now established. He wished to shorten everything,— the road from the prison to the tribunal, and the passage from the tribunal to the scaffold.

In conformity with his orders the court began its sitting
at midday, with no other show of state than this: three straw-
bottomed chairs, a pine table, two lighted candles, a stool in
front of the table.   The chairs were for the judges, and the
stool for the accused.   At either end of the table also stood a
stool,— one for the commissioner auditor, who was a quartermaster; the other for the registrar, who was a corporal.   On
the table were a stick of red sealing-wax, a brass seal of the
Republic, two ink-stands, some sheets of white paper, and two
printed placards spread open,— the first containing the declaration of outlawry; the second, the decree of the Convention.   The tricoloured flag hung on the back of the middle
chair: in that period of rude simplicity decorations were
quickly arranged, and it needed little time to change a guard-
room into a court of justice.   The middle chair, intended for
the president, stood in face of the prison door.   The soldiers
made up the audience.   Two gendarmes stood on guard by
the stool.

Cimourdain was seated in the centre chair, having at his
right Captain Guéchamp, first judge; and at his left Sergeant
Radoub, second judge.   Cimourdain wore a hat with a tricoloured cockade, his sabre at his side, and his two pistols in
his belt; his scar, of a vivid red, added to his savage appearance.   Radoub's wound had been only partially stanched; he
had a handkerchief knotted about his head, upon which a
bloodstain slowly widened.

At midday the court had not yet opened its proceedings.
A messenger, whose horse could be heard stamping outside,
stood near the table of the tribunal.   Cimourdain was writing,
— writing these lines: —

"Citizen Members of the Committee of Public Safety,— Lantenac
is taken.   He will be executed to-morrow."

He dated and signed the dispatch; folded, sealed, and
handed it to the messenger, who departed.   This done, Cimourdain called in a loud voice: " Open the dungeon! "

The two gendarmes drew back the bolts, opened the door of the dungeon, and entered.

Cimourdain lifted his head, folded his arms, fixed his eyes on the door and cried: "Bring out the prisoner!"

A man appeared between the two gendarmes, standing beneath the arch of the door-way. It was Gauvain.

Cimourdain started. "Gauvain!" he exclaimed. Then he added, "I demand the prisoner."

"It is I," said Gauvain.

"Thou?"

"I."

"And Lantenac?"

"He is free."

"Free?"

"Yes."

"Escaped?"

"Escaped."

Cimourdain trembled as he stammered: "In truth the castle belongs to him; he knows all its outlets. The dungeon may communicate with some secret opening. I ought to have remembered that he would find means to escape; he would not need any person's aid for that."

"He was aided," said Gauvain.

"To escape?"

"To escape."

"Who aided him?"

"I."

"Thou?"

"I."

"Thou art dreaming!"

"I went into the dungeon; I was alone with the prisoner. I took off my cloak; I put it about his shoulders; I drew the hood down over his face; he went out in my stead, and I remained in his. Here I am!"

"Thou didst not do it!"

"I did it."

"It is impossible!"

" It is true."

" Bring me Lantenac! "

" He is no longer here. The soldiers, seeing the command-ant's mantle, took him for me, and allowed him to pass. It was still night."

" Thou art mad! "

" I tell you what was done.'"

A silence followed. Cimourdain stammered: " Then thou hast merited —"

" Death," said Gauvain.

Cimourdain was pale as 'a corpse. He sat motionless as a man who had just been struck by lightning. He no longer seemed to breathe. A great drop of sweat stood out on his forehead. He forced his voice into firmness, and said: " Gendarmes, seat the accused."

Gauvain placed himself on the stool.

Cimourdain added: " Gendarmes, draw your sabres." His voice had got back to its ordinary tone. " Accused," said he, " you will stand up." He no longer said " thee " and " thou " to Gauvain.

CHAPTER III

THE VOTES

GAUVAIN rose.

" What is your name? " demanded Cimourdain.

The answer came unhesitatingly: " Gauvain."

Cimourdain continued the interrogatory: " Who are you? "

" I am Commander-in-Chief of the Expeditionary Column of the Côtes-du-Nord."

" Are you a relative or a connection of the man who has escaped? "

" I am his grand-nephew."

" You are acquainted with the decree of the Convention? "

" I see the placard lying on your table."

" What have you to say in regard to this decree? "

" That I countersigned it; that I ordered its carrying out; that it was I who had this placard written, at the bottom of which is my name."

" Choose a defender."

" I will defend myself."

" You can speak."

Cimourdain had become again impassible. But his impassibility resembled the sternness of a rock rather than the calmness of a man.

Gauvain remained silent for a moment, as if collecting his thoughts.

Cimourdain spoke again: " What have you to say in your defence? "

Gauvain slowly raised his head, but without fixing his eyes upon either of the judges, and replied: " This: One thing prevented my seeing another; a good action seen too near hid from me a hundred criminal deeds. On one side an old man; on the other, three children,— all these put themselves between me and duty. I forgot the burned villages, the ravaged fields, the butchered prisoners, the slaughtered wounded, the women shot; I forgot France betrayed to England. I set at liberty the murderer of our country; I am guilty. In speaking thus, I seem to speak against myself; it is a mistake, — I speak in my own behalf. When the guilty acknowledges his fault, he saves the only thing worth the trouble of saving, — honour."

" Is that," returned Cimourdain, " all you have to say in your own defence? "

" I add, that being the chief I owed an example; and that you in your turn, being judges, owe one."

" What example do you demand? "

" My death."

" You find that just? "

24

" And necessary."

" Be seated."

The quartermaster, who was auditor-commissioner, rose and read, first, the decree of outlawry against the *ci-devant* Marquis de Lantenac; secondly, the decree of the Convention ordaining capital punishment against whosoever should aid the escape of a rebel prisoner. He closed with the lines printed at the bottom of the placard, forbidding " to give aid or succour to the below named rebel, under penalty of death; signed " Commander-in-Chief of the Expeditionary Column, — GAUVAIN." These notices read, the auditor-commissioner sat down again.

Cimourdain folded his arms and said: " Accused, pay attention. Public, listen, look, and be silent. You have before you the law. The votes will now be taken. The sentence will be given according to the majority. Each judge will announce his decision aloud, in presence of the accused, justice having nothing to conceal."

Cimourdain continued: " The first judge will give his vote. Speak, Captain Guéchamp."

Captain Guéchamp seemed to see neither Cimourdain nor Gauvain. His downcast lids concealed his eyes, which remained fixed upon the placard of the decree as if they were staring at a gulf. He said: " The law is immutable. A judge is more and less than a man: he is less than a man because he has no heart; he is more than a man because he holds the sword of justice. In the four hundred and fourteenth year of Rome, Manlius put his son to death for the crime of having conquered without his orders; violated discipline demanded an example. Here it is the law which has been violated, and the law is still higher than discipline. Through an emotion of pity, the country is again endangered. Pity may wear the proportions of a crime. Commandant Gauvain has helped the rebel Lantenac to escape. Gauvain is guilty. I vote — death."

" Write, registrar," said Cimourdain.

The clerk wrote, " Captain Guéchamp: death."

Gauvain's voice rang out, clear and firm. "Guéchamp,"
said he, "you have voted well, and I thank you."

Cimourdain resumed: "It is the turn of the second judge.
Speak, Sergeant Radoub."

Radoub rose, turned toward Gauvain, and made the accused
a military salute. Then he exclaimed: "If that is the way
it goes, then guillotine me, for I give here, before God, my
most sacred word of honour that I would like to have done,
first, what the old man did, and, after that, what my commandant did. When I saw that old fellow, eighty years of
age, jump into the fire to pull three brats out of it, I said
'Old fellow, you are a brave man!' And when I hear that
my commandant has saved that old man from your beast of
a guillotine, I say, 'My commandant, you ought to be my
general, and you are a true man; and, as for me, thunder!
I would give you the Cross of Saint Louis if there were still
crosses, or saints, or Louises.' Oh, there! are we going to
turn idiots at present? If it was for these things that we
gained the Battle of Jemmapes, the Battle of Valmy, the
Battle of Fleurus, and the Battle of Wattignies, then you
had better say so. What! here is Commandant Gauvain, who
for these four months past has been driving those asses of
royalists to the beat of the drum, and saving the Republic
by his sword; who did a thing at Dol which needed a world
of brains to do,— and when you have a man like that, you
try to get rid of him! Instead of electing him your general,
you want to cut off his head! I say it is enough to make a
fellow throw himself off the Pont Neuf head foremost! You,
yourself, Citizen Gauvain, my commandant, if you were my
corporal instead of being my superior, I would tell you that
you talked a heap of infernal nonsense just now. The old
man did a fine thing in saving the children; you did a fine
thing in saving the old man; and if we are going to guillotine
people for good actions, why, then, get away with you all
to the devil, for I don't know any longer what the question is
about! There's nothing to hold fast to! It is not true, is
it, all this? I pinch myself to see if I am awake! I can't

understand. So the old man ought to have let the babies
burn alive, and my commandant ought to have let the old
man's head be cut off! See here! guillotine me! I would as
lief have it done as not. Just suppose: if the children had
been killed, the battalion of the Bonnet Rouge would have
been dishonoured! Is that what was wished for? Why,
then, let us eat one another up and be done! I understand
politics as well as any of you: I belonged to the Club of
the Section of Pikes. Zounds, we are coming to the end! I
sum up the matter according to my way of looking at it. I
don't like things to be done which are so puzzling you don't
know any longer where you stand. What the devil is it we
get ourselves killed for? In order that somebody may kill
our chief! None of that, Lisette! I want my chief; I will
have my chief; I love him better to-day than I did yesterday.
Send him to the guillotine? Why, you make me laugh!
Now, we are not going to have anything of that sort. I have
listened. People may say what they please. In the first
place it is not possible!"

And Radoub sat down again. His wound had reopened.
A thin stream of blood exuded from under the kerchief, and
ran along his neck from the place where his ear had been.

Cimourdain turned toward the sergeant. "You vote for
the acquittal of the accused?"

"I vote," said Radoub, "that he be made general."

"I ask if you vote for his acquittal."

"I vote for his being made head of the Republic."

"Sergeant Radoub, do you vote that Commandant Gauvain
be acquitted,— yes or no?"

"I vote that my head be cut off in place of his."

"Acquittal," said Cimourdain.   "Write it, registrar."

The clerk wrote, "Sergeant Radoub: acquittal."

Then the clerk said: "One voice for death. One voice
for acquittal. A tie."

It was Cimourdain's turn to vote. He rose. He took off
his hat and laid it on the table. He was no longer pale or
livid. His face was the colour of clay. Had all the specta-

tors been corpses lying there in their winding-sheets, the silence could not have been more profound.

Cimourdain said, in a solemn, slow, firm voice: "Accused, the case has been heard. In the name of the Republic, the court-martial, by a majority of two voices —"

He broke off; there was an instant of terrible suspense. Did he hesitate before pronouncing the sentence of death? Did he hesitate before granting life? Every listener held his breath.

Cimourdain continued: "Condemns you to death."

His face expressed the torture of an awful triumph. Jacob, when he forced the angel, whom he had overthrown in the darkness, to bless him, must have worn that fearful smile. It was only a gleam — it passed; Cimourdain was marble again. He seated himself, put on his hat, and added: "Gauvain, you will be executed to-morrow at sunrise."

Gauvain rose, saluted, and said: "I thank the court."

"Lead away the condemned," said Cimourdain. He made a sign: the door of the dungeon re-opened; Gauvain entered; the door closed. The two gendarmes stood sentinel,— one on either side of the arch, sabre in hand.

Sergeant Radoub fell senseless upon the ground, and was carried away.

CHAPTER IV

AFTER CIMOURDAIN THE JUDGE COMES CIMOURDAIN THE MASTER

A CAMP is a wasp's nest,— in revolutionary times above all. The civic sting which is in the soldier moves quickly, and does not hesitate to prick the chief after having chased away the enemy.

The valiant troop which had taken La Tourgue was filled with diverse commotions,— at first against Commandant Gau-

vain when it learned that Lantenac had escaped. As Gauvain
issued from the dungeon which had been believed to hold the
marquis, the news spread as if by electricity, and in an instant
the whole army was informed. A murmur burst forth; it
was: " They are trying Gauvain; but it is a sham. Trust
ci-devants and priests! We have just seen a viscount save a
marquis, and now we are going to see a priest absolve a
noble! "

When the news of Gauvain's condemnation came, there was
a second murmur: " It is horrible! Our chief, our brave
chief, our young commander,— a hero! He may be a viscount,— very well; so much the more merit in his being a Republican. What, he, the liberator of Pontorson, of Ville-
dieu, of Pont-au-Beau; the conqueror of Dol and La Tourgue,
— he who makes us invincible; he, the sword of the Republic
in Vendée; the man who for five months has held the Chouans
at bay, and repaired all the blunders of Léchelle and the
others! — this Cimourdain to dare to condemn *him* to death!
For what? Because he saved an old man who had saved three
children! A priest kill a soldier! "

Thus muttered the victorious and discontented camp. A
stern rage surrounded Cimourdain. Four thousand men
against one,— that should seem a power; it is not. These
four thousand men were a crowd; Cimourdain was a will. It
was known that Cimourdain's frown came easily, and nothing more was needed to hold the army in respect. In those
stern days it was sufficient for a man to have behind him the
shadow of the Committee of Public Safety to make that man
formidable; to make imprecation die into a whisper, and the
whisper into silence.

Before, as after the murmurs, Cimourdain remained the
arbiter of Gauvain's fate as he did of the fate of all. They
knew there was nothing to ask of him, that he would only
obey his conscience,— a superhuman voice audible to his ear
alone. Everything depended upon him. That which he had
done as martial judge, he could undo as civil delegate. He
only could show mercy. He possessed unlimited power: by

a sign he could set Gauvain at liberty. He was master of life and death; he commanded the guillotine. In this tragic moment he was the man supreme. They could only wait.

Night came.

CHAPTER V

THE DUNGEON

THE hall of justice had become again a guard-room; the guard was doubled as upon the previous evening; two sentinels stood on duty before the closed door of the prison.

Toward midnight, a man who held a lantern in his hand traversed the hall, made himself known to the sentries, and ordered the dungeon open. It was Cimourdain. He entered and the door remained ajar behind him. The dungeon was dark and silent. Cimourdain moved forward a step in the gloom, set the lantern on the ground, and stood still. He could hear amidst the shadows the measured breath of a sleeping man. Cimourdain listened thoughtfully to this peaceful sound.

Gauvain lay on a bundle of straw at the farther end of the dungeon. It was his breathing which caught the new comer's ear. He was sleeping profoundly.

Cimourdain advanced as noiselessly as possible, moved close, and looked down upon Gauvain. The glance of a mother watching her nursling's slumber could not have been more tender or fuller of love. Even Cimourdain's will could not control that glance. He pressed his clinched hands against his eyes with the gesture one sometimes sees in children, and remained for a moment motionless. Then he knelt, softly raised Gauvain's hand, and pressed it to his lips.

Gauvain stirred. He opened his eyes, full of the wonder of sudden waking. He recognized Cimourdain in the dim light which the lantern cast about the cave. "Ah," said he, "it is you, my master." And he added: "I dreamed that Death was kissing my hand."

Cimourdain started as one does sometimes under the sudden rush of a flood of thoughts. Sometimes the tide is so high and so stormy that it seems as if it would drown the soul. Not an echo from the overcharged depths of Cimourdain's heart found vent in words. He could only say, "Gauvain!"

And the two gazed at each other,— Cimourdain with his eyes full of those flames which burn up tears; Gauvain with his sweetest smile.

Gauvain raised himself on his elbow and said: "That scar I see on your face is the sabre-cut you received for me. Yesterday, too, you were in the thick of that *mêlée*, at my side, and on my account. If Providence had not placed you near my cradle, where should I be to-day? In utter darkness. If I have any true conception of duty, it is from you that it comes to me. I was born with my hands bound,— prejudices are ligatures: you loosened those bonds; you gave my growth liberty, and of that which was already only a mummy you made anew a child. Into what would have been an abortion you put a conscience. Without you I should have grown up a dwarf. I exist by you. I was only a lord, you made me a citizen; I was only a citizen, you have made me a mind. You have made me, as a man, fit for this earthly life; you have educated my soul for the celestial existence; you have given me human reality, the key of truth, and, to go beyond that, the key of light. O my master! I thank you. It is you who have created me."

Cimourdain seated himself on the straw beside Gauvain, and said: "I have come to sup with thee."

Gauvain broke the black bread and handed it to him. Cimourdain took a morsel; then Gauvain offered the jug of water.

"Drink first," said Cimourdain.

Gauvain drank, and passed the jug to his companion, who drank after him. Gauvain had only swallowed a mouthful. Cimourdain drank great draughts. During this supper,

Gauvain ate, and Cimourdain drank,— a sign of the calmness
of the one, and of the fever which consumed the other. A
serenity so strange that it was terrible reigned in this dungeon. The two men conversed.

Gauvain said: "Grand events are sketching themselves.
What the Revolution does at this moment is mysterious. Behind the visible work stands the invisible; one conceals the
other. The visible work is savage, the invisible sublime. In
this instant I perceive all very clearly. It is strange and
beautiful. It has been necessary to make use of the materials
of the Past. Hence this marvellous '93. Beneath a scaffold-
ing of barbarism a temple of civilization is building."

"Yes," replied Cimourdain. "From this provisional will
rise the definitive. The definitive — that is to say, right and
duty — are parallel: taxes proportional and progressive; military service obligatory; a levelling without deviation; and
above the whole, making part of all, that straight line, the
law,— the Republic of the absolute."

"I prefer," said Gauvain, "the ideal Republic." He
paused for an instant, then continued: "O my master! in
all which you have just said, where do you place devotion, sacrifice, abnegation, the sweet interlacing of kindnesses, love?
To set all in equilibrium, it is well; to put all in harmony, it
is better. Above the Balance is the Lyre. Your Republic
weighs, measures, regulates man; mine lifts him into the
open sky. It is the difference between a theorem and an
eagle."

"You lose yourself in the clouds."

"And you in calculation."

"Harmony is full of dreams."

"There are such, too, in algebra."

"I would have man made by the rules of Euclid."

"And I," said Gauvain, "would like him better as pictured
by Homer."

Cimourdain's severe smile remained fixed upon Gauvain,
as if to hold that soul steady: "Poesy! Mistrust poets."

"Yes, I know that saying. Mistrust the zephyrs, mistrust

the sunshine, mistrust the sweet odours of spring, mistrust the flowers, mistrust the stars!"

"None of these things can feed man."

"How do you know? Thought is nourishment. To think is to eat."

"No abstractions! The Republic is the law of two and two make four. When I have given to each the share which belongs to him —"

"It still remains to give the share which does not belong to him."

"What do you understand by that?"

"I understand the immense reciprocal concession which each owes to all, and which all owe to each, and which is the whole of social life."

"Beyond the strict law there is nothing."

"There is everything."

"I only see justice."

"And I,— I look higher."

"What can there be above justice?"

"Equity."

At certain instants they paused as if lightning flashes suddenly chilled them.

Cimourdain resumed: "Particularize; I defy you."

"So be it. You wish military service made obligatory. Against whom. Against other men. I,— I would have no military service; I want peace. You wish the wretched succoured; I wish an end put to suffering. You want proportional taxes; I wish no tax whatever. I wish the general expense reduced to its most simple expression, and paid by the social surplus."

"What do you understand by that?"

"This: First, suppose parasitisms,— the parasitisms of the priest, the judge, the soldier. After that, turn your riches to account. You fling manure into the sewer; cast it into the furrow. Three parts of the soil are waste land: clear up France; suppress useless pasture-grounds; divide the communal lands; let each man have a farm and each farm a man.

You will increase a hundred-fold the social product. At this moment France only gives her peasants meat four days in the year; well cultivated, she would nourish three hundred millions of men — all Europe. Utilize Nature, that immense auxiliary so disdained; make every wind toil for you, every water-fall, every magnetic effluence. The globe has a subterranean net-work of veins; there is in this net-work a prodigious circulation of water, oil, fire. Pierce those veins: make this water feed your fountains, this oil your lamps, this fire your hearths. Reflect upon the movements of the waves, their flux and reflux, the ebb and flow of the tides. What is the ocean? An enormous power allowed to waste. How stupid is earth not to make use of the sea!"

"There you are in the full tide of dreams."

"That is to say, of full reality."

Gauvain added: "And woman, what will you do with her?"

Cimourdain replied: "Leave her where she is,— the servant of man."

"Yes. On one condition."

"What?"

"That man shall be the servant of woman."

"Can you think of it?" cried Cimourdain. "Man a servant? Never! Man is master. I admit only one royalty,— that of the fireside. Man in his house is king!"

"Yes. On one condition."

"What?"

"That woman shall be queen there."

"That is to say, you wish for man and woman —"

"Equality."

"Equality! Can you dream of it? The two creatures are different."

"I said equality; I did not say identity."

There was another pause, like a sort of truce between two spirits flinging lightnings.

Cimourdain broke the silence: "And the offspring, to whom do you consign them?"

" First to the father who engenders; then to the mother who gives birth; then to the master who rears; then to the city that civilizes; then to the country which is the mother supreme; then to humanity, who is the great ancestor."

" You do not speak of God? "

" Each of those degrees — father, mother, master, city, country, humanity — is one of the rungs in the ladder which leads to God."

Cimourdain was silent.

Gauvain continued: " When one is at the top of the ladder, one has reached God.   Heaven opens,— one has only to enter."

Cimourdain made a gesture like a man calling another back: " Gauvain, return to earth.   We wish to realize the possible."

" Do not commence by rendering it impossible."

" The possible always realizes itself."

" Not always.   If one treats Utopia harshly, one slays it. Nothing is more defenceless than the egg."

" Still, it is necessary to seize Utopia, to put the yoke of the real upon it, to frame it in the actual.   The abstract idea must transform itself into the concrete: what it loses in beauty, it will gain in usefulness; it is lessened, but made better. Right must enter into law, and when right makes itself law, it becomes absolute.   That is what I call the possible."

" The possible is more than that."

" Ah, there you are in dream-land again! "

" The possible is a mysterious bird, always soaring above man's head."

" It must be caught."

" Living."   Gauvin continued: " This is my thought: Constant progression.   If God had meant man to retrograde, he would have placed an eye in the back of his head.   Let us look always toward the dawn, the blossoming, the birth. That which falls encourages that which mounts; the cracking of the old tree is an appeal to the new.   Each century must do its work: to-day civic, to-morrow human; to-day the question of right, to-morrow the question of salary.   Salary and right,— the same word at bottom. Man does not live to be paid nothing. In giving life, God contracts a debt. Right is the payment inborn; payment is right acquired."

Gauvain spoke with the earnestness of a prophet. Cimourdain listened. Their *rôles* were changed; now it seemed the pupil who was master.

Cimourdain murmured: "You go rapidly."

"Perhaps because I am a little pressed for time," said Gauvain, smiling. And he added, "O my master! behold the difference between our two Utopias! You wish the garrison obligatory, I the school. You dream of man the soldier; I dream of man the citizen. You want him terrible; I want him a thinker. You found a Republic upon swords; I found —"

He interrupted himself: "I would found a Republic of intellects."

Cimourdain bent his eyes on the pavement of the dungeon, and said: "And while waiting for it, what would you have?"

"That which is."

"Then you absolve the present moment?"

"Yes."

"Wherefore?"

"Because it is a tempest. A tempest knows always what it does. For one oak uprooted, how many forests purified! Civilization had the plague; this great wind cures it. Perhaps it is not so careful as it ought to be; but could it do otherwise than it does? It is charged with a difficult task. Before the horror of miasma, I comprehend the fury of the blast."

Gauvain continued: "Moreover, why should I fear the tempest if I had my compass? How can events affect me if I have my conscience?" And he added, in a low, solemn voice: "There is a power that must always be allowed to guide."

"What?" demanded Cimourdain.

Gauvain raised his finger above his head. Cimourdain's eyes followed the direction of that uplifted finger, and it seemed to him that across the dungeon vault he beheld the starlit sky. Both were silent again.

Cimourdain spoke first: "Society is greater than Nature. I tell you, this is no longer possibility — it is a dream."

"It is the goal. Otherwise of what use is society? Remain in Nature; be savages. Otaheite is a paradise,— only the inhabitants of that paradise do not think. An intelligent hell would be preferable to an imbruted heaven. But, no,— no hell; let us be a human society. Greater than Nature? Yes. If you add nothing to Nature, why go beyond her? Content yourself with work, like the ant; with honey, like the bee,— remain the working drudge instead of the queen intelligence. If you add to Nature, you necessarily become greater than she: to add is to augment; to augment is to grow. Society is Nature sublimated. I want all that is lacking to bee-hives, all that is lacking to ant-hills,— monuments, arts, poesy, heroes, genius. To bear eternal burdens is not the destiny of man. No, no, no! no more pariahs, no more slaves, no more convicts, no more damned! I desire that each of the attributes of man should be a symbol of civilization and a patron of progress; I would place liberty before the spirit, equality before the heart, fraternity before the soul. No more yokes! Man was made not to drag chains, but to soar on wings. No more of man reptile! I wish the transfiguration of the larva into the winged creature; I wish the worm of the earth to turn into a living flower and fly away. I wish —"

He broke off. His eyes blazed. His lips moved. He ceased to speak.

The door had remained open. Sounds from without penetrated into the dungeon. The distant peal of trumpets could be heard, probably the reveille; then the butt-end of muskets striking the ground as the sentinels were relieved; then, quite near the tower, as well as one could judge, a noise like the moving of planks and beams, followed by muffled, intermittent echoes like the strokes of a hammer.

Cimourdain grew pale as he listened. Gauvain heard nothing. His reverie became more and more profound. He seemed no longer to breathe, so lost was he in the vision that shone upon his soul. Now and then he started slightly. The morning which illuminated his eyes waxed grander.

Some time passed thus. Then Cimourdain asked: " Of what are you thinking? "

" Of the future," replied Gauvain.

He sank back into his meditation. Cimourdain rose from the bed of straw where the two were sitting. Gauvain did not perceive it. Keeping his eyes fixed upon the dreamer, Cimourdain moved slowly backward toward the door and went out. The dungeon closed again.

CHAPTER VI

WHEN THE SUN ROSE

DAY broke along the horizon,— and with the day an object, strange, motionless, mysterious, which the birds of heaven did not recognize, appeared upon the plateau of La Tourgue and towered above the forest of Fougères. It had been placed there in the night; it seemed to have sprung up rather than to have been built. It lifted high against the horizon a profile of straight, hard lines, looking like a Hebrew letter, or one of those Egyptian hieroglyphics which made part of the alphabet of the ancient enigma.

At the first glance the idea which this object roused was its lack of keeping with the surroundings. It stood amidst the blossoming heath. One asked one's self for what purpose it could be useful? Then the beholder felt a chill creep over him as he gazed. It was a sort of trestle, having four posts for feet; at one end of the trestle two tall joists upright and straight, and fastened together at the top by a cross-beam, raised and held suspended some triangular object which

showed black against the blue sky of morning.   At the other
end of the staging was a ladder.   Between the joists, and directly beneath the triangle, could be seen a sort of panel composed of two movable sections, which, fitting into each other,
left a round hole about the size of a man's neck.   The upper
section of this panel slid in a groove, so that it could be
hoisted or lowered at will; for the time, the two crescents,
which formed the circle when closed, were drawn apart.   At
the foot of the two posts supporting the triangle was a plank
turning on hinges, looking like a see-saw.   By the side of
this plank was a long basket; and between the two beams, in
front and at the extremity of the trestle, was a square basket.
The monster was painted red.   The whole was made of wood
except the triangle,— that was iron.   One would have known
the thing must have been constructed by man, it was so ugly
and evil looking; at the same time it was so formidable that
it might have been reared there by evil genii.   This shapeless
thing was the guillotine.

In front of it, a few paces off, another monster rose out
of the ravine.   La Tourgue,— a monster of stone rising up
to hold companionship with the monster of wood.   For when
man has touched wood or stone they no longer remain inanimate matter; something of man's spirit seems to enter into
them.   An edifice is a dogma; a machine, an idea.   La
Tourgue was that terrible offspring of the Past called the
Bastille in Paris, the Tower of London in England, the Spiel-
berg in Germany, the Escurial in Spain, the Kremlin in Moscow, the Castle of Saint Angelo in Rome.

In La Tourgue were condensed fifteen hundred years (the
Middle Age), vassalage, servitude, feudality; in the guillotine one year,—'93; and these twelve months made a counterpoise to those fifteen centuries.   La Tourgue was Monarchy; the guillotine was Revolution,— tragic confrontation!
On one side the debtor, on the other the creditor.   On one
side the inextricable Gothic complication of serf, lord, slave,
master, plebeian, nobility, the complex code ramifying into
customs, judge and priest in coalition, shackles innumerable,

fiscil impositions, excise laws, mortmain, taxes, exemptions, prerogatives, prejudices, fanaticisms, the royal privilege of bankruptcy, the sceptre, the throne, the regal will, the divine right; on the other, this simple thing,—a knife. On one side the noose, on the other, the axe.

La Tourgue had long stood alone in the midst of this wilderness. There she had frowned with her machicolated casements, from whence had streamed boiling oil, blazing pitch, and melted lead; her oubliettes paved with human skeletons, her torture-chamber,—the whole hideous tragedy with which she was filled. Rearing her funereal front above the forest, she had passed fifteen centuries of savage tranquillity amidst its shadows; she had been the one power in this land, the one object of respect and fear; she had reigned supreme, she had been the realization of barbarism; and suddenly she saw rise before her and against her, something (more than something) as terrible as herself,—the guillotine.

Inanimate objects sometimes appear endowed with a strange power of sight. A statue notices, a tower watches, the face of an edifice contemplates. La Tourgue seemed to be studying the guillotine. She seemed to question herself concerning it. What was that object? It looked as if it had sprung out of the earth. It was from there, in truth, that it had risen. The sinister tree had germinated in the fatal ground. Out of the soil watered by so much of human sweat, so many tears, so much blood; out of the earth in which had been dug so many trenches, so many graves, so many caverns, so many ambuscades—out of this earth wherein had rolled the countless victims of countless tyrannies—out of this earth spread above so many abysses wherein had been buried so many crimes (terrible germs) had sprung in a destined day this unknown, this avenger, this ferocious sword-bearer, and '93 had said to the Old World, "Behold me!" And the guillotine had the right to say to the donjon tower, "I am thy daughter."

And, at the same time, the tower—for those fatal objects possess a strange vitality—felt herself slain by this newly risen force.

25

Before this formidable apparition La Tourgue seemed to shudder. One might have said that she was afraid. The monstrous mass of granite was majestic, but infamous; that plank with its black triangle was worse. The all-powerful fallen trembled before the all-powerful risen. Criminal history was studying judicial history. The violence of by-gone days was comparing itself with the violence of the present; the ancient fortress, the ancient prison, the ancient seigneury where tortured victims had shrieked out their lives; that construction of war and murder, now useless, defenceless, violated, dismantled, uncrowned, a heap of stones with no more than a heap of ashes, hideous yet magnificent, dying, dizzy with the awful memories of all those by-gone centuries, watched the terrible living Present sweep up. Yesterday trembled before to-day, antique ferocity acknowledged and bowed its head before this fresh horror. The power which was sinking into nothingness opened eyes of fright upon this new-born terror; the phantom stared at the spectre.

Nature is pitiless; she never withdraws her flowers, her music, her fragrance, and her sunlight from before human cruelty or suffering. She overwhelms man by the contrast between divine beauty and social hideousness. She spares him nothing of her loveliness, neither wing or butterfly nor song of bird. In the midst of murder, vengeance, barbarism, he must feel himself watched by holy things; he cannot escape the immense reproach of universal nature and the implacable serenity of the sky. The deformity of human laws is forced to exhibit itself naked amidst the dazzling rays of eternal beauty. Man breaks and destroys; man lays waste; man kills; but the summer remains summer; the lily remains the lily; the star remains the star.

Never had a morning dawned fresher and more glorious than this. A soft breeze stirred the heath, a warm haze rose amidst the branches; the forest of Fougères permeated by the breath of hidden brooks, smoked in the dawn like a vast censer filled with perfumes; the blue of the firmament, the whiteness of the clouds, the transparency of the streams, the verdure, that harmonious gradation of colour from aqua-marine to emerald, the groups of friendly trees, the mats of grass, the peaceful fields, all breathed that purity which is Nature's eternal counsel to man. In the midst of all this rose the horrible front of human shamelessness; in the midst of all this appeared the fortress and the scaffold, war and punishment,—the incarnations of the bloody age and the bloody moment; the owl of the night of the Past and the bat of the cloud-darkened dawn of the Future. And blossoming, odour-giving creation, loving and charming, and the grand sky golden with morning spread about La Tourgue and the guillotine, and seemed to say to man, "Behold my work and yours."

Such are the terrible reproaches of the sunlight!

This spectacle had its spectators. The four thousand men of the little expeditionary army were drawn up in battle order upon the plateau. They surrounded the guillotine on three sides in such a manner as to form about it the shape of a letter E; the battery placed in the centre of the largest line made the notch of the E. The red monster was enclosed by these three battle fronts; a sort of wall of soldiers spread out on two sides of the edge of the plateau; the fourth side, left open, was the ravine, which seemed to frown at La Tourgue. These arrangements made a long square, in the centre of which stood the scaffold.

Gradually, as the sun mounted higher, the shadow of the guillotine grew shorter on the turf. The gunners were at their pieces; the matches lighted. A faint blue smoke rose from the ravine, the last breath of the expiring conflagration. This cloud encircled without veiling La Tourgue, whose lofty platform overlooked the whole horizon. There was only the width of the ravine between the platform and the guillotine. The one could have parleyed with the other.

The table of the tribunal and the chair shadowed by the tricoloured flags had been set upon the platform. The sun rose higher behind La Tourgue, bringing out the black mass of the fortress clear and defined, and revealing upon its summit the figure of a man in the chair beneath the banners, sitting motionless, his arms crossed upon his breast. It was Cimourdain. He wore, as on the previous day, his civil delegate's dress; on his head was the hat with the tricoloured cockade; his sabre at his side; his pistols in his belt. He sat silent.

The whole crowd was mute. The soldiers stood with downcast eyes, musket in hand,—stood so close that their shoulders touched; but no one spoke. They were meditating confusedly upon this war,—the numberless combats, the hedge-fusillades so bravely confronted; the hosts of peasants driven back by their might; the citadels taken, the battles won, the victories gained; and it seemed to them as if all that glory had turned now to their shame. A sombre expectation contracted every heart. They could see the executioner come and go upon the platform of the guillotine. The increasing splendour of the morning filled the sky with its majesty.

Suddenly the sound of muffled drums broke the stillness. The funereal tones swept nearer. The ranks opened—a cortége entered the square and moved toward the scaffold. First, the drummers with their crape-wreathed drums; then a company of grenadiers with reversed arms; then a platoon of gendarmes with drawn sabres; then the condemned,—Gauvain. He walked forward with a free, firm step. He had no fetters on hands or feet. He was in an undress uniform, and wore his sword. Behind him marched another platoon of gendarmes.

Gauvain's face was still lighted by that pensive joy which had illuminated it at the moment when he said to Cimourdain, "I am thinking of the Future." Nothing could be more touching and sublime than that smile. When he reached the fatal square, his first glance was directed toward the summit of the tower. He disdained the guillotine. He knew that Cimourdain would make it an imperative duty to assist at the execution. His eyes sought the platform; he saw him there.

Cimourdain was ghastly and cold. Those standing near

him could not catch even the sound of his breathing. Not a tremor shook his frame when he saw Gauvain.

Gauvain moved toward the scaffold. As he walked on, he looked at Cimourdain, and Cimourdain looked at him. It seemed as if Cimourdain rested his very soul upon that clear glance. Gauvain reached the foot of the scaffold. He ascended it. The officer who commanded the grenadiers followed him. He unfastened his sword, and handed it to the officer; he undid his cravat, and gave it to the executioner. He looked like a vision. Never had he been so handsome.

His brown curls floated on the wind; at the time it was not the custom to cut off the hair of those about to be executed. His white neck reminded one of a woman; his heroic and sovereign glance made one think of an archangel. He stood there on the scaffold lost in thought. That place of punishment was a height too. Gauvain stood upon it, erect, proud, tranquil. The sunlight streamed about him till he seemed to stand in the midst of a halo. But he must be bound. The executioner advanced, cord in hand.

At this moment, when the soldiers saw their young leader so close to the knife, they could restrain themselves no longer, the hearts of those stern warriors gave way. A mighty sound swelled up,—the united sob of a whole army. A clamour rose: "Mery! mercy!" Some fell upon their knees; others flung away their guns and stretched their arms toward the platform where Cimourdain was seated. One grenadier pointed to the guillotine, and cried, "A substitute! A substitute! Take me!" All repeated frantically, "Mercy! mercy!" Had a troop of lions heard, they must have been softened or terrified, the tears of soldiers are terrible.

The executioner hesitated, no longer knowing what to do.

Then a voice, quick and low, but so stern that it was audible to every ear, spoke from the top of the tower: "Fulfil the law!"

All recognized that inexorable tone. Cimourdain had spoken. The army shuddered.

The executioner hesitated no longer. He approached, holding out the cord.

"Wait!" said Gauvain. He turned toward Cimourdain, made a gesture of farewell with his right hand, which was still free, then allowed himself to be bound.

When he was tied, he said to the executioner: "Pardon. One instant more." And he cried: "Long live the Republic!"

He was laid upon the plank. That noble head was held by the infamous yoke. The executioner gently parted his hair aside, then touched the spring. The triangle began to move,—slowly at first, then rapidly; a terrible blow was heard—

At the same instant another report sounded. A pistol-shot had answered the blow of the axe. Cimourdain had seized one of the pistols from his belt, and as Gauvain's head rolled into the basket, Cimourdain sank back pierced to the heart by a bullet his own hand had fired. A stream of blood burst from his mouth; he fell dead.

And those two souls, united still in that tragic death, soared away together, the shadow of the one mingled with the radiance of the other.

THE END.